**Also available from
Sophie H. Morgan**

Her Wish
His Command
Touch of Magic

SOPHIE H. MORGAN

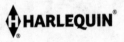

ISBN-13: 978-1-335-47604-3

The Witch is Back

Recycling programs
for this product may
not exist in your area.

For questions and comments about the quality of this book, please contact us at CustomerService@Harlequin.com.

Harlequin Enterprises ULC
22 Adelaide St. West, 41st Floor
Toronto, Ontario M5H 4E3, Canada
www.Harlequin.com

Printed in U.S.A.

To Joe Shillito, soon to be, I'm sure, a household name in fantasy fiction. Without your eternal positivity (and incessant nagging), this book would have stalled around page fifty. A true friend, a great writer and never to be matched at singing "Club Tropicana."

Thanks, pal.

CHAPTER 1

*E*mma hated birthdays. And there were very few things she *hated*.

She had a long list of things she didn't like. Public speaking, people making fun of her dog for his (lack of) looks, creating curses, horror movies, being late, witch high society, karaoke…they all held a spot on the list. But birthdays held a special spot on another, shorter list. Underlined, written in red ink and with three exclamation points.

Her human friend insisted that she couldn't hate birthdays. What was there to hate?

Attention, Emma had always supplied. It was an easy answer, one Leah always laughed off. And it was half true. Emma really did hate the attention. If given the choice between everybody in a room raising a glass, all eyes on her, or letting twenty thousand spiders crawl over her body, it was a no-brainer. Come one, come all arachnids.

Witches didn't celebrate birthdays. Why celebrate a day you were born? Where was the achievement? Witches celebrated *magic*. The lineage, the strength, the rarity. And despite the debatable achievement of being born into a respectable family, Emma's magic was less potent than watered-down vodka. Such was the way of younger siblings. Society—followed closely by her mother—had written her off as useless as far as magical status was concerned. No, her usefulness lay elsewhere.

Her other reason for hating birthdays. The reason that had steered the course of her life ever since her mother had seen her playing with a Higher family's son and seen a golden ticket. There were, after all, two ways a family could rise to Higher family status. One way was to distinguish themselves with magic.

The other was to marry into it.

But that was the past. And now she was here, in Chicago, surrounded by humans and their human preoccupation with being free to live as they wanted, following hearts and passions and squeezing every drop of the lemons life gave them. Which was how Emma found herself reluctantly taking a shift manning front of house at her bar, after their full-time bartender had thrown caution to the excessive wind that gave the city its nickname and followed her boyfriend to Seattle. Well wishes and all that, but damn her for leaving Emma in this position.

Emma wasn't good with people. She loved watching them, but shove her into a situation where she had to make small talk and be interesting, and it had the same effect as using a sickening curse on a house plant. The leaves would wither and drop off, just like any conversation she was forced to be part of. The fact that she co-owned a human bar sometimes made her question her own mind.

But this wasn't really *her* business. It was theirs. Hers, Leah's and Tia's—Tia, her best and only witch friend. Gloria Hightower had sure made an elemental mistake the day she'd forbidden her eight-year-old daughter from playing with the lesser Emmaline Bluewater. Anyone could see that forbidding

Tia to do something was the quickest way to get her to jump right in. Both feet, no floaties, a daredevil grin on her face.

And thank the Goddess for her—and for Toil and Trouble, which, while not Emma's first choice of a career, had indisputable fringe benefits. Like how it really, *really* ticked off her mother.

The thought invariably brought a half smug, half guilty smile to her face.

She'd spent the past hour crouched behind the polished walnut bar that ran the length of the thirty-foot space, checking wine bottle levels and serving the occasional customer. At least the business crowd didn't expect banter, and since most came in like they were entering Noah's Ark—two by two— she was pretty much treated as an extension of the bar's furniture. No complaints here.

Now, finished with inventory, Emma rose from her crouch and placed her notepad on the counter. Her eyes swept the large space, double-checking all was okay. It seemed to be. Suit jackets had come off, ties loosened, heels slyly kicked off under tables. That had been important to Emma, that Toil and Trouble be a place people could relax. Nothing formal, not somewhere you felt judged.

Aside from that, Tia and Leah had taken the reins, from the gigantic wide-screen on the exposed brick wall at one end that silently played the news headlines, across the tables and booths outfitted in wine leather, to the small stage they used for karaoke nights, live music and other live performances. One man had even rented it to ask his girlfriend to marry him, (Emma's idea of hell). Fortunately for him, his girlfriend had said yes.

Emma just hoped for his sake she'd gone through with it. The fallout otherwise wasn't pretty.

"Hey, cutie." Leah's voice acted like a sudden beam of light, interrupting that dark path of thought. Emma straightened from where she leaned on the bar as her friend bounced up to her. The street doors rocked from Leah's usual pace of eighty miles per hour.

A perky blonde human in jeans, a peacoat and a Cubs cap, Leah radiated vitality. If the humans ever wanted to solve the energy crisis, they could hook her up to the grid and have done with it. The woman lived at breakneck speed and figured she had two hands and twenty-four hours in a day for a reason.

Emma adored her. "What are you doing here?"

"What a welcome. All it needs is a party popper and some balloons to be complete."

"I just meant, I thought you were at the shelter today."

Leah's grin was easy as she slid onto a bar stool. "I finished my shift and thought I'd swing by, see how you were doing."

In addition to co-owning the bar, Leah volunteered at a local animal rescue shelter. It was actually where she and Emma had first met. Emma's dog, a mixed breed—the polite way of describing Chester, who seemed to take traits from a dozen dogs—had been Leah's recommendation. They'd been fast friends, with Emma also taking some shifts with Sloane, her half sister, when she had spare time.

"Fine. Good. It's been slow." Which had been the idea behind the three of them deciding to stick Emma on afternoons. Less need to banter.

Leah spied her notepad. "You know, it's amazing." She pulled the notebook and pen toward her and began to doodle a broomstick. "All that power and you still use a pen and paper."

The hair on Emma's neck prickled. "Leah."

"Please." Leah waved away her concern, even though she did lower her voice. She began on a cauldron. No matter what Emma and Tia told her, Leah refused to believe cauldrons weren't a part of witch culture. "Nobody's going to take me seriously."

Still, Emma tamped down the urge to check the compact in her stowed purse. You never knew who could be eavesdropping through a mirror. "It's not good to rely on too much *magic*." She mouthed the last word.

Leah leaned in. Her voice, though quiet, brimmed with bottled enthusiasm. "And why is that? If I was a witch, I'd *so* abuse my powers."

Emma's fingers tap-tap-tapped on the counter and she gave Leah a pained glance. It was forbidden to reveal to any human that witches existed, except if given permission by the High Family. Any witch that broke that law found themselves on the nasty end of a curse. And that didn't even take into account what they did with the human.

Leah caught the look, held up her hands. "All right, fine. I'll stop. With that. And now I get to focus on the real reason I came by." She dug in her bag and withdrew a sequined party hat. It was pink and ferociously ugly. "Happy birthday!"

Holy… Emma blanched. "I'm not wearing that."

"Oh, come on. It's fun." Ignoring her weak protest, Leah stood on the stool's rungs to attach the hat to Emma's head.

The elastic dug into her chin. She sulked. "You know I don't like my birthday."

"C'mon. I've let you ignore all your birthdays thanks to your weird aversion—"

Emma choked. "Let me ignore them? You hired a stripper for my birthday last year. *And* you forgot to pay him." She'd had to suffer walking through town in mortified silence with a half-naked firefighter to the nearest ATM.

"You could've just spelled him to forget."

She could have tried, but mind magic had never been her forte. Ask her to nurture a plant to health, she was your girl. Complicated spells that dealt with memory were a whole different ballpark. She could've ended up trapping him in his own mind or making him fall in love with a lamppost. Better a little humiliation for her than trying to detach a human from an inanimate object.

Leah rolled her eyes, either too naïve or too human to grasp the magnitude of what mind magic really meant. "Anyway, not the point. Let's celebrate another year of you."

Ugh. "How long do I have to keep this on?"

"Until you get a birthday kiss." Leah waggled her eyebrows. "And I know just the man."

Emma's groan was heartfelt. Leah had the worst taste in men, and Emma knew some pretty terrible guys. Warlocks took arrogance and polished it to a high shine. She didn't have that much experience, having only really dated in the past couple of years when…well, when *he* hadn't come for her. But dates seemed like a lot of work.

Men expected her to be pretty and laugh at the right time and toss out witty comments that edged on flirty. Unfortunately she was all-around average—brown hair, brown eyes, brown personality. Too timid, too shy. Too serious. Even the nice guys had barely restricted their yawns behind their menus. Any witty comments were kept to herself for her own amusement. As always.

And then there was the other factor. Bastian.

The name sent a ripple of emotion through her. None of it good. And much too complicated to explain.

"I don't want to date right now" was all she said to Leah's expectant expression.

"I swear, I am going to drag you out of the nest, Emma Bluewater, whether you like it or not. At some point in your life, you are going to have fun on your birthday."

"I'm meeting Sloane for a movie tonight. You know I can't cancel on her. Even if I wanted to ditch her for a man."

Leah sighed, adjusted her cap. A lock of sunny hair drifted

out to curl against her cheek. "You really crush the dream I'm nursing that *male witches*," she mouthed, "are good lovers. They can't be if you're this against dating. Or maybe they are and that's why. We don't measure up." She gauged Emma's expression. "Are they? You'd tell me, right?"

Emma smiled and took back the pen and paper to cross out the witch doodles. "Any new rescues today?"

Leah gave her a speaking look but surrendered with good humor. They chatted about the shelter for a bit—well, Leah talked and Emma listened—and whenever anyone came up to the bar, Leah distracted them with cheerful small talk while Emma filled the order. Must be her birthday, Emma thought wryly. Usually she was pushed to "put herself out there."

"Before I forget," Leah added as a woman paid for her two Cokes and carried them off. "You, me, Tia, drinks tonight. *After* the movie," she said when Emma opened her mouth to counter. "I know I'm working, but Tia promised to mix us up something special." A set of dimples appeared. "Something witchy this way comes."

"Last time Tia made drinks, I ended up with pink hair."

"And you looked so cute. A little fun is just what you need. Drinks," Leah commanded with a firm nod. "We're doing drinks. And I will finally get a potion right." Even though she was human, Leah was convinced she'd one day master the art of potion-making. Or the perfect witchy cocktail, in any case.

On that topic, she cocked her head. "We still got any of that powder you mixed up last time? You know, the one that tasted like raspberries and lost fantasies."

Emma gave in as always with a grin at Leah's romantic description. "Falayla root. It's in the storage room." And packed one hell of a punch when added to cocktails. For a witch, it gave a nice, dreamy buzz. For a human, it hit like five shots at once.

"I'll check if we'll need more for the drinks I'm planning."
Leah winked and jumped off the stool. "Hold tight."

Emma watched her friend walk off, watched the men in the
room watch her go. Leah had that essential feminine something that men seemed to react to, a sway to her hips that drew
attention, even with the cap. Maybe the cap helped. Maybe
men liked seeing a sports team on a woman's head. Emma
certainly wasn't an expert.

Seeing nobody else to serve, she dragged over the box of
bottles she'd carried up earlier and bent to restock the under-
the-counter fridge.

Splitting her attention between the job in hand and the
mirror behind the bar, she'd unloaded all the white and was
starting on the pink stuff when a draft that whispered winter was on its way snaked around her ankles. A shiver worked
down her spine and she shrugged her shoulders out, sliding
a bottle into the fridge. Odd she'd feel the draft down here.

She slid another bottle next to its sibling when movement
in the mirror distracted her. Reflected, a man stood near the
register, half turned away as if looking back at the doors.

Something struck her as oddly familiar about his stance,
the exact detail of his face in profile. Intuition made her chest
tighten as she stared at the mirror.

That was when he swiveled and said, "Hello?"

Emma's heart thumped so hard against her ribs she could've
sworn she heard them crack. When wine spilled over her fingers, she realized she'd snapped the wine bottle's neck. She'd
lost control of her magic.

He'd always had that effect on her.

No. It couldn't be him.

But she found she couldn't move from her crouch, even
with the wine and blood mixing until her cuts stung like crazy.

Turn, she willed, stomach squeezing as she caught a quick flick of his eyes in the mirror. Blue.

Like *his*.

"Hello?" he repeated. "Is anyone here?"

That masculine voice, whiskey-rich silk, hit her in the gut. A thousand thoughts pushed forward as black sparks fizzed and popped in front of her eyes. Oh yeah. The whole breathing thing. She inhaled. Exhaled. It didn't help. She wondered what her odds were of creating a portal where the customers wouldn't see it.

Run?

The idea slapped her back. Where the hell had her backbone gone?

She pushed to her feet, holding tightly to a neutral expression like it was a life preserver in the middle of the ocean.

Captain, we're going down.

Not on my watch, she told herself, bracing as she cleared the counter.

Her gaze tangled with his immediately. Like a piece of weather magic, a lightning bolt shot through the center of her, sizzling her skin with an almost painful intensity. His gorgeous face had only ripened with time, the cheekbones sharp, the lips soft in all that masculinity. He wore a shadow of dark honey stubble, his hair the same shade cropped close but with enough thickness to have locks brushing his forehead. That beautiful, undeniable face, like the navy eyes, revealed nothing except a flash of something she couldn't define. Just one more question left unanswered.

The first one being where he'd been for the past seven years after he'd run out on her without even a note.

She fisted a hand, the one that had smashed the wine bottle. Focused on that small pain instead of the hurt that throbbed at her center. "Bastian."

For a moment, they took each other's measure before he offered one of his practiced smiles. "Emmaline. It's you."

Her throat felt thick, blocked. "What…" She swallowed, took a breath. It didn't help. "You're here." In her bar. In her haven.

"I'm here," he confirmed. His smile turned teasing, though it didn't reach his eyes. "C'mon, is that any way to say hi to me?"

In her head she saw it, her hand shooting out, a poison ivy spell flying free to wrap around him. Not deadly, but oh-so-painful. It was so satisfying she almost believed she'd done it.

"Hi." The word was toneless, not that he noticed.

"Good start." He winked. Held out his arms. "Now, how about a hug for your fiancé?"

CHAPTER 2

Someone's sharp intake of breath played across Emma's ears, neatly underscoring Bastian's damning question. She realized a beat later it had come from her. Her chest felt tight, as if someone had cast a crushing curse, ribs impacting until her lungs struggled to draw a second proper breath. She'd take that over having to talk to him. *Him.*

Bastian Truenote. The warlock she'd been friends with at ten, been obsessed with at fifteen, been engaged to all her life. Her first kiss. Her best friend, aside from Tia. The man who'd abandoned her when she'd been twenty-one, when they'd been starting wedding plans. *Without even a note.* Thank the Goddess he'd left one for his parents or they'd have all thought he'd been murdered.

He might not have been, but any respect and standing she'd had in witch society had been shot point-blank. Along with any belief he'd cared for her.

Cut to her holding her chin up against the catty mothers and their daughters who talked behind their hands of "poor Emmaline." Too boring to keep a man like Bastian, a society prince, even with a contract in place. And that wasn't even taking into account her own mother's icy condemnation when she'd learned Bastian had left.

You can't do anything right.

She hadn't seen him since. Nobody had.

And now he was here. Standing on the other side of the bar, his expression easing from smiling to quizzical at her continued silence.

She needed to say something. What did you say to a prodigal ex-fiancé? Hint: two words, seven letters. Starts with *F* and *Y*.

"You're bleeding." Bastian's voice made her jerk. A frown almost made its way onto his brow before it lost momentum. She wasn't surprised. Frown lines indicated someone with the capacity to be serious. Bastian had never worried a day in his life. That used to be what she'd adored about him, when her own life was pinned together with so many screws and thumbtacks that could bust at any second.

Emma glanced at the small cut at the base of her thumb. Blood welled, enough that it would need to be cleaned. She could heal it with a few words, but not in front of the humans. She'd had to adapt to human ways, so she did have a first aid kit. It was in her office.

She'd have to take him there—away from the bar where Leah would bounce out at any moment. She just couldn't deal with questions right now.

She wet her lips, took a moment to concentrate on the words. "We can talk in—in my office."

"Sure," he said with easy confidence. The spotlights caught darker blond highlights in his hair as he moved with inherent grace.

She glanced around, hesitating when she realized she'd be leaving the bar unmanned. But while practicality was nestled in her DNA, this was a catastrophe in the making. She slid her cell from under the bar, keeping a wary eye on Bastian like she would a vicious dog, and messaged Leah a quick *bathroom break* text. Leah, like most humans, was glued to her cell, so she'd pick up the message.

Keeping her hand elevated, Emma jerked her chin and turned. She could sense Bastian follow, as if her body was still attuned to his.

They didn't speak as she led him at a fast clip down the hall and into the office. As soon as she stepped foot through the doorway, Chester barked once and spun in a delirious circle before losing his balance and falling with a grunt. He was up again in a second and dashed over to her legs, where he leaned his small bulk against her calves. Small pops of joy flooded through their bond and with them, a spark of magic.

Grateful, she leaned to scratch him behind his ears. At least she had him in her corner.

"I don't want to alarm you," came the butterscotch tones behind her. "But there's some kind of small beast on your leg."

If only she'd taught Chester to attack. "He's my dog."

She straightened, turned enough to see doubt flicker in his face. "Are you sure?"

Her jaw tightened. Any words she longed to say would have suffered because of it, so she just gave Chester another stroke.

"What breed is he?" Bastian eyed him. "Or species, should I say? Is he part warthog? Pygmy goat?" Chester trotted over, sniffing the air around Bastian's calves before plopping his butt on the carpet. His tongue lolled out his mouth and his tail began to buff the floor. Bastian gave a short laugh and bent to pet him. "Odd-looking thing."

"Sorry my dog doesn't live up to your standards," she managed, pleased that the tone was tart enough to be served with vanilla ice cream.

Surprise replaced the doubt. Little wonder, since the girl he remembered would've never dared reproach him. He smiled, inviting her to share it. She still couldn't see it in his eyes and wondered at the absence. "I was joking."

"Mmm." It was the most she could manage. It was easier when she didn't look at him. "He's part basset, part terrier, maybe part bloodhound. Nobody really knows." And she couldn't care less. Appearances were less than nothing to her.

"You didn't want to pick just one?" She could hear his grin, the one he'd always worn, in his voice.

For once she was immune. She wasn't about to swoon over somebody who insulted her dog. Chester was chunkily built and short, his nose was too big and his ears too long, and nobody would pick him to be in a beauty pageant. But he was adorable and he loved her. No matter if she sometimes couldn't get her words out or read too much or preferred to sit at home on Saturday nights writing in her journal about the trips she and Sloane planned to take. Chester loved her anyway.

Chester wriggled and panted and flopped onto his back, crooning his delight as Bastian obliged with a stomach rub. She gave both males a dark glance. Unfortunately, Chester sometimes loved indiscriminately.

"Yes, you're a good boy." Bastian lifted a hand and a dog treat appeared. "Do you mind?"

Chester spotted the treat and froze for a heartbeat before he scrambled up and planted his butt on the floor in a sit. Even so, his rump wiggled so much, he was practically vibrating.

Emma sighed. As if she could say no now. She nodded.

Bastian held the treat out. Chester quivered and looked at her.

She couldn't help the smile. "Yes," she said quietly.

The dog took the treat and galloped over to his dog bed where he crunched. Pieces went everywhere.

Bastian rose out of his crouch, dusting off his hands. "Not your average familiar."

Considering most witch familiars were perfect, prideful animals, that was an understatement. But Emma figured she and Chester were a pair, both out of place in a world that demanded flawlessness. Familiars were meant to help nurture the spark of magic in a witch by way of a spell the witch had to perform that linked the two. Chester was a joyful spot in her soul, a dog that longed only to be with her. Considering how lonely she'd always been, that was nothing short of magic.

She folded her arms, a barrier. "So?"

"So, what does your mom say about him?" A lilt in the words, a searching glance, as if they were sharing a secret. Once, he'd made fun of Emma's mom, Clarissa, somehow making the day-to-day seem bearable because he was there with her. Until he wasn't.

Ignoring him, Emma rounded her desk and put the furniture as well as her chair between them. She placed her hands on the chair's high back, grounding herself. "Why are you here, Bastian?"

He tucked his thumbs into his pockets. "Can't I just be in the neighborhood?"

"No."

"Anywhere in the world is our neighborhood," he pointed out. "The brilliance of magic."

"And here I thought you'd—forgotten the way home." The words ripped from her, halting though they might be. The sheer rudeness dizzied her, a kind of giddy thrill snapping some of the ropes that had been tied to how this man thought of her. Along with any lingering confusion or guilt. She'd sooner be mad than feel those.

His eyes narrowed infinitesimally, but an easy enough smile curved his lips. "And here you are a long way from it." He nodded at the office. "I never would have pegged you as the kind to leave society. Or own a bar."

Emma bit her tongue before any more retorts wriggled loose. It seemed once she'd started, the devil wouldn't leave her be. She shrugged, lifted her chin.

"So serious. At least that hasn't changed."

She didn't like the threads of memory he was tugging on, aware that if he pulled on the wrong one, the torrent of hurt and anger and guilt would gush out.

And she *had* changed. He just didn't get to find out how much.

At her silence, he began to wander around the office, which usually felt roomy and now shrank to the size of a dollhouse. She kept an eye on him as she pressed her hands flat against the leather chair. Her thumb screeched.

He caught her wince, turned immediately. "You haven't healed that yet?"

Before she could jerk away, he was on her. Or at least his hands were as he lifted her injured one. She did pull away then, or tried to, but he held her with easy strength and examined the cut.

He flicked his gaze up, navy meeting brown. Something leaped between them. Unexpected. Unwelcome.

She refused to acknowledge the jump in her pulse and tugged again on her hand. "I don't always use magic here."

He let her go this time. "It's just me. Go ahead—heal it."

She ignored him and bent to extract a first aid kit from her bottom desk drawer. She fumbled with the latches. They opened at a look from him.

"*Don't help me.*"

His eyebrows shot up. "Okay. Sure."

She set about getting all the necessary bits from the kit, relieved to have a task to focus on instead of him.

"Nice hat, by the way," he said after a beat. "Cute."

The heat in her cheeks dialed up to blistering. That stupid sequined party hat. Of course, because having to face a man who'd literally run away from her wasn't humiliation enough. Why not go the whole way and get out her diaries from when she was fifteen, where she'd composed an ode to his eyes?

She wiped that from her mind before he could catch any hint. She might not have mastered mind magic, but Goddess knew Bastian had always had the knack. Most witches learned to block from the cradle, but if you were comfortable with someone, you could let your guard down. And she *knew* Bastian had often picked up impressions from her in the past.

Well, not now. All she wanted him to feel was nothing.

And the endless itch from some poison ivy. That would be sweet.

She steeled herself. Allowed the devil a free pass. "It goes with my outfit."

He blinked.

She counted it as a victory. She pushed ahead. "It's been a long time."

A pause. "I've been traveling."

"My postcards must have gotten lost." The words may have been quiet, but they had bite.

"Emmaline…" He floundered, obviously caught off guard. "Weren't we friends once?" Something moved behind his eyes as the question lay in the air.

By how fast her heart was beating, blood should have been pulsing out of the cut. *Friends?* If they had been, wouldn't she have rated some kind of goodbye, or at least a warning? That he'd been about to totally screw her over?

She fumbled with the Band-Aid, having already cleaned the cut. Normally she'd have used magic but having cut off her own nose, she gritted her teeth and soldiered on until the cut was sealed.

"Friends?" It was all she could say without breaking into a wild laugh. Brown strands of hair fell in front of her eyes, obscuring her vision. She didn't move to tuck them back, preferring the distorted image of him.

His frown found purchase for a second this time before smoothing away to another practiced smile. "Yeah. I don't think I have a single childhood memory without you in it. And that includes the time you accidentally lit Clarissa's rose garden on fire, remember that?" His grin invited her to come with him down memory lane.

Considering her punishment had included going without food for a day, while working on fire magic for the entire twenty-four hours, she resisted.

"What are you doing here, Bastian?" she repeated, cursing the wobble in her voice. Cursing that she'd broken down and asked.

They'd had a binding engagement contract, written by her father and signed by his mother, as was traditional. Emmaline Bluewater and Sebastian Truenote were meant to get married, in the time from dawn on her twenty-first birthday to the eve of her twenty-fifth. Four years to get the job done. To see it through. To say "I do."

But he'd decided to say "I don't," go off and travel the world, find himself—or some such BS. He'd left in the middle of the night, no warning, no message to anyone but his parents the night of her twenty-first. *I'm sorry, but I can't marry Emmaline.* Plain words that said everything.

While she'd been starry-eyed as a teenager and would have happily taken Bastian's hands and made vows, Emma would now sooner get up in front of a crowd of people, in her underwear, and recite the entire *Fifty Shades of Grey* book than slip his ring on her finger.

If Bastian thought he could come back and smile at her and she'd let the past years of humiliation slide, he was dead wrong.

"I'm very busy. You need to go."

She fought the urge to shift under his stare. Time stretched like overchewed gum, only the background noise of the bar masking the thump of her anxious heartbeat.

"Yes," he said finally with slow deliberation. She could almost hear the cogs whirring as his brain worked. "You are. I shouldn't have come in the middle of a workday." This time his smile was wide and open and charming as ever. It could have melted a chocolate bar. Even if it was as fake as a glamour spell. "We can catch up at the party."

He was already moving to the door before she worked her brain around his sentence. "What—what party?"

"The party. You didn't hear?" He reached down and scratched Chester, the traitor's hopes fixed on another magical dog treat. "My parents are throwing me a welcome home party. I know," he added as if she'd protested, "but they haven't seen me in a while and it's important to them."

"You were gone a long time. They missed you."

There it was again, the hint of darkness that was instantly swept away when he cleared his throat. "It'll be sociable. Food, drink. You're busy now, so we can talk then."

"Bastian—"

"I'm surprised your mom hasn't let you know. Clarissa was always on top of those things." He patted Chester once more. "It's tomorrow night. Black tie, as always, at the Truenote manor. They'll expect us to start off the dancing, so wear comfortable shoes."

"Bastian—" she tried again, growing frantic at what he was describing. Goddess, to avoid that, she'd tie him to a chair here and force the reunion. Better they do it now than in front of all witch society. But as he paused to hear her speak, her tongue went thick. "I can't…" She fought for words, any words. "I don't…" Helplessly, she stared at him.

"Hey." His tone gentled and for one minute, he looked like *her* Bastian. The young man who'd made excuses to get her out of dancing or brushed her hair back away from her face as if he cared. The reminder stung like a thousand cuts, bitterness the salt that kept them open. "I know you're not sold on these things, but we'll dance, do our duty and then find a spot in the garden." A note of something tinted his voice as he added, "Like we always did."

Like we always did. Because he expected she would just fall at his feet like an adoring girl?

It took her a moment to realize the grinding sound came from her teeth.

She unlocked her jaw. She didn't want to talk to him or be around him and the confusing storm of emotion he unearthed. But if his parents were throwing a ball, he was right. Clarissa would be calling and would insist on Emma attending. Maybe it would be better to put off their "reunion." Maybe she'd be able to sort out what to say, how to act.

Coward.

"I'll see you then." He turned to go, paused, looked back. His eyes swept her body, leaving her skin flushed. "You look good."

She stubbornly refused to say anything to that garbage, especially as it felt false. And she *hated* that her pulse skipped regardless.

His eyes lingered. "And happy birthday, Emmaline."

"Emma," she said a beat later, but he was already gone.

With his scent lingering on the air like the remnants of a spell, for a moment she did feel like shy, scared Emmaline again. It terrified her. That quickly gave way to a hot lick of anger that he'd sweep into her life as easily as he'd left it.

Chester pawed her leg and then bumped his head against it.

With a short breath, she nodded. "You're right. We have to do it, so no point dwelling."

After all, she had Leah to deal with first.

And Goddess knew what Tia was going to say when she found out that Bastian was back.

Emma glanced down at Chester. "We'd better hide the potions."

CHAPTER 3

The initial meeting had been harder than he'd expected.
When Bastian stepped from the portal he'd created
from the bar into the bedroom his parents had maintained,
he gave in to temptation and dragged his hands over his face
before simply covering it.

He hadn't handled it well.

Understatement. He'd handled Emmaline about as well as
if he'd tried to pick up butter with hot hands.

As he'd prepared to see the girl he'd once been engaged to,
the girl he'd trusted and loved, it hadn't crossed Bastian's mind
that she'd have changed. Of course, he'd known she'd look
older than the sweet twenty-one-year-old he'd run from. He
just hadn't expected to be confronted by such a direct stare
from those quiet brown eyes.

It had thrown him off enough that he'd briefly forgotten his
plan. The plan to don his old persona like a tux and be Bastian
Truenote: charming, devil-may-care, universally adored. He'd
imagined sweeping into the bar—a bar, Emmaline owned a
bar?—displaying his smile and watching her melt for him.

Instead, he'd been thoroughly, if quietly, reprimanded and sassed. By a girl who'd once turned crimson if he so much as walked into the room.

He'd fumbled for control of the situation, but she'd blocked him at every turn.

The girl he'd practically abandoned at the altar would have thrown herself into his arms. That Emmaline had been slight, waif-like, with hunched shoulders and a serious expression except for the occasions he'd wheedled a shy smile from her.

This new Emmaline was…different. Even with the same brown eyes, the same brown hair, the same clothes that helped her blend so well with the humans she'd chosen to live with, she wasn't his sweet Emmaline. The one he'd left to protect.

Unless she'd played a part in why he'd run.

That suspicion had nibbled at him for seven years, had kept him away so he wouldn't have to uncover the truth, but now he had no choice but to face it.

The Emmaline he'd known, or thought he'd known, had accepted their impending marriage. Had looked forward to it in her own demure way, and had been pushing for a quick wedding. Unlike him.

Emmaline had been his best friend, but he had chafed against the childhood contract, the demands on how he spend the rest of his life. The pressure he'd felt to play the perfect part. And now here he was playing a part again. The part of a man who hadn't discovered the truth about the Joining—an unconventional clause buried deep in their engagement contract, a clause with the sole purpose of draining him of his familial magic.

The part of a man who hadn't tried to tell someone and discovered a silencing hex had been placed on him by Goddess knew who.

A man who couldn't shake the suspicion that his best friend, his fiancée, had known and had betrayed him for all the power she didn't have.

And so he'd run. It had been the only thing he could think to do. Run and he'd be free of the contract. Run and the problems were left behind, along with everything and everyone else.

But now his family was facing a worse threat.

On the heels of that thought, he dropped his hands and padded to the door. Opening it, he crossed the threshold into the wide paneled corridor that boasted portraits of Truenotes going back centuries. He felt his ancestors glare at him in disapproval—imagination? A spell? He'd never figured it out—as he crossed to a door five doors down.

He knocked with his knuckles, soft. "Mom? You awake?"

There was a beat of silence before a papery-thin voice answered. "I'm awake. Come talk to me."

Bastian steeled himself before he twisted the knob. When the door swung open, he managed not to flinch. Unlike yesterday, when he'd first laid eyes on her after portalling in from Egypt.

Diana Truenote half reclined in a bed fit for royalty. A four-poster carved from walnut, draped in silk canopy curtains a shade of blue only found in the night sky, it drowned the frail woman, who struggled to sit up on his arrival.

He crossed the room in quick strides, forestalling her. "Don't, Mom. You should be comfortable."

"I'm fine. I wish you and your father would quit fussing." Her words would have made more of an impact if she hadn't started coughing. She lifted a handkerchief, pressed it to her mouth.

At his look, the chair in the corner skidded over to Bastian like an obedient pet and he dropped into it, smoothing out any worry lines. His mom didn't need to see his anxiety.

When her attack had finished, he nodded at the water carafe. "Need a drink?"

"I'm fine. Don't fuss." She slumped against the pillows, arranging her hands neatly on the coverlet. They were thinner than they should be. Diana had always been slender, but in the past seven years, she'd gone from slender to skin and bones. She reminded him of a piece of wood that had been whittled down to a toothpick.

Her golden hair, the hair he'd inherited, was now dull, straggling down her shoulders and thin in places. Tanned skin had lightened to look like vellum he could see through to the veins below. Eyes that had always laughed were hollower, sunken, reddened.

It destroyed him.

She smiled. "How was the big reunion?"

His laugh was brittle. "It could have gone better." He leaned forward, steepling his hands and resting his arms on his knees. "I think...she was pissed at me."

"No." His mom might be sick, but she still had enough about her to be gently mocking. Her familiar, a cat with black-and-white markings, stretched from its position at the base of the bed before making its way to Diana's lap. It began to purr as she stroked. It, too, was worse for wear, fur patchy, eyes watery.

Before, it had been elegant, like most familiars. Unlike Emmaline's mongrel. He almost laughed at the memory of that ugly face, which still somehow managed to be cute. He had no idea how she'd got that past her mother, who she'd always striven to please.

Bastian pursed his lips. Just how much had she done in her efforts to be a good daughter?

In response to his mom's teasing, he gave her a baleful look.

Humor briefly lit her features. "Maybe she was caught by surprise," she suggested.

"She didn't seem surprised. She seemed pissed to see me."

And surely if she craved power, or wanted him for a husband, she'd be ecstatic that he was back. He clung to that, the way a small boy clings to his mother's hand.

His mom's laugh was weak but still a laugh. "My poor boy. A woman who isn't falling over herself for one of your smiles?"

He shook his head, impatient. "Emmaline isn't some woman. And she always...well, you know what she was like."

"She worshipped you."

He frowned. His mom didn't know the whole of it so she couldn't share his doubts. Still... "I wouldn't say worshipped."

"You were her port in the storm." Diana scratched the cat behind its ear and its purr increased. "Her fiancé. Her best friend. Of course she worshipped you. But time has a way of changing that. She's not the same girl you knew."

"I'm getting that." He stared at his shoes. Unsettled. Goddess, he didn't want to be here, forced into this again. To look at her and wonder.

A pause. "Bastian, if you're not ready—"

"No," he interrupted, eyes flashing up. "This is my mess."

"Not really." Her smile turned wistful. "But there's no turning back the clock." Her hand reached out, covered his. "I'm sure she'll do as you ask. She used to adore you. I'm positive you can win her over to your side."

He nodded, breathing in and exhaling any doubt. There was no room for it. What use was the past now? It was the past for a reason. Emmaline had to agree.

His mom began to cough again and his hand tightened underneath hers.

She had to.

★ ★ ★

Emma stepped from the portal, eyes adjusting to the darkness that surrounded the Truenote manor. In true Southern style, it was painted ghost white, with fancy columns and a wraparound porch and gorgeous oaks that lined the long drive. Lights flickered in the trees and around them, floating and dancing in the breeze aided by magic. Portals opened up here, there and everywhere on the gravel drive as witches and warlocks from Higher families arrived for the welcome home party.

Emma had opened hers and Tia's portal out of sight in the woods that surrounded the property. She needed a moment to calm herself before stepping into target range. And privacy to remind Tia not to go casting a curse on Bastian when they got inside, even if that would be satisfying.

Her friend continued to seethe beside her as she had done since she'd learned of his return. With sharp, irritated movements, she adjusted the strapless violet sheath she wore. "Arrogant dick," she muttered, moving on to check her hair. It was perfect, as was her dress, but then everything about Tia Hightower was just so.

She exemplified what a Higher family daughter should be—beautiful, poised, powerful. Everything Emma wasn't.

It helped that Tia didn't have much patience with the society world. Of course, being the heir to a Higher family did have some perks. Unlike Emma, who was scorned for running a human bar, Tia's involvement was laughed off. She could, and did, do and say what she wanted.

And thank the Goddess for it or she'd never have become friends with Emma all those years ago, and helped her when she'd truly needed it.

Loyalty was big with Tia, as she proved now, drawing a hex bag from her clutch.

Emma eyed it. "I thought I hid all those."

"Not all." Tia smiled. It had *danger* written all over it. "Won't look so handsome when warts break out across his face."

"No hex bags." Emma held out a hand.

"It'd be fun."

"No."

"Just imagine it. In he comes, waving to the society he abandoned, all of them smiling at him in adoration since Golden Boy can do no wrong—but oh, wait, is that a wart? No, it's two. Or three or ten. Suddenly, Golden Boy isn't so golden."

Emma stamped on the laughter, knowing it would only encourage her. She gestured. "Give me it."

"Fine." Tia relinquished the bag.

Emma considered her. "And the other one."

"What other one?"

"You knew I'd make you give me this. Which means you have a backup."

"But Emma," Tia whined. "The bastard hurt you. A little harmless payback is due."

She shook her head, having had time to form her strategy for dealing with Golden Boy, as Tia called him. "I don't want him to know how bad it was. I just want to get through tonight. Please?"

Tia's shoulders drooped and she let out a gusty sigh. "You're much better than I am." She reached into her cleavage and pulled out another hex bag.

Emma took them, concentrated. Smoke uncoiled before both bags lit up, a small blaze that burned out in seconds. Those twenty-four hours working on fire magic had paid off. Kind of. Ask her to set something larger on fire, it might take her a week. Maybe a few days with some energy drinks.

She dusted off her hands and then passed them over her

hair, which was loose over her shoulders. She wore one of her older dresses, a simple black sheath cut to the knee. Black didn't draw the eye.

Most witches went the opposite route and preferred color, like Tia, whose violet silk made her seem like one of those pretty candies wrapped in foil. It set off her brown skin and black hair to perfection, making the gold specks in her hazel eyes pop.

"I can't believe he had the nerve to come to the bar," Tia said into the pause. She shook her head, her lip curled.

The whole thing seemed surreal to Emma now. Bastian showing up, letting the cat out of the bag. Leah was still recovering from the shock that Emma had a long-lost fiancé. She'd been stunned into silence for a full minute before demanding all the details. Emma's birthday drinks after the movie had been spent discussing Bastian and all that revolved around him. The harm he'd caused, the emotions he'd devastated. This was why she hated birthdays. They never brought about anything good.

She'd been glad to escape for a shopping trip the next day with Sloane, who was unaware that Emma's past had shown up like a body she'd thought buried. Instead, the teen had agonized over purple or pink nail polish, as if that held the key to making friends. Emma's nails remained unpolished—maybe for that very reason.

"Anyway. Screw him." Tia tilted her head to the entrance, where witches and warlocks from Higher families and their less lucky counterparts streamed in like fish up a river. "Ready?"

Emma inhaled. "Sure."

The two stood still for another minute.

"Give me ten seconds and I could make another hex bag?"

A smile broke through Emma's ice. She slid a mock-warning look to her friend. "No hex bags."

"Fine, fine, fine." Tia indicated. "Shall we, then?"

They stepped out of the trees and onto the gravel. It crunched under their heels as they navigated the drive then hiked up the steps. The invitation that had appeared on her bedroom mirror—along with a pointed note from her mother about how she expected Emma to reflect well on the family—had said midnight. The witching hour. Cute. Probably Bastian's idea.

Emma's breath grew shorter as they entered through the grand doors and headed for the ballroom. Already people were starting to notice her, fans flapping harder, whispers buzzing behind them. Some titters that twisted Emma's nerves, which were already wound so tight that any minute she'd start vibrating like an overwound alarm clock.

"Oh, Goddess." Tia's mournful murmur jerked Emma's attention away from a group of society matrons that were openly pointing at her. "Here comes Maybelline."

Maybelline Pearlmatter was one of the biggest gossips in society and got away with it purely because her family happened to be one of the oldest. Amazing what societal deafness generations of power could buy. She dressed only in shades of green and always wore a feather in her hair.

Emma spotted it bobbing toward them through the crowds that packed the ballroom.

She eyed the distance from where she stood to the corner she used to hide in as a kid.

Tia's hand locked around Emma's wrist. "Don't even think about it."

"Tia, darling!" came the exclamation not ten seconds later. Maybelline burst free from the groups like a head from a tight dress, arms outstretched. Her dress was a voluminous affair of emerald satin paired with a peacock feather stuck in a pale green turban. Wisps of her blonde hair curled out from under the turban to frame a face with a jawline that was as sharp as her tongue.

Maybelline had always been extraordinarily kind to Emma,

considering how much fodder she was for the gossips. But the older witch did have a tendency to latch on to someone, calling attention to herself and her companion. Not Emma's idea of a good time.

An invisibility charm would be good right about now, she thought as she held still next to Tia, who was embraced with enthusiasm. Then again, maybe if she stayed still enough, Maybelline wouldn't know she was there.

"It's been too long!" Clouds of scent wrapped around the three of them as Maybelline drew back. "And you're looking stunning as usual. Now, I know we've talked before, but Henry—"

"Ancient history, Maybelline." Tia's voice was firm at the mention of Maybelline's son. Emma almost expected a sign reading *Keep Out* to appear in front of her.

The older woman sighed. "But you would make me such beautiful grandchildren." She spun to Emma in the next beat. "And Emmaline Bluewater, as I live and breathe. You're looking…" She hesitated as her eyes slicked down Emma's dress, which was the antithesis of Maybelline's and every other witch's here. "…healthy," she finished. "Although a little color in your cheeks would work wonders."

"Hello." Emma's voice was barely a wisp of sound.

"Still shy?" Maybelline clucked her tongue. "I'd have thought Clarissa would've defeated that by now."

Clarissa Bluewater had definitely tried to get rid of what she viewed as her daughter's impediment. Emma pursed her lips and said nothing.

Maybelline patted her hand. "But at least you return with glory, my dear. All those sniggering idiots are now eating crow. Some literally." Her smile turned catty. Emma didn't want to ask, but then as always with Maybelline, she didn't have to. The older witch wasn't one for playing coy. "Your mother has been on a tear, her head high and triumph blazing on it as if she had trumpets playing wherever she goes. And if anyone dares to say anything, her punishments are...creative."

Emma's forehead lined, even as her eyes darted around at the mention of her mother. Reactively she smoothed any wrinkles out of her dress.

"Triumph?" Tia lifted an eyebrow. "What triumph?"

"Bastian's return, of course."

Emma didn't see how Bastian coming back could equal triumph for her mother, but she didn't care. All she wanted to do was find Bastian, have him say whatever he needed to say, cut him off at the knees with some well-chosen words—well, a gal could dream—and then take the fastest portal home. She had a pint of mint chocolate chip in the freezer that promised to be warmer than any of these people.

"Sorry, Maybelline." She gestured in a random direction. "I'm going to find...um, Bastian." His name felt intimate on her tongue.

"Of course, go, go! Lovers reunited—always makes for a great story." Maybelline sighed, and then glanced slyly at Tia again. "You know, Henry—"

Emma headed off with an apologetic glance at Tia. She circled the room, as close to the walls as she could get, trying to blend in with the furniture that lined them even as everyone else gathered in groups, talking and laughing and drinking from gold flutes filled with champagne.

Still, it made a pretty spectacle, with the vines wrapping around internal columns and the lush tall plants creating a greenhouse kind of feel. Bastian's mom had always liked greenery, especially at the grand parties she'd used to host, and the evidence she still did grew vibrantly on every wall. Some of the vines even flowered with small pink buds that smelled as fragrant as a summer rainstorm.

Emma paused next to one that wasn't yet fully developed and touched a finger to it. It bloomed instantly, opening up and embracing the light flooding the room from the chandeliers that floated above. Her lips curved.

"I forgot you could do that."

Bastian's voice made Emma jolt so hard her teeth bashed together. She spun, one hand out on the column for balance. "*Damn it.*"

"Sorry." Sincere apology rang in his voice. "I thought you'd hear me. Though it's so loud in here, that was probably stupid."

She had to look at him. It was customary for one party of a conversation to look—however briefly—at the other.

Any minute now.

Emma breathed out. Forced her eyes up. Immediately wanted to curse.

Of course he was gorgeous, dressed in a tux as crisp as an apple and looking just as delicious. He and Tia should have been the ones engaged to each other. They'd have made perfect children, with perfectly strong powers.

Her chest was tight as she nodded at him. "Bastian."

Something moved in his face, but she couldn't guess at the emotion before it was gone. "Been here long?"

"No."

"Did you come with Clarissa?" He glanced toward the sea of witches and warlocks pretending oh-so-badly that they weren't dislocating their necks to see what was happening. "I didn't see any flying monkeys on the drive."

"No." She ignored his joke and gestured to where Maybelline still had Tia cornered. "I came with Tia."

"Sure, I remember her." He waved at her friend and blinked when Tia only used one vocal finger to wave back. He pursed his lips. "Yeah. I definitely remember her." He turned back to Emma, hands finding homes in his pockets.

The chatter of the crowd swirled around them as neither said anything. They used to be able to stand together like this, comfortable, at ease with the silence.

Now it was as if they were both naked and trying to pretend they weren't.

Emma's cheeks blazed as the image grew in her mind, an image she quickly stomped on before Bastian picked up the stray thought. Damn mind magic.

She struggled not to let the resentment that she had to be here show, her determination to hold on to some dignity anchoring it back. She knew it wasn't really fair to blame solely him for everything that had happened, but it was easy. She was happy to stick to easy.

"You're different," he said, breaking the impasse. He leaned his weight on a column. Blue, blue eyes stared at her. "You used to have a lot to say to me."

Oh, she had things to say to him. "I grew up."

"I noticed." His eyes slid over her, ensuring each inch of skin tingled. Her resentment turned into a chokehold. "A whole new Emmaline."

"Emma," she corrected.

"Emma." It was soft, intimate, like the inside of a petal brushing down her neck.

Her hands curled into fists. "You wanted to talk?"

"Later. Can I get you some champagne first?"

She shook her head.

"Then—"

"Excuse me! Excuse me, everyone." A voice she recognized as Alistair Truenote's rang out, magically enhanced to rise above the din in the ballroom. Everyone's heads turned to the raised dais where he and Bastian's mom stood. Well, where Alistair stood. Diana Truenote half reclined on a padded velvet chair, smile as bright as ever even though her skin matched her house's façade for paleness.

Emma was distracted from her concern as Bastian cursed at her side. "Damn it. I told him I wanted to talk to you first."

"Talk to me?"

"Yeah. I— Look, Emma." He grabbed for her hands and she had an impression of heat and strength before she pulled them free. "I'm sorry, I wanted to speak to you but Dad... well, he's Dad."

Alistair was accepting a champagne glass from a server and encouraging everyone else to do the same. "It's time to celebrate the moment we've awaited," he said with a booming laugh, as filled with vitality as his wife wasn't. He was a handsome, robust man, very similar to his son except he was built solidly like a tree trunk, and Bastian was lean. His beard was trimmed close, blond streaked with silver, which perfectly matched the hair he wore just as closely trimmed to his head. For one hundred and seventy, Alistair was looking...

Well. She sighed. Perfect.

Odd one out, raise your hand.

"Emmaline... Emma." Drawing her attention back, Bastian stepped closer, his words tumbling over each other. "I know this isn't an ideal way to do it, but here we are. I came back for you."

Emma's heart jerked like it had been hit with a lightning bolt. Next to her hand on the column, another bud exploded into a full flower.

Out of the corner of her eye, she saw Alistair lift his glass. "Shall we toast?"

Bastian made a quick movement. "This isn't how I pictured it...but hell." He ran a harried hand through his hair. "Emma, I need you to marry me."

"To the reunited happy couple!" Alistair sang out. "Bastian and Emmaline!" His words resonated round the room like an echo.

Or a wave against a cliff, over and over again, eroding it. Eroding who she was now back to meek Emmaline who would have fallen into Bastian's arms at so little. Emmaline who was always in second place. Who he'd abandoned and left desperate for a way out.

"*No!*" The word blasted out of her, anger licking up her insides until she choked on the heat.

Bastian's face twisted in shock. "Emmaline."

"My name is Emma," she managed, voice catching as she tried to breathe.

"Please." Bastian grabbed for her free hand, keeping it locked in his. A passionate plea.

Every hackle rose as she went stiff. Just because he was back, he thought all it took was his dad announcing their engagement? Him spouting a few empty compliments? Did he really think she was that simple? Had he no respect for her at all?

Had he ever?

She blanched as everyone lifted their glasses to them, smiling with their lips if not with their eyes. Some would still be bitter that she, of the lower echelons, caught a Truenote. A Truenote, after all, was top tier. A Truenote could do no wrong.

"*Please.* I need to marry you."

She opened her mouth, but her throat was so thick, the words wouldn't come. Except for the one that resounded again and again and again in her head. "*No.*"

"Emma." Bastian looked deep into her eyes. "If you don't marry me, my mom will die."

CHAPTER 4

If you don't marry me, my mom will die.
The words didn't make sense to her. It was as if he'd started speaking Latin, or one of the old tongues that Emma's mother still brought up and pointed to as languages she should know "as a Bluewater."

She waited for him to laugh. Not that it was funny, but he *had* to be joking. Marry him? Now. After seven years of being the frog the prince hadn't wanted to kiss.

She stared at him, watching his eyes. They chilled her. No joy, no humor. Just one hundred percent, grade A serious Bastian. She could count on one hand the times she'd seen him with those eyes.

Had she ever seen him with those eyes?

"What?" she finally managed, since staring at him wasn't helping.

He pinched the skin between his eyebrows as his dad continued his toast. "We can't talk here." He grabbed her hand and threaded his fingers through hers.

She yanked at his hold and broke free. "I'm not going any-where until you explain."

His eyes flashed, frustrated, as he opened his mouth. What-ever he'd been about to say was lost as Alistair—the gift that kept on giving—gestured to them. "And now our leading couple will open the dancing. Bastian?" He motioned to his son, seeming truly happy. Or truly drunk.

Emma wished she'd thrown back a bottle or two herself as she stared with dread at the hand Bastian held out.

"Please." Bastian gritted it through a courteous smile, dip-ping his head and looking up through his lashes.

Please what? Please don't cause a scene? Please don't say no? Please don't run out of here screaming?

Well, she wouldn't have run. Like any respectable witch, she'd have created a portal and hauled ass through it.

The moment stretched out long enough for whispers to start hushing through the crowd. Bastian's right eye twitched.

Damn it.

Emma didn't try to disguise her reluctance as she accepted Bastian's hand. Hers slid into his like it belonged and she shook off a chill as he turned and led her into the center of the ballroom.

Her stomach twisted as she faced him, his other hand com-ing around to rest on the small of her back to ease her closer. Her left hand drifted to rest ever so lightly on his shoulder, touching as little as possible.

She tried not to absorb how broad he felt or how memo-ries washed over her, being this close to him. He smelled like days spent talking in the bayous. Like crisp autumn nights hanging out in the Garden District. Like childhood and what came after.

She swallowed against the rising tide of emotion as the first strains of music started. "I hope I remember how to do this."

She didn't even realize she'd said it aloud until he gave her a faint smile. "Just follow my lead."

Easy enough for him to say when that was all she used to do. But now she had no choice but to obey as he swept them into a dance.

Very aware of the eyes on them, Emma concentrated on not stumbling for the first few bars, looking everywhere but at his face—much too close to her own. He danced with confidence, not losing a beat even with all his years away, the hand on her back guiding her with ease.

She waited until the next few couples joined them before she pounced.

"Explain." It was soft, but a demand, nevertheless. She was done being passive.

He darted a glance at her, eyes very dark, before focusing on the swirl of the dancers. His terse words shocked her when they came. "My mom is sick."

Instant sympathy beat away the dark emotion, at least for a moment. "I'm sorry." And she was. Diana had always been nice to Emma, despite the obvious social-climbing machinations of her mother.

"Yeah." He contemplated the musicians as they twirled their way. "I need you to marry me."

Need. Not want.

The phrasing sliced through her and she wrestled with the urge to be sick. "What does one have to do with—with the other?"

A moment stretched between them, the wail of a violin akin to the scream Emma locked inside.

"It was just a cough at first," he said, low enough that anyone dancing nearby wouldn't hear. "A tickle. Then it spread to her lungs. Now she can't keep food down and her hair is starting to fall out."

Emma frowned, uncomprehending.

"She's dying, Emmaline." His jaw hardened into cement. Navy eyes flamed brighter with suppressed magic. Something like accusation glittered before he closed them.

The words floated, sharp darts that pricked at Emma's composure as she lost a step. She almost stopped dancing, but his hand tightened on hers and forced her to continue. *Right. Can't let on that anything is wrong. That isn't society's way.* "She can't be."

"She is."

She stared as her feet moved in the old patterns, trying to understand. Witches didn't get sick. Not really. They maybe caught a side effect from a spell, and there was the odd malady that had evolved to create havoc in witch kind. They weren't immortal; just long-lived. But Diana was still young, only one hundred and fifty-odd years old.

Emma twisted her neck. Diana was slumped in her chair onstage, Alistair next to her as if neither desired to dance. His arm was around her. She'd have thought it was affection—it was widely known that the Truenotes had an unusual love match rather than the more typical soulless pairings—but now saw it was for support. Shock, sympathy, sadness swirled together as she shook her head to try and still the tornado. Her attention swung back to their son. "What is it?"

His whole body was tense enough, she thought she could flick him and a hairline crack would thread through his body until he finally collapsed from the pressure.

"It's us. Me." The words were saturated with despair. "She's dying… My mom is dying because we didn't get married by the time stipulated in the contract."

Her frown grew more concentrated, her voice more halting. "Bastian, that…that doesn't make— Well, it doesn't make sense." She'd read the contract. She'd had to, for many reasons, but this…this wasn't the done thing. There was a time limit in every engagement contract, yeah, but if exceeded, then it went before the High Family to decide the fate of the couple. People didn't *die* from not completing it.

"I know. But it doesn't mean it's not true." He drew in a breath that sounded like it came from the soul. "She started to get sick a few years ago. It was only mild, nothing to rush back for, or that's what she told me. But I talked to Dad…she's been getting worse, especially in the past two years. We didn't know what was causing it. Dad…he wanted me to come home, be with her, but I needed to find answers. And I found them a week ago in Egypt."

Emma watched him, hardly daring to breathe.

He flicked her an inscrutable look. "I went digging in one of my friend's houses. He's a warlock who collects valuable books and has an archive filled with musty tomes full of information most people have forgotten." He chose his words carefully. "Apparently engagement contracts, if not fulfilled, used to have nasty side effects for their witnesses. There's a curse written into ours, Emmaline, because it's phrased like a traditional contract." He shook his head, just a little, as if he still couldn't believe it. "If we didn't get married by the time you turned twenty-five, our witnesses to the contract—your dad and my mom—sicken until the curse eventually consumes them."

It was like a blow from behind and she reeled, fingers going lax in Bastian's as he doggedly continued the dance neither of them had wanted.

Her dad…it obviously couldn't affect him. He'd died ten years ago in a freak potion explosion at his job working in the laboratory of a magical cosmetics company. Her mother had hated that he'd worked and had forbidden anyone to grieve. Emma had worn a black stud in her right ear under her hair so her mother wouldn't see.

But Bastian's mom.

It was unbelievable. It couldn't be true. *Why* would anyone…

Her mother's face, smug in the arrangement she'd nurtured to fruition, loomed in her mind. Her mother. A witch who was renowned for her creative tricks. She would have ensured a clause was put in like this. Only she could be that conniving, actually using medieval engagement contracts as a basis for Emma and Bastian's. No wonder she hadn't pitched a fit when Bastian had pulled up sticks and flown the coop. She'd been annoyed, put out, but ultimately accepting. Goddess, she'd even allowed Emma to move away from New Orleans.

Because she knew, at some point, her daughter would be standing right here as Bastian begged her to marry him so his mom wouldn't die.

Sourness hit the back of her throat. Walls closed in around her, clamping her as Bastian spun them into a turn around the other couples. False smiles aimed their way as they twirled and got lost in the melee. No way out.

Her skin had felt hot moments ago; now she could rival a corpse for temperature. This couldn't be happening.

Vows were serious in their world. Humans may *say* until death do they part, but as far as Emma had observed, it was more like until divorce do they part, with one human taking the house and the other taking the contents, down to the last insignificant baseball card.

But witches worked with words and binding rituals. Vows held power. If she walked to the altar and faced Bastian and went through with the ceremony, she would always be tied to the warlock who'd run from her. And who'd only returned because he was desperate. If his mom hadn't been dying, he'd never have come back. To her. For her.

She viciously cut the thought in two. That was Emmaline emerging from the closet Emma had shoved her in. The Emmaline whose deepest desire was to have Bastian turn around one day and declare his love. Declare that even without the contract he would choose her.

Years had passed, she'd moved on. Mostly. And now here she was, in a well-lit ballroom, the toast of society, dancing with the golden prince. A scenario any woman would kill to live. A man begging her to marry him. But not because he chose *her*. Because she was the other name on the contract. And what a contract it had proven to be.

Her heart constricted and she closed her eyes briefly. "No," she murmured, pained. She didn't want this. The box around her tightened.

"Emmaline?" A hoarse note in his voice had guilt rippling through her. "Please. I know you're not the girl I used to be friends with." He hesitated and his hand tightened where it held hers. Their legs brushed as they spun. "I know I'm asking a lot. But it's my mom."

And there it was. It was his mom. No matter how resentful she was, how hurt she was, how much she didn't want to marry someone who was forced to marry her, she couldn't sentence someone to die just so she could leave Bastian the way he'd left her.

Once again, she'd lost. Bitterness tangled with sympathy, but she choked out the word. "Okay."

Bastian didn't breathe for a long moment, enough that his lungs protested the restriction. He gulped one in, eyes locked on Emmaline's—Emma's—face as he continued to move them both through the old steps drummed into him from childhood. She was pale, her eyes haunted. She couldn't look less like a blushing bride. But she'd said...

"Okay?" he echoed, voice gravelly. "You'll do it?"

Her chest lifted as she took in a breath. Unhappiness rode

her face. Yet... "I'll marry you." He barely heard the words, but she'd said them.

Relief was a typhoon that soaked him, his guilt and worry drinking it in like desert plants. He wanted to drop to his knees, weakness making him so suddenly dizzy that his smooth movements hitched. He fought the ridiculous urge to cry. And ask why she was relenting. Had she known all along that he'd be forced to this, that there was even more to the contract's hidden clauses than he'd told her? Would she really be willing to drain him of his magic?

But if she had, why would she have refused in the first instance?

Was it a game to make him think she didn't know or didn't care?

He couldn't worry about that now. He had to focus on what mattered. Magic may have been his family's legacy, but his mom was his family's heart.

"Thank you," he whispered, and at that moment the past didn't shadow the gratitude he felt. "Thank you, Emmaline."

Her name joined the last musical note as the band finished their number. Bastian drew them to a stop, staring down at her. Other couples broke apart to wander off, brushing past them. Almost together, they withdrew their hands. Discomfort crawled across his neck. He didn't put a hand there, aware eyes would still be on them. To that end, he presented his arm to lead her off the floor.

She didn't move, gaze shuttered. "I have—some things I need to say."

His arm remained, even as some of the relief diverted into suspicion.

Both a desperate urge to know the truth and a dizzying kind of panic at the idea had him pushing his arm closer, a silent demand to take it. "Not here."

She blinked, mouth pursing as she swept a look around at their audience. He tried not to let her obvious reluctance bother him as she gave in and let him steer her off the dancefloor.

People tried to intercept them, of course. Society matrons disguised as well-wishers, old so-called friends of his whom he'd only spent time with because they'd grown up in the same Higher family social circle, catty witches who were all eyes for him and teeth for Emmaline. Or would have been if he'd slowed down.

"We need some alone time" was all he said, a stab of guilty pleasure in his chest at Emma's vibrant blush.

He squashed the feeling as he led them across the veranda, down the back steps, and drew her into the folly his dad had created years ago as an anniversary gift for his mom. Memory enclosed them as much as the hedges and trees hiding them from view.

This was where they'd always escaped to, often with a bottle of champagne that Bastian had snagged. They'd wandered the folly or found the stone love seat at its center and talked, gossiped, bitched. Well, Bastian had, and Emmaline had listened. She'd always listened and just…let him be. Everyone had let them be—they were, after all, encouraged to spend time together. To grow the bond. To ensure they were following the plan.

His thoughts turned dark and a hint of that earlier panic spiraled through him. Did he want to know?

Yes.

No.

Yes. He gulped a breath of air, sweet with heat. He'd missed New Orleans and her idiosyncrasies, including the air you could almost drink. He'd missed a lot. And whose fault was that?

Only the faintest of music reached the center of the folly,

where he stopped. Emma immediately stepped away from him. She closed her hand into her palm like a fist.

Awkward, he gestured. "You want to sit?"

"No."

He nodded, took another breath. Unintentionally mirroring her, he closed one hand into a fist at his side. "What do you have to tell me?"

Something strange flashed across her face before she turned to the hedges. She began to fiddle with the tiny leaves. "I have conditions before we do this."

"What conditions?" She'd already have him, and through him, his family's magic, at her disposal. The contract specified that she would be able to drain that power for her own use. What more could she ask for? His gut roiled at the possibilities.

Her arms wrapped tight around her stomach. He didn't think she'd noticed, but the flowers blooming on the hedges around her had withered into husks. Not a great sign.

He watched the vertical crease slide between her eyebrows, a line that had always made an appearance when he'd dared her to do something she thought outrageous. She'd always been so serious, but Goddess, sometimes she'd made him laugh.

"I know it has to be a true marriage," she said, her voice so like the one that had haunted his dreams when he'd first left, his soft-spoken best friend, that emotion pincered his heart.

He struggled past it. "Is that what you want? A *true* marriage?" He infused carnal meaning into the word, unsure how he felt about that. How could he sleep with her if he didn't trust her?

He'd never thought about bedding Emmaline much when they were young. But in any case, Emmaline had apparently gone, and he was left with Emma.

Emma was standoffish. She was silent, reserved. Angry. She didn't laugh like each moment was stolen. She didn't *laugh*. He couldn't even equate her in his mind with the girl he'd kissed once when she'd turned eighteen. A friendly gesture, nothing more. She'd gone scarlet and hadn't talked to him for the rest of her birthday. He'd found it sweet.

His gaze settled on her lips now. They were parted, shallow breaths emerging from them. Kind of sexy if he thought about it, how they almost made a bow. He watched them shape the word she spoke.

"No."

He couldn't remember ever hearing that word from her in the past and now he heard it entirely too much.

He forced himself to say the words he needed to in order to close the deal. "We can have a true marriage, Emmaline. If that's what you want."

Something about what he'd said made an angry glimmer appear within her brown irises. Color bloomed in her cheeks. "Thank you for your sacrifice," she said in a tone that rode the line between snide and simpering. "But you won't have to lower yourself to that."

Lower himself? "We'll be married," he said slowly, searching her face. It held no answers, no hint of what she wanted him to say. What he could do to make her happy to agree. He just hoped she hadn't learned any of her mother's tricks while he'd been gone. Or had she learned them before?

He *hated* this. All the questions that popped up like hands at a press conference. He desperately wished he could go back to a time when it was just the two of them against the world. His closest friend.

"I shouldn't have phrased it like that." She pressed her lips together. "Maybe a better word would be *official*. I know this marriage has to be official, but it will be in name only."

"In name only?"

She seemed to pick her words carefully. "I'll marry you, but we won't live together and be a—a couple. I'll live in Chicago. I'll still work at the bar. At my own place."

He wanted to ask why she'd chosen a bar, why she'd left, but this wasn't about them becoming friends again. This was about saving his mom. Keeping Emmaline happy was key to that.

"And me?" he prompted.

She shrugged. "You can do what you want. Like you always have."

Ouch.

"You want to live separate lives." He repeated it for clarity.

She nodded.

Vows were for life. That was just understood in their society, which was why marriage contracts and family bloodlines were so important.

He cocked his head. "Don't you want children?"

The color that had just vacated her cheeks hurried back. He almost grinned at the familiar sight. Her arms drifted to her sides. "Maybe," she whispered.

Testing her, he eased closer, slipping into his old charming façade. "You know how kids are made, right?" He swirled a finger, had a strand of her hair dance playfully around her face.

She shot him a look. "Yes."

"Then you know we'd have to be together at least some of the time. And a lot closer."

She batted her hair. "Stop it."

"Make me."

"You're a child."

"Yes." A true grin pulled at his mouth as an exasperated breath puffed from her.

"Fine. Let me revise that. In name for now." She pointedly ignored his teasing so he let her hair drift down. "Maybe we could, I don't know, revisit it again in twenty years."

"Ten." He didn't know why he'd countered. Maybe he was

just being an ass, but he was also a man and she wore irritated well. "But we can live apart for now. If that's what you want."

"Don't pretend you want to be married," she said. "I'm just saying what we're both thinking."

He didn't even know what he was thinking anymore, but he did know he needed her to marry him. So he nodded. If it was possible, her mouth pulled even tighter.

What had he done now?

He moved on. "Okay, living apart. For now. You'll keep your job, I can do whatever."

"Or whoever."

Swear to the Goddess, he thought he'd heard that wrong. A full thirty seconds passed. "You did not just say that."

Irritation mixed with obvious embarrassment, but she jerked a shoulder. "I'm serious. I'm not really going to be your wife. I don't expect fidelity."

A weird, misplaced anger completely at odds with his doubts stewed in his stomach. "Well, you should. Hell, Emmaline—"

"Emma."

"—I'll be your husband. You really want me to cheat on you?"

Her chin jutted up. "It won't be real."

"Real enough." He wasn't sure why he was angry; she was giving him a free pass. He still had to figure out how to shut down the Joining clause, but she was agreeing to marry him, letting him have his single rights, and was saving his mom. That was all that mattered.

He hung his head, annoyed, frustrated with the situation. No matter how they got to this place, they were stuck with each other. The least he could do was make it as easy on both of them as possible.

"Fine," he almost snapped before catching himself and evening the tone. "Thanks. So, totally separate lives. Once the rings are exchanged and the kiss seals the deal, we'll be off to our own corners."

Her hands fidgeted at her sides. "Yes."

"Great." He felt itchy, and it wasn't helping things. He should be celebrating. He was getting what he needed. "But until then," he continued, still with the tight edge to his voice, "I think it's best if I move in with you."

Her mouth dropped open.

Before she could say her favorite word, he held up a hand. "Hear me out. The Divining will start now that the official engagement has been announced. You know it's designed to test us, to see how we'll match as a couple. It'll be easier for the magic to work if we're together." And wouldn't it be interesting to see what the Divining picked up?

It was a witch tradition, one of those long-held ones that they didn't stand a chance of skirting. Every couple had to undertake the Divining. At the basest level, it was a chance for witch families to show off their offspring. The magic assessed a couple's strengths and compatibilities as they emerged as a potential new power unit. It was the crowning glory to an engagement.

Nobody knew exactly how the magic worked to test each partner and weigh up their traits. A spell would be cast by the High Family, and the magic would take on a life of its own, judging, testing, deciding as the couple went through their regular lives, revealing the individual traits that they'd bring to the partnership. Traits would show up written on their wrists underneath official tattoos. Brands to wear with honor. Apparently.

Eventually the magic would show its decision and would form rings they'd wear for the rest of their lives. Some couples got gold, others silver, some platinum, others cobalt or emerald. Each precious stone or metal with its own meaning and power.

But it wasn't just the Divining that had prompted Bastian to insist on moving into Emmaline's house. He needed to keep an eye on her, to make sure she'd actually go through with it. Even if he had to swallow the past and put on his charm like new clothes every day, he would get her to that altar.

For now, at least, Emmaline fell in with his plans as she gave a short, less-than-gracious nod of reluctant agreement.

He let out a breath and with a thought, two glasses of champagne appeared in his hands. He held one out. "A toast to us then, my bride."

She accepted it, a telltale shake in her hand making the bubbles fizz.

He lifted his glass, ignoring that the bubbles in his own glass trembled. "Thank you, Emmaline. Emma. Really. I'll do anything I can to get this over and done as soon as possible."

A flash of something on her face. "Naturally."

He paused, having the feeling he'd put his foot in it again. He used to be good at this, but being away from the witch circle for all these years had robbed him of more than time, it seemed. He doubted he'd fit in so easily with his society friends now, and to tell the truth, he had little interest in the invitations that had piled high in the days since his return. She might not be Emmaline anymore, but he wasn't the old Bastian either.

He focused on her face and the task at hand. "We'll get through the Divining and the wedding and then be done with each other. At least for the next decade."

She tipped her glass and drank.

His gaze slid to her throat as she swallowed. He should be happy. Right? But everything felt so…shaky. He needed her to *want* to marry him. He needed to feel in control so this sick, panicky feeling that she'd back out would retreat. From somewhere far away, he heard himself say, "I think we need something to seal the deal."

She eyed him. "Wasn't that what the champagne was for?"

With her sudden nerves obvious, his settled. He floated the champagne out of their hands with a thought. "Nothing bad. Just a kiss."

"Forget it."

He caught a flash of something from her, an emotion she felt so strongly she was projecting out from behind her shields. It was there and gone before he could identify it.

He eased closer. "We're going to kiss at some point. Might as well get the first one over with."

"Charming," she drawled, although her eyes had widened.

He didn't allow himself to grin at this flash of sass. "Take one for the team."

"The team?"

"You and me. We're a team now."

She shook her head. "We're not. And we're *not* kissing." But she hadn't stepped back or walked away, and if he wasn't mistaken, her pulse was throbbing at the base of her throat. He had a sudden urge to put his mouth there, nip it.

That alone almost sent him bolting from the folly. This was Emmaline, remember? And all that went with her.

But she did have such a good mouth.

He kept that mouth in his sights as his chest brushed hers. He wanted to slide his hands over her hips, but instinct told him she'd rabbit if he pushed it.

So, instead, he angled his head down. "Just a kiss."

Her response was a rapid in-drawn breath.

He kept his approach slow, slow enough that she could break away and run. Say no. Scream. Shout an immobilizing spell.

All she did was stare at him with those soft, wide brown

eyes. Looking into them brought out a peculiar emotion, something he didn't want to examine.

She was quivering just a little when he lowered the final inch, her mouth damp and soft. He rubbed his against it, enjoying the textures, the novelty that this was Emmaline. She parted her lips ever so slightly and he sipped at her. Her feet drifted closer, head angling back.

Taking his cue, he kissed her deeper, stroking her tongue with his.

Electricity in its purest form seared him down to his soles. His arms slid around her, held tight. His fingers dug in.

Goddess, she tasted like sugar and spice and all things infinitely *not* nice. Definitely naughty. And the realization made a groan stir in the back of his throat even as everything hardened.

He needed to stop. He'd said just a kiss.

With a surprising depth of disappointment, he lingered once, twice, and then pulled back to look into glazed eyes. The force of his desire to drop his head, to forget their deal blew through him, making his hands tremble.

He swallowed before he forced himself to loosen his grip and step back. Into reality with all its issues.

As she flushed bright red and whatever soft emotion he'd seen on her face twisted into a frown, his gaze wandered to the flowers on the hedges. Funny. There suddenly seemed to be twice as many.

CHAPTER 5

*E*mma counted off the seconds as they walked back into the ballroom. Faces wreathed with smiles as fake as some of the glamours older witches wore turned their way. She ignored them, barely touching Bastian's arm as he escorted her. She badly wanted to grip it for support, her legs unsteady enough that they could be on a rocking ship. *Start the countdown.*

Twenty…nineteen…eighteen…

But she wouldn't be gripping him anytime soon. That stupid kiss…

Her stomach clenched at the memory, even as she turned fury inward as well as outward. What had he been thinking? What had *she* been thinking?

Pride, that was what she'd been thinking. He'd been so sure a kiss would disarm her; she'd seen it in his face. He'd wanted to turn back time, for her to become the swooning girl in his arms.

So, pride had swaggered up, tapped her on the shoulder, beat its chest and assured her they could stand there, unmoved, stiff as an object hit with an immobilizing spell.

Idiot, she berated herself. She'd have been better off sneering at his idea. Now he'd know. Because there had been…just a moment…a sheer fraction of time…when she'd softened.

And now she hated herself for that curiosity, the shiver that had snuck up her like an international cat burglar and stolen her memories of who held her. It had just been so long since a man had kissed her.

That was all it had been. A reaction, a freak incident.

A hell of a kiss.

She smoothed the scowl before the partygoers spotted it.

Tia frowned at her from the crowd, jerking her chin at Bastian in a *What the actual fuck?* motion. Her friend was confused at the engagement announcement. She could join the club. They could meet every Wednesday and Friday and recite a pledge: *Emma is an idiot and a pushover.*

Emma shook her head in a slight movement. Later, when they were alone, when they were back in Chicago. Home. Then she could explain. It would have to be one of her other conditions—she wouldn't lie to her best friend. Even if she'd wanted to, if she didn't explain, Tia would assume she'd fallen back into Bastian's arms and would likely strip her hide off with her tongue, bundle her into a portal and keep her restrained in the bar's office while she tried to cure the spell that had obviously been put on her. What were friends for if not to cure curses?

But Goddess, what would she tell Sloane? Nothing, she decided in the next minute. At least not yet; it wasn't like she was planning on leaving to rejoin New Orleans society. Separate lives meant she could keep Bastian and Sloane separate, too. Just as she'd managed to keep everyone else down here ignorant of her greatest secret. Keeping Sloane safe was more important than anything Bastian could do to her.

Speaking of, Tia's eyes shifted to Bastian and narrowed.

When she glanced back at Emma, she lifted a hex bag with her head cocked in question. Since Emma had patted her down, she dreaded to think where Tia had pulled that from.

It did make her lips tip up, though. She shook her head again and kept moving forward with Bastian.

Fourteen...thirteen...twelve...

Music played in the background as they continued to walk. She wasn't sure if Bastian had a direction in mind or if he was just putting on a show, displaying the engaged couple as if they were an act in a zoo.

Eight...seven...six...

She sure felt like an exhibit, people staring, whispering, noses going into the air behind delicately fluttering fans. Her stomach twisted as she realized everyone was looking at them. Her breathing grew shallow and heat flashed to her cheeks, her nape. Goddess, she hated attention.

Four...three...two...

"Emmaline."

One.

Emma's fingers dug into Bastian's arm. He shot her a searching look even as he turned them to face the woman who'd spoken.

Her posture was perfect, her features classically beautiful and sharp enough to cut ice cubes for a dozen drinks. Platinum hair was artfully piled into curls atop her head, her dress a deep shade of crimson. Her eyes were as brown as the ones they drilled into, if cooler with the ever-present disappointment.

Emma swallowed over the lump that always appeared in her throat. "Hello, Mother."

Bastian tipped his head in polite, if equally cool, greeting. He never had been a fan of her mother's. "Clarissa."

"Bastian. How nice to see you've returned" was the neutral response. "You look tanned."

He nodded, his expression guarded. "I spend a lot of time in Africa."

"My, my." Clarissa's lips nudged up into what was either a tight smile or an involuntary spasm. "You must tell me about it sometime. You and my daughter will come to the house for dinner."

"If you'd like," Bastian said.

Emma didn't speak. She knew her agreement wasn't necessary.

As predicted, her mother moved on. "May I be one of the first to offer my congratulations and wishes for a successful marriage."

No words of happiness, Emma noted. She supposed that wasn't a necessary ingredient in the witch world.

Bastian didn't say anything, his gaze fixed on Emma. She realized he was determined she should reply, hold up her end of this engagement.

"Thank you, Mother," she managed. And stalled.

Clarissa's lips thinned. "She speaks. I was beginning to wonder if I should search you for a hex bag."

Emma's throat constricted. Her tongue felt thick and clumsy in her mouth as she cast about for something to say.

"As you can see, her lessons in social graces never did improve." Clarissa sighed, the short, irritated noise that had resonated throughout Emma's childhood. "Perhaps a refresher is in order, Emmaline. You're going to be married to an important man. Even if he has a tendency to scamper about." The insult was scathing but Emma barely heard it.

A refresher? Horror filled her at the idea, images flashing through her head.

Bastian's arm went taut under her hand. "I don't think we will need your guidance, Clarissa." His tone was one she'd rarely heard—quiet steel, a sword hidden in the shadows.

Clarissa tipped her chin down. "There's no need for the pretense. We all know why you've returned."

He arched his eyebrows, every muscle tense.

She appraised him. "You're here to fulfill the contract at last. I know Emmaline may not be powerful or beautiful, but I assure you, she can be biddable."

Biddable. Like a dog.

But then, was her mother wrong? She was just standing here, letting the insult slam into her.

She may have moved out, got a job, lived independently, renamed herself. But with her mother, she'd always be meek, quiet Emmaline.

Blood surged to her cheeks with humiliation.

"Why did you decide to return now?" Her mother looked at him expectantly, too used to being obeyed to consider the rudeness in her question.

Even as the thought crossed Emma's mind, she caught the glint of mockery buried in those chips of brown ice. Disgust reared up as the realization sank in. Oh, Clarissa knew. And she was poking the sore spot for fun.

A hot emotion closed around Emma's throat. *How far did apples fall from the tree?*

Bastian was cool beside her. "Duty. Friendship. Family."

"Of course," Clarissa murmured. "What else would it be."

The hum of power under his skin sank into Emma, like a static shock at where they touched.

"On that note, I need to have a word with my daughter in private. About our plans for the future." Her gaze switched to Emma, unaware of the powder keg beside her. "Motherly advice for the Divining. That sort of thing."

She didn't wait, only turned and headed to a retiring room earmarked for the guests to sit a spell.

Bastian's eyes were dark. "Future plans?" he asked lightly. "Sounds nefarious."

"It's never anything but." Her joke fell flat. She shifted, uncomfortable.

His hand touched her chin. "You don't have to go."

Her knight in shining robes. Except now she knew a damsel couldn't depend on anyone. Sometimes they needed to face the dragon alone.

"I won't be long. We can act the happy couple when I'm back."

He bit back whatever he was going to say. Nodded.

Emma dropped her hand from Bastian's arm and, without looking at him, trudged after her mother.

Or began to. After five steps, an invisible hand smacked her on the butt.

She stopped dead. He did not. He couldn't. He wouldn't.

Angling her head back, Emma let loose some of the anger she felt at being trapped and channeled it into a full dead-eyed glare at Bastian.

Who merely shrugged. "It's what teammates do." He smiled then, and this was a warmer temperature. It slid into Emma's body and rippled like sunshine, banishing some of the shadows from dealing with her mother.

Still, she narrowed her gaze. "Don't." She might have said more, but Clarissa would be irritated to be kept waiting.

She found her mother in the blue retiring room. The Truenotes had used every shade of the color in an effort to wrap the guests in feelings of calm, a striking and comforting sensation. Emma had often retreated here at a Truenote ball until Bastian could find her.

The colors did their best, but Clarissa Bluewater was too much their match.

"Are you trying to embarrass the family?" was her opening

salvo, as soon as Emma stepped foot into the room. Emma kept quiet, as she'd learned long ago that this wasn't a question to answer. Clarissa waved a hand. "That's what you wear? On the night of your official engagement? The night we've been waiting for since you drove the Truenote boy off?"

Emma twisted her hands together, chest tight.

Clarissa's breath whistled through her teeth. "He's back, Emmaline. Do you understand that? We get a chance to finally follow through with this marriage and get everything we've wanted. You might finally be useful, but only if you don't run him off again."

Bastian wasn't going anywhere, not while his mom was sick. But Emma didn't raise that, just nodded.

"That means dressing like a woman a man like Bastian would want." Clarissa's eyes raked down her body. "This doesn't show off your figure, it positively reeks of mourning and it is *not* something a Truenote née a Bluewater would wear."

"Sorry, Mother."

"You know I do this for the family. It's for all of us."

Emma had her doubts about that but took the path of least resistance and continued to nod.

Clarissa examined her dress again with obvious distaste. "If society hadn't already seen you wearing that funeral sack, I'd fix it. As it is, for any event in the future, I want you to report to the mansion first so I can approve of the outfit. No mistakes can be made. All eyes will be on you."

A headache pounded behind Emma's eyes. She'd known that the engagement becoming official would be the talk of the witch world—they'd all been waiting on it for decades. But to hear it said so baldly was like sticking her hand into frog spawn. Completely sickening. And, just like frog spawn for certain potions, the engagement was completely necessary.

"Now, we don't have much time," Clarissa continued, pacing up and down the short runner provided between two facing couches. "The Divining could begin as soon as tomorrow once the High Family are called on to do the spell. So I want you to remember the family in everything you do. Try and emphasize the powerful traits. In fact, I'm not sure you shouldn't come back to the mansion now Bastian has returned."

Panic slapped out. "*No*."

Clarissa stopped midstep. Her head turned, one eyebrow raised. "No?" she echoed.

Emma balled her hands, nails sinking into her palms as she dragged up a breath. "Bastian said—he said he wanted to see Chicago," she improvised. "With me. Bonding. And all that."

"Hmm." Clarissa's eyebrow retreated next to its twin. "He always was peculiar. Maybe you two *were* destined for each other." She shook her head and continued to pace. "Fine. Then you'll stay where you are, but stay alert. I will not have you embarrass the family any more than you already have by driving off the boy in the first place. Practice your magic: essentials, potions, hexes. And get a haircut, I can see seventeen split ends from here."

"Yes, Mother."

"And for the Goddess's sake, speak as little as possible. Nobody wants a fool who can barely get above a whisper in the family, not when she doesn't even bring substantial powers into the mix." Clarissa cast her eyes to the heavens. "I curse your father for leaving me in charge of this family. At least your brothers have the gift in spades. You, unfortunately, take after your father too much."

How right she was. Her dad had been an expert at keeping secrets, if nothing else. Sloane was the best example of that.

Clarissa held out a hand and a silver compact adorned with

the Bluewater crest appeared in it. She handed it out. "This is a direct line to me. I want you to give me an update any time a Divining brand presents itself."

Emma nudged her legs into moving, slowly bringing herself to Clarissa's side. She reached for the compact and Clarissa's magic snapped out, locking her in place. Immediately she felt the drain, a consequence of the leech power her mother had hidden from their world. She always used it as punishment, ever since Emma had been young. It felt as though someone was tugging on her insides, stretching to the point of pain. If Clarissa continued, soon Emma's nerve endings would be screaming. Her breath came in small pants but she forced herself still. Struggling wouldn't do any good.

Clarissa waited a good ten seconds for Emma to feel the warning before she delivered a vocal one. "Don't screw this up, Emmaline. Flatter him. Obey him. Fuck the boy if you have to, but don't let him leave again."

Shock rooted Emma to the spot at the crude suggestion.

Clarissa pressed the compact into her hand and released the magic. "Your brothers have made the family name shine. Now it's your turn. Don't disappoint me."

Emma had never been so thrilled to breathe Chicago air. As soon as she stepped foot out of the portal, Tia threw up her arms.

"Dude, what the hell?" Before Emma could speak, she shook her head. "No, wait. We need Leah and we need some Cauldron cosmos."

Emma had opened the portal directly into her office, so all Tia had to do was tow her through the back and out front to the bar. Emma tossed the mirror behind her as they left. If it was a direct line to Clarissa, chances were she could eavesdrop.

It was past two in the morning. The bar was closed, but

Leah would still be cashing out the register and wiping down. Sure enough, when they came down the passageway, Leah sat on a stool, a stack of bills and a large glass of ice water in front of her.

"You're not going to believe this," Tia announced as they strode in.

Leah's stool wobbled as she flinched and let out a muted yip of alarm before she recognized them. "Hell, guys." Her hand flew to her chest as she breathed out. "Next time get a gun. It'd be faster."

Tia pointed to the stool next to Leah. "Sit, Emma."

Leah eyed Emma as she obediently rounded the bar to hoist herself next to Leah. "Well? How did it go?"

"Not yet." Tia shook back her shoulders and gestured at the counter with a small flourish. A cocktail shaker and several ingredients appeared in a puff of purple smoke.

Emma arched an eyebrow. "Feeling a *Bewitched* vibe, T?"

"Gives it a little something extra."

Leah clapped her hands together. "Cauldron cosmos. That means something happened at the party. Dish."

"Get me a drink first," Emma muttered, slumping.

Leah reached out, fingered the material of Emma's dress as Tia got started on the mix. "This is what you wore?"

Emma slid her a look.

"I know, but c'mon. This belongs in the section politicians' wives shop in. Demure, boring. Camouflage for the dead."

"That's her go-to." Tia picked up an ice pick and hacked at a block, keeping an air shield up around it to save them from flying ice.

"You know, I've heard some friends are nice." Emma split a sour look between them.

Tia added a pinch of something pink that sparkled and a

large splash of some liquid that came in a pink bottle. "Real friends tell the truth, and truth? It hurts, baby."

Barely restraining from rolling her eyes, Emma nodded at the notes on the counter. "Do you need help?"

"No, all done, really." Leah bundled them together. "I'll put these in the safe and when I get back, I want to hear everything."

"She will, too." Emma watched her friend go. "Last time she made me describe the appetizers."

Tia snorted. "She's not the only one. Sloane has an unbelievable appetite to know everything."

"Just remember she's barely thirteen."

"By thirteen I'd cast my first hex."

"Well, she's human."

"Half."

"With no powers."

"Yet." Tia shook her head. "Not relevant yet, in any case." She capped the cocktail shaker, picked it up and then let it go in midair. It hovered there. She nodded to Emma. "You always know when it's the best consistency."

Emma didn't have the best control over her limited telekinesis, but she'd had a lot of practice with this. She flicked her fingers and had the cocktail shaker vibrating like a cat on a washing machine. Leah came back in and watched, delight curving her face.

"I'll never get over that," she said, with a wistful tone. "Can I try mixing the next round?"

Emma quit shaking, reeling in the cocktail shaker until it rested on the counter. "Sorry. I have to get back for Chester."

"Then next girls' night." Leah threw herself back onto her stool. "I think I've almost got it."

Tia and Emma shared a look. The last cocktail that Leah

had made had had way too much jasmine powder in it and they'd all ended up without a voice for a few hours.

Leah caught the exchange. "Hey, come on. It was better than the time before when I made Tia vomit blue."

A snorted laugh escaped Tia as she conjured three chilled martini glasses and began pouring the concoction into them. "You think bringing that up is going to help?"

Leah accepted her glass. "Shows some improvement, right?"

"She's like sunshine bottled." Tia passed Emma her glass. "You clearly didn't grow up in the witch world."

"No, but speaking of..." Leah looked at Emma over the rim of her glass. Expectation widened her eyes like a child about to be told a bedtime story.

Emma stared at the pink froth on her drink. When she breathed out, small ripples skated the surface. They got bigger and bigger. Just like Bastian asking her to marry him. The consequences would change her life in so many ways...

Well, she'd made the decision and now she had to live with it. She'd had experience with that.

She squared her shoulders, lifted her glass. "I'm getting married." She gulped half of the drink down as Leah spluttered.

"Oh, yeah." Tia clinked her glass with Leah's. "Right there with you, pal."

"What... How... When...?" Leah stopped, exhaled. Took a drink. Wiggled her shoulders as the magic hit her bloodstream. "That was needed. Now, spill."

Emma swirled her drink, choosing to focus on it rather than her friends. "I had no choice."

Tia's glass hit the counter. "He forced you? Give me ten seconds to hunt up a hex bag and I'm going nuclear on his ass."

"Tia."

"Don't worry; it won't be traced back to us. I've gotten better at hiding the energy signature."

Emma wasn't touching that with a ten-foot wand. "Tia. His mom is dying."

"What?"

Emma explained, setting out the facts like toys at a tea party. When she'd finished, Leah stared at her a minute before gulping down the rest of her cosmo.

Tia slid her a grimace. "You'll feel that tomorrow."

"That's tomorrow's problem." Leah's head bobbled as if it couldn't decide whether to shake or nod. "Wow. Emma. Wow."

"I know."

"And you can't get a quickie divorce once the clause has been met?"

"No such thing," Tia answered, eyes glued to Emma's face. "So you're getting married, but it's completely platonic."

Emma viciously suppressed the memory clearing its throat. "Yes. I told him that I'd still live here, work here. He can do whatever. Far away from me."

"And how's that going to work when he sleeps with someone else after the vows?"

Emma shrugged, indifferent. At least, it was a cousin to indifference. In the ballpark. She could see it from where she stood.

"Right." Tia pursed her lips. "I know that face."

"What face?" Leah caught the last drops of cosmo on her tongue.

"What Ms. Emmaline has not told you was that she was infatuated with Bastian Truenote since…well, forever."

"That was years ago," Emma insisted, annoyed. "Before he abandoned me."

"Try telling that to your face because I can already see it."

That annoyance circled Emma's blood, along with the potent cocktail. "See what?"

Tia jabbed a finger. "The gooey, he's-so-dreamy shit. You like him being back."

She gaped for a couple of seconds. "*No!*"

"You do. He's going to come back in, make you fall for him and then sleep his way through society, and I'll have to watch him break your heart all over again."

The picture painted was much too vivid. Emma would have preferred a misty watercolor. "I told you, I said he could. We'll live separate lives."

"It's not a good idea. And what about Sloane?"

"What about her? I'm not going to let them near each other." The idea made panic stretch gossamer wings inside Emma's chest and she put a hand there as if to steady it. "Bastian was the perfect son."

"You mean, until he ditched you."

"Thank you for the reminder."

"Just see you do remember."

"Look, he *was* always doing everything as a warlock should, followed all the rules and customs." Sloane's troubled and shy face came to mind and Emma's heart pinched. Her resolve hardened. "Even if I was stupid enough to fall for him, I doubt he'd like me being so close to Sloane. Or you," she said pointedly to Leah, who had a somewhat dreamy look on her face. "It wouldn't be proper."

"Maybe he'll fall in love with you and wouldn't care," Leah proposed and then watched as both Emma and Tia snorted out laughs. "What? It could happen."

Emma smirked. "Someone's had too many cosmos."

"Seriously." Leah kicked her, missed, and almost fell off the stool. She huffed as she resettled. "Whatever, I'm dying to get a look at this guy. What's he look like?"

The words left Emma unbidden. "Like sunshine and sin." She held up her hands as Tia threw up hers. "She asked!"

"Oh, boy." Leah's shoulders wriggled. "Is he going to be around?"

Emma knocked back the rest of her drink. Braced. "He's moving in."

"*What?*"

Tia's noise resembled a teakettle on the boil. "I didn't make these strong enough."

CHAPTER 6

*B*astian planned his next steps as carefully as if he was organizing one of the archaeological digs he'd been involved in the past few years. He stood just to the side of the doors of Toil and Trouble, so anyone inside couldn't see him, revving himself up for the encounter.

The memory of Emmaline's fingers biting into his arm, her reluctance to go with Clarissa at the ball, had kept him up all night, pacing back and forth. Were they planning something worse? Or had it really been about the Divining?

However Emmaline was involved, he now knew Clarissa had her own suspicions about why he'd left. It didn't necessarily follow that she'd been the one to cast the silencing hex, but she'd definitely be the top suspect on his list for choosing the traditional engagement contract that now put his mom in jeopardy.

As much as it galled him, Clarissa would win. And it would be a win for her since she likely planned on taking advantage of the power Emma would gain through the Joining.

He leaned heavily against the brick of the building as he

tried to put that aside and get his head in the game. Emmaline wasn't happy. Whether it was because she was playing puppet to her mother or because she didn't want to marry him for her own reasons, she could retreat at any point.

He needed to win her over. He could do it, he was sure. They'd been friends once.

Hadn't they?

He silenced the doubting voice. If this was going to work, he couldn't constantly question everything she said or did. He'd go crazy. He needed to establish some kind of friendliness again. After all, even with separate lives, she was going to be...his wife.

He twitched and then exhaled in irritation. Enough. He twisted to face the door. It gave under his push and warmth rushed to greet him. He only hoped Emmaline would eventually do so with half as much enthusiasm and without Tia and her hex bags in tow.

Chatter filled the room but it wasn't overwhelming, pods of conversation between groups or pairs, a couple of singles reading or staring at their cells.

Behind the bar was a human, short but amply made, wearing a Cubs cap. She chatted easily to the older man she poured a beer for, winking at him and making him laugh as he collected his change.

He headed her way, stopping directly in front of her. "Hi."

"What can I get you?" She glanced up with a ready smile, only for it to freeze. "Shit."

"What?" He glanced behind him, just to make sure an axe-wielding psycho hadn't wandered in.

"Nothing." Color streaked along her high cheekbones. "Uh, sorry. I...stubbed my toe."

"Okay," he said slowly, believing that about as much as he

believed in ancient curses bringing mummies to life, like some of the more superstitious humans he'd come across.

"So." She stared at him as if seeing something other than his face. "You'll want a drink. Or maybe something to eat?" She gestured at the cake stands that crowded this end of the bar, all covered by glass domes. Inside each were treats that called out to his sweet tooth—plump muffins, glossy cakes, cookies as big as a man's hand.

"Coffee would be good." He weakened. "And maybe one of those muffins."

"Sure." She filled his order without asking how he took his coffee. Then stared at the black liquid. "You're Bastian."

Surprise chased confusion. "Yeah. How'd you know?"

"You've been mentioned."

Pleasure snapped at surprise's heels. "I have? All good I hope."

"You hope for a lot." Before he could say anything else, she smacked her head. "I didn't ask if you took cream or sugar."

"A little cream would be good. Maybe a bit of sugar."

"No problem." She fetched the items, let him doctor it himself. "You're here to see Emma?"

Bastian swirled the spoon in the liquid, the white rippling through the black until they were one. He cast an appraising glance at the woman. "Is she here?"

"In the back. Want me to grab her?"

"I'll have this first." Curiosity compelled him to ask, "Do you work here full-time?"

"In a way." She braced her hands on the counter. Her nails were painted a fun bright pink. "I own a third of the place."

Bastian took that on board with a slow blink. He hadn't known a human also owned the bar; he'd assumed it was just Emmaline and Tia. He'd have thought it was hard to conceal magic use otherwise—though Emmaline had said she kept her powers to a minimum here, he conceded, lifting the coffee cup and blowing across the steaming surface.

Why a bar? The question continued to plague him. From what he'd seen at the ball, she still considered attention as the missing circle of Dante's hell. Maybe he could ask and begin bonding that way.

He sipped, made a noise of appreciation. "You make good coffee."

"One of my many talents." She held out a hand. "I'm Leah."

"Bastian." He accepted and was rewarded with a surprisingly firm shake. "But you already knew that. What gave me away?" Did Emmaline have a photo of him from days long gone? The thought brought with it an unanticipated amount of pleasure, which was immediately crushed by his better sense.

"Let's just say her description was dead-on." She grinned, leaving him to wonder exactly how he'd been described and how much Leah knew. Her expression held a certain knowing, but it was impossible that she'd know *everything*, human as she was. He buried his curiosity behind another sip of truly excellent coffee.

"A man who doesn't immediately demand to know more about himself." Leah pursed her lips, all laughing eyes and mischief. "I didn't dare dream you existed."

"Not going to lie, I have been told I am a woman's dream man before," he tossed back. See, he remembered how to do this.

She sighed dramatically. "And *pop* goes my little hope balloon. Now you'll either further dash my hopes or you'll split that muffin with me."

She talked to him like they were already friends, as if they'd known each other their entire lives. Strangely charmed by the vivacious human, Bastian held out a hand. "Got a knife?"

Leah's smile widened. "You pass the first test, anyway."

His heart stuttered. Had that been a Divining test? Or were those words a coincidence?

He'd woken up with an intricate tattoo stamped on his wrist. A calligraphic *B* and *E* joined at the top by a crown. The High Family had cast their spell and the magic was now around him, waiting to prove his magic, his nature and how compatible he and Emmaline were.

Would it also ferret out the truth?

Did he want it to?

Speaking of, Leah's gaze dropped to his outstretched hand and exposed wrist. "Cool ink. *B* and *E*? Dude, way to commit."

He gulped more coffee. "You could say."

"I get you. All in, balls out."

He choked on a laugh, burying it with a broad grin. And moved to phase one of his plan.

"I'm here about the job vacancy."

The reaction he got was not encouraging. Leah looked as if he'd handed her a pile of dog shit. Cold. So much for instant friendship.

"I don't know if that's such a good idea."

"I promise I'm a hard worker." He produced an old winning smile, projecting honest innocence for good measure.

Leah was silent a moment, clearly unmoved. Again, Bastian wondered exactly what she'd been told.

"You'll have to run it past Emma," she said finally.

"Great."

"And Tia, our other partner."

"Great," he repeated, forcing confidence. *Joy.* "Point me in their direction."

Leah regarded him. For a human, she had a pretty good hard stare. He felt it like a chill across the back of his neck.

Then she sighed, rolled out her shoulders. "Look, I've never been one to judge on hearsay. But what you did to Em was pretty crappy." Her head jerked as if erasing that. "Definitely crappy."

So she knew the bare bones.

He didn't bother trying to defend himself. "I'm here to make up for it."

"Are you? Or are you here for you?"

That hit close to home, and he flinched.

"Like I said, I don't know you and I'm always happy to be proven wrong. So if you're going to be in her life, please don't screw her over."

He opened his mouth to hotly debate that but shut it with a click of teeth. What was the point?

"She's in the kitchen." Leah gestured behind her. "Tell her you have my vote but you're on probation."

Emma had ditched the hangover from last night's debauchery and was happily piping spiced apple cupcakes with salted caramel frosting when she heard footsteps approach.

Assuming it was Leah, she didn't bother looking up, determined to pipe a perfect rose onto each cupcake. If she could get these out for the afternoon, the afternoon drinkers would demolish them before dinnertime. And Sloane was always partial to a sweet treat. They had plans to go to the movies—there was some rom-com Sloane was dying to see—and she'd texted earlier to let Emma know she'd passed the English test she'd been studying for. Definitely felt like a cupcake was in order.

She was swirling the nozzle up to the point when— "You bake?"

Her hand convulsed; frosting pulsed out of the bag to the counter. She stared at it a minute, then raised her eyes to Bastian.

His eyes went from her to the white frosting and then began

dancing. "Sorry. I think people usually try and give a little warning before that happens."

She almost smiled before she came to her senses. She bit down on it and held the piping bag to her like a weapon. She would not be amused by him. She wouldn't feel anything.

"Bastian," she greeted. Calm. Collected. As if she didn't have flour in her hair or melted butter on her sweater. "We didn't—I didn't expect you so soon."

He wandered in, dressed as mouthwateringly as always, though this time in broken-in jeans and a simple T-shirt despite the cool weather.

"I didn't know you baked." He tilted his head. "The goods on the counter—yours?"

"Yes."

"You've got talent."

"You tried them?"

He paused. "Well. I didn't get a chance."

So, like always, an empty compliment. Acid soured her stomach. She turned her back and got a cloth to wipe up the escaped frosting. As she concentrated, his gaze burned into her.

"I wanted to talk to you," he said, and without his face to complicate matters, his voice was average. Really. It wasn't masculine silk that teased her skin. She couldn't have felt less affected. "Obviously, we agreed I'd move in."

Something she was already regretting. "Yes."

"But I think we should do more. I should do more."

Appalled wasn't a strong enough word for how she felt about that idea. "Why?"

Apparently she hadn't disguised her feelings very well. His tone stiffened. "I know we said we'd lead separate lives, but there'll inevitably be some function or some event or something that means we'll be together. Let's just say, I think it'll make it easier on both of us if we're on good terms."

Her lips flattened. "You want it to be like it was before."

He was silent. Then, "I'm not stupid. I know something is off." He hesitated. "You know you could always tell me anything. If something else is going on." A strange kind of urgency threaded through his words, an underlying meaning that made a small amount of sweat break out on Emma's forehead. What did he know?

When she didn't respond, his eyes hardened a second before he closed them. When they opened, all she saw was the usual aimless charm. "I know we've changed. That you don't think of me that way anymore. And I'm sorry. I really am, Emma."

He didn't even know what he was sorry for. Anxiety forgotten, pinpricks of wrath dappled her body. She managed a nod. It was the best she could do.

"Maybe we won't get to how we used to be. But I'd like to…start fresh. New. I'd like to know you."

Emma steeled herself against the words. Bastian had always had a way with them. She didn't care. She didn't want to know him. She knew enough.

Even if he made sense. Even if it was practical.

Goddess damn it all.

"You want to spend time together. Here," she clarified.

"I want the bartender job."

Emma swayed back as if punched. *Why don't we have chairs in here?* "It's a human bar," she stressed. "With humans."

His eyebrows cocked. "I assumed."

"You'd have to be nice."

"I'm always nice."

That was so patently untrue that a snort escaped her. He looked startled before his lips quirked.

"I like humans," he offered. "I've had to be around them a lot. It's surprisingly refreshing to be around people who don't rely on magic."

Shock punched her a second time, but she curled her hand around the counter before it could knock her out.

Mistaking her silence for refusal, he pushed harder. "I can learn all the skills if you don't want to use magic. I'm pretty good with my hands."

Not. Going. There.

"And it'll be good for us to spend time…connecting."

"Bastian," she managed around the thickness in her throat. "Are you sick?"

"No?"

"Did you take something? Drugs?"

"No."

She lifted a hand. "How many fingers?"

His lips twitched. "Did you have this much of a mouth when we were younger?" His gaze drifted to the appendage in question.

She felt it tighten in instinctive annoyance. So obvious he would go the route of flirtation. Bastian never could deal when someone didn't like him. She hated that it affected her.

"You can have the job," she said at last. Maybe it was actually a good way of keeping him away from Sloane. "I'm not promising we'll end up friends. But we could use the help."

"Do you need to run it past Tia before I end up with an STD?"

She grimaced, ran a sticky hand through her hair before she recalled the frosting. Great. "I'll tell her." And wouldn't her friend be delighted? Especially in light of the BS she'd been prophesizing. She'd have to cite Sloane. Tia loved the girl as well, and it wasn't like Sloane was legally allowed to hang around the bar. Emma was pretty sure Tia would agree that keeping him busy at the bar was the best way to keep Bastian from finding out about her secret. About her sister.

"I'll start tonight."

She wanted to remind him that she was the boss, but it would've looked petty of her. "You *sure* you want to do this? It's real work." So, maybe she had to work on pettiness.

Faint amusement lightened navy to cobalt. "I like new experiences. So, boss, should we shake on it?"

"We didn't shake on getting engaged."

"Which makes it even more important we do something official now. Unless you prefer the old-fashioned seal-with-a-kiss method."

At the withering stare she shot him, he nodded. "A handshake it is."

He closed his fingers around hers, palm kissing palm. A wave of unwelcome heat spiraled lazily from where they touched.

His eyes were pure navy again when he spoke with soft determination. "I'll make you like me yet."

The only reaction she felt that deserved was a quiet snort.

As predicted, Tia wasn't very happy about the arrangement. And by "not very happy," read "extremely pissed."

"He worms his way in everywhere, doesn't he?" she'd fumed when she'd been told. "Golden boy just has to snap his fingers."

Even when Leah had pointed out he was free labor for a month and when Emma had reluctantly pointed out that if he was going to hang around, might as well keep him contained to one place, Tia had muttered darkly about watching out for her clueless best friend.

So that boded well. Maybe Emma would make sure he and Tia never worked overlapping shifts. Still, Bastian was a big boy. Emma was sure he could handle one pissed-off witch. Well, two if you counted her, but she was less the hex bag type, more the "feel my wrath through my frosty silence" type. Generally speaking. Not that Bastian seemed to be that moved by that method. In fact he didn't seem to notice it at all.

It was just like they were already married.

He'd left to get his things, check on his mother. Emma tried not to let that concern soften her heart.

Instead she concentrated on being relieved she had time alone. She needed to consider an aspect of the marriage that had slipped her mind with the whirl of…well, everything, last night. An aspect that, had Bastian known about it, would probably make him even less keen to marry her.

The Joining clause. A clause that gave her the power to siphon his magic from him after their vows—which would then allow Clarissa to use her leech power to take it from Emma.

Just when you thought things weren't complicated enough.

She'd considered it as she'd finished the cupcakes and made a start on the sugar cookie dough, which needed to be refrigerated overnight. As bad as the Joining clause was, she was disinclined to tell him about it. It wasn't like he had any choice in going through with the marriage and honestly, what good would it do anyone for him to know? At least, right now. He was stressed enough about his mother, and this would only divide his attention.

And fine. She didn't want to involve him yet. Things were strained enough between them without adding yet more drama to the mix. Better she try and figure out a way forward without him. Keep to their corners and interact just the smallest amount.

Part of her—and it wasn't a part she was particularly proud of—whispered that it would serve him right if she didn't do anything about fixing the clause. But that wasn't right and she knew even as the idea tiptoed across her mind that it wasn't something she could ever truly consider. As much as he deserved to bathe in a fire ant trap, his magic was his family legacy, part of him. She wouldn't take from him like he'd taken from her.

But there had to be a way to block her mother's hidden clause, and with that in mind, she'd sent a message through her mirror to the brother she was closest to. Kole already knew about the clause, having been with her when she'd discovered it. He was also extremely talented with magic of all types and had a bunch of contacts from his travels. Hopefully he'd have some idea of how to help. And if not, she'd have until the ceremony to decide whether or not to tell Bastian the truth before it all kicked off.

She hadn't stayed long at the bar after making that decision, choosing to walk Chester home in the rain instead of portalling. She lived about twenty minutes from the bar and she always preferred to walk, even if the air was heavy with drizzle. Chicago was known for its blustery showers, cool weather and arctic winters.

The very opposite of New Orleans's balmy days and humid nights. The thought always made her smile.

She wasn't smiling now as she sat on the edge of her bed with Chester in her lap trying to shove his face in front of hers. She doubted anyone would smile faced with a thirteen-year-old on FaceTime who was going for the world record in sulking.

"Chester," Emma scolded, putting her hand on his head and pushing him back down. The familiar popped back up like he was made of rubber. He loved Sloane and the feeling was usually returned.

Except for now, since Emma had told Sloane she might be late for the movies and they'd have to reschedule. Something she tried never to do. The girl lived with her aunt; her mom had died in childbirth, and her aunt worked as a nurse all hours to support them both. As a result, Sloane was left on her own a lot and was shy around new people. Her guidance counselor at school had suggested the Big Sister program as a way of coming out of her comfort zone. Not that the primary reason for her being so awkward—knowing she was part witch all her life—was something they could help with.

Having found out about Sloane through a letter in her dad's belongings, the truth cleverly hidden by a spell he'd taught Emma when she was young, Emma had deliberately moved to Chicago to find her after Bastian had left. To be there for her. Considering they had to keep the true family connection a secret—Clarissa wasn't a witch you cheated on easily—Emma had signed on with the program as an easy way of explaining why she was hanging around. She sometimes thought a different "big sister" might be able to help Sloane come out her shell more, but they helped each other. When she knew someone, Sloane was sassy and smart and fun. Having some experience of living behind a wall, Emma was trying to get her to make new friends using tricks she'd learned herself.

Emma glanced at Chester. Always drawn to the needy, she thought. For all the good it did her.

"I told you; something came up. An old...friend." Emma winced at how that sounded. Sloane was very sensitive and saw herself as being a low priority.

Sure enough, hurt came into the teenager's soft brown eyes. "Sure," she murmured, the camera wobbling. "You must want to see them."

"Not really." Emma tried not to lie too much, considering Sloane's childhood had pretty much sucked. Her mom had died giving birth to her, their dad had snuck away as much as he could to portal to her but then he had died as well, and even now Sloane had to be kept a secret from the witch world until she was ready. If she ever was. It had all left her feeling a little lost, abandoned, and Emma had promised to always be upfront and put her first.

With that in mind, she sighed. "It's complicated. I'll tell you more when I see you. But he's a warlock, which means we have to be extra careful."

"Because of your psycho mom?"

Emma snort-laughed. "Yes. Promise me you won't just show up." She pushed Chester down again when his nose snuffled the screen. He didn't understand how Sloane could be there and not be there at the same time. A pang of happiness slid from him to Emma and she let it comfort her. At least someone was happy.

She focused on the truth. "Bastian was my childhood friend. I haven't seen him in years. But he knew my family intimately. It's possible he might see the connection."

Sloane's eyes grew wide, a flush on her round cheeks. "A warlock? Is that different to a witch?"

"Not really. Just fancier sounding."

"What can he do? Can he do telekinesis? Tia lent me this book and I read all about how some warlocks can float things ten times their body weight." Glee appeared. "I would so kick some ass if I had that power."

A mini-Leah. Goddess save them all. "I'm not sure what he can do anymore, but he used to have some telepathy and telekinesis."

"So cool." She slouched. "You sure I can't meet him?"

"Yes."

"What if, like, you and he started dating? Then we could trust him and I could get to ask him all about his magic."

"We are *not* dating."

"Oh." With the mercurial nature of teens, Sloane looked disappointed. "That's a shame. We could have gone shopping and picked you up some new clothes."

"What's wrong with my clothes?" Emma asked, even though she'd heard the budding fashionista's opinion. Several times. In person and in writing.

Sloane did an eye roll as well as any other teenager. "You look boring. I heard witches always dress stylishly."

"You heard that, huh?" Emma did her own eye roll. "So sad for you to have got stuck with the boring witch for a sister."

"I know, right?" Sloane crossed her eyes. "I promise not to show up, but maybe if he sticks around and you realize he's not gonna betray me to the dark-bitch-momster, then we could talk?"

Emma checked the laugh at the description because the possibility filled her with dread. She settled for: "We'll see," having heard the overused parenting phrase on a human show years back. Turned out, it was overused for a reason.

She checked the time. Bastian hadn't said when he'd show up, but he'd been gone for four hours. He was bound to be there soon; she'd texted him the address.

"Is he sleeping in your bed?"

Emma almost dropped the phone. "Sloane!"

"My aunt says girls shouldn't sleep with boys in the same bed."

"Your aunt is right." Even if it did bring to mind an image of…

Well. Never mind that.

She cleared her throat. "He'll be sleeping on the couch. It's his first night and he'll need me to show him where everything is. It might run late, which is why I have to cancel."

"Oh." Sloane chewed on this, her free hand fiddling with her brown bob. Emma had tried to convince her not to cut it a month ago, but the girl had seen a celebrity she liked with a bob and that had been that. She looked cute, but far too grown-up for Emma's liking.

"I'd prefer to go to the movies, Jellybean," Emma said softly, using the forbidden nickname she'd given Sloane years back. She stifled a smile at Sloane's long-suffering look. "Tomorrow, yeah? I'll bring you the cupcake I made for your doing so well on your test."

They hung up not long after. Emma fell back on the bed, stroking Chester's head as he wriggled his way up her side to place his heavy head on her chest with a contented sigh. She stared up at the ceiling.

Already she'd had to disappoint someone she loved because Bastian had come back.

Just this once, she vowed with a frown. Nothing else would change. Her world would not revolve around him. Not again.

CHAPTER 7

$\mathscr{B}$astian had to admit he'd been curious about where Emmaline lived. This was her hidden oasis, the world she used to escape from her mom, from witches, from society. He wondered what Emmaline's home would say about her.

The first thing to note was that she lived in a cozy, if somewhat shabby building. Presumably when she'd moved from New Orleans, she'd not only stopped relying on Clarissa for a home, but money as well. Emmaline had cut herself off from everything familiar. She'd got out. As had he.

And yet they'd both ended up exactly in the same place.

The second thing to note was that her apartment was small, mostly one room, with things everywhere. The front door opened into a short entranceway, where an end table with a photo frame and a glass bowl for odds and ends sat below coat hooks that housed a couple of jackets and Chester's leash. The hallway extended into an open-plan living space, a beige L-shaped couch sitting on a patterned rug marking off the main area, and a kitchen just off from it. A breakfast bar slid in between them, stools topped with plush leather pushed in neatly. Bookcases lined the walls, the occupants piled haphazardly, some books, some DVDs, a small potted plant that was thriving, unsurprisingly. A large TV sat on an oak unit, more plants around it. Picture frames hung on walls painted a light gold and pieces of glass art squeezed in where there was space around the room.

The third thing to note was that she didn't like him in her space. Ever since she'd let him in five minutes ago, she'd been watching him drift around. She hadn't spoken since greeting him at the door and he could see her nerves, like a fine row of strings in the air he could pluck.

Charm her, he reminded himself.

He glanced at the closest picture. It held a photo of Emmaline and her two co-owners, all laughing, a party hat perched on Emmaline's head—like the one she'd been wearing the other day.

She still celebrated her birthday, then. Witches might not celebrate them as a rule, but he'd always made a point to get her a cake, buy her a present, sing. And her eyes would be less haunted for a while. He'd hoped someone would carry on the tradition when he'd run. He hadn't wanted to think of her alone on her birthdays. Even if...well, even if.

Birthdays were not a comfortable topic, so he moved on and glanced at the next photo frame. *Thank the Goddess.* "The pyramids?"

"Sorry?"

He turned, gestured to the frame. "You've been to the pyramids?" He'd seen them three years ago, up close as he'd portalled inside, and remembered it having been an almost holy experience.

"Ah, no." She combed her fingers through her hair, leaving it disheveled. Cute. "I'd like to go, but..." She trailed off, then caught her shoulders, pushed them back. Challenging him to pity her.

He absorbed that without reaction. When he looked closer at the photo, he realized it had been cut from some kind of travel magazine. "You should go. You'd like it." He'd said it automatically, but he wasn't sure what "Emma" liked. He'd known Emmaline, or thought he had, but this was someone else entirely. "Well, if you like breathing in air so hot you can almost taste it, and bugs as big as your nose."

She didn't blink. "You've been." It wasn't a question, but he answered with a nod.

"Yeah, and honestly, it's great. The hieroglyphics alone are something to see. And my friend, Ethan, lives just off the banks of the Nile near Cairo—he has his home glamoured so the tourists don't stumble onto him. He's got these stunning old tomes. You should see them; some are so brittle, you're scared to even go near them but the imagery…" He glanced up, trailed off.

Her gaze had turned puzzled, as if he'd begun speaking a foreign language halfway through.

Feeling a flush of embarrassment, he spotted another picture frame, this one of the Amazon. He pointed. "More bugs, torrential rainfall, but amazing cultures hidden in there. You'd love the flora." He figured that was a safe bet since her home was outfitted with plants. At least that hadn't changed. A feeling of gladness warred with the ever-present doubt.

He moved his eyes along the other picture frames, spotting Edinburgh Castle, a Bali island, the Great Wall of China, Sydney Opera House…

"Why haven't you traveled?" he asked, turning to face her. She clearly wanted to.

Her gaze on his was steady as she appeared to search for an answer.

"I have responsibilities" was what she finally opted for. "Some of us do." As he absorbed the insult's punch, she gestured at the couch. "I don't have a spare room."

"I've slept on worse." Besides which, he could always transmogrify it into a bed if it proved lumpy. He slid his rucksack off his shoulder, placed it next to his temporary bed. "Thanks for this, Emmaline. I know it feels a little weird now, but it'll work out." He hoped.

Her look turned doubtful, but she didn't speak against him. "Your shift starts at eight, so you have time if you want to go into the city."

"Sure, we can do that." He was easy. "Somewhere you want to go for dinner?"

She blinked. "Ah..."

"Italian still your favorite?"

"No. I mean, yes, but... I meant if you wanted to go into the city. Alone."

He took the second hit on the chin. "You really don't like me, huh." It would be hypocritical to get upset since he had so many unanswered questions about her. Guess he was hypocritical. He forced a smile. "How about I cook?"

A beat passed. "You're serious?"

"Sure. I've learned some things. Do you like paella?"

He headed for the kitchen, swerving to avoid Chester, who spat out a bone he was carrying, dropping down and proceeding to gnaw on it with low grumbles of glee.

Emma trailed him. "You cook?"

"I mean, I'm no master chef, but I can throw ingredients together." He motioned to the stools. "You can watch and talk to me."

She didn't move.

"Please?"

With slow resignation, she slid onto a stool. A beer appeared in front of her and she closed her hand around it, lifting it up to drink.

Another surprise. Emmaline was a common beer drinker. He bet that would have made Clarissa screech if she knew.

He conjured a paella pan and the ingredients he needed. "You got a sharp knife, cutting board?" He got them out when she pointed. "So. Tell me. Why did you open a bar?"

Silence met his question.

His knife slid through the chorizo as he chopped, concentrating on that, allowing her time to face the fact that she'd have to talk to him for this to work. And it had to work.

When she spoke, her voice was taut. "Why not a bar?"

"You don't seem the bar type."

"And what type am I?"

He shrugged. "The bakery type." Indicating the antique teacups everywhere, he added, "Or a tearoom."

Her eyes narrowed but Goddess knew what he'd said wrong. Then she said, "Predictable. Boring."

"I like bakeries," he contradicted, irritated that she was taking everything the wrong way. "I don't think they're boring."

"Maybe I like bars." Her chin went up and he didn't think he'd ever seen such a contrary expression on Emmaline's face.

"Okay." He focused down again because looking at her was proving difficult. He finished the chorizo. "What else don't I know?"

Silence again.

"You know me." He almost missed the low words.

"Not really." He stared at the chopping board. "I knew Emmaline. Or I thought I did." He opened his mouth, but the silencing hex stabbed into his throat, crackling up it like Pop Rocks. Only with more discomfort.

As he struggled, her heard her say, "I thought I knew you, too. Apparently we were both wrong."

Pain bloomed in his chest now as well. He surrendered to both and put down the knife. "Maybe we're moving too fast. I'll go out to dinner."

He expected her to hand him his coat. Instead, he heard a sigh.

"I still like cupcakes," she said in a soft voice. "My favorite color is still yellow. I still prefer to read a book than dance at a ball."

It was a small offering, but it was enough. He cleared the remaining discomfort from his throat. "That's good to know." He continued prepping for the next couple of minutes as she watched.

"I like your place," he said, searching for something neutral to talk about.

"Right."

"I do," he protested on a surprised laugh.

"It's small."

"So are mini-muffins but that doesn't mean I don't like them."

Her lips pushed into a hesitant smile and a pang shot through him. She glanced around. "It suits me and Chester."

"I thought you might have used a TARDIS spell when I saw the outside," he commented, referring to the spell that made spaces bigger once you pushed past the curtain of glamour.

"I could have, but I wanted to live like they do."

"They? Humans?"

She tensed. Assuming he was being derogatory? He knew the extreme sticklers in witch society looked down on humans, but he'd never subscribed to that. Probably thanks to his parents, who had always blazed their own trail. They were lucky their family name held so much power or the society sharks would've ripped the sheer niceness out of them decades ago.

"I don't know about you," he said, conjuring his own beer. Needing it. "But I like how free they are."

Surprise reflected back at him. "Yes. Exactly." She pursed her mouth and added, "And this place is completely opposite to my mother's mansion."

He supposed that *would* be a selling point. Better a tiny warm home than a giant icy prison.

"After a while..." She shrugged. "There didn't seem a need to expand."

"Well, I like it. It suits you."

"Because it's small and artless?"

The sly humor from her was unexpected. He liked it. "Technically I still live at my parents' house."

Her fingers toyed with the wet label draped around her beer bottle. "You never settled anywhere?"

He hesitated, feeling like they were moving into dangerous territory. "I liked—like—Egypt a lot. Even considered getting a home there, but I like being able to pick up and find the next dig."

"Of course you do." She looked away from the label, forehead creasing. "'Dig'?"

"Archaeological," he clarified, choosing to ignore her comment. He felt a nudge and smiled down at Chester. He threw him a piece of sausage. "I help out on digs as an antiquities expert."

She looked taken aback. "Are you?"

"Sort of. I specialize in occult items."

Her chin lowered in a nod. "Right." She hesitated. "And you like these digs?"

"I really do."

Emma seemed to argue with herself for a minute before asking, "Why?"

Was she that reluctant to get to know him that she had to

force it? "I like the comradery between the team. I like the work, sweaty, hard, but when you unearth something that came from a different time…it's a magic all its own."

"You work? Wait, no. More important—you *sweat*?"

His grin was quicksilver, a flash of amusement at her sass. "It's a late development."

"I thought you were just…" She trailed off, hunting for words. "…partying."

"Maybe when you knew me—when I was twenty-one. On a dig site, I'm the guy who starts sawing Zs at ten p.m. This bartender gig will be the latest I've stayed up past my bedtime in a while."

The word *bedtime* sat uncomfortably between them, draping long arms around both their shoulders.

"Well," Emma said without apparently having an end to the sentence. Her cell went off and she lurched for it. Whatever the message read had her lips curving upward.

Another pang made his jaw harden. "Boyfriend?" He hadn't considered that. Hadn't even asked.

She looked up, startled.

"I didn't…" He tapped his fingers on his bottle, uncomfortable. "Sorry if this has caused a difficult situation."

"It's not that." But she didn't explain anything more.

And he supposed he didn't have a right to it, but again. Secrets.

The pang became harder to keep inside.

An awkward silence descended again and with it, a flutter of anxiety. He needed to do something, to remind her that she wanted to go through with this.

It came to him and he set the paella to simmer, turning to her.

"I almost forgot."

He snapped his fingers and a cupcake appeared in between

them, chocolate with yellow frosting, complete with small birthday candle.

As she stared, he picked up the little cake and touched a finger to the wick. Raising it slowly, he tugged a flame into life. It flickered merrily.

"It won't be as good as yours, I'm sure, and it's late, but here." He held it out. "Your favorite flavor and color. Happy birthday. Again."

"Bastian…" Her voice was shaken. Wide eyes looked from the cake to him, clearly seeing more than sponge and frosting. "You don't need to— I don't want— This is…unnecessary."

He continued to hold the cake out. "I'm sorry I missed your other birthdays."

She jerked a shoulder, glancing down at her twisting hands.

"I'd like to make a pledge now that no matter where we are, as your husband, I'll always come back for your birthday."

"No, you don't have to… I don't like my birthday anyway."

"You used to."

Her eyes met his. Even without words, they spoke to him. He felt his heart twist. "Please?"

Finally she dipped her head in a jerky nod. "Fine."

Something unclenched inside. "Make a wish, then."

"Stupid." But she did blow out the candle.

A thin trail of smoke curled upward as he passed it over. Her fingers brushed his. They were cold.

"What did you wish for?"

She didn't look at him, only slid off the stool. "I didn't. I have everything I want. Sorry, I just realized… I have to go meet someone."

His mood curdled. "Who?"

Her forehead pinched and he realized he had no right to ask. He looked at the stove. "The paella is almost ready."

"I'm not hungry. I hope your shift goes well."

"You're not coming?"

She shook her head and left the room, taking her cell with her.

Bastian stared at the paella pan, gut roiling, until the stench of burning caught his nostrils. Just one more thing ruined.

CHAPTER 8

Unsurprisingly, Bastian was a perfect bartender. He was always on time for his shifts, always happy to help out or bring up supplies from the cellar, always friendly with the customers. Real friendly, Emma reflected, watching from the corner of her eye as she wiped down a section of the bar. That practiced grin of his had more than a few female hearts fluttering and a lot more than a few slipping their number across the bar.

Bastian hadn't encouraged it overtly, but the man was always *on* like a light bulb that had no dimmer setting.

Well, she amended, except for the times she caught him watching her. She didn't even know what to call that expression. She didn't delude herself into thinking it was desire. More like…he was waiting for something.

For her to drop at his feet again? She'd sooner explain to him about Sloane.

Who had, unfortunately, developed an interest in Bastian, especially after Emma had relented and explained the whole situation. She supposed it had all the components for a teenager to be enthralled—drama, unrequited love, secrets upon secrets, curses. She'd tried to downplay it all, but there wasn't really a way to downplay it that much.

Worse still was that Leah had shown her sister a picture of Bastian when Sloane had helped out on one of her shifts at the shelter. Emma didn't even ask how Leah had a photo of him, but she cursed that she'd shown it to Sloane. Like waving a red rag at a bull, showing a gorgeous guy to an impressionable teen. Sloane now had it in her head that Emma and Bastian's story could be some great romance. She was also pushing to meet him, which Emma was finding harder and harder to avoid. They'd argued last night on the phone and when she'd finally hung up and ventured out of her bedroom, Bastian had been right there, checking who she'd been arguing with, was she okay, could he get her a drink…

She sighed, rubbing the cloth in slow circles as Bastian continued to talk to three women in their early twenties. He was mixing them up the bar's witchy signature cocktails—sans real witchiness. One of them laughed, flipped her hair over her shoulder and angled closer. So obvious.

Emma firmed her jaw and scrubbed the wood with more determination. Even without this thing with Sloane, it wasn't getting any easier. He'd been back in her life for over a week. They even had a routine going like a regular couple. He would already be up by the time she ventured out of her bedroom, usually waiting with a myriad of different breakfasts, every day a new one from a place he'd visited.

Just because she hadn't traveled didn't mean she had to miss out, he'd said.

She hated him more for being so genial while she felt fit to burst with resentment over the past. Resentment and a small amount of guilt, she thought with a pang, but forced it aside. No point dwelling on that.

After breakfast, he disappeared to visit with his mom or do whatever he did, and she headed to the bar to bake or do admin or to kill time so she didn't sit at home clock-watching for the minute Bastian would turn up.

He'd made a point of always being "home" for dinner, whether that was formal sitting-at-the-breakfast-bar dinner or takeout on the couch in front of Netflix. He hadn't argued with any of her choices, insisting she watch what she wanted.

The only time he'd got short with her was on the second night, when she'd told him she was going out. She'd never been the best liar, so when he'd asked her why, she'd mumbled that it wasn't his business and fled. From then on, she'd made sure to make plans with Sloane in the day. She really didn't need to give him anything to be suspicious about.

The truth was, she couldn't relax with him. Her skin felt tight, fizzy, her stomach taut with nerves and bitterness. She hated that he seemed so relaxed, so easy when she felt this way and ended up making passive-aggressive comments like she was Sloane's age.

He didn't even call her on it—he just accepted the role of punching bag. And so she felt on edge and unsatisfied and petty. And suspicious herself because *nobody* was that nice. What was his game? Why on the Goddess's green earth was he taking this without a fight?

"I think that spot's clean."

Emma looked up from the bar into Leah's amused face. She dabbed once more out of principle, before tossing the cloth aside. "Thought you had a date?"

Leah screwed up her nose. "He didn't like dogs. What does that say about him?"

"Some people don't."

"Would *you* trust someone who didn't like dogs?"

"I don't trust anyone."

Leah laughed as if that was a joke, then shrugged. "He also didn't open my door for me or pull out my chair. And I don't care what they say—yes, I can open my own damn door, yes, I can pull out my own damn chair, but is chivalry dead? Is it too much to ask for a dog-loving gentleman to sweep me off my feet?"

"Probably."

"Don't you know any—" she wiggled her eyebrows "—that would be right for me?"

Emma tipped her chin in warning toward Bastian who, admittedly, was at the other end of the bar. And seeing that it was ten p.m. on a Saturday, the volume level was cranked up to call-the-cops loud.

Still, Leah was suitably chastened. "Sorry. Forgot he was here."

"You're too nice for that world." Emma meant it. If you got a pat on the back, you should check for a knife. "And they're all snobs."

Leah leaned her elbows on the bar, plopped her chin in her hands. "Fine. Let me die alone."

"You have three dogs and two cats."

"So not the point." But she laughed. "In lieu of a hot night with an accountant, I'll take a Hex on the Beach, heavy on the Hex."

"I'll make that." Bastian's words in her ear.

Emma jerked, cracking her elbow on the bar. Pain shot up her arm in an arc of fire and she yelped. "*Damn it.*"

He watched her, wide-eyed. "Sorry. Thought you'd heard me."

"With my latent ninja-hearing skills?" she said bad-temperedly. "My ability to hear a pin drop? Or maybe you think every woman in here is watching you."

Leah raised her eyebrows at that.

Bastian's gaze was shuttered, but maintaining the polite, easy smile of the past week, he said, "No, I just thought… I'll make that drink."

"I can make the damn drink." Emma made an effort to be calm, her heart still thumping hard. "That woman is waiting."

He nodded, strode off to the customer, sliding on his charm.

Leah raised her hand. "Uh, what was that?"

"What?" Emma avoided her gaze and set about making Leah's drink.

"You bit his head off—though you need to work on your insults. 'Ninja-hearing skills'?" She shook her head. "Work with Tia. She's got a mind for them. Once said to someone that they were more disappointing than an unsalted pretzel."

Emma worked up a faint smile.

"Seriously. Last I heard you guys were doing the friendship thing. He's being all nice, what's with the 'tude?"

Emma hesitated. "I just… I can't."

"Can't…finish the sentence?"

"Can't deal. He's too… He's *too* okay about the whole thing. And it makes me feel like…" She dragged a hand through her hair, which she'd left down to hide behind. "Like I'm being unreasonable about the whole him-leaving thing. Like I should be over it because he is. Or appears to be," she added, thinking of that look he got sometimes.

"Which brings out the inner bitch," Leah concluded. "Honey, if you don't want to do this, kick him out of your place, we'll fire him. Hell, Tia would pay you to. She's had a face like someone ate all the marshmallows out of her Lucky Charms all week."

"The annoying thing is he's right." Emma rolled out her shoulders to try and release the tension. "If we're going to be—to be married, wouldn't it be better to be able to speak to each other without wanting to push him into a convenient well and walk away whistling?" She coughed. "For example."

Leah didn't bat an eyelid. "Sure. But if you can't get over it…"

"I know." Emma made a sound like a teakettle. "I know."

"…you should get under him."

Emma dropped the cocktail shaker and only a push of telekinesis saved it from going splat on the floor. "*What?*"

"Just kidding." Leah gave her an impish grin before she grew serious. "Maybe—and don't curse me or anything—but maybe you should consider telling him how you feel."

"I get it. You're joking again."

Leah held up her hands. "Hear me out. You can't get past what he did, he's tiptoeing around you because he obviously knows you're angry about something. You're both playing nice and that's not how you clear the air. Even friends fight to clear the air."

Emma cast her a meaningful look.

Leah grinned. "Best friends realize when the other is right," she added. "But seriously. Maybe it's the only way forward."

"Leah…that's the worst idea." Emma's head mirrored the jagged movements of the cocktail shaker she rattled. "I'm not going to offer up my soul to him to laugh at. Or to pity." Or to offer a fake apology for how he hadn't thought twice about her.

"Fine. Your life, your future husband."

Emma's stomach twisted. She didn't speak, concentrating on building the Hex on the Beach in colorful layers.

Leah just didn't understand. She hadn't seen how ridiculously infatuated Emma had been with Bastian. He'd been her hero, her best friend, her world. Any piece of kindness from him, she'd taken to mean he liked her, too. Any time he sought her out, she glowed as the chosen one. Every time he brought her a cupcake on her birthday, she knew she was one birthday closer to her twenty-first when they could start planning their wedding and the beginning of their lives together.

She wasn't stupid; she knew, even at the time, that he hadn't been infatuated with her like that. He'd liked her as a friend, maybe his best friend, but he hadn't looked at her with hot eyes or touched her with the intent for more. She'd known she was less important to him than he was to her. But she hadn't cared. She'd depended on him, and he'd let her down in more ways than he knew.

She'd been good old predictable Emmaline, someone he could put down like a toy he was finished playing with, and she'd be happy when he picked her back up.

"Hello?" A man's voice, annoyed, rose above the crowd. "Can I get some service over here?"

Both Leah and Emma looked over at the demand. Leah rolled her eyes and held out a hand. "I'll finish my drink off. You go serve Mr. Manners there. Unless you want me to?"

"I need to push myself, right?" So saying, Emma slid Leah the drink and took a breath. She walked the short distance to the waiting customer. "Sorry. What can I get you?"

"A glass of red and a scotch neat. And some quicker service, if that's possible." The dimmer lights didn't mask his displeasure.

Emma didn't say anything, having learned over four years of owning a bar that dealing with customers meant you had to have a higher tolerance for BS. It wasn't worth making an enemy out of someone who could drop money and convince people to come here. Besides, some people just liked to complain.

She poured the red wine, did the same for the scotch. The man stared at her with pinched eyes as she returned with them and told him his total.

"You know," he said, taking out a leather wallet and sliding off a bill. "I'm pretty sure your boss doesn't pay you to talk with your girlfriend there."

Emma smiled, as she'd learned to under her mother's tutelage. As fake as this guy's "Rolex." She took his money to the register, aware of his glower, annoyed that he wasn't getting a response.

When she handed over his change, he made a point of putting it away. "Here's a tip." He lifted his chin as if imparting what he believed was a great one-liner. "Do your damn job and save the gossiping for later."

"Is there a problem here?"

For the second time in five minutes, Emma jolted at the sound of Bastian's voice. Her hand slipped across the bar and knocked the guy's wineglass. It wobbled, splashing some of the contents onto his shirt.

Great.

The guy looked at his shirt and then at her, his eyes wide. "That's Hugo Boss, you damn idiot!"

"Hey," Bastian warned.

Emma's heart drummed harder as she gripped her hands together. "I'm so sorry." The guy's expression was utter fury as he dabbed at the blotch with his fingers, only succeeding in rubbing it in. The stain was eating the fabric like Ms. Pac-Man. Emma winced. As a result, her voice was timid when she added, "We'll pay for the—the dry cleaning bill, sir. And next round's on the house."

"What? Speak up, for God's sake."

Bastian tensed. "You want to find a better tone."

Emma's throat squeezed but she took another breath. "I said," she tried, that breath constricting in her chest. Her toes curled in her shoes as she willed herself louder. "You'll get free drinks for the hassle and we'll pay the dry cleaning bill. I… We…" She faltered as his sneer widened. "So…rry."

"You will be." The guy jabbed a finger at her.

The only warning was—well, there was no warning. The next thing she knew, Bastian had the guy's shirt in his grip, pulling him across the bar and succeeding in getting not only more red wine but scotch and whatever else stained the surface across the fabric.

Oh, good Goddess. Emma gaped, mind racing. Should she conjure a hose? A horn? A wrestling commentator?

Bastian jerked the guy's head up to his. His eyes were a dangerous blue. "I'm sorry," he said evenly. "You were too far away. What did you say?"

Presumably not used to being jerked around like a ragdoll—compliments of Bastian's added strength via telekinesis—the guy's mouth flapped like laundry hung on a line in a stiff wind.

Emma looked to Leah in disbelief. Pointed.

Leah toasted her with a drink.

"I suggest," Bastian said, still in that chilling, even tone, "you apologize and leave the bar now." He released his hold, his magic shoving the guy back across the counter to flounder on the other side.

The man stared at both of them, then at the audience they'd attracted. His cheeks went a muddy red before he smoothed a trembling hand down his stained shirt. "Trust me," he said, his voice echoing his hand, "I am never coming here again. You're insane. I could sue."

Bastian didn't blink, didn't smile, didn't nod or tip his head or do anything but resemble a scary-as-hell statue. The old Bastian would have winked and charmed his way out of it. This was *not* the boy she'd once known.

Emma watched the man stride off to where his date stood, aware of a dizzy kind of rage blooming inside her. "What did you do?" she managed.

Leah sidled over with a calm, confident expression. "Ex-

cellent dinner theater, guys, but don't you think you should…
ah, smooth things out? A bit more?" She smiled blandly, as
if she hadn't just reminded Emma to work some magic, and
headed for a towel to mop up the spill.

Right. Emma closed her eyes and reached for some kind of
calm. Pushing away the buzz of scandalized customers, she
started an incantation for blurred memories. She was almost
at the end when she heard Bastian join in, his hand sliding
into hers.

Her instinctive reaction was to pull away but she withstood
it. He did have a better grasp on mind magic than her. Anyone did. Tia was the one who—in those rare instances they'd
needed a blurred memory spell—usually painted memories a
soft watercolor. With Bastian at the helm, the witnesses and
the man himself would remember that there had been some
excitement, but nothing too bad or eye-opening.

Leah pretended to be absorbed in the spot she was cleaning,
just as if she didn't have a keen knowledge of witchcraft and
was merely a harmless, oblivious human. *Yeah. When frogs fly.*

Spell done, Emma dropped Bastian's hand. She tried to push
down the rage, needing to explain why he'd been wrong, why
he shouldn't do it again. Calm. In control. But the rage just
bounced back like Jell-O. And it spread.

"What a dick," Bastian said, with a frown. It segued into
one of his easy, vague smiles before her eyes. "Guess he learned
his lesson."

It was the smile that did it.

Emma's jaw felt wired shut, her teeth clamped so tight it
hurt. She pointed out the back. "Now." It was all she could
say in public.

Leah made a low whistling noise and tossed the cloth over
her shoulder. "I'd go with her, if I were you." She turned to

take some drink orders, a quick nod to Emma conveying her approval.

Emma didn't wait, just turned on her heel and marched out. She'd worn flats with low heels and they clicked angrily, followed by Bastian's slower tread.

She took him into the office where Chester snoozed, so tired out from a run that although his tail wagged like fury when they entered, his body stayed ensconced in his bed. Even the sight of that tail and the *hello-how-are-you-I-missed-you* vibes coming down their bond failed to dull the keen blade of Emma's anger.

"Close. The. Door," she ordered when Bastian would have left it open.

With eyebrows high enough to reach under his hair, he did so. "Why do I feel like I've been summoned to the headmaster's office?"

Of course he'd joke. Everything was a joke. An act. A performance. Nothing was real with him.

Goddess, she was so mad, and she couldn't get her words out. They lined up, waiting their turn, but her tongue felt thick and stiff as she tried to figure out what to say.

"Emma? Look, if you're upset about what that jerk said—"

"No." The word snapped out like a whip. She paced to her desk, braced her hands on it. She'd never been a violent person, but hitting him seemed like a great idea. Her chair flew backward as a pulse of anger ripped out of her.

Bastian stepped forward, wary. "Emmaline?"

She whirled on him. "I'm not her."

He stopped, confused. "What?"

"I'm not her. I'm not Emmaline."

His shoulders stiffened, but his face stayed as smooth as a frozen pond. "I know you're upset, but—"

"I'm not upset. I'm not a tender flower that needs your protection. I don't need *you* to fight for my honor." She was having trouble looking him in the eye, but she trembled with fury.

He held up his hands. "Excuse me, I was only trying to help."

"I don't need it. I don't need *you*."

A spark of anger electrified his face. "Emmaline…"

"No!" She screeched it and some papers flew up as if a sudden wind had kicked them into the air. "She's gone. She left when you did."

Something sharpened in his eyes. "What do you mean? What happened when I left?"

His ignorance fanned the flames.

"I moved on, Bastian. I'm not her. I don't need you to rescue me anymore. Don't need you to smile at me, or be nice to me, or to act like we're friends."

"I thought we went over this," he gritted out. "I thought we agreed—"

"Well, turns out, I can't. I can't smile and pretend the past doesn't exist. It happened."

"You're not making any sense."

"What did you think would happen? Did you think you'd come back and I'd throw myself at you?" She jabbed a finger at him. "Emmaline was weak. I made myself strong."

He made an aborted motion, as if he was going to grab her arm, but stopped himself. "What do you mean, strong?" His words flashed out, surprising her with their intensity. "What did you do?"

Chester whined from his bed, sitting up. Even that couldn't distract her.

"Enough," she seethed. "It's enough. Enough pretending."

"Yes," he shot back, his jaw so tight, his cheekbones looked jagged. "Enough pretending. Tell me what you did. Tell me, Emmaline. Tell me." He sounded like he was begging.

She clutched her head, shook it. "I can't do this—*we* can't do this. You need to leave."

"I can't."

"Leave!" she shouted, her voice a thunderclap in a storm. "You're so good at it."

"Em—"

"You didn't even say goodbye." The words burst out of her, seven years in the making. "You were just *gone*. I needed you and you were *gone*."

He twitched, gone rigid. "I left a note."

"For your parents. I didn't make the cut?"

He rubbed the back of his neck, tension vibrating around him. "It's not like that."

"Yes, it is. You couldn't have made it more obvious how little I meant."

His eyebrows slammed together. "That's bull."

Her laugh was short and sharp enough to cut into skin.

He flinched. "It is," he insisted. "You meant something—you *mean* something."

Emma felt the lie like a blow. "And that's why you fled the country with only *I can't marry Emmaline* as a reason?"

"I didn't 'flee.' I just…" He grimaced. "I can't… It's complicated."

"I'm sure." She swallowed past the lump in her throat. "Do you know…what it was like to get up the next day and be told you'd left me?"

"I didn't leave *you*." But he didn't look at her.

"Yes, you did," she confirmed. "That fact was rubbed in my face at every opportunity. *Poor Emmaline. Bastian had to run to get away.* And my mom…"

His attention was keen. "What? What did she do?"

"It doesn't matter." She dragged in an unsteady breath. Her knees were trembling, her weight unbalanced. "None of it matters now." Disgusted with herself, she shook her head. "I don't even know why I bothered. It's not like you care."

"Emma." Bastian's strained voice stole over her senses, trying to weave its own magic. "You don't know— You have to understand." Frustration simmered in his eyes.

She could sympathize. She could back off and play her role again. But she'd had enough of this falseness. Leah was right.

"What I understand is that the boy I needed abandoned me. Left me to the wolves. No explanation. No apology. Nothing. For seven years, I heard nothing. And now you're back, and we have to get married, and you expect me to forget everything. Smile, laugh. Do my part, play my role like you. Why not, right? You don't think you have anything to be sorry about. You've always done what's easiest." Her jaw firmed as she stared into his pale face. "And the worst thing is? I didn't even expect you to do any different."

Unable to keep looking at him, she whistled for Chester and headed for the door.

As she passed Bastian, he touched her arm. "Emmali—"

At the touch, a pulse wave of emotion burst from her. She couldn't control it. It rippled over him, his eyes going pure black at the major use of magic as he opened to the memory she unintentionally released. His hand clamped around her arm and he shuddered.

The backlash was keen and Emma's teeth gritted as a small amount of pain knifed through her system. It would be nothing like what Bastian was experiencing as he relived the memory of her being told he was gone, that he'd left her. Of the moment she realized she was alone and—

She ripped herself free, shaken at the memory read. Pure betrayal ripped through her. "How dare you?" she seethed. The idea of what he could have read had her heart pounding.

He stared at her, cheeks as white as death.

She didn't say anything else—what was there to say? She stepped out of his reach and walked to the door. Opening it, she snapped her fingers for Chester and created a portal to her hiding place. She managed to close the portal on the other side before she dropped to her knees, burning up with old pain and humiliation. Sand rubbed against her palms as she flattened them, then dug them into the beach.

"So close to discovery," she murmured to Chester, who belly-crawled up to her. "Thank the Goddess I managed to pull out in time."

As she sat in the cool quiet of the beach next to Lake Michigan, no others around due to the freezing weather so late on a Saturday night, the full extent of how badly she'd veered off course sank in. So much for calm. So much for control.

She winced at the thought that he'd relived her pain. At least that was all he'd relived. At least now he'd stay away. What that meant for the Divining, she didn't know, but it had been a week out of the month already and no new tattoos had etched into her skin.

The magic clearly had weighed her and found her lacking, like everyone else.

Her sigh was whipped away by the wind. The cold stole into her bones, but she continued to sit on the beach, her familiar huddled by her side, the lapping waters in front of her and regret at her back.

CHAPTER 9

*B*astian did the only thing he could think of. He went home.

He'd never admitted to himself how much he'd missed the place, the parents he'd left behind on his great rush to escape. If he'd admitted it, he might also have admitted that he could have fought harder to stay, could have tried to find another solution. And that had been a reality he'd been hiding from, long before the news that his mom was sick. Because the truth was Emmaline was right—he'd also run because it was easy.

He felt ripped open, exposed, a layer of filth coating his insides that he wouldn't be able to clean with a hot shower. Emmaline's emotions battered him, the memory still knocking around his head, his magic having picked it from her mind. She'd been projecting so hard and he'd been wide open when he'd touched her. It had been like a bomb going off.

Her despair and bitterness…he could taste it like ashes and wine. That and desperation.

The portal opened up in the hallway and tonight he knew his ancestors were real, their painted faces condemning him as he dragged his feet toward the parlor most favored by his mom. It was barely ten thirty. Before, his parents would have been up past the witching hour, but now, who knew?

Fortunately he heard his dad reading one of his mom's favorite romances aloud, his booming voice only slightly quieter than usual, but what he'd consider soothing. They could have used a spell to make the pages read themselves aloud, but he knew his dad would think that "the easy way out" and not good enough for those he loved. It would have normally made Bastian smile, but his emotions were too raw, too shredded for that. All he could think was that he hadn't followed his father's example. "The easy way out" had been a door he'd often walked through.

Emma's accusations pricked him again and he dragged in a breath as unsteady as a table with three legs. Then he made himself move, knocking once on the jamb as he entered. "Hey, guys."

His mom looked up from where she reclined on the green velvet couch, a lap blanket over her legs and her familiar over the blanket. "Hey, sweetie," she said, a smile lighting up her features, even with the bruises under her eyes.

His dad lowered the book with an echoing smile. "Come to relieve me of book duty?"

Normally Bastian would have made a joke about not reading sex books with his parents, but when he opened his mouth, nothing came out. He cast a lost look at his mom.

She pursed her lips, gaze moving over his face. All sorts of maternal alarm bells must have rung because the next minute she directed a speaking look at his dad. "Ali," she said, voice soft, a little raw. It hurt Bastian to hear it. "Would you get me a glass of water?"

"Of course." Alistair picked up her hand, kissed the backs of her fingers. "I'll be five minutes."

Nobody mentioned magic or the carafe of water that was sitting on a table two feet away.

Bastian sank into the big armchair that matched the couch and which sat at a right angle to his mom, opposite the chair his dad had taken. An antique wooden coffee table bridged all three, piled with books, magazines, tissues, pills, a bowl of uneaten popcorn. His mom hadn't regained her appetite. His heart, already oozing blood, convulsed at the sign she wasn't getting better.

"What's up, baby?"

The endearment made his throat close. He slumped back, using one hand to rub his aching forehead. "I fucked up." In so many ways.

Normally his mom would have tsked, would have scolded him like he was a teenager. Even Truenotes would be frowned upon for swearing. Now she sat in silence as an imaginary clock ticked off seconds in his head.

"I fucked up," he repeated, dropping his hand. "Didn't I?"

Kindness shone out of Diana's eyes. "Yes."

Like someone had cut his strings, Bastian slumped forward, resting his elbows on his knees and dropping his head into his hands. "Fuck," he said again, helpless to think of any other word.

"Let me guess. Emmaline found her spine?"

He rubbed burning eyes. "You could say that. She let me know how it was when I left. For her, I mean." He held his hands there, struggled to say something about the hex. Choked on the words. "There's more to the story, Mom. I just... I can't say what."

"You could try."

The magic closed a hand around his throat, sinking in electric fingernails that crackled internally. He pressed the heels of his hands into his eyes and then dropped them. He gave a small shake of his head. "You know I wouldn't have hurt her."

If his mom was disappointed he didn't say more, she hid it well. "I know."

"I would never have hurt her," he repeated, the wash of despair from Emma flowing up him again. Breaking him.

His mom sighed at his statement. "You wouldn't mean to." She studied him, pale, sick, but still a mom. Coming to some sort of a decision, she struggled up.

"Mom—" Bastian made a move to help her but she waved him back.

"My darling boy." She stroked her familiar's head, smiling absently as it purred and craned its head under her touch. "You're my son and I love you. I know you didn't think of it as 'abandoning' Emmaline."

That was the truth. And it killed him that his parents couldn't know the real reason. Or the main one, he admitted.

"You were both young. Too young, but those mistakes are mine and your father's also." Her lips pinched before she shook that off. "Looking back, it's easy to see you chafed at the gilded cage we'd made for you, even though you liked Emmaline. Of course you wanted to live your life a bit first, experience it away from being a Higher family son or a fiancé. We don't blame you for that."

I was doing it for the family, he wanted to yell. *For us. For Emmaline, so she didn't have to go through with it.* Surely his childhood friend would've hated herself when she realized the consequences of their marriage. That she'd have stolen the essence of who he was through the Joining clause.

For if the crash of emotions had clarified anything, it was that she'd been hurt by his disappearance. She hadn't been mourning the loss of his powers.

But…she was still hiding something. There had been a

touch of guilt at the end, just a hint, that kept him wary. Unable to let go of the old suspicion.

His mom grimaced and his gaze shot to her. He was halfway out of his chair before she clucked at him bad-temperedly. "Don't start feeling sorry for me, Bastian Aloysius Truenote."

"Mom." An automatic grimace at the dreaded middle name. Suddenly he was thirteen and trying to explain how the furniture had magnetized to the ceiling.

His reaction made laughter return to her face before it turned considering. "You got to live your life. But Emmaline...she was the one left behind."

He flinched. "She moved to Chicago."

"Yes. But not immediately. You know what witch society is like. Higher sons can do no wrong, especially when a family's as old as ours. They blamed her for your leaving, and her mother did nothing to quell the rumors." The dark glint in her eyes told Bastian exactly what Diana Truenote thought of that lack of maternal instinct. "She got whispered about, laughed at, teased, humiliated."

He considered how small he could make his body to match how he was feeling.

"And she endured it in silence. The poor girl." His mom gazed at a point off in the distance. "I did what I could, but our interference only made it worse. I was proud of her when she left. Nobody expected Emmaline Bluewater to do anything but wilt under her mother's hand. Nobody expected her to do much of anything."

Familiar suspicion bubbled up with its twin, regret. And yet the regret trumped suspicion as he pictured what it must have been like. "I didn't mean for it to look like I ran from her."

"I know. You thought of you. You were young and selfish, and the young *are* selfish. But that girl adored you, Bastian. Really and truly loved the air you breathed. When you left, it devastated her." His mom continued to calmly peel the flesh from his bones as her words sank into the heart of him. "She came over here every day for a month to ask about you. Wanted to make sure you were okay. It was so obvious she wanted to ask if you'd passed on any messages, but she couldn't bring herself. You remember that Emmaline: shy, halting, blushed if you looked directly at her." She shrugged. The movement triggered a hacking cough, the rattling sound alarming him.

Knowing she'd only scowl if he offered help, he gripped the chair's arms, resigned to being useless. A pattern, it seemed, with him.

Winded when the fit trailed off, Diana scratched behind her familiar's ear. Caught her breath. When she continued, her voice was hoarse. "I know it's hard to hear, and I don't want to hurt you. But I want you to know, your leaving has been good for her. It got her out of her mother's shadow, got her to experience some of the world. I even heard her giving some lip to Natalia Fieldstone at the last Equinox ball when that unpleasant woman commented on Emmaline's hair being the color of mud."

Bastian's mouth made a barely there curve. "Yeah, she's got a tongue on her now." It was different. New. But he could admit spirit suited Emmaline.

Emma.

I'm not her, she'd cried.

And *I made myself strong*.

How?

"I'm glad she told you, though." Diana reached out a hand and as if it had crossed the gap between them, Bastian felt her soothing touch across his cheek. "No marriage can be built on pretense. Truth builds; lies tear down. Now at least with the air clear, you can see what you're left with. Build on it."

She couldn't know how painful her words were. The truth might have set them all free—if he was only *free* to share it.

For the rest of his life and his marriage, he would have to look at his wife with doubt, and she would look at him as nothing more than a spoiled, selfish kid who'd run out on her for no reason.

"You could always start giving me grandchildren," Diana suggested, chuckling as Bastian's face flushed with heat. "Well, she is going to be your wife," she pointed out. "You'll share a bed."

Bastian studied his shoes. "We're not talking about this."

"Oh, come on," she teased. "I know she isn't a supermodel, but Emmaline is pretty in her own way."

That wasn't the issue here. Yes, Emma was pretty in her own way. With the long sweep of brown hair, those expressive eyes framed by dark lashes, and the slow smiles that robbed a man of his breath until he felt the only way to regain it was by stealing it from her lips.

That kiss.

But. Always a but.

"Bastian?"

He shook his thoughts away. "Give us time, Mom."

"Fine." She smiled, a smile that sagged at the edges, tiredness painting itself with lavish strokes. "You know now, Bastian, her truth," she reminded him. "And you're not the same young man that left."

No, he wasn't. Whether that was a good or bad thing, he was harder, slower to trust and more guarded. So was she. He hoped she hadn't had anything to do with the contract, but he couldn't be sure. Not when her guilt had brushed up against him. How could he trust without knowing what she felt guilty about?

A decision slid into place. The hex may choke him, prevent

him from talking about the contract clause or the conversation he'd overheard, but this was a truth he could know. A question she could answer. And maybe they could move past it. Past everything.

Emma hadn't expected him to be there when she returned but as she opened the door, Bastian stood up from the couch. Panic fluttered in her throat and the edges of a portal manifested, her will to flee so strong.

She wasn't a coward, she reminded herself. Just...

She wasn't sure what she was.

She closed the door behind her and Chester, her familiar gamboling over to Bastian to throw himself at his feet, belly side up. The TV was on and provided a murmuring backdrop of voices.

"Hello." The word was neutral. Not angry, not questioning.

Bastian bent to give Chester a quick stroke, but his eyes remained on her. When he spoke, his voice matched hers. "Hello."

They faced each other as if squaring off to combat. The idea sent a flood of exhaustion into her bones and she almost swayed. "I don't want to argue, Bastian."

"Me neither."

Her fingers found her opposite sleeve and began to pick at it. She hated this. She hated that the air rippled with the echo of her voice pouring out old hurts, that it thickened with the reminder of his memory read that had given him a front-row seat to her humiliation.

They stood in silence that yawned like jaws.

Too many thoughts crossed his face before, finally, he cleared his throat. "I'm sorry."

The old Emmaline might have been knocked off her feet into a swoon.

Emma relinquished her sleeve and folded her arms. "For what?"

"For leaving you without explaining why." His expression turned pained. "For leaving you to deal with the fallout and not realizing there'd be one. For leaving you for so many years. For leaving you…" He stopped. Closed his eyes. "For leaving you alone. I'm sorry. Emma."

She stiffened the walls around her heart. She wouldn't break that easy.

"Pretty words," she said.

"I mean them."

"Words come easy to you, Bastian." They always had.

His jaw ticked.

She gripped her sides where she could reach, searching for courage for what she had to ask. "So, tell me now. Why you left. The real reason."

Something dark flickered in his eyes, his face. It made everything inside her tense in instinctive reaction.

Chester's claws on the wooden floor and a shampoo commercial on the TV should've provided a break in tension, but neither of them even glanced away.

Finally, he gritted out, "All I can tell you is that I was young and stupid."

That was the explanation she was getting after seven years of silence?

Resentment built inside her in waves. "That's it? That's all you have to say?"

He ran an agitated hand across the back of his neck. "What do you want me to say?"

She made a noise. "Good night, Bastian."

He made a grab for her but she smoothly moved out of the way, a happy outcome of putting in her time at the "business end" of the bar.

"What do you mean good night?" he demanded.

"I'm tired. In general, but also of the games." She faced him, taking comfort from the way Chester frolicked over and leaned his slight bulk against her leg. "What do I want you to say? How about the truth?"

"Because truth is so important to you." There was a definite tone to his words.

Rage jumped into the fray, cuddling resentment like a close friend. "Excuse me?"

"Why don't you tell me some truths, Emma?" His voice was hard. So were his eyes. "Why did you want to marry so quickly at twenty-one? We had years."

Her cheeks flushed hot. "You know why," she evaded, heart picking up its pace.

"Do I?"

"You want me completely humiliated, is that it?" Her fingers curled into her palms to keep her emotion inside. She didn't want any plant fatalities and the fern in the corner already drooped. "Fine. I wanted to marry you—was eager to, in fact—because I fancied myself in love with you. Okay? There's the great humiliating truth we both knew. I was pathetic enough to settle for having you in any way I could, as quickly as I could."

To his credit, not that she wanted to give him any, he was visibly taken aback. His throat bobbed as he swallowed.

Emma found strength in it. Why the hell not continue at this point? "Face it, Bastian. You're not only the firstborn, you're the Truenote heir. Your magic is one of the strongest in society. Doors opened for you. But you ignored all of that because you—you couldn't stand the idea of marrying me. The shy idiot. Number five in a weaker family with weaker magic. No b-beauty." She stumbled over the word, hating to even admit that a sliver of herself had valued that at the time.

"No." He made an aborted move toward her, his hand reaching out and then fisting when she stepped back. His face took on an edge of frustration. "*No*," he repeated, hard. And then, after a moment, "I couldn't stand the idea of marrying *anyone*."

She blinked.

"I had everything," he continued, picking his words carefully. "And I was an idiot who thought running away was easier."

"Than what?"

His expression was strained. "Having to face you. Marriage."

She wrapped her arms around herself. Her skin felt raw from keeping magic locked inside. "You wanted the freedom to choose."

He opened his mouth as if to say something, then seemed to choke. Lines appeared around his eyes as he paused for an extended moment. "I did," he said, the words torn from him as if they'd been buried deep. A small amount of shame shadowed his face.

"And here we are anyway."

"Here we are." He lifted his chin and resolution replaced the shame. "And now I have to ask you for the truth."

Her laugh was cracked, much like her brain would be after this conversation. "You've had far too much as it is."

"And yet not enough." The air crackled as he seemed to gather himself. "Earlier, in the office. The memory read."

Her lips thinned.

"I know you feel guilt." His eyes burned, locked on her. "Please. Tell me. Why do you feel guilt about me?"

She'd sooner have gone over all the slights and snubs and tears again. This was not an area she wanted to get into. Sloane and the Joining and…everything. The path ahead was too dangerous to travel.

The silence thickened and he began to look gray. "What did you do?" he whispered, the words hoarse.

Alarmed, she stepped back. "Nothing."

"Emma…"

"I…" Goddess, why could she never think quickly? "I… guess it might have been because…" Should she tell him about the Joining? She batted the idea back down instantly. Kole hadn't been in touch with a solution and things were complicated enough. She'd already exposed herself too much for one evening.

Coward, her inner voice whispered, but she ignored it, searching for a different reason to feel guilt. Inspiration put up a hand and she grasped it. "Because my mother was so eager for the wedding to happen."

If anything, his face went darker.

She hurried on. "I was a doormat—let's be honest. I'd have waited until you were ready, but my mother…she was eager to get us married. I just went along with it, even knowing you weren't going to be pleased." In a way, that was true. Clarissa had been forceful in arranging for the engagement to be officially announced and had already been discussing the Divining. Emma hadn't argued because—well, she'd never argued. Her mother could've asked her to float herself over a cliff and Emma would've done so.

He absorbed this in silence. She couldn't read his expression, couldn't tell which way he was tipping. Her foot bounced in agitation as she watched each thought flicker across his face.

He had to believe her. She had no hands left to play—she couldn't tell him about Sloane either. That was too important a secret and the more people that knew, the less safe her sister was. From Clarissa, from that whole world.

"So," he said finally, apparently accepting her words. A soundless breath eased from her as her shoulders loosened. "Where do we go from here? We're stuck together in this."

Ouch. "Why do you always make it sound so bad to be stuck with me?"

"What?" Lines dug into his forehead. He shook his head abruptly. "No. If anything, you're stuck with me. I know I'm a bad bargain."

"Please. Spare me the false modesty."

"Oh, trust me, it's not false." He leaned his hips back against the couch. "Goddess knows I'm far from perfect."

"Right. Tell me one thing about you that isn't." She offered the challenge with a good deal of mockery.

He considered. "I can't grow a mustache."

"Bastian."

"I'm serious—it comes in all patchy. Very George Michael."

An inappropriate laugh huffed out of her. The rightness of the moment struck like the chimes of a clock and she recoiled, refusing to get lost in it.

"So?" he repeated. "Where do we go from here? Do we stick to our corners? Unwilling to trust."

Bending to Chester, she stroked his head and hid her face, absorbing the *love-you-love-you* vibes of support. Emotions clashed inside her like a version of pinball. She knew his preference was to avoid difficult topics, but he'd come here. He'd said sorry. And she thought he meant it.

It didn't mean that all the resentment and bitterness and hurt washed away like footprints in the sand.

"It wouldn't be like it was." The TV almost covered her murmur, but he heard. She met his gaze. "It can't be. I'm not her." She'd screamed the words at him, but now, here, she needed him to truly understand that. The adoring girl was gone. After everything, she'd had to be stronger, so she'd carved Emma out of Emmaline. For Sloane, for herself.

He stared at her. "I'm not him."

The ring of truth made the words hard to hear. They also lent her a touch of sadness. A kind of mourning for them both. The kids they'd been.

He was right. He'd been young—they both had.

Selfish. But young. A mistake. They'd all made them.

She hated that he knew how hurt he'd made her. But now he knew, it was kind of freeing. Like she didn't have to hide as much. Like she didn't have to lock up the bitterness.

She didn't think they'd ever get to where they'd been, where she trusted him with all her secrets, but this was as clean a slate as she could give him.

"I really did hate you," she whispered into the unsettled silence.

Navy eyes stared back at her wordlessly.

"But I don't want to hate you anymore." And that was the most honest thing she could've said. She watched him as he watched her, that new neutral expression hiding all but some of the pain. "We can try. To move forward. I can't promise we'll be friends."

"Married but not friends?"

"Some witches prefer it that way."

"Not me. You know the example I had." A quirk of his lips as he referred to the beyond rare love match his parents had. It slipped off again as he squared his shoulders. "We need to be honest with each other. Going forward. It was our mistake. It shouldn't be our future. Equal partners going forward."

Sloane's face came to mind, not to mention the Joining clause, and Emma shifted, trying to keep any guilty motions to a minimum. "Of course."

He nodded. "So. Partners, wife?" He strode forward, held out a hand.

She slid her hand into his, breath hitching as rougher skin than she'd anticipated rubbed against hers. "Partners. Husband." Unnerved by the feelings aroused by touching him, she cleared her throat. "Maybe friends. But this time, you'll have to work for it."

A genuine grin—maybe the first since he'd been back—curled upward. "Did I mention I like the new sass?"

She couldn't help it. "No, because you know I don't need or want your opinion." But she smiled.

He barked a laugh. "No more putting me on a pedestal then."

"Please. If anything, I should be up on one for even considering this."

"I could worship at your feet." To her surprise—and unease—his smile went lazy. "I might even like it."

"You keep your fetishes to yourself."

"So, handcuffs are a no?"

He laughed aloud at her expression and she crossed her eyes at him in response.

It felt...right. Like the clock had turned back, except not, because she was more herself now. And maybe so was he.

The moment held and it slowly dawned on her that he still held her hand. Worse, he was rubbing his thumb along her palm. Tingles chased down her skin as she swallowed.

Something bright moved between them. Her stomach clenched.

"Emma?" Her name was a husky question. He drifted closer.

She had no idea what she'd have said, but as her mouth opened, a hot pain seared her wrist.

Gasping, aware of Bastian hissing simultaneously, she

clutched at her skin. As she watched, a dark line drew from their tattooed initials to form another branch. In cursive lettering, the word *compromise* wrote itself out.

The pain faded and with it the weird moment. At least she hoped so. She took a large step backward to help.

Bastian examined his wrist, which now bore the same word. When he caught her looking, he dropped his arm behind his back. Nodded with a rueful curl of his lips. "No turning back now."

Her stomach roiled but she nodded in response. "No turning back."

CHAPTER 10

They didn't retreat to their corners. Even after the weird almost-kiss, they'd decided in the spirit of getting to know each other again to get a drink, get some popcorn and watch a movie. Or they'd tried, but soon figured out they had vastly differing views on what constituted a "good" movie. They started out polite, but after half an hour they'd thrown off that civility, reminded of their agreement to always be honest. Politeness killed friendships in the long run.

And Emma discovered she *enjoyed* fighting with Bastian. The puzzled air he got when she disagreed with him, as if still getting used to the new reality, never failed to make her smile. He'd figured that out at about four a.m. when she'd got him arguing white chocolate versus chocolate chip cookies and she'd sniggered in the middle of his passionate speech on the side of classic chocolate chip.

"I miss when you were agreeable," he'd lamented to the ceiling and hadn't seen the floating pillow until it hit him in the face.

Emma had finally conked out halfway through some action movie Bastian knew every line to and had woken up five minutes ago at Chester's pained *needtogoooutneedtogoout* vibes coming down the bond. An unfamiliar knitted blanket was draped over her.

She fingered the blanket, uneasy. Bastian must have conjured it. Thoughtful. Sweet.

Nothing to read into, she decided. The actions of a kind-of friend. She pushed the unease away.

Sitting up, letting the blanket fall to her lap, Emma smoothed a hand over her hair. It felt like a bird had set up its forever home in there, unsurprising since she tended to be a restless sleeper. No wonder Bastian had disappeared. He'd probably gone home to sleep since she was technically on his makeshift bed. Unless he'd taken hers.

Refusing to let the image settle, she swung her legs off the couch.

And promptly stood on Bastian's sleeping body.

Her foot slipped as she tried to avoid contact. Her mangled thoughts attempted to manipulate the air to cushion her, but speed had never been her thing and she could only yelp as she landed half on top of him.

His breath fled him in a pained *oomph*. His eyes snapped open, a grimace twisting and mixing with a what-the-hell expression.

She levered herself up, cheeks hot. Playing it off, she stared at him staring at her. "Morning."

"Morning." He blinked sleep from his eyes. "You planning on doing this every day when we're married? It's a different wake-up call than most wives perform." Wickedness flashed in the blue. "Though a similar position."

Yep. Conjure a coffin; she was dead. "You—you shouldn't say stuff like that."

He fiddled with a piece of her hair that had drifted forward. "Who else should I say it to?"

"Can't you just say morning?"

"I did." He tucked the stray piece behind her ear, grazing skin that shivered in response. "You look different."

"My cheeks aren't usually red."

He grinned. "I'd say more pink. But that's not it. You seem…" He studied her, gaze wandering over her features. A kind of breathless anticipation held her immobile as she waited for him to finish. Finally he just shook his head with a quirk to his mouth. "I don't know. Ignore me. I'm not used to such an aggressive hello in the mornings."

Emma swallowed the butterflies, forcing them down to the deepest pit of her stomach. "I didn't know you were here. I slipped."

"You had the couch."

"You could have had my b-bed."

He didn't comment on the obvious stutter. "Seemed ungentlemanly. Besides, I've slept on plenty of floors. It doesn't bother me."

"Bastian Truenote sleeping on floors?" She couldn't keep the skepticism out of her voice.

"I've even been known to have a beard."

"No."

"Yes."

"I don't believe you."

"I have pictures."

She laughed and his expression froze. "What?"

"Nothing." He rocked his head back and forth on the carpet in a facsimile of a shake. "I just don't think I've heard you laugh for a while."

There went the damned lump in her throat again. She cleared it. "Maybe you're not as funny as you think."

"Maybe," he murmured.

He had the air of someone who'd discovered something

new and it was starting to freak her out. Or maybe that was the realization that she was still lying half on top of him.

"Oh, Goddess." She scrambled up, flushed and all patting hands. She didn't know what to do with them after so they fluttered like birds who'd just escaped a cage. As Chester shot her a mournful look, she sagged in relief. "I have to walk Chester." And escape. No, not escape, she amended. Just... get some fresh air.

"Okay." He swung himself up in one easy, athletic motion. Rumpled looked good on him. While she probably looked like she'd traveled fifteen thousand miles with only the clothes on her back. Equality, her butt. "I'll make breakfast. Pancakes?"

She still couldn't get past the fact that he cooked. He who'd grown up with a cook and maids and a myriad of servants to all but cut his food for him. She nodded shyly and whipped off with Chester to get that fresh air.

When she returned thirty minutes later, he had the plates all ready to go on the breakfast bar under a warming spell. She excused herself to wash up and dress in new clothes, putting on mascara and then taking it off because she didn't want it to seem like she was making an effort, before joining him.

"I could get used to this." The scent of warm, buttery pancake made her salivate. "I mostly eat takeout." Well, that or Sloane offered to cook, and how embarrassing was it that a thirteen-year-old could do better than her? Something the girl never failed to crow over.

"I could teach you?" he offered.

An automatic no was on her lips before she clamped them together. *Try*, she reminded herself. "Nothing too complicated?"

"I'll go easy on you." The light words did something funny to her. He didn't seem to notice, spearing a forkful of pancake dripping with enough maple syrup to fund Canada for a year. "Got plans today?"

It was Sunday, which meant she was hanging with Sloane at the shelter. She opted for a half-truth and avoided looking directly at him. "I'm volunteering at the shelter."

"The one you got Chester from?"

Her familiar wagged his butt on the floor from where he sat by Bastian, eyes big and wide and pleading for pancake. She nodded.

"Is it a big operation?"

"Fairly. They get a lot of rescues."

"I'm surprised you don't come home with them all." Her surprise must have shown. "I remember how you used to act around animals. You loved them."

Animals never judged. Well, she amended silently, most didn't, though some could be as snobby as Higher witches.

"Not practical," she said instead, focusing on cutting her pancakes into neat squares.

"And you always do the practical thing?"

"Of course."

"Of course," he murmured. "Maybe I could meet you and we could get some lunch?"

Her eyes shot up. "No!"

He blinked. "No?"

"I mean, ah…" Heat crept into her face. "I…already have plans. With my mother."

"You're hanging with your mother?"

She studiously dragged a piece of pancake through syrup. "With the Divining and all, she wants to…go over stuff. Everything. And the contract."

There was silence. When he spoke, his voice was measured. "Contract?"

"Yeah."

"What about it?"

Emma's mind blanked. Goddess, she was such a terrible liar, but she couldn't have Bastian coming to the shelter. She plowed ahead, little grace, all determination. "Um. You know. Legally binding clauses and parties of the third part." Wow. Convincing. She swallowed more pancake. "Boring stuff, I won't...bore you with."

The weight of his gaze was hard not to shift under but she fixed an easy smile to her face.

"Want me to come?" he asked lightly. "I might be able to help."

"No! No, I mean, no." *Brilliant, Emma.* "It's fine. I won't subject you to Clarissa any more than absolutely necessary." She smile-grimaced and then pushed away her plate. "That was great. Really."

If someone had paid her a million dollars to read his thoughts right then, she'd have to refund the money. She held his gaze, projecting nothing but innocence as he studied her. When he finally looked back at his plate, tension melted from her shoulders and she slumped with a relieved breath.

"Got dinner plans?"

The way he rocketed from subject to subject left a girl dizzy. "Sundays usually mean Chinese takeout. I'm happy to split the bill."

"We're going to have to talk about this takeout dependency."

She laughed and his face did the scientist thing again. "Stop looking at me like that."

"Like what?"

"Like I'm a monkey that just learned to talk."

He grinned. "What's your favorite restaurant?" A smooth change of subject, she noted.

She shrugged. "Probably Cesario's. Italian," she clarified.

"I'm spending the day with my mom, too." He gave her a thin smile. "But after that, you, me, Cesario's. Bottle of wine."

"Why?" It came out unbidden. Unnerved.

"Because I like to drink wine with Italian. So?"

It was dinner. They were adults and…they were hungry. And they were getting to know each other again. Their new motto/mission statement. She forced a casual expression even as her palms sweated. "Okay."

"It's a date!" Leah crowed. Her butt wriggled in her seat, a pretty good impression of Chester when he'd been given a Milk-Bone.

Emma glowered next to her where they sat at the shelter's reception desk. She'd clocked in an hour ago and had innocently brought up the invite when Sloane had gone to help clean out the kennels with another volunteer her age. She had adamantly not wanted to work with a stranger, but Emma was trying to slowly challenge her to meet and talk to new people. She just hoped she'd done the right thing.

However, she was regretting bringing up the dinner plans immensely. "It's *not*. It's dinner."

"With your fiancé."

"Yes."

"And that's not a date?"

"No."

"Will there be wine?"

"Leah."

"Are you going to change?"

"Of course. I'm wearing clothes that smell like dog."

Leah lowered her voice. "Will you put on lacy underwear?"

Emma took a beat. "Why?"

"You're right. Maybe too obvious. But at least wear something sexy. Is he a legs-and-butt man or is he all about the girls?"

"Oh, my Goddess."

"It's a valid question so you know how to dress." Leah tapped her lips with a pen. "He strikes me as a leg man. A short skirt is always a winner."

"It's *not* a date."

"Uh-huh." Leah smiled with a cheery air, switching hats from annoying best friend to shelter volunteer as two men holding hands walked into the airy reception. "Hi, how can I help you today?"

The shorter of the two, with curling blond hair, beamed back. "We're here to pick up Winston."

Leah's smile turned gooey. "Congratulations! It's an amazing thing you're doing."

"We can't wait. We bought out the pet store."

The taller affectionately squeezed his partner's hand. "He's going to be spoiled rotten."

"No such thing. So we have most of the paperwork already completed, so if you can just fill out these last few forms I'll go get Winston."

The paperwork was completed in minutes and soon Leah was back with a French bulldog that was completely black but for a white tail. It wagged like crazy and he jerked on the lead when he saw the two men.

"He knows his daddies already," Leah commented with a laugh.

"Hey, boy." The shorter blond bent to his haunches, held out his arms, and the room filled with his laughter as the dog bounded over and scrabbled to get onto his knees.

They left happy, and with them went Emma's reprieve.

"So what does this mean? Are you attracted to him?"

Emma wasn't sure if it was humans in general or Leah in

particular that jumped to conclusions like a cat on a fleeing mouse but either way, she wasn't letting the subject go.

"I told you. It's dinner. We had it all out, what happened in the past. He apologized. We're..." She circled a shoulder irritably. "Trying to figure out where to go from there."

"I know, I saw the cool tattoo change."

Emma tilted her wrist to the light and stared at the new addition. It was beyond weird to think more branches would descend from this, ultimately spelling out their compatibility and power as a couple. It was beyond weird to think of them as a couple.

She shrugged it off. "We're actually trying to get to a place where we might be friends again now that it's behind us. He suggested a friendly dinner. That's all."

"But is that all you want to be? Friends? Or does he hope— do *you* hope—that it'll lead to something more romantic?"

"No." It was decisive. "I went down that road before. We're getting married; we're better off as friends. If we can even be that. I still don't know if I trust him." Not to mention everything she was keeping from him...

"That makes no sense." Her friend pursed her lips. "So if he kissed you, you'd...?"

Emma's body flooded with heat then chilled in rapid succession. The garden provided an excellent example of what might happen if Bastian kissed her. Again. "That won't happen."

Eyebrows arched, Leah looked far from convinced. And she didn't even know about the first kiss. Emma had kept that from everyone. She knew just how they'd react, and it hadn't meant anything. Not really.

Switching tactics, Emma jabbed a finger at her. "I thought you were on my side."

"I am."

"Then why are you pushing for this to be a date?"

"Because." Leah's shoulders lifted. "I want you to be in a happy marriage with a man who deserves you."

Emma scowled. Flicked a pen so it rolled across the desk. "Well, now I can't say anything."

"Jury's still out on him, by the way, and whether he *is* that guy, but I like that he's man enough to admit he was a dick and actually apologize. And again, I don't see why it would be a disaster to have a romantic relationship with your *husband*."

"You're not a witch," Emma muttered.

Leah's lips quirked. She picked up the runaway pen and tapped it on a pad in front of her. "Have you told Tia?"

"No."

"Are you going to?"

Emma slid down in her chair. "No."

Leah smiled, satisfied. "It's a date."

Sloane appeared about an hour later, shoulders hunched, nodding as the girl next to her talked rapidly, hands going a mile a minute. There was a definite uncertainty to Sloane's posture, but a trace of a shy smile, so Emma had hopes it had gone okay.

She didn't say anything then, but after their mutual shifts had finished, she hustled Sloane to their favorite place for milkshakes. She opted for vanilla, Sloane for some disgusting-looking monstrosity that had chocolate and toffee and brownie pieces and whipped cream and chocolate shavings.

"Your aunt will kill me if you're sick later," she said, staring at the huge—ha—drink.

"Please." Sloane snorted. "Aunt Debbie will be at work. And didn't you hear? Teenagers have cast-iron stomachs. Even half-human ones."

"I hope you're right." Emma stuck her straw into her own conservative drink. "Anything that comes with a spoon isn't a drink. Just saying."

Sloane gave her a beatific smile and dug in.

They were silent for a moment, absorbing the bustling atmosphere of the old-fashioned diner, which had memorabilia that ranged from signed autographs to the very tacky singing-and-dancing bass plaque. Sloane sometimes liked to mess around with the jukebox, being a fan of the Motown era. Human music was contraband in deepest society so Emma was new to a lot of the songs Sloane played, but she'd decided her girl had good taste.

Emma sucked some of the melting shake up through her straw and asked, in a very casual way, "So, how was your shift?"

Sloane jerked a shoulder, idly swirling her spoon to reach a brownie piece near the bottom. "It was okay. I played with Mikey some."

Mikey, an adorable mixed breed—best guess was a cross between a Labrador and a beagle—was Sloane's favorite because he was just as shy as her. Emma had hopes she could talk Sloane's aunt into adopting him, but it was all about picking the right moment.

"And how did it go with Louise?"

Sloane gave her a look that said the teen knew exactly what Emma was doing. "It was okay."

"On a scale of one being finding matching socks in the morning and ten being an awesome milkshake with your favorite big sister?"

Sloane snort-laughed and the sound warmed Emma from her toes. "You're such a nerd."

"Takes one to know one." Emma's foot nudged her under the table. "Come on. Are we talking okay, you got through it, or friend potential?"

Sloane hesitated. "She said a bunch of her friends are going to the movies tonight if I wanted to go."

"That's great!" Emma beamed.

"You're weird." But there was no heat in her words as she stirred the spoon around. She had such a pretty face, all heart-shaped and round cheeks, but it was shuttered a lot of the time. She preferred to hide. Emma could relate.

But that wasn't good for either of them. Which was why she put up with Leah's not-so-subtle pushing to challenge herself—and it was in fact Leah who'd given Emma the idea to do the same for Sloane.

"Do you want to go?"

Sloane's shoulder jerked.

Emma's lips met and she pressed them together as she studied the young girl. "I know it's scary," she said softly.

The teenager at last looked up and her expression was taut. "What if they make fun of me?"

"Why would they make fun of you? Apart from for your poor taste in drinks."

Sloane didn't even smile, just listlessly began to stir the drink again. "I'm— I can never think what to say around new people. What if they think I'm weird?"

Yep, this girl was *so* Emma's mirror. Her heart ached for her because at least Emma had developed her safe space, had in fact designed her life to suit her for the most part.

"I don't think you're weird."

"That's because you're weird."

"Hey, I resemble that remark."

That got her to smile at least.

"You don't have to go, but the movies might be a good way to start hanging out with new people. You don't even have to talk for a lot of it and if you're not enjoying yourself, you can call me and I'll come get you with a fake emergency."

Too late she remembered she had plans with Bastian, but

she discarded that. If Sloane needed her, she'd ditch Bastian. Somehow.

"Just promise me you'll think about it. Did she give you her number?"

Sloane nodded. "I said I had to check with Aunt Debbie."

"Good. But remember our motto this year."

Emma watched as Sloane performed another spectacular eye roll. "Be brave," the girl parroted with a snarky expression that suited her better than the uncertain pinched look.

Be brave.

Emma would have to remember that herself.

"How's Bastian?"

"None of your concern."

"A warlock who looks like he could be a movie star is in town to marry you and it's not my concern?" Sloane crinkled her nose. "Surely if he marries you, we can trust him."

"I told you; that isn't how magical marriages work. They're arranged for all sorts of reasons—power, money, genetics. Trust, friendship, love don't enter into it." You had to be one of the upper set to choose your spouse. Emma had always wondered why Bastian's had been arranged, but then, he'd never made a stink about it.

Until he'd left.

"Whatever." Sloane poked her drink. "Can't I at least be in the wedding?"

"I wish you could, Jellybean."

The beginnings of a pout formed, but worse was the hurt in her sister's eyes. Emma put out a hand to her. "You know, if I was really getting married to someone I loved, I would have you front and center with me. But it would be dangerous for you."

"Isn't that for me to decide? I want to be with you."

Goddess. "You're so young still."

"So? I'm old enough to decide."

"Sloane, you get that I'm not just talking about some insults, right? My mother is free with her hands and more so with her magic. I don't want you hurt."

Sloane slumped and she let out a breath that told Emma she'd won. For now. "Okay, but…after you're married…you're not going away with him, are you?"

Emma snorted, made sure her voice was light and scornful. "Please. We've got our own trip to focus on. We just have to get through this next month and then Bastian will leave. And everything will be just the same."

If she kept saying it, it was bound to come true.

"Now, tell me what boys you like."

"Emmaaaa." Sloane made a face and just like that, they were normal sisters again.

Still, hours later, even with the words *Bastian will leave* firm in her mind, Emma stared with growing panic at the pile of clothes on her bed.

Nothing was right. Nothing.

She'd tried on everything in her closet and conjured more besides. Every piece sent the wrong message. Either it was too formal or too baggy or too date-like. She wanted an outfit that said, *I know we're just friends even if we're about to be legally encouraged to jump each other's bones.*

A chill, casual outfit. One that still made her look halfway attractive.

Not that she wanted Bastian to *be* attracted to her, but she did have some female pride even after living with her mother for twenty-one years. And considering Bastian looked like he'd been touched by Adonis as a baby (legend, never certified), she didn't want everybody in the restaurant to think he was on a pity date. Not that it was a date.

With a strangled scream at her own thoughts, Emma burrowed into the clothes.

She felt a wet nose touch her hand seconds later.

"It's too late," she told Chester, speaking through a cashmere sweater. "I've made a nest."

He yipped.

"Nope. Only room for one."

Another nudge. A pulse of reassuring love came down their bond.

Despite herself, Emma's lips curved. "Fine." It was uttered in a reluctant tone she only half had to fake.

She heaved herself out of the clothes, blinking at the rush of bright light. She could do this. The trick was to not think about it. What would she wear to go to dinner with Sloane, or Leah and Tia?

Half an hour later, she examined herself in the mirror, turning to glance at her familiar. "What do you think?"

He barked once.

"I hope you're right." She passed a critical eye over the simple teal dress that Leah had bought her last Christmas. It was a ribbed knit jersey and flowed over Emma's body like water. She'd never have picked anything like this herself. Her go-to style was muted with the odd bright color for contrast. This was beautiful, but it did pop like a bauble on a Christmas tree.

But as she'd been pulling a Sabrina in the mirror, turning in circles to try on outfits, her temperature rising as she got more and more frustrated with herself, it had caught her eye. It was just above the knee with a polo-neck and long sleeves, giving the right balance of skin on show. It was a day dress you could wear for night. And a warlock would appreciate color. Not that she cared.

She'd thrown on some tan ankle boots with a chunky heel and had even let herself add some mascara and nude lipstick.

It didn't scream *date* to her. Did it?

Maybe the silver studs were too much.

"Emmaline?"

Bastian's voice made her heart sputter like a speedboat trying to get the motor started.

Not a date. Why be nervous?

"Coming." She grabbed for her cell, her purse and a reality check, and headed out of her bedroom, Chester padding at her heels.

Bastian stood to one side, looking at her framed picture of the Egyptian pyramids. She took in his smart trousers and gray sweater in mute appreciation. His body made the items into sinful poetry, each swathe of fabric a line composed to his…well, his raw appeal.

She hated that she could still feel such a powerful attraction when her mind knew it was stupid. Surely her brain should be strong enough to govern her body?

She made a conscious decision to put her eyes back in her head and put on a bright, unaffected voice. "I haven't eaten since lunch so dibs on garlic bread."

His eyes were smiling as he turned. They blinked, darkened as he ran his gaze over her. She supposed he hadn't seen her in bright colors since Clarissa used to pick out her clothes, and they'd never flattered.

"Emmaline Bluewater, is that you?" His tone joked, but he was staring. A lot.

To say it was unnerving was like saying the Nile was a stream.

The dishes in the sink rattled in warning.

She grabbed hold of her nerves, packed them down. Goddess. As if it wasn't bad enough she was still attracted to him; she could *not* let him see the effect he had on her control.

She needed to move so she did, stepping away from her door and heading to the kitchen to…do what, she didn't know.

"I take it that's your way of saying I won't embarrass you?" She played it off with a casual tone as she changed Chester's water, careful not to spill on her dress. Normally she'd do it with magic, but she didn't trust the faucet not to go Niagara Falls on her.

"You'd never embarrass me."

The sincerity in his voice was just as sexy as his ass. Damn it.

Too much, it was too much. She needed to break the tension. She didn't think twice, spun in a full circle to change her outfit. "I'll take that bet."

He took one look and a genuine laugh rolled out, deep and rich and thoroughly amused. "Okay. You could embarrass me if you wore that."

"You don't think it suits me?" Her cheeks heated as she pretended to be absolutely fine dressed as a giant hot dog. It was worth it in the name of friendship. Better that than that dark, hot navy stare that undressed as it went. A shiver started low and rolled up her body as she shifted in place.

"I didn't say that." He came forward, laughter still creasing his cheeks. "Though if we're talking couple's costumes, I think it might be more appropriate if I was the hot dog and you were the bun."

Words failed her. Like they always did when he did this… flirting thing. Was she supposed to say something flirty back? Was that what friends/platonic husband-and-wife duos did?

He was within touching distance now. The sweater looked soft. She wondered if it would feel that way if she reached out.

"Cat got your tongue?" he teased.

Get it together. "I don't think—I should encourage you." Her stomach knotted at the hesitant way the words emerged.

Usually, this was the point her date would blink, try and

hide surprise at her shyness, the way her sentences would stop-start like an escalator on the fritz. Maybe flinch, depending on the dick quotient, as Tia called it.

Of course, this wasn't a date and Bastian did none of those things. Instead, he shrugged.

"You should absolutely encourage me. Isn't that what a wife does for her husband? Besides, I think you secretly like it."

She hoped he didn't know that for certain. She didn't think she was projecting, but she knew if an image was strong enough, he could pick up on it.

Throwing up another layer onto her shields, just in case, Emma pulled off a sneer. Or what she hoped was one. "I do not."

His dimple flashed. "Do."

"Don't."

"Do."

"Don't."

"Yeah, you do, and you know how I can tell?" He snagged a finger over her cheek. Electricity snapped through her, stealing her breath. "These get red."

"That's because I'm embarrassed for you."

"I'm not the one dressed as a wiener."

"You're just acting like one?"

He laughed again, making his expression dance. He looked more like the Bastian she remembered than he had since he'd come back. She couldn't decide if that was a good thing. "Emmaline Bluewater." He shook his head, and then snapped his fingers. A portal opened in the center of the room.

"Must be the hunger," he said, gesturing for her to precede him. "So let's get you fed."

Locking her knees, she restored her dress and walked through the portal with him close behind. It closed at his command and she found they were within a block of the restaurant.

Drizzle peppered her skin as they began to walk.

Bastian conjured an umbrella, held it up above her.

"Too late to play the gentleman," she told him. "I've seen it all now."

He held open the door to Cesario's, letting her pass, but catching her when she drew abreast of him. "Not yet, but would you like to?"

The laugh bubbled up and she shook her head. He was a bad influence.

"There you are!" Tia's voice interrupted, surprising enough to shake Emma free of Bastian's warm gaze. "We've been waiting for you."

She swung her head around and spotted her friend standing at a table for four. Leah sat next to her, a resigned expression on her face.

CHAPTER 11

"$\mathcal{D}$id I ever tell you," Bastian said, his words joined like children linking hands, "that I like the color blue? In fact," he went on, with the air of someone imparting something truly interesting, "it's my *favorite* color. And Emma's is yellow."

Emma shared a look with Leah, who'd foregone another drink in favor of chocolate chip cookies, citing her day-long hangover from the last batch of Cauldron cosmos. Her friend hid a grin behind another bite.

Tia snorted from her position, sitting on the far end of the bar, back to the wall. "Should've put money on it." She tipped her empty martini glass to Emma. "To the reigning champ."

Bastian did a double take, put an offended hand to his chest. "'Scuse me? I'm still in this. I can hold my drink. I'm strong. I can hold anything. Boxes. Suitcases. One time, I held a whole mummy sarcophagus *by myself.*" He leaned in, cupped a hand around his mouth as if to shield it from Leah, and loud-whispered, "I might have used some magic, though."

Emma couldn't help but be charmed. After a long, excruciating dinner, during which Tia had jumped on everything Bastian said, her friend had then ushered them all into Toil and Trouble for some after-dinner drinks. She should've known a competition would've blossomed; Bastian had never turned down a challenge and Tia knew Emma could drink anyone under the table. Her uncharacteristic party trick that always amused. And now, the poor guy was what she could only term drunk off his spectacular ass.

Whoops. Edit that to remove "spectacular." Clearly, she'd been affected by the drinks, too. Clearly.

Still, she'd thought Bastian would hold out longer than two Cauldron cosmos and two Broomstick Bellinis. He'd complained at first that the drinks were too sweet, but that hadn't stopped him from throwing them back, even when Tia had supposedly made the last batch stronger.

The drinks seemed to have unlocked his mouth, and he wouldn't stop telling them all "little-known facts."

It was charming, damn it. She'd never really seen him less than put-together, even when he was pleading for his mom or apologizing to her. He'd been a little rumpled, maybe, but rumpled in a way that only emphasized his perfection.

Sprawled on a bar stool that would have wobbled over if Emma hadn't kept correcting it with what little telekinesis she had, he was sloppy and rambling. His hair was in disarray from him repeatedly pushing his hands through it, and he'd taken off the sweater half an hour ago, complaining it was too hot. Every time he waved his arms around—which happened when he thought of something new to tell them—the muscles in his arms flexed and her magic pulsed inside her. Along with certain other things that would remain nameless.

Leah grinned. "Magic, Bastian? Whatever do you mean?"

Emma shot her a warning look. Just because he was somewhat worse for wear didn't mean they should play this game.

She didn't know this Bastian, didn't know if he'd turn her friend in. Or demand they erase her memory. Leah's life was too big a risk to pin on a maybe.

His mouth made a lopsided smile. "I used to dabble."

Uh-huh. That might have been treating the truth as an elastic band he could stretch, but she supposed technically it *was* the truth.

"And you know what else?" He flicked a hand and a coin appeared, weaving around his fingers in a trick no magician could do.

How much had he drunk? Or how low was his tolerance?

And still, she had to be impressed with the amount of control he had over the coin even while three sheets—make that six—to the wind. Telekinesis was a skill and only the most powerful could manipulate objects with precision. Not like her balancing the stool with broad sweeps.

Just another example of their incompatibility.

The depressing thought swaddled her like a baby.

Leah made appropriate *ooh* and *ahh* noises.

Bastian grinned, made the coin disappear. "I still practice," he said, lifting his glass to his lips. He stared at it when he came to the baffling realization it was empty. "There's a lot of pressure. To be perfect."

Emma straightened.

From across the room, Tia scoffed. "And here I thought it just came naturally to you," she drawled.

Bastian leaned in to Leah from where she stood on the other side of the bar. "She doesn't like me."

"I noticed."

"I don't really care."

The snort that left Tia held layers of emotion, the top note being reluctant amusement.

"And I'm far, far, *far* from perfect. Pick a point in the distance, then multip…mutil…times it by a hundred miles. I have flaws."

"Now it's getting interesting." Leah pushed her half-eaten cookie to him. "Eat something, handsome."

"I love cookies. You make the best cookies," he threw at Emma like a compliment grenade.

It landed in her hands and she had no idea what to do with it. Or the ridiculous warmth that came with it.

"Emmaline knows. Sorry. Emma. She hates when I call her that." He picked out a chocolate chip. "Flaws on top of flaws beneath blond hair. But when you're a firstborn son of one of the most powerful families, you have to bury them. You have to be the best son, the best friend, the best warlock."

Emma jackknifed up. "Ah…"

Leah's expression froze like she had no idea what to do.

Tia's legs swung to the side as if preparing to jump and tackle Bastian.

Who hadn't even noticed he'd dropped the *W* word. "I try, but you know what, perfect is *boring*. Look at Emma." He followed his own instruction, his navy gaze focused a little off-center. "She's never been perfect."

What warmth remained was chased out by a clutch of annoyance.

"Yeah? Well, you've always been an ass," she retorted, perilously close to a pout.

He didn't even seem to hear that, head cocked, studying her with a deepening frown. "If only I knew if I could trust you."

He knows. Sloane's image formed in her mind before she hastily coated her shields again so he couldn't pick up on it.

"You have secrets." It was a mumble, a complaint as he continued. "You hide things. Maybe you're hiding what I think; maybe you're not."

It was like talking to the Riddler. She shared an uneasy glance with her friends. "What do you think I'm hiding?"

"The reason," he stressed. Unhappiness flooded his eyes. "*The reason*. The betrayal."

She blinked. "I, uh…" She didn't have any words for him. She looked to Leah, unsure. Did he know about the Joining? But if he did, why wouldn't he have said something?

Leah tapped the cookie. "Time to eat."

Tia's feet hit the ground as she jumped off the counter to stride over. Her expression was intent. "What I want to know is whether she can trust *you*."

"*Tia*."

"I think so," he said seriously. "As long as she doesn't betray me again."

Uneasiness tasted sour on her tongue. Seriously, what did he know?

"How did I betray you?" The question was out before she thought better of it.

Those unhappy eyes slanted toward her. "I can't say."

"Because it's bull," Tia retorted. "It was you—Emma never betrayed *you*."

"Hope not." He shrugged. "We'll see. But I do owe you. For my mom. Even if what you…" He stopped abruptly, one hand going to his throat.

"Is he choking?" Leah slipped off her stool and made to go to him.

Bastian's shoulders abruptly relaxed and he shuddered. "Keep forgetting," he muttered. "Stupid."

Leah cocked an eyebrow. "Could he be allergic to some of the special ingredients?"

"I don't think so." Emma put out a hand. "Bastian? You okay?"

He glanced up and smiled, as if the past few minutes hadn't happened. "Hi."

She smiled back, unable to help it.

Tia cleared her throat. "You didn't really answer my question. Can *she* trust *you*?"

Enough. "This isn't your business," Emma returned, irritated.

"You're my friend. It kind of is."

"So if I went to find Henry?"

Warning darkened Tia's face. "Not the same thing."

"Yeah, it is."

Bastian clapped his hands to get their attention. "It's fine, Emma," he told her, finally picking up the cookie Leah was all but shoving at him. "She's your friend. She's annoying as hell. But she has a point."

Emma stared at him. She had no words. Again.

"Still." He chewed thoughtfully. "Some things should stay private. Like what we're going to do about sex."

Leah chuckled. "Aw, man, he is so wasted."

He had to be. She'd never seen a man this chatty. This… Honest.

The word clicked the light bulb in her head and her hand shot out, grabbed Tia's arm. "You need to come talk to me."

"I'm still talking to Bastian."

"No, you're done." Emma dragged her over to the far side of the bar, where she whirled on her. "What did you do?"

"What?"

"Nobody gets that honest without a little help. Man, I should have seen it earlier."

Tia folded her arms. A dead giveaway. "What?"

"You put a truth potion in his cosmo, didn't you?"

Tia's chin lifted. "So?"

Oh, jeez. Emma was tempted to put her head in her hands.

"What the hell? That breaks about ten thousand codes of ethics."

"Please, witches don't *have* ethics."

It chafed because she was right.

"And I had to know the truth. What his intentions are. What his real feelings are. I'm worried."

"How many times, Tia? This. Isn't. Your. Business!" When Tia opened her mouth, Emma interrupted. "You're treating me like a child."

"I've seen the way you look at him."

"I don't."

"You don't look at him?"

"Well, sure, *sometimes* I look at him. But, I don't, you know, *look* at him."

A beat passed. "I'm not sure if it says more about you or me that I followed that." Tia shook her head, pushing the topic. "I can see the old you in your eyes."

"Ouch." Emma pulled back, hurt sliding in like a knife between her ribs.

"I'm serious. They have stars upon stars. And worse, he's starting to look at *you*."

Emma's pulse bumped. "What?"

"I mean, obviously he's got some trust issues we didn't know about but even so… Okay, have you ever baked something and it's unusual but you think you like it so you keep trying it?"

"He is not looking at me like that." Hell, *she* wasn't the one who'd had the truth potion. Why should she admit she'd noticed some of the long looks sent her way?

"Hey, it was either this or a hex bag."

"No hex bags." Emma sighed, ran a hand over her hair. "I shouldn't have worn the dress."

"No."

Miffed, Emma sent her a look. "I'm going to take him home. Before he spills any more secrets."

"Hey, aren't you glad you know he doesn't trust you? It means you can figure out how to be stealthier about Sloane."

Emma wasn't admitting anything. "What if he spills the magic secret completely and Leah can't pretend anymore?"

Tia had the grace to look shamefaced. "Yeah, I didn't think about that. The good side is that one out of three truth potions have foggy memory as a side effect."

"Bastian's skill is mind magic."

"Right." Tia shrugged. "Damage is done anyway. Just let me ask a couple more questions."

"*No.*"

"We all right here?" Leah joined them.

Emma looked past her.

"He went to the bathroom. What's up?"

Emma poked a finger into Tia's shoulder. "She roofied him."

Leah's mouth fell open.

"Goddess, you make it so dramatic." Tia poked Emma back. "I slipped a small truth potion in his drink is all."

"A truth potion." Leah considered. "Yep, that explains it. Hey, can I have a batch for this guy at the shelter? I think he likes me, but I'm not sure, and not to go all girly-girl, but I don't want to just ask him…"

"No," Emma told her.

"Buzzkill."

"I'm *fun*, goddammit." She was getting tired of everyone saying how serious she was.

Leah patted her shoulder. "Yes, you are. Under planned, controlled circumstances." She grinned at Emma's scowl. "How long should the truth thing last then?"

"Six hours at most, depending how much she gave him."

"He'll sleep it off. But I haven't had a chance to ask—"

"No."

"Buzzkill."

"He has a right to his secrets. Would you want someone to truth potion you?"

"All's fair in love and witchcraft."

"You're all nuts. I'm going home." Emma walked over, grabbed her coat.

Leah appeared next to her. "You should at least ask him how he feels about you, beyond the trust thing."

"Not you, too." Emma enunciated the next part for both of them. "We're not even friends, let alone anything else."

She may as well have been trying to sell her friends land in Florida for a bargain; they looked that unconvinced.

It played on her mind as she collected Bastian and nudged him out of the bar. The cold night air soaked into her exposed skin as she made them walk the blocks home, figuring it couldn't hurt him. Or her, since three cosmos was more than her usual amount. Practical Emma again, she thought with a grimace.

He kept trying to open portals, but considering his loosened state of mind, she didn't want to chance them ending up on some kind of dig site in the middle of a crowd. To her dismay, he found it amusing when she kept closing them, and they fought a strange kind of tug-of-war over the portals all the way home.

By the time Chester greeted them, she was worn out. Bastian was a lot stronger magically than she was and going up against his will was like arm wrestling with a heavyweight boxer.

She dropped her keys, greeted her dog, and hesitated by

the couch. Would he need help getting to bed? Should she let him have hers when he was this gone?

Bed and *Bastian* were two words that didn't belong in the same sentence, she decided uneasily.

He didn't seem to share her worries as he dropped onto the couch. He sprawled, six feet whatever inches of solid beautiful male. All he was missing was a beckoning finger.

She turned and walked in the opposite direction. "Want some water?"

"Sure. I can get it."

She swiveled, put out her hands as she would to traffic. "No. I got it."

"I'll help." He'd pushed to his feet and was already ambling over. He'd left his sweater behind, and his beautifully defined arms were clearly displayed by his T-shirt.

"You'll help me get water from the fridge?"

He dimpled at her. "I'm here to make your life easier."

"Riiight." She elongated the word, then waved at the fridge. "Go for it."

"Have I said thanks for everything you're doing?" He stepped forward.

Why was he so close?

Duh. The fridge was behind her.

Emma scuttled out of the way, bracing her back against the breakfast bar as he brushed past her to open the fridge door and grab a bottle. "You've said thank you."

"I mean it." He closed the door, holding the bottle by its neck. "It's amazing. You're amazing."

Her stupid pulse leaped again. "Anyone would do the same."

"No." He shook his head and came closer. She tried to go through the breakfast bar to the other side, but the wood held firm. Drat. If she could just remember the words to the ghosting spell... "Not everyone would. Not every witch would. But you've always been different."

She didn't dare speak.

"Sometimes I think I can trust you." Consideration reflected in both the words and the warm navy gaze he dragged over her. "Because I *like* you."

"Good." She tried to sidle to the side, but his arms came around her, bracing him against the bar and leaving her trapped between the counter and his body. Panic battled desire. "We're meant to be getting back to friends, right?"

"No. I mean, yeah, but it's more than that. Lately—" He stopped, clearly frustrated. "Lately, when I'm around you, I watch your mouth."

It parted at his words.

"And I remember that night in the garden."

Goddess, he smelled good. Emma struggled not to lean in and bury her nose in his neck.

"It's such a bad idea," he murmured, his gaze moving to hers. Locking there. "We have a plan. Friends. And there's the trust thing but...my gut tells me to trust you."

"O-okay..."

"You're Emmaline," and he looked baffled by the words even though he'd said them. "But..."

But *what*?

She would *not* ask.

What she should do was push him back or duck under his arm or cast a spell or use a broad wave of telekinesis so she could escape to her room. That would be the sensible, practical thing to do for their long-term goal of staying friends in a platonic marriage.

She stayed where she was.

"Do you like me, Emma?"

She hesitated, somehow feeling the question was more

loaded than what it sounded. Finally she nodded, helpless to speak. Her throat felt thick.

"That's good. I want you to like me. I want to make you smile." He lifted a hand, grazed fingers over her lips. "I want to see this mouth smile."

She swallowed.

"This mouth…" he repeated, and his voice dipped. "All I can think about is this mouth."

That potion should be outlawed. She had no idea what to say, literally lost to the sensual web he was unintentionally weaving.

"I want to kiss you."

The darkly spoken words came like a lightning punch from a shadowed alley. They hit her solar plexus and she wheezed. So sexy.

He didn't seem to mind, one corner of his mouth hooking up into a dimple. "That surprises you. It surprised me. And then I tried to ignore it, but the truth is that I want to kiss you. One more time."

She stared up at him, weak at the knees, in the head. Her magic teetered on the brink. "Oh, Bastian," she breathed. "You're going to regret saying that."

"Probably." His smile dropped, replaced with an intent look. "But if I'm going to regret anything, might as well regret this."

And before she grasped his meaning, Bastian kissed her.

CHAPTER 12

It was heat and magic and desire and all Emma could think, as her hands blindly flew up to grip Bastian's shirt, was *more*.

He didn't go slow, didn't ease her in. And she loved that he didn't think he needed to, that he didn't think of her as shy, sweet Emmaline who needed to be coaxed.

Instead, he kissed her like a woman he had to have. His lips plundered hers, his arms tight around her, the bottle of water dropping to the floor. His mouth moved with absolute purpose and that purpose was to drive her out of her freaking mind. And he did it *well*.

Dizziness washed up her body and she vaguely heard a clatter from the cupboards, something smash as her lips clung to his, her body pressed snugly against him.

His mouth left hers and she tightened her grip on his shirt. *Not yet, not yet.*

"Open," he breathed. "Open for me."

Her moment of incomprehension fled when he kissed her again, and this time she parted her lips. He took full advantage, his tongue teasing hers, his hands sliding over her body, learning it. Everywhere he touched, heat spread, arrowing to her core. Her breasts flattened as she leaned even farther into him. Sensitized nipples rubbed cloth and her breath hitched.

He heard, his mouth growing hotter, more ardent as his hands gripped her hips and boosted her up onto the bar. He nudged her legs open, stepping between them, all without breaking the kiss.

The man had skills. She was aware of his heart beneath her hands and how it thundered, a pair to her own. She flattened her hands, loving how his pecs jumped in response, how his grip tightened on her hips as she slid them over his chest. Across his nipples.

A phantom hand began to slide up her thigh and she jerked in surprise. He recaptured her mouth instantly, a smile flavoring the kiss. And that telekinetic hand continued to tease up her thigh. Too slowly.

She bit him. He growled in response.

This wasn't her. This wild, needy creature. She was the serious witch, the awkward date. Where had this need come from, this desire to rip off her clothes and his and have him hold her down with his weight. Come into her.

Bastian. It had always been Bastian.

Her hands fisted at the thought. She broke the kiss, shuddering when he took the opportunity to lick down her neck to the base, where he gently bit.

"Emma." It was a groan against her skin. "I want you."

Another dish smashed from the open cupboard behind him.

No. This had to stop. He wasn't in his right mind. Neither was she.

"Stop," she whispered, unable to push him away. "We need to stop."

The phantom hand hesitated, mirroring his mouth. He was breathing hard. "Why?"

"Because." She swallowed, tasted him. "We had a deal."

"Let's talk about that."

She saw he was about to kiss her again, knew she'd weaken if he so much as laid lip on her, and took the coward's way out. She threw up a hand. "*Incantartum.*"

Bastian dropped like a rock amidst the broken china.

Emma grimaced. "Sorry," she murmured to his sleeping form. "But you'll thank me tomorrow."

As she'd expected, Emma was plagued by half dreams that focused on hot mouths and strong hands. And feelings of dread and guilt and a small amount of concern. She'd thought she was over this, over him.

Did you really, though?

It didn't really matter. Once the Divining was done, Bastian would go anyway. What was the point in thinking too much about feelings, regrets, secrets? She'd chosen her path and she was sticking to it. No matter how good the man's mouth was.

She gave up trying to sleep at six a.m., threw on some clothes, snuck past Bastian as she motioned for Chester, and together they hit the park early. It was busier than she'd thought and what with Chester's sudden love for a poodle that he wouldn't quit following around and a detour to get fresh bagels, it was past seven when she returned to her apartment.

She didn't halt when she saw Bastian standing by the breakfast bar, but the little hop-skip probably hadn't fooled him. "Oh. H-hi."

Was she supposed to pretend The Kiss hadn't happened? Was she supposed to breeze through like she went around catapulting herself onto men on a weekly basis?

To her surprise, an expression of discomfort settled on Bastian's face. Maybe he had no idea what to do either. She wasn't sure if that helped or hindered.

"Morning," he said in his lovely deep voice, and the husky echo of his *I want you* sounded in her ears.

Even if someone had paid her a thousand bucks to do so, she couldn't have stopped the heat that spilled into her cheeks.

He gestured to the floor. "I, ah, cleared up the mess."

That she'd made because her magic had gone AWOL during The Kiss. Oh, boy.

She held up the white paper bag. "I brought bagels!"

"Great." He shoved his hands into the pockets of his jeans. "Emma…" He stopped, seemingly running out of words. She knew the feeling.

She went to put the paper bag on the breakfast bar, hesitated for a second at the image of Bastian pressing her against it. She tried to wipe the memory out of her mind, but it looked like she'd need some baking soda and vinegar because it stubbornly refused to lift.

"Should I apologize?"

Her head whipped up. "No!" Her voice sounded appalled, which was good, because that's how she felt. For one thing, he'd been under the influence of alcohol and a potion. For another…she knew it had been stupid and impulsive, but it had possibly been the most exciting moment of her life. If he said he was sorry, that made it cheaper in some way.

He didn't seem convinced. "I woke up with shards of china in my hair. It's a bit hazy how they got there, but I'm pretty sure you wouldn't have knocked me out if you didn't have good reason."

She cringed. "You didn't do anything. Wrong, I mean." The beginning of his sentence registered. "Hazy? You don't remember?" She tried to decide if that was good or bad.

He rocked back on his heels. "I remember drinking at the

bar. I remember coming back here." The wall behind her suddenly must have been fascinating. "I remember…kissing you."

And on a scale of one to humdinger, how did that rate for you?

She pushed that to the back of her mind in case he accidentally picked up on it. As if this wasn't awkward enough. "That's pretty much it."

"And you put a sleeping spell on me because…?"

Oh, Goddess.

She fidgeted with the paper bag, the crinkling sound covering up the awkward silence. "You welshed on the deal," she finally said, trying to play it off light, carefree. "One kiss, right?"

"Right." He pursed his lips and memories hit like a flood. She tore her gaze off them as he added, "Sorry about that."

She shifted from foot to foot. "In the interest of honesty, ah, it wasn't entirely your fault."

She actually felt the weight of his gaze. "You wanted to kiss me?"

Holy Mother Goddess. Her cheeks burned as she sidestepped the question. "Tia may have…well, she might have… I didn't know until after and I would have stopped her but… she, ah…"

Bastian's eyes widened. "She put a truth potion in my drink." Before she could do more than nod, he stepped into her, body vibrating with tension. "What did I say?" he demanded. "Did I say anything about why I left?"

She blinked. "No…"

If anything, he looked disappointed. One hand swept the back of his neck as he jerked a nod. "Right. 'Course not."

"Do you have something to tell me about why you left?" she asked, curiosity nudging nerves out of the way.

His gaze whipped to her, then back to the floor. He didn't say anything for a moment that stretched to an uneasy point.

Then he huffed an amused breath. "I can't believe Tia got one over on me. With all the times my friends pulled that prank on each other, I'd have thought I'd remember the taste of a truth potion."

Emma refused to acknowledge her disappointment. She didn't really have the right to it, considering what she was keeping from him. "I think it tastes different with alcohol. But I hope you're not too upset; I know it's a violation."

He waved that off. "Please, it's kids' games, like I said." Speculation crossed his face. "Just tell your friend if she wants to play kids' games, she'd better watch her back."

Goddess save Emma from witch society.

She restrained herself from rolling her eyes and instead said, "I got sesame or plain."

Both were toasted and on plates in the next five minutes, and with that done a stilted conversation was taking place. With the memory of The Kiss hovering, it was hard to act normally, as unsophisticated as that was.

Emma turned with an overwhelming sense of relief as her cell chimed. Except it wasn't her phone.

Dread drummed in time with her heart as she slid the compact out of her purse. Only Clarissa ever messaged her through the mirror. Not like she had other friends in the witch world, besides Tia.

She smoothed her hair, pinched her cheeks, breathed in and out as she caught Bastian's stiffening posture, and opened the gold compact.

To find Kole's face looking back at her. "Hey, squirt," her older brother said with a grin. "Miss me?"

A rush of pleasure made her lips curve involuntarily. "Kole. I thought you were still at sea."

"Just got back this morning. Did the dutiful son thing and then thought I'd hit you up, see how you're doing." His eyebrow, the same color as his and her hair, lifted. "With the Truenote dick."

Bastian looked torn between annoyance and amusement. Emma stifled a smile, shifted to make sure Kole couldn't see that the man in question was in her apartment.

Out of her four older brothers, Kole was the closest to her in age and therefore the one she'd spent the most time with. He was six years older, so while she was growing up, he'd mostly been at boarding school. But when he'd been home, he'd plagued her like a brother should, unlike her other siblings, who'd taken after Clarissa and alternately ignored and/ or scorned her. He now researched water magic with other scientists, which meant he was rarely at home. He'd always been the smart one.

"Kole," she admonished, half meaning it. "We're over that."

"You cried. I still owe him broken legs. But the reason I'm calling, I found a warlock to block—"

Panic made her hurry to cover his words. "We're over it, Kole. Look." She lifted her tattooed wrist so he could see the proof. "And we're *all* here."

Looking far from convinced, he let it go when he realized what she meant. "Mother must have been on him like slime on a frog when he got back into town. Poor dick didn't stand a chance." He smiled as he said it, knowing Bastian could hear him. Because he was actually ten. Before she could comment, he added, "All I can say is he's getting a treasure."

"Kole," she said, touched.

"I am going to be one hell of a brother-in-law, after all."

Funny guy. "I can cast spells through the mirror," she reminded him.

"Must have been practicing, since you couldn't even build a proper snowman with Sloane's help last time I was in town."

She let out a high-pitched cackle, heart ramming her ribs

at the mention of Sloane's name. "You can control *water*," she objected, trying to breeze past it. Nothing to hide here.

"Yeah, yeah. With the Exhibition coming up, all I'm saying is—"

"Exhibition?"

"Mother didn't… Of course she didn't." Disgust appeared on his face, so similar to hers but much more handsome. "An Exhibition ceremony has been arranged to celebrate the match. You know how society likes to judge."

And how Clarissa would do anything to show off the family. Except she knew Emma wasn't as strong as the other Bluewaters, lastborn and all…which meant another mirror message was in her future, demanding she practice. Or worse, go over to the manor to practice.

Her body chilled at the thought.

"I can help?" her brother offered, clearly reading the despair.

Bastian wandered into her line of vision, eating a bagel, and an idea bloomed in her mind.

"Maybe. I'll get back to you. I think it's better if you concentrate on other things." Like breaking the Joining clause. Sloane. Everything that went with her.

On the wavelength they'd fine-tuned when they were young, he nodded. "All right. You free for lunch? We can catch up. I have some news." His eyes gleamed with underlying meaning.

"Absolutely." And thank the Goddess. She might at least be able to let one of her secrets go. It was getting tough to juggle them all, even as a woman.

They spoke for a few more minutes, arranging for him to pick her up at the bar, before she snapped the compact closed. She looked at it a minute and then placed it on one of the end tables, next to a drooping plant. Magic leaped to her fingers as she touched the leaves, urging the fern to thrive again.

If only everything was so easy.

"Kole doesn't live at the manor with the rest?" Bastian asked when she walked over and sat on the couch, ensuring there was a lovely Chester buffer in between. Her familiar was all about the bagel, using big eyes to his best advantage, though he did spare a tail wag for her when she sat down.

She curled her legs up and wrapped her arms around them. "He's in research out on the Atlantic for most of the year."

"I always liked him." Bastian flicked her a look that was pure teasing. Normal. "Apparently not returned."

She relaxed. Kole's call couldn't have come at a better time. Everything was back on even footing and they could...not forget, but...skip over the kiss.

"Who's Sloane?"

Damn it. She forced herself not to freeze. "I volunteer with a program for teens. Kole's hung with us a few times." Proud of how casual she sounded, she smiled.

"Ah, cool. Maybe I could meet her at some point if she's important."

"Maybe."

He hesitated, reading the brush-off for what it was, before choosing his battles. "I was going to meet up with Ethan, that friend I told you about, today. The one who lives off the river Nile." His plate disappeared back to the kitchen at a gesture from him. "I was going to ask if you wanted to come join us."

"To Egypt?"

"Yeah."

She wasn't sure why she was so surprised. It wasn't like they were talking a long plane ride. It was just a portal away.

To meet his friend. In Egypt. As his fiancée.

Mixed feelings about that. Longing, uncertainty, some small pleasure that he didn't mind introducing her as his soon-to-be wife. To his friends.

Goddess, get a hold of yourself.

She shook off the mooning stage and said, "Maybe another time."

"Sure. I think you'd like Egypt." He tapped his finger on his knee. "Remind me why you haven't gone again?"

She lifted a shoulder, unable to put it into words. Well, not words she could say aloud. The truth was she'd been saving for a long time to take Sloane away on a fantastic trip the old-fashioned plane ride way. Sloane and she had been planning their route for the last year and both were beyond excited to experience it all for the first time together.

Not that she could tell Bastian that without revealing just how important Sloane was. She changed the subject. "Did you hear what Kole was saying?"

"Yes. He thinks I'm a dick."

"Besides that." She took a breath, the unease edging back in. "There's going to be an Exhibition."

He gave a careless shrug. "Annoying but not surprising. Most Divinings have one."

Emma squeezed her knees tighter. She didn't want to admit what she was about to admit, but for the sake of friendship—not to mention common sense—it was necessary. "I need to practice."

"Practice?" His expression softened. "It's not a competition, Emma. You show up, you show off a trick or two, you get cake. Or that's what happened the last time I went to one. Cake's still a thing, right?"

She wasn't in the mood to laugh. "Mother won't think of it like that."

"So?"

So. As if it was just that easy.

"You stood up to her once," he pointed out, and that same

dark something shifted in his face. "Or you wouldn't be here. Right?"

That wasn't exactly what had happened. She didn't want to go into it. "I'm not as strong as you." It pinched her pride, but she squeezed the question out. "Will you help me?"

"Again, not a competition. Just... I don't know, do something with flowers."

She could just picture Clarissa's face if her only daughter made a few potted plants bloom. "It's not enough."

He flattened his lips, a frown settling heavy on his forehead. "Why do you even care what they think?"

She didn't. And she did.

When she didn't respond, he gave her a soft nod. "I'll help, of course I will. Not that I know how."

Relief body-checked her and she impulsively reached out and caught his knee. "Thank you."

He stared at her hand. "No problem."

Emma took the hint and removed it, clearing the awkwardness in her throat. "Today?"

"Egypt," he reminded her. "Kole."

"Right." She bit her lip. She wasn't sure when the Exhibition was; she'd have to get that out of Kole that afternoon, if Clarissa didn't message first. But she wanted to be ready and Bastian was one of the most powerful people she knew.

You could ask Tia, an inner voice pointedly reminded her.

She brushed that well under the rug and put a table on top of it for good measure.

He took one look at her crestfallen face and sighed, just as he had when they'd been teenagers and he'd taken pity on her. "I'm at the bar tonight," he said. "You can come by and we'll practice there."

"In front of humans?"

"Unless you want to learn to work with fire or lightning, I think we can keep it quiet."

She wondered if he remembered how much he'd spilled last night. "Leah's working."

They shared a stare: her desperately neutral, him weighing it up.

He remembered something, but how much she didn't know.

"I'll distract her," he said finally. "Eight sound good?"

She nodded.

"Great." He stood. The air rippled over his clothes as he changed to ones more suited to hotter climes. "I'll get off now while it's still early there."

"What time is it?"

"They're seven hours ahead so..." He consulted his watch, counted forward, "Around two thirty in the afternoon." He grimaced. "Not so early. At least Ethan has air-conditioning."

"That's the warlock you were telling me about?"

"Yeah. You'd like him, he likes to bury himself in work, too."

She scowled at him, which only made him grin. Then he'd created a portal and was gone.

CHAPTER 13

$\mathcal{E}$mma enjoyed her lunch with her brother, relaxing as she only could with certain people, especially when Sloane joined them halfway through. Kole had found out about their half sister with Emma so while it remained a secret from the rest of their family, Kole had invested time and effort in getting to know the young girl. They talked about life, hobbies, movies, books—anything but her relationship with Bastian and the tattoo on her wrist. She'd worn long sleeves, but it peeked out just to mess with her. And so did Sloane, when she brought it up, complaining that she wasn't allowed to meet Bastian or go to the wedding.

"Consider yourself lucky." Kole had tweaked her nose and laughed as she'd glared at him. "Those things are boring, Jellybean. How about we throw her a party—a going-away party for Bastian."

Emma rubbed her forehead as Sloane ran with that idea like it was a one-hundred-meter sprint.

Kole had made his opinion of the engagement clear, especially as he knew the entire story of what had happened seven years ago. He knew, however, that if Emma was going along with this marriage, she had good reason, so he let the subject slide with only minimal grumbles. He really was her favorite brother.

Especially as he'd handed her the first piece of good news since this whole thing had started. Apparently he'd asked around and had heard of a powerful warlock who could infuse a blocking spell into an inanimate object. Once enchanted, the object could block any curse.

"Just have to track him down." Kole had squeezed her hand. "Give me a week or so. What kind of thing would work?"

"It would have to be something he'd wear all the time. Something that wouldn't raise his suspicion when I gave it to him."

Her brother didn't ask whether she was sure that not telling him was the smart thing. He didn't like Bastian and didn't trust what the other warlock might do if he learned about the Joining clause. "How about a ring? You could give it to him at the ceremony."

Relief made Emma light-headed. "Perfect." She really was lucky to have him on her side.

She was not so lucky at trying to convince him to stay away from the bar. Considering he hadn't been back for a few years, he apparently wanted to play big brother, do a walk-through, knock on the walls and pretend he understood how it sounded when a wall was solid.

She strode arm in arm with him through the double doors, having dropped Sloane off at her house. Any second, she thought, with an inner grin. Three. Two. One.

Leah's blond curls jerked up as if she'd scented him from by the bar. She screeched, drawing attention from the Monday-afternoon crowd, and barreled over, throwing her petite body against his. Emma dove to the side to avoid being pancaked.

"Big brother Kole," Leah crowed, linking her arms around his neck. She'd decided when they'd first met that she was going to adopt him as a brother. Kole, who'd had limited experience with humans and no experience with a human like Leah, had accepted it with good grace. They'd been like siblings ever since. Well, Emma amended. Kind of siblings.

He grinned down at Leah. "What was your name again?"

She swatted him. "Emma didn't tell me you were released from prison. What's it like showering without eyes on you?"

"Strange. You could help me out with that, come by my house, watch through the glass…"

Leah laughed, delighted that her playmate was back, and linked her arm through his, drawing him to the bar.

"She's kidding," Emma reassured the nearest patrons as they blinked. She caught up with them as Leah was pushing Kole onto the stool nearest the register. "Leah," she admonished, "you're scaring the customers."

"She shouldn't be out in public." Kole swiveled on the stool, took a look around. "A good crowd for a Monday afternoon."

"We do okay." Leah hiked a thumb at the glass domes covering Emma's recent bakes. "Your sister's baking helps. I keep saying we ought to hire a chef, pull in the real lunch crowd, but you know Emma."

Emma folded her arms. "Because I'm sensible, *I'm* the bad guy?"

"I've only just got her to switch from vanilla ice cream," Leah told Kole in a mock-whisper.

"You're meant to be my brother." Emma nudged him. "Defend me."

"Vanilla is a perfectly acceptable flavor. For old ladies."

"You suck."

Leah grinned. "Beer?"

"One. Then I have to get home for dinner. Mother wants to discuss—" He shot a look at Leah who rolled her eyes.

"The secret's out, Kole. I know you listen to Manilow in the morning while you're gelling your hair."

"Cute," he told her. "Shoo. You're not meant to know this stuff." He'd realized Leah knew the big secret a couple of years ago and had not taken it well. Not because Emma and Tia had broken the rules, but because he didn't want anything to happen to Leah. Was there any real doubt why Kole was the only person in her family Emma got on with?

"Talk to your sister." Leah held up her hands. "She forced the knowledge down my throat, even when I was screaming for her to stop."

He snorted. Pointedly turned his head to the side. "She wants to discuss *something*," he told Emma.

Something to do with the Exhibition, no doubt, which Emma had been less than happy to learn was in a couple of weeks, toward the end of the Divining month. A good show to round everything off. Sweat licked her temples at the thought. Goddess, she hoped Bastian wasn't all talk when he said he could help her.

Leah plunked a beer in front of Kole, sneered when he pulled out his wallet. "Your money's no good here. You just have to tip." She tapped her cheek.

He grinned, boosted himself forward and put a smacking kiss where she'd indicated.

"Did she say anything about me?" Emma asked him, referring to Clarissa. She'd so far heard nothing from her mother, which could either be a good sign or a sign of impending doom.

Kole tipped his beer back, took a swallow. "She asked me if I'd spoken to you. I said I'd told you about the Exhibition." He hesitated.

Emma's stomach sank. "She wants me to go over to the manor, doesn't she?"

"I can stall her, Em." He nudged her shin with his foot. "Don't stress. But I would practice because Clarissa can only be stalled so long, and she *will* want to inspect you at some point." He grimaced in sympathy.

"Okay, I *have* to meet this person," Leah said, leaning on the bar.

"No," Emma and Kole said together, horror uniting their voices.

"C'mon, this chick can't be that tough."

Kole snorted. "Chick," he repeated, shaking his head. "Yeah, you're not meeting her."

Leah opened her mouth to retort, then raised her head at a shout down the bar. She nipped off to fill an order.

"So," Kole said, swiveling to face Emma more. "How is your soon-to-be ball and chain? Has he explained why he ran away?"

Emma summed up her thoughts about that question with a speaking look.

"I'm just asking."

"He's good. We're fine." She toyed with the idea of telling Kole he was sleeping on her couch, but she wasn't sure how the brother in him would react to that. "We're taking the time to try and be friends again." Or something. Guilt made her hunch her shoulders. Friends didn't keep secrets like the ones she was.

"Again?" Kole tapped his beer with a finger. "Like before when you used to follow him around and lap up any attention he threw your way?"

Stung, Emma frowned. "It wasn't always like that."

"Maybe, but that's what it looked like. So?"

"No." Emma's frown deepened when Kole looked far from convinced. "I'm serious. I don't kowtow to him now."

"Just be careful. You're not telling him about Sloane, either, right?"

Emma used her magic to flick him between his eyebrows. It was something she'd got really good at when she was younger. You know, because of all the practice.

She felt a poke in her side a second later, right where she was ticklish, and almost fell off the stool.

But at least he was grinning again. "All right, I get the hint. I trust you," he said. "For now. But he'll have to meet big brother at some point."

"Sure." Like way, *way* in the future.

Fortunately, Kole stayed long enough to chat with Leah and flirt with a couple early drinkers who approached the bar with swinging hips, but not long enough to bump into Bastian, who was early for his shift.

Unnecessary since Mondays were never a busy late crowd. Of course, there were the high-powered lawyers and bankers and stockbrokers—fill in your high paying job with stress up the wazoo here—who quit their jobs late and came in to throw back a drink or five, but on the whole, Bastian had plenty of time to spend with her. Especially since Leah was handling most of the clientele, leaving the two of them to a private conversation as she flirted for tips.

They'd started with the basics—Bastian had asked her what particular gifts she had.

Which were pretty much slim to none. She had a touch of telekinesis, an affinity with plants and she made a decent potion. None of which was going to wow the snobbish society dames and their sneering daughters. She didn't point that out. She didn't need to. Bastian had grown up there, too.

"I know it's not much." Emma flicked her fingers at a beer mat, sent it spinning.

It spun, reversed, then spun the other way again, up and up and up, until it was pirouetting like a ballet dancer.

"Show-off."

His smile made her glad she and her weak knees were perched on one of the bar stools. "I only do the best tricks for the pretty ladies."

Do not *blush*, she warned herself. Especially since, for Bastian, handing out compliments was like passing around a bowl of popcorn. They had no substance and you felt hungrier after.

"If that's your best trick," she said with an arch tone, "we're both screwed."

He laughed, the sound easing into her like warm honey.

She shifted on the stool. "You've, ah, obviously developed your telekinesis."

"Yeah. It's got more precise. Comes in handy when you're on a dig and you suddenly fall down a hole into an ancient tomb."

Her eyes bugged out. "That happened to you?"

"No."

"Jerk."

His dimple danced. "Nothing so dramatic. But for brushing sand or dirt away from delicate objects, you learn to be extra careful."

The affection in his voice made dual feelings of fascination and envy war within her. "How did you get into that?"

He propped his elbow on the bar, his chin in his hand. It put his face closer to hers, which, with The Kiss still emblazoned on her mind, was not a good idea. Any minute now she'd move away. Sixty seconds and she'd do it.

She breathed in cinnamon and fallen leaves, a scent she'd always associated with him and his magic. And wanted.

"Archaeology?" Bastian mused, returning her to her question. "Well, after I…"

"Left. You can say it. I won't start screaming at the ceiling."

His mouth twitched. "After I *left*," he said with a dip of his head, "I didn't really know what to do. I moved around, traveled, saw a lot of things I wanted to see, saw some things people I tagged along with wanted to see. I got caught up with this group of archaeological students from NYU who were doing the summer thing out in Mexico." His eyes went a little glassy, lost in memory. "I thought it sounded kind of boring, but I'd been on my own for a while and didn't like the idea of wandering aimlessly again. So, I went with them and met Dr. Frankell."

A stab of jealousy at the obvious admiration reared up and snagged her by the throat. "A woman."

"Now, now, Emmaline. No need to be jealous."

She spluttered.

"She's happily married to the love of her life," he informed her over her choking noises. He reached out, snagged her hand and rubbed it with his thumb. The resulting tingle curled her toes.

She tugged at his hold. "I'm not jealous."

"Of course not. Well, anyway, she's a very experienced woman."

Emma's expression flatlined. "I'm sure."

He clucked his tongue. "What a naughty little mind you have there. I'm shocked." He squeezed her hand and let it go. "Experienced in her field. She showed us how to map out grids, how to dig, how to uncover artifacts. What we should be looking for. How cultures are built in our minds from one shard of pottery. How stories are woven from the bones left behind."

Emma blinked.

He ducked his head, and she could swear he looked a shade embarrassed by his rhetoric. "From the time I first held a brush and discovered a piece of history, I was hooked."

"You didn't seem to be that interested in history before."

He shrugged. "This is like living it. Discovering it. Not reading in books."

Despair gathered in Emma. Like what she did, he meant.

"And they do all of it by hand," he marveled. "I can cheat some, use my powers, find the interesting stuff, but one of the guys, George, he works quadrant by quadrant and doesn't find anything for days, and still he gets up early to go work his sector."

"And you're right there with him."

"Yeah. Sometimes, if I'm very careful, I'll move an object under the sand so he discovers it."

"That's nice."

"I'm a nice guy."

"Ha." But she was smiling.

He gazed at her, mirroring that smile. He was so close and it was like it was just the two of them.

If he broached the small gap, if he leaned in a little more…

A noise from the other end of the bar popped the bubble. He straightened. "We're, ah, not here to talk about me, anyway. We're talking about your powers."

He said it quietly, so she didn't worry that anyone had overheard. She just made a face and wriggled her tense shoulders in their thin sweater. "Fine. But you mean lack of, right?"

Something flickered in his face. "Does it bother you? The… smallness of your gifts."

Ouch. Although she realized he wasn't trying to be hurtful, he'd succeeded anyway.

"No." She lifted a shoulder and let it drop. "I just know what everyone else thinks."

"You wouldn't ask for more if you could?" The intensity of his stare surprised her into a small, awkward laugh. Ah, the irony...

"No. At least, I don't think so. What do I need with a lot of powers?" She indicated the crowd. "I'm living in the human world. Magic isn't exactly an advantage—at least not if you're sticking to ethics."

"Didn't know witches had those," he quipped, something easing in his expression. Even so, he continued to study her as if her words held the key to a greater truth. What truth, she had no idea.

In any case, he soon moved on. "You're too tense. Magic is natural for us. Just breathe." He reached out, stroked a finger down her throat. "In." His finger trailed back up. "Out." As if that was going to help her relax.

Despite the ball of lust tightening in her belly, Emma breathed with him, forced her shoulders down from where they hung out with her ears.

"Good," he praised. "Now." He put the mat back in front of her. "Lift this."

She shot a furtive look around.

"I've cast a curtain spell; they won't see anything."

"Must be nice to be so powerful."

"It doesn't take much. I've just used it a lot." He lifted his eyebrows at whatever he read on her face. "Gutter mind. On digs."

"Oh." She focused on the beer mat. Then looked back at him. "You sure nobody will see?"

"Emma..."

"Fine." She breathed out as instructed and stared at the mat. With one hand, she gestured to lift it up. It hovered two inches above the bar.

"Can you do it without your hands?"

She bit her lip. "Not really. It takes a lot more concentration."

"We'll work on that. Looks more impressive if you don't use your hands. Besides, it can come in handy, so to speak."

Conjured by his words, the memory of the telekinetic hand grazing her thigh punched into Emma's mind. The beer mat smacked back onto the bar.

He looked in question at her.

She avoided both the look and the question by pushing the mat to the side. "I told you I didn't have much."

"Okay. So, what about your plant stuff? I know you can make them thrive. Can you make them die?"

"Why would I want to do that?"

"To really piss off an enemy?" He grinned. "What else?"

Her shoulders moved in a restless motion. "I don't know." Her inadequacy all but choked her.

"Can you create flowers out of nothing?"

"From a seed?"

"No, from nothing. Say I wanted a flower, right now, could you do a conjuring?"

She picked at the idea like a hangnail. Examined it from all corners. "I'm not sure. Usually I have to start with something."

"Okay." Thoughts raced across his face. "I have an idea. But we'll start basic." He closed his hand into a fist, then turned it around to open it, a small brown seed now sitting in his palm.

No surprises that Bastian could master that advanced magic.

"Is there anything you can't do?" she muttered.

He attempted a bashful look. "If it's telekinetic or mind-related, not really."

She exhaled thinly. "It's a wonder I'm not fending off attacks." At his lifted eyebrow, she explained, "From the mothers who want your bloodline mixed with theirs instead of mine."

"Not like we have a choice with that, thanks to the contract." It came out sharp and she shot him a surprised glance.

He wagged the seed in his palm as if he hadn't just snapped at her. "How fast can you make this grow?"

Apparently he wasn't going to explain the hostility. Fine. "I don't know. It's never been about speed."

"Amen to that."

He sent her a long, lascivious look that was clearly meant to make her laugh, rather than stir up anything hot. Ever the overachiever, he managed both. She let his weird hostility go, tucking it away to examine later, and snorted in response.

Bastian put the seed on the counter. "Grow it."

Well, that at least she could do. Ever since she'd taken her first steps, she'd been able to make plants thrive, flowers bloom wildly. They'd always reacted to her emotions, flourishing brilliantly when she was happy, withering when she was sad.

Now she focused on the seed, able to see the flower in her mind's eye. Magic hummed in her blood, pushed against her skin and then drifted out like a warm summer breeze to surround the seed.

With a magical nudge, she urged it to peek out, to take its first look at the world, to bloom and grow. A few sparks of silver magic surrounded the seed, growing as it too grew until the beautiful flickers of magic fizzled into nothing to reveal a sunflower lying on the bar.

Bastian picked it up, twirled the stem. "Impressive."

Her eyebrows drew together. "Hardly." Nature magic was one of the least skilled—almost anyone could do it with a bit of practice.

"You know, if you keep putting yourself down, I'm going to have to start reacting." He tapped the sunflower on her nose, making her jolt. "As your future husband, I will promise at that altar to defend you from all comers. That, sweet Emmaline, includes yourself."

"I'm shaking in my boots," she said, deadpan.

"That mouth." He released a breath, looking to the heavens as if the Goddess would help out. "Yes, it's uncomplicated, but you made the seed grow in under a minute. Without the aid of potions or an incantation. That's skill."

That took her aback. She was so used to thinking of her magic as weak, she hadn't thought of it in those terms. And neither had her mother.

"But I think you could get faster. A bit showier if you can 'burst' the flower from the seed." He nodded to himself. "We'll practice. It'll look great for our act."

"Our act?" she repeated, lost.

"Yeah. You're worried your magic won't be flashy enough? Well, we'll combine our talents and give them one hell of a show."

CHAPTER 14

*B*astian didn't sleep well. He hadn't been sleeping well for months, but last night's reason had a name, an attitude and soft pink lips.

Emma…

The morning after he'd begun his tutoring of Emma's powers and roughly thirty-six hours after their second kiss, Bastian stared up at the ceiling as he lay on the couch. And tried to push the memory of those seeking lips out of his head.

It was Emma, he reminded himself, as he punched the pillow and resettled. Shy, sweet Emma. Old-childhood-friend Emma. But as a reminder, it was losing power. His hormones just nodded sagely and agreed that yep, it was Emma. Sassy, sexy Emma.

Trustworthy Emma?

When he'd heard about the truth potion, half of him had leaped in terrified excitement at the prospect of finding a way around the silencing hex. He should've known something so simple wouldn't have worked—the hex was still clearly being refreshed. And yet, things would've been so much easier if he could have asked Emma straight-out what she knew. If she'd really meant that she wouldn't know what to do with a lot of power.

Because…

Because he wanted to give himself permission to like her, he admitted.

The small mirror he carried as a conduit chirped with his mom's chime. It flew across the room at his will and he smoothed a thumb across the surface to answer it, relieved to have a distraction.

His mom's thin-boned face wavered before settling into a solid picture. The bruises under her eyes were dark, but those eyes shone when the connection was made. "Do the ladies go for that scruff on your face?"

He had to smile. "Hey, Mom."

"Hi, baby. I didn't expect you up so early."

"Then why the wake-up call?"

"I had an idea and I wanted to run it past you. We want to invite you and Emmaline to dinner."

"Emma," he said automatically, running the invitation through his mind like a ribbon through his fingers. "She prefers Emma. Dinner?"

"Yes. We don't really know the girl—woman—and if she's going to be my daughter-in-law, that shouldn't be the case."

It made something inside him shift to hear that. He squirmed. "It's not like it's going to be a real marriage, Mom."

"Are there rings involved?"

"Well, yes."

"Are you going to stand at an altar under a full moon and recite the binding words?"

"Okay, but—"

"That reminds me—have you done any planning for the wedding?"

He blanched. It was enough for him to deal with the engagement, let alone plan a wedding. And he couldn't see it being at the top of Emma's list either.

His mom's sigh reached through the mirror. "That's what I thought." She pursed her lips. "We'll hire someone. But you'll still have to be somewhat involved."

"Why? I just show up and say the right name, right?"

Apparently weak jokes and weddings didn't mix. Or so his mom's expression said.

He hadn't even really thought about wedding prep. He knew it had to happen ASAP after the Divining to restore his mom, but hell, he was a guy. Name one guy who lived to pick out flowers and rings and bands...when he hadn't picked the bride.

Even if he did like her.

In any case, he voted yes to the idea of hiring someone. A witch wedding planner could pull something together in no time. He wondered if Emma had thought about it at all, if she'd dreamed what the day would be like. She probably had at twenty-one. Now...

"Even more reason for you and Emmaline—Emma—to come to dinner tonight. We can talk basics then. I've asked your father to dig up some names. One meeting, Bastian," she said to his silent groan.

He only did it for effect, to be normal. In truth, he would coat himself in flowers and skip down the aisle if it meant his mom getting well.

She lifted up from where she reclined, faltering as her arms gave way. His heart stuttered. She pushed a piece of paper through the mirror. He grabbed it and glanced at the scribbles.

"Names of three wedding planners in the magical community," his mom said, confirming his suspicions. "And how is six o'clock for dinner?"

He resigned himself to the inevitable. "Great. We're having roast beef, right?"

"It's your favorite, isn't it? Unless Emma is a vegetarian?"

He thought of the other night, with her shoveling his paella into her mouth. "No, strictly a carnivore."

"Good. I'm sorry about the early time… I just get so tired these days."

"It's fine, Mom." He tried to sound lighthearted even when that heart was so heavy, it would sink to the bottom of the ocean in eight point two seconds. "You know me, I can always eat."

"Apologize to Emma for me."

"I don't need to. She's not like that."

Something he'd said made his mom cock her head. "Oh? What is she like?"

Many adjectives came to mind, not all suitable for a mom to hear. "Nice."

"Do me a favor: never tell her that. Nice." His mom shook her head, frowned as if it had hurt. "What woman do you know who'd ever want to be described as 'nice'?"

"You raised a heathen, what can I say?"

"Don't I know it. Six o'clock," she said, and he repeated it. "We'll welcome her into the family."

He ignored the weird pang in his chest as he gave his mom a nod.

An hour later, one conjured cup of Starbucks and a few episodes of *Friends* down, Bastian had still not successfully ignored the weird feeling his mom had given him. Like he and Emma were really getting married.

Though, if they were *really* getting married, he mused, leaning back against the couch and eyeballing Emma's door, things would be different. He wouldn't be out here on the couch, for one thing.

Images of a bed and Emma's body had barely begun to dance in his mind when her bedroom door opened, startling him into bobbling his take-out cup. She emerged, dressed in jeans and a gray sweater that weren't at all like the blue number she'd had on that night. He'd noticed she didn't tend to wear colors. A damn shame. In that teal number, she'd about stopped his heart.

"Morning." He fought not to stare. Instead he concentrated on Chester, who trotted up to Emma to say hello. She stroked his head idly. "Ah, I conjured coffee. You want?"

"I can grab some."

"No, seriously. What's your order?"

"You're sure?" His exasperated noise made her grin. "Okay. Thanks. I'll have a mocha latte."

"Thought you didn't have a sweet tooth." He handed over the drink, taking care not to brush fingers. Not for any specific reason.

"When did I say that?" She headed to the kitchen and he trailed behind.

"I just never see you eat a lot of sweets." He leaned on the infamous breakfast bar, blocking memories with determined focus.

She slid bread into the small toaster. "I didn't know you watched what I ate."

He watched her too much. He let it slide. "Speaking of eating, got plans for later?"

A warm red seeped into Emma's cheeks. "No. Well, maybe. I'm not sure."

He opted to believe the first answer. "Great. We have dinner plans."

"Oh?" One of her hands came up to her throat, fiddled with the necklace she wore.

"My mom invited us to come to dinner."

Her hand dropped. "Oh."

He rolled his shoulders, grimaced. "I know it's a bit meet-the-family, but she said she wanted to know her daughter-in-law."

Emma's eyes got a bit rabbity. "Even though we're not going to have a real marriage?"

"I mentioned that."

"And?"

"She wants to meet her soon-to-be daughter-in-law," he repeated with emphasis, taking a sip of his latte. "And to start planning the wedding."

It was as if he'd said he'd decided to pursue a career as a second-rate charm purveyor, hawking trinkets to humans at hokey psychic shops.

He slumped. "I know, but she's right. It has to be planned. Don't women love that stuff?" He tried a hopeful smile. Got a squinty look back. "Okay, so we'll both suffer through it. She gave me some names of witch wedding planners. All we need to do is pick one, take one meeting about what we want and then show up on the day."

"You don't really believe that, do you?"

"Let me have my delusions, Emma."

She smiled at that. "A wedding." It was as though the concept was foreign to her. "I guess I never thought about the actual, ah, wedding." And the idea was apparently disturbing. The toast popped and she got it out, methodically buttering it from a tub she got from the fridge.

He looked at her in surprise when she handed him the plate.

"For the coffee," she explained.

He accepted it with a thanks. "If it helps, think of it as a party." He bit into the toast, chewed. Swallowed. "A really big one where we promise to be linked for eternity."

"You know, Tia isn't the only one who can work hex bags."

A joke, he said internally as he forced his instantly tight muscles to unclench.

She pushed her hands through her hair before they dropped to her side. "A wedding. Planning a wedding." She shook her head.

His hand grabbed hers from across the bar, squeezed. All by itself without permission. "One name, one meeting," he repeated, resisting the urge to stroke the skin beneath his. "Show up on the day. And then I'll leave you alone." He forced a grin. "That's what you want, right?"

"Right." She licked her lips.

His gaze zeroed in. His body leaned…

He dropped her hand like it was on fire. "Okay, so it's six o'clock. Tends to be fairly casual." For some reason, he added, "My mom likes color." He fingered the edge of her sweater. "Do you own anything besides black and gray?"

She swatted him away.

He dodged. "Should have used telekinesis," he mock-lectured and then found himself on the painful end of an invisible forehead flick. He rubbed it with a wry grin. "Touché."

"Six, then." Her expression was resigned, arms hugging her stomach. "Am I meeting you there?"

Since he spent a lot of time in the day at home, it was a fair assumption. "I'll swing back to grab you." He fed the last of his toast to an ever-patient Chester, hiding his smile at Emma's frown. "Have a good day, dear."

On his way out the door, he stopped, and driven by the devil, swung back. "Hey, my mom also loves sexy lingerie, so if you could—" He ducked out the door with a wide grin before the take-out coffee cup made contact.

★ ★ ★

"Emmaline." Diana Truenote's voice was warm as she leaned on her husband's arm for support, her eyes even more so. She held out a thin hand, which was cool as Emma slid hers into it. "Or Emma, now, isn't it?"

Emma nodded. Good manners compelled her to add, "Emmaline is fine, if you prefer."

"I prefer what you prefer." Diana squeezed her hand. "I always forget how grown-up you look, but then, I suppose we don't see you that often."

If it was Clarissa who had been speaking, it would have been a barbed dig. With Diana, it was hard to detect any hints of disapproval, though Emma sifted through the words carefully.

"Thank you for having me," she said, and then stalled. Her brain emptied as social panic set in.

Oh, Goddess. They were looking at her—all three of them. Watching. Waiting. Shouldn't she at least be given a stage and a microphone and some one-liners to warm up the crowd with before going improvisational?

Alistair beamed from Diana's other side, his jolly face slightly lined, hinting at his age, but so much like his son that it was almost hard to look at them together.

That's what Bastian will look like in one hundred and forty years or so, she thought. *Everyone is going to envy me.* Her belly jittered.

"She's been looking forward to it all day," Alistair said as he greeted his son with a clap of his hand on Bastian's shoulder.

"And you haven't?" His wife angled her head back, the light catching how thin her skin looked, turning it translucent.

Emma felt a clutch in her heart. She slid a look at Bastian, saw the tension in his jaw. Before she could think better of it, she used the telekinesis she'd been practicing (at his decree) to touch his hand.

He startled, then shot a glance at her. She continued to face head-on, embarrassed at the impulse. At least until she felt the sensation of a phantom hand covering hers in thanks.

"Of course I have," Alistair was saying as Emma forced her attention back to the tableau. He winked at her. "Now I get to spend my evening with two pretty ladies."

He'd always been sweet to her, and an incorrigible charmer. Nobody had to look far to wonder where Bastian had picked up his ways. But tonight, having made somewhat of an effort, she did kind of feel pretty. She'd tried on multiple outfits, settling on a knee-length black skirt and a boatneck sweater she'd seen in a magazine. She'd conjured it in cerulean blue and was over conscious of the way it drew the eye. She already wished she'd worn gray—like Bastian, who, after teasing her about color, wore a gray sweater with slacks. With his rumpled hair and a hint of scruff on his jaw, put him in a magazine and he could sell anything. Perfect.

There's a lot of pressure. To be perfect. His words from that night came back to her. He'd been drunk, but also under a truth potion and, not for the first time, she picked away at what that might mean. That entire episode had only produced more questions.

Her thoughts scattered as Diana gave a small tug on the hand she still held. "Come inside, we'll have drinks in the parlor," she said. Her small smile was edged with tiredness.

Realizing she needed to sit, Emma allowed herself to be escorted to a small room at the back of the house that she hadn't been in before. Filled with knickknacks, it was clearly a favorite space. A family room. And she'd been invited in.

The tug at her heart was vicious and she told herself to ignore it. It was all a façade. She wouldn't be family. Not in any real sense.

Bastian touched a hand to the small of her back as she hovered. "You good?" His lips brushed her ear and she shivered.

With a jerky nod, she drifted into the room, unsure of where to go. Luckily Bastian made the decision, urging her to sit on a couch done up in green velvet. He sat next to her, close enough that his thigh nudged hers.

His mom settled opposite, his dad bending to murmur something in her ear. Her head turned a quarter inch so they locked eyes and she smiled. There was something there, a connection between the two, that made Emma feel as if she were intruding on a private moment.

"We thought we'd have drinks first," Alistair said to her. "Then roast—you like roast, Emma?"

She nodded. She felt tongue-tied, and with her, that meant she would likely talk in stop and starts. Better to be quiet and dignified.

"Good. Can't understand vegetarians." Alistair shook his head, baffled. "If we let cows breed and breed without making use of them, what happens then?"

"I think they become our overlords," Bastian said with a dry touch.

"You joke, but anything is possible, son. You managed to come out ugly when your mother and I are such stunners."

Emma tensed at the insult, gaze whipping back and forth, but Bastian just grinned.

"If anything, it's a miracle I came out so good-looking with a toad for a father. That, and Mom's genes."

"Nice save, darling." His mom waved a hand at Alistair. "If you're expecting the drinks to grow legs, either cast a spell or forget it."

He caught her hand, kissed the knuckles. "Virgin H2O?"

"With a twist."

"Emma?"

Still getting used to byplay that didn't have a mean undertone, Emma startled at her name. "Ah…water's fine."

"You needn't have water on my account," Diana said. "Un-settled stomach is all."

They all knew it was more than that, but Emma didn't comment. "Okay. Um…" What was appropriate with in-laws?

Bastian pressed his leg against hers. "I'll have a beer, Dad. Emma?"

She nodded gratefully.

As with Diana, everyone acted as if it was normal. Again, the differences between this family and the Bluewaters paraded in front of her. Wearing neon clothing just to make the point.

For one thing, if she'd gone mute in front of her mother, Clarissa would have lost her temper. For another, if she'd asked for beer, she'd have been subjected to a lecture on how beer was a common drink and Bluewaters weren't common. Then again, the Truenotes had achieved the kind of blue-blooded success Clarissa craved; they didn't need to try so hard. She still wasn't entirely sure why they'd agreed to sign that stupid engagement contract to begin with. Bet they were wishing they hadn't. The truth sat like a rock on her chest as she accepted the beer.

When they all had their drinks, Diana turned to her with expectation. "So, Emma. You live in Chicago now, correct?" At Emma's nod, her smile cranked up a notch. "What made you settle there?"

Concentrate on simple sentences, she reminded herself. Less likely to hint at Sloane then. Her hands twisted in her lap as she took in a breath. No need to be nervous. What did it matter if they liked her?

"A human I met told me about it," she said carefully. "She, ah, said it was full of art and food and culture. And cold." A quick smile. "I liked the idea of cold."

"So do I sometimes, when it's August and I'm fixing to melt," Diana agreed. She took a sip of water, glass trembling.

She ignored the weakness. "And you run a bar? Do you enjoy that?"

"Mom." Bastian slung an arm over the back of the couch, almost across Emma's shoulders. "Interrogation much?"

"I'm just getting to know her. She's our guest."

"There's the third degree, which you aced. You've moved onto fourth."

Emma again held her breath but unclenched when Diana aimed an arch—but clearly unoffended—look his way.

"It's fine," she told him, focusing on his thigh that pressed against hers, the heavy feeling of his arm so close to her. She felt enclosed, protected. Attention back on Diana and Alistair, who'd poured himself a scotch and sat next to Diana, their hands clasped, she pondered what to say. "It's different. A challenge."

"Tia Hightower is your partner, if I recall. She always struck me as smart," Alistair commented, swirling his scotch.

"She is. And we have a third business partner. A—a human." Unsure how the society couple would take that, she braced.

"I always used to love having humans on my team," Alistair said, a finger to his chin thoughtfully. Catching her confused look, he added, "When we did research with potions and lotions, we'd always have some humans in the know to bring their experience to the research. All sanctioned by the High Family, naturally," he continued. "Humans are in high demand in certain sectors of the business circuit. For those of us who can see beyond our egos." He winked.

"I know what you mean," Bastian cut in. "On our digs, I'm always amazed by the leaps in logic humans make. We've often made an important discovery because of my team's instincts. And when you consider what we're digging up—admittedly, I like the magical finds, but even so, some of the older human antiquities are…" He trailed off with a sheepish smile Emma found annoyingly endearing. "Anyway, Leah—Emma's business partner—has the same…zest for life that I see in my teams." He nudged Emma. "She's the fun part, right?"

She frowned. "I'm fun."

"Tia's bold," he carried on, "and you're smart."

Before she could argue with that succinct diagnosis, Alistair tipped his glass to her. "He's right, you were always a smartie." A teasing glint in his eye. "We were grateful when you and Bastian became friends. Hoped he would follow your example and crack a book sometime."

"I went by the osmosis theory," Bastian said lazily.

"A son of mine who didn't read," Diana mourned. "I used to buy him books as a child and would find them propping up furniture or used as projectiles."

"She exaggerates," he told Emma, who was fascinated by this window into a Bastian she hadn't known. "And I *did* learn to like books. Some books."

"All Emma's influence, I'm sure."

All three turned to look at her and the beer bottle she'd been lifting to her mouth froze. They were waiting for her to speak, she realized, to say something unbelievably witty. To sparkle as Bastian's fiancée should. Nerves circled her throat.

Why was it that when she was alone with him she could fire back sassy rejoinders, but when faced with his parents, her brain glitched and suggested *I like pudding* as an acceptable comment?

"I don't know." Her hands squeezed each other as she frantically tried to think of something to say. "He usually tried to get me to go to Bourbon Street."

Bastian winced. "Traitor."

Diana faced him. "I knew it! I knew you used to sneak off there."

"But with Emma." A winning smile. "A good influence."

"Sounds like she was just as wild as you were."

Emma found she liked the idea of that. Wild Emma. Better than serious. People never seemed to realize that what they took for seriousness was shyness. And fine, there was some practicality in there, too. Still. It got old.

Wild Emma.

Diana suddenly coughed, a hard, wracking sound that came from her lungs. Alistair immediately smoothed a hand over her back, soothing her as he came up with a handkerchief. Diana pressed it over her mouth. Her eyes watered.

Bastian's thigh was rigid. Emma angled a look at him, skated her eyes over the tight corners of his mouth, the stiffness in his jaw as he stared at his mom.

Diana finally took in some breaths, raw ones that had Emma wincing. Diana's water glass flew from the side where she'd perched it to hover in front of her. She took it with a murmured thank-you to her son, sipped.

Alistair rubbed her back. "Always one for the center of attention, my wife."

Emma stared in shock. How could he make light?

When Diana gave a choked laugh, when Emma saw the shadows in Alistair's eyes ease, she understood.

They were a unit, she thought, longing she didn't acknowledge wisping through her. A true partnership. More, they were a love match. Something she'd constantly marveled at as a girl and more than one family had sneered at—behind their hands, naturally, as nobody wanted to offend the Truenotes.

What would it have been like growing up with parents like these? Would she have yearned for a love match of her own instead of a cold, practical arranged marriage?

Had Bastian?

"Why don't we have dinner?" Diana said, voice only slightly

hoarse. "And turn the focus back on Emma and Bastian's wedding."

"Mom…" As his father had done, Bastian acted normal. And whined.

"There's a lot to plan."

"We're going with one of your names."

"But she'll still want to know your preferences. A venue."

"We'll have it here." Bastian turned to Emma. "That is, unless you'd prefer it somewhere else? The Bluewater manor?"

She quickly shook her head. Twice. "Here's fine."

Undaunted, Diana pushed on. "Flowers, cake, music, guest list. All to be discussed over a nice roast."

Emma and Bastian shared a look of quiet suffering as they all rose to walk to the dining room.

Well, she thought, at least they weren't asking her questions about herself anymore.

Dinner lasted for two hours, with conversation flowing like the wine Bastian's dad poured with abandon. Maybe too much abandon—his voice got progressively louder, and toward the end he'd started to profess a desire to see the Grand Canyon that same night.

They'd finally made an escape from the table when Bastian had stood and tangled his hand in Emma's, saying that they'd walk off some of the meal in the gardens before they went home. She'd finally relaxed, no longer as jittery as she'd seemed at the beginning. True to his mom's nature, Diana had clearly read Emma's nerves and had kept up the conversation, including her but not putting her on the spot as she'd unintentionally done at the beginning.

Now they headed for their old place in the gardens at a slow, easy pace. They were out of sight of the house, lost in the folly. Their hands brushed as they walked side by side and neither moved farther away. The stars were easy to see out here, diamonds spread out on black velvet, and he lifted his face appreciatively to take in the sights and smells of a home he'd put to the back of his mind for seven years.

"Sorry about that," he said after a moment of walking in comfortable silence. "I think Mom is a little caught up with the idea of a wedding." More so than he'd anticipated, considering the circumstances. "I think it takes her mind off... well, things."

Emma's shoulder nudged up in a half shrug. Her expression was elsewhere.

Probably normal, considering the slight awkwardness behind the discussions. Bastian kicked a pebble, watched it dash across the ground. After all, nothing like planning a wedding when everyone knew the real motivation wasn't love but survival.

He was working out whether to address that when she stopped and wrapped her arms around herself. "I'm sorry."

He stopped, too, though his heart jolted once against his ribs in anticipation. "For what?"

"Being rude." She chafed her arms as his expectations dimmed again. "Being quiet. For not being able to talk. I must have embarrassed you."

His hand flew out, caught her arm. He hadn't thought through the action but found he couldn't now release her. "Embarrassed me?"

She didn't look him in the eye, focused instead on his hand. "I get so nervous in groups. I'll try harder next time."

His brain worked as he tried to puzzle it out. "I know you're not comfortable in big groups." She never had been. He wouldn't call four a big group, but he'd never been shy like her. "Why would that embarrass me?"

Now she did look at him. Like a page in a book, he read

frustration, annoyance, shame. The last killed him. "They're your parents."

"Last I checked."

"I'm meant to be your…" She squirmed. "You know. Fiancée."

"Last I checked." His voice came out huskier.

She shot him an impatient look.

His brain was obviously slow because he just wasn't connecting the dots. "You're going to have to spell it out for me, Emma."

"Just forget it." She tried to pull away, but he held on. She huffed, looking everywhere but at him. "I'm shy, Bastian."

"I know."

"I'm shy and I'm not good with groups and I go quiet and can't think of what to say. And they're your parents." When he remained silent, clueless, she ground her teeth. "How could they possibly think I'm good enough for you?"

Something in his chest screwed tight, making it hard to get a decent breath. Why did she care?

"Emma." And that was it, the whole of what he could think to say.

Emma waved her free arm back toward the house. "I just sat there, tongue-tied. I bet your mom thinks I'm an idiot."

"You agreed that roses are the best flowers. She loves you."

"You can't be serious!" She made a small noise that inadvertently went straight to his groin. Of course, the fact that she was het up, eyes alight and cheeks ablaze, also played into it. She was glorious when she was animated. "I don't want to be a weight around your neck. The embarrassing wife."

"You won't be." He'd never even thought about her social awkwardness past the first week or so. Couldn't think of anything now except to make her feel better. "Your being shy is part of you. Just like this cute nose." He tapped it, teasing, sliding his finger down the bridge. "Or these lips." He dragged his finger across her satiny cheek, grazed her bottom lip and forgot his own name when her lips parted with a shaky breath.

With effort, he dropped his hand. She looked confused, a little hazy. "Being shy isn't a reason to be embarrassed. And some warlocks fantasize about a quiet wife."

That got to her and he saw her fighting back a smile. It lightened something inside him, the part that hated to see her distraught.

She was quiet a moment. "I wanted your parents to like me."

His heart hurt. He swept his thumb over her forearm, reassuring. "They do." He meant it; he'd seen his mom looking with approval at Emma throughout and his dad didn't relax that way around just anyone. And as for his feelings...

What a mess this all was.

Blocking the confusion swirling in his chest, Bastian fell back on teasing. "I think they'll find it refreshing to have somebody quiet in the family."

She chewed her lip. It made him light-headed with the need to take over. To *take*. At least this, his attraction, was simple. It was just acting on it that would make it complicated. More complicated, he absently amended, tensing as her lip slid from her teeth, wet and plump.

"I'm just not used to that."

He'd lost the thread. "What?"

"Family." She said it in such a wistful tone, his poor heart squeezed again.

He drew her toward him, not stopping until she was a few inches from his chest. "Well, you're stuck with us now."

Her smile was hesitant, shy. "You think they liked me?"

He gazed at her, everything compacting in his chest, in his stomach, until that light-headedness evolved into a dizzy feeling. And the truth came out, complex and thorned. "I like you."

It felt like a monumental admission, but all she did was laugh.

"I'm serious," he insisted. He looked into eyes he'd once described as ordinary brown. "The more I know you, the more I like."

"Read that in a romance novel?" But the blush was back.

It gave a man ideas. His mind went a little hazy.

He began to reel her in, lost to those twin flags of color. "I like how you speak and how you move and how you care about people." And how that said louder than words that she couldn't have been involved in the contract. Surely. He heard the hitch in her breath as her breasts brushed his chest and knew his breathing wasn't too steady either. "I like your eyes and your smile and your legs."

"M-my legs?"

"Mmm." He lifted his free hand, thumbed her bottom lip again. He didn't know if it was intentional, but when her tongue grazed his thumb, he went rock hard.

"I like this mouth, Emma." His voice was raw. "I really like this mouth."

"Bastian…"

He knew an invitation when he heard it. He bent down and took that mouth like he'd been aching to do ever since that night. Gentle, he told himself, even as he quivered. Easy.

She opened for him at his nudge. Their tongues entwined, sending a shot of desire through his blood like aged whiskey.

His hands tangled in her hair as the heels of her hands dug into his waist. It drove him crazy, the feel of her body against his. The sweet pressure made him nip her lip, soothe the action with his tongue. She made the sexiest sound in her throat and her mouth became more aggressive. Just like that, the kiss spun out of his hands and flung him into a sensual tornado. His hands tightened on her as she rocked against him. It was like holding fire and he considered himself lucky to be burned.

He only lasted a few heartbeats before he groaned, ripping his mouth off hers to press it to her forehead. "Come home with me." Screw complicated.

"We live together." He was gratified to hear the tremble, how breathless she was.

He laughed softly against her neck. "Decision made easier, then."

He couldn't stop kissing her, her forehead, her cheek, down to her neck. He bit gently and felt her shudder echo through his own body. She felt so good against him. He could only imagine how amazing it would feel without all these clothes in the way.

She clutched him as he kissed the base of her throat. Then tension—and not the good kind—crept into her shoulders. "Bastian. We can't."

"I think we just proved we can and we should." Still, he pulled back, breathing ragged. If he'd thought she was red before, she was lobster at this point. Even more so when she glanced down at the grass and the mass of wildflowers that had bloomed at their feet.

He grinned; she glared.

"We talked about this," she said. The snippy tone didn't work considering how she was still breathless.

"So? Let's put it back on the table."

"Table?" Her lids drifted closed as he stroked a finger across her collarbones.

He stared at the pulse in her throat, how it fluttered. "Hell, anywhere you want it."

"Bastian…" She pulled in a breath, pressed her lips together. When her eyes opened, there was resolve in them. "We should stop."

"You sure?"

"Yes."

He leaned down, nipped her lip. "Then why are you still holding me?"

She followed his gaze where she still clutched him. He'd never seen anyone move so fast as she backed up.

He let out a breath. She was probably right.

She was still hiding something from him, but the fork in the road had been reached. Either he had to accept that she might have known about everything but had been forced into it by her mother—which was almost justifiable, he reasoned—or he had to keep himself back from her. And he was fast coming to the conclusion the second wasn't an option.

"It's a bad idea." She folded her arms, but not before he saw the twin points of her nipples saluting him. His mouth went dry, head veering into foggy territory again.

"I've been thinking about that." Since his hands wanted to reach for her, he mirrored her pose and crossed his arms, leaning casually on his back foot. "Why is it such a bad idea?"

Her mouth dropped open.

"Is that an invitation?"

That made it snap shut.

Even from where he stood, he could swear he heard her back molars grind. "We said we'd be friends."

"That is friendly."

"That's how you are with your friends?"

"Sure."

"Then maybe that's why you have so few."

The wryness only made him want her more, and his reservations were easily buried. Time to let go of the past. Even just thinking it made him feel like he'd shed a coat whose pockets had been filled with rocks. He gave her a wide smile, re-lieved to have made a decision to let her secrets lie. "Emma, we're getting married."

"I heard that."

"Would it be bad for a husband and wife to have sex?"

"It's complicated."

It really was.

"You're leaving after this," she barreled on before he could say anything. "I think it could get messy if we tried to be any-thing more than friends. We should be practical."

Just like that, without warning, memory snuck up on him and his smile dialed down to childhood nostalgia. "Shy, sen-sible Emmaline." He used his telekinesis to tug her top like a boy in the playground. "Don't you ever want to go a bit wild?"

She batted at the invisible hands. "Being sensible isn't a bad thing."

She had a point, and he admitted that letting his base de-sires win probably would only make everything more com-plicated in the long run.

But he'd already boarded the Runaway Express and passed Complication Station, and she needed to get on this train. "Maybe we should put a pin in it. Just think. Weigh up the pros and cons." His eyes caught on her lip, which she was bit-ing again, and his throat went dry. His next words were in-voluntary. "I'd make it worth your while, Em. I'd make you scream."

CHAPTER 15

I'd make you scream.
Just think.

How did he expect her to think about anything else? Fortunately Emma had a day of baking ahead of her, some to put out in the bar, some to freeze for when she was busy doing paperwork or admin. Her mind was occupied with measuring, sifting, stirring, whisking—

—and then Bastian's voice would pop back into her head like a determined boomerang.

With her keen sense of knowing, Tia had launched at Emma as soon as she'd slipped into the bar that morning. Emma had barely shaken out her umbrella when her friend was on her, demanding to know what was going on.

Since Tia's premonitions weren't strong enough to include images, just a heady sense that something important would happen, Emma had evaded by telling her about the dinner with Bastian's family. She focused heavily on how sick Diana was, not only because Tia was a secret marshmallow, but because she needed the reminder of why she'd agreed to this marriage.

Reminder: it hadn't been so she could fall into the trap that was Bastian Truenote. Again.

Even if she felt even guiltier now for keeping the Joining clause from him.

But there was a solution, she reminded herself. She hadn't created the clause, but she'd fixed it. That was enough.

She beat the mixture for the cookies by hand, needing to work off the tension.

It wasn't fair of him to capitalize on her attraction to him, especially by contrasting the idea of casual sex—which was what it would be even if they *were* getting married, right?—with her sensible nature.

She beat harder. It wasn't a crime to be sensible. Especially when she had a history of getting in too deep with him and watching him leave.

Shy, sensible Emmaline.

A scowl threaded her brow. She was so tired of being the sensible one. The practical one. Just once, she'd like to shock everyone and throw caution to the wind.

Don't you ever want to be wild?

Goddess, yes, she did. Maybe this was her chance, if she played it right. Eyes wide open to what this was—and what it was not.

But was it wrong to sleep with Bastian when she was keeping so much from him? Or since it would be casual, just bodies coming together, did it not even matter?

A noise broke through her mental game of back and forth. Her compact chimed, insistent and shrill, from her purse where she'd stashed it on the floor by the door.

She stared at it, dread coiling in her stomach. Maybe it

would be Kole, she reasoned, as she dragged her feet over to her purse. She fished out the compact, opened it up.

Immediately her throat closed. Her tongue seemed to have grown two sizes as she struggled to speak. "M–Mother."

"I thought I could never be shocked over how much you continue to disappoint me, Emmaline." Cruel, arctic tones sliced through the mirror to cut away at her self-esteem. "Explain yourself."

Tension gathered into knots at the base of Emma's spine, through her shoulders and neck. "I don't understand."

"Don't be an idiot," Clarissa snapped. Her haughty face was perfectly made up, the elegant grand lady with an ugly glint in her eyes that the small mirror couldn't disguise. "I know it's second nature with you, but please, for once, try and act like a Bluewater."

She'd heard this all before. "What have I done, Mother?"

"Did you dine with the Truenotes last evening?"

"Yes."

"You *dined* with the Truenotes."

Sweat moistened her temples. "Yes?"

"Stupid girl. How could you have accepted their invitation without consulting me?"

Emma had no idea how to answer that. Which, as it turned out, wasn't a big deal, since Clarissa motored on regardless.

"We are the bridal party, Emmaline. We should have had Bastian over first. It is our responsibility and our privilege to extend an invitation."

"Sorry, Mother."

"I don't want you to be sorry, I want you to think these things through like the daughter I tried to create. You will have important responsibilities as Bastian's bride, Emmaline, and it's obvious you're already falling short."

A tremor made the compact quiver, but Emma forced herself to hold it steady.

"We obviously can't undo this mess you've created, so you and Bastian will dine at the manor tonight."

"I have plans—"

"No." Clarissa barely bothered to acknowledge her before continuing. "And I want to see you beforehand. Goddess knows what kind of impression you made on the Truenotes without proper instruction or inspection. What did you wear? No," she said in the next clipped breath. "I don't want to know. The damage has been done. You will come to the manor tonight at six sharp and present yourself for inspection. I also want to see what you are planning on for the Exhibition. I will not have our family embarrassed by your pitiful magic."

Emma's stomach roiled at the idea of all of that. "I don't— I mean, I don't think… Well, I mean, it's…"

"For the Goddess's sake, Emmaline." Her mother's lips pinched. "Talk properly."

A swallow got stuck in her throat. Emma fisted her free hand hard, so the nails bit into her palms. The pain helped ground her and she managed to take a breath. And another. "Bastian might not be free tonight." *Either*, she finished in her head.

"Emmaline, I do not have time for excuses. Why don't you shock us all and not be a disappointment this time? I'll see you at six."

Clarissa's image faded to white before the mirror returned to normal, revealing Emma's pale face. Not even pale, she thought, disconnected. She looked like she was about three days from death.

Her hands began to shake and the compact dropped from her nerveless fingers. She brought them to her face, pressed them into her eyes, practicing inhaling and exhaling.

Then she dragged her cell from her back pocket and dialed Bastian.

He answered on the third ring. "Couldn't stay away, huh?"

"I'm so sorry."

His voice took a sharp turn into concern. "What is it? Is something wrong?"

Emma stared at her shoes. Black flats. Sensible. "My mother called."

"Oh?" His voice turned cool, as it always did on the subject.

"She was…was…"

"Emma? What did she say? Do you need me to portal to you?"

"*No.*" She didn't want him to see her so pitiful. *Get it together.* "She was angry that I'd had dinner with your family and you haven't with her."

He took a beat that stretched to a couple of years. "Right," he said eventually with a heavy dose of resignation. "Sounds petty enough for Clarissa. I take it our presence has been demanded."

"I'm so sorry."

"It's fine." It didn't sound fine to Emma's ears and she bit back another sorry. "We'll eat, we'll drink, we'll drink more." His voice brightened. "Maybe we'll explore and accidentally break something."

She wouldn't have thought it possible so soon after a call with her mother, but his attempt at humor tickled her throat, enough to make her smile.

"Dinner. Okay." He cleared his throat. "Well, what time do you want me to pick you up?"

The smile fell. "I have to go first for the inspection."

"Inspection?"

Damn. That had slipped out. "Never mind. Just come at seven."

"You sure you don't want me to come with you? I'll face the wrath of Clarissa."

"No. Just…don't be late?"

"Promise. Hey, you want me to wear jeans?" he teased, provoking a helpless laugh. "I'll wear jeans in front of your mother if you want. Say the word."

He'd always been able to make her smile. Any time after a Clarissa bomb had exploded, she'd succumbed to this black, icy feeling that numbed every part of her, like she'd fallen in a dark frozen lake. Bastian had always known how to get her smiling again. He'd brought the sun.

Her heart ached at the memory.

"Emma?"

"Formal's better," she said softly. "Thank you."

"What are fiancés for?" He hesitated. "You sure you're okay?"

Emma leaned hard against the wall. Was she okay? "I'm fine."

"Once more with feeling."

"Thank you," she said again.

"Not what I meant, but I'll take it. Are you bringing Chester?"

"Yes." This was what her familiar was there for, to help her face down threats even if they came in the form of her own family. Their bond would help keep her level. It didn't matter that Clarissa hated the sight of him, citing his common breeding as unbecoming of a Bluewater. It had been too late by the time she'd laid eyes on him; the binding ritual had been struck. It was one of the only things Emma had come close to battling her mother about.

Speaking of her familiar, Chester was already headed her way from the office. She didn't like to have him in the kitchen when she baked, unhygienic and all, but her distress had resonated down their bond. The hurried noise of his toenails clattered as he dashed down the hall. Soothing love came down from him, as well as sparks of magic in case she needed a defense. He didn't realize that it was an emotional attack, not physical.

"Emma?"

"Yeah?"

"Are you still thinking?"

Tension balled low in her body, this one a completely different kind. Her toes curled in her pumps. "Yes."

"And?"

A flash of his lips on hers. His hands twisted in her hair. "I don't know."

"I'll take that. For now. And then, Emma? I'm going to take you."

He hung up before she could figure out if she found that statement annoying as hell or unbearably arousing. Chester whined at the door as if sensing her confusion.

Didn't matter anyway. She had something even worse to do now she'd passed the bad news on to Bastian, and that was break her previous plans with Sloane. Her belly clutched at the idea. Yet more plans broken.

She pressed the cell phone against her mouth as she let Chester in with a sweep of telekinesis. He bounded over on a huffing sound, throwing his little body against her legs. The vibration of his tail wriggled from his body to hers and had a small smile curving her mouth—because who wouldn't smile at that? She dropped a kiss on his nose and then pressed Sloane's number.

The teen hated talking on the phone, but Emma felt it was easier to misinterpret a text than a call. Especially with this kind of news.

She winced when Sloane answered, having hoped it would go to voicemail and she could prolong this a bit longer. *Coward.* "Hey, Jellybean."

★ ★ ★

"Tell the truth," Kole murmured to Emma out of the corner of his mouth. "Tell me you don't feel like one of the von Trapp kids when she makes us do this."

Emma stifled a smile, an unbelievable event under the circumstances. She'd been in the Bluewater manor for thirty minutes and had had to endure her mother's disapproval on her outfit choice—her simple black sweater and pants now swapped for a demure green sundress, despite it being winter—her disapproval of Emma's Exhibition plans, her disapproval of Emma's choice of familiar, and her disapproval of Emma's existence.

Okay, so she hadn't voiced the last one, but you didn't need a wand to spell that out.

Having white-knuckled her way through all that, Emma was now lined up with her siblings in the foyer, ready to receive Bastian when he arrived. Clarissa had always thought it showed a unified front, a strong show of both power and class.

But Kole was right. It also made them look like the von Trapp children ready for Maria to step in and make their lives better. If only.

Clarissa was going down the line, starting with the eldest, Johannes, following on to Peter, and now pointing at Christopher's bow tie and instructing him to make sure Bastian heard about the latest development in his potion research. He nodded with a grim expression. That didn't mean a lot; Christopher was always grim. But then he'd had to endure more years of living under Clarissa than she had.

Clarissa moved on to Kole and her face wrinkled as if a lemon had materialized in her mouth. "That suit will not do, Kole."

He made a show of looking down. "What's wrong with it?"

"It's brown."

"Yes, it is."

"Bluewaters should not wear brown suits."

"Is that in the family grimoire?"

She gave him a withering glance. "You got your sense of humor from your father."

Far from insulted, Kole nodded. "And my stubbornness from my mother. The suit's fine, Mom."

Clarissa hated her children calling her the informal name. Still, Kole earned six figures and was successful in his research career. Enough so that he'd earned the High Family's attention and approval. As such, his slack was cut a lot longer than Emma's.

"Your hair is not brushed," she said finally. She gestured and his hair waved as if a comb had been run through it.

Kole shuddered. "I hate it when you do that."

"Then I suggest next time we have company you do it yourself, so people don't mistake you for a tramp."

"Gee, I do miss this motherly advice when I'm away."

Emma stared at her shoes, fighting an urge to smile. She loved her brother, even if her heart hammered at the way he lipped off.

Clarissa's shadow fell on her. Emma swallowed, pushed her gaze past the sapphire pendant her mother wore, past the unsmiling mouth to the cobra-like eyes that—surprise, surprise—were far from pleased.

"Your hair," she said.

Emma's hand flew to her head.

"So much of it. You look like a streetwalker."

Kole snorted. "You really haven't been out of the manor for a while, have you?"

"Enough, Kole." Clarissa's cool eyes surveyed Emma's face. "Fix your hair."

Emma stared back, unsure what she meant. Cut it? Dye it? Uncertainty colored her movements as she again ran her hand over her head.

Clarissa sighed, gestured. Every strand of hair on Emma's head yanked back in a vicious tug, winding together into a high updo. She bit down on a yelp as her scalp pinched. Her mother didn't even notice.

"It will do. And we've already done as much as we can with the rest of you." Her attention moved wrathfully to Chester, whose tongue was dripping slobber onto the polished marble. "Why did you bring that mutt?"

"He goes where I go." Emma's hand rested on Chester's head.

"He embarrasses the family."

Emma didn't say anything to that. No need to state the obvious—that he was a perfect match for her.

With one last disdainful sniff, Clarissa lifted her gaze and let the matter drop. "As for conversation, I expect you to let your brothers lead it. I'm sure Bastian has been bored enough these past couple of weeks. Let him enjoy some stimulating conversation." Dismissing her daughter, she clipped off in her heels to check something with one of the maids.

"I don't think Larry, Moe or Curly could muster up stimulating," Kole commented quietly to her. His hand found hers, gave a squeeze.

She cast a weak smile at him. He was sweet to worry, but she'd dealt with much worse. Hell, if all Clarissa wanted from her this evening was to be quiet, it was a job she couldn't fail at.

Nerves jittered in her stomach as she listened with half an ear to Kole talking about a movie he'd just seen, completely oblivious or completely indifferent to the scowls being shot his way by their brothers. All she wanted was to get through this as quickly as possible. She already knew it was going to be humiliating; why extend the suffering? But in her need to match the more established Higher families, Clarissa often spun dinner out over several courses and hours. Emma dreaded it.

Added to that, Sloane hadn't taken the broken plans well.

The hurt in her sister's voice echoed in Emma's ear as she shifted her weight. She'd tried to explain, but all Sloane had heard was that she wasn't important enough and that the witch world held more allure—despite Emma's fervent reassurances to the contrary. Sloane had again protested that she could meet Bastian as Emma's volunteering program "little sister," not her *little sister*, and insisted they could pull it off.

Emma had no interest in pulling it off. Running a con on a man like Bastian was asking for trouble. Despite promises of milkshakes the next day, Sloane had barely uttered a yes before making excuses and hanging up.

Looked like she needed a new potion to show the teenager. Even if Sloane couldn't do magic yet, she liked to mess around with potion ingredients. It usually won her over.

Bribery. She was such a good sister.

"Bastian Truenote," intoned the snobbish butler who'd been with their family for dozens of years.

Emma's head was tight with nervous tension as Bastian strode in, beautifully outfitted in a navy three-piece suit. He wore polished brogues and even a pocket square in his jacket pocket. Confident, charismatic, gorgeous as any movie star. She'd never felt so inadequate, standing in a line with her much more successful siblings in her mother's manor. He may say how hard it was to try for perfection, but he made it look like he'd been born to it.

She braced herself as he swept a look over the line of them. He nodded at her brothers, pausing on Kole, who'd angled his chin in a cocky challenge, before he finally settled on her. A private smile curled his lips, and her shoulders eased somewhat. And that pocket square turned a matching green.

CHAPTER 16

*B*astian had never warmed to Emma's brothers. Three were older than him, the gap spanning a few decades to a handful of years. The three eldest ones had always been pompous, stuffed with the lessons Clarissa had drilled into all her kids. Even though the Bluewaters weren't a Higher family in truth, they'd clung to the fringes, unbearably close to being one of them. Emma's father had worked backbreaking hours to send Emma's brothers to the boarding schools Higher families attended, even though Emma had told him once her mother had a bone-deep hatred that any of the family had to "work." Emma's dad had been the last son of a Higher family, bought with Clarissa's family's money.

No changes in the next generation there, he thought as they all sat around the antique dining table in the grand dining room, everybody dressed up in formal clothes. Nobody joked or teased, all very proper and stiff-backed. He thought of the night before, remembered Emma looking up at him, saying how she wasn't used to family. His heart twisted.

Except for Kole and Emma, he amended, taking a bite of

sinfully good lamb (at least the Bluewaters had an excellent chef going for them). The two siblings were their own family. They sat next to each other down the table, as far from the proper places of honor as Clarissa could stick them without resorting to a kiddy table. Her attempt at reminding Bastian she had the control here, he supposed, with a handy stab of humiliation for Emma. Not that she seemed to notice.

The brother and sister had that secret language of family—a joke told in the way Kole quirked his lips at something one of the painfully boring brothers said, the dab of a napkin from Emma implying a mock scolding.

Something eased inside him at the knowledge she'd had reinforcements here.

But Kole didn't pull punches when it came to threatening Bastian. Amusement, rich and warm, tickled him when Kole sent him another challenging look, having caught Bastian's gaze lingering on Emma.

In Bastian's defense, she looked so pretty under the floating candles suspended high above them. Her skin glowed, even if she did seem pale. The hairstyle opened up her face, and while he preferred it loose, he couldn't deny it brought attention to her eyes and her strong cheekbones. It was hard to remember a time when he'd thought she was ordinary-looking.

"Are you looking forward to the Exhibition, Bastian?" Clarissa held her wineglass loosely, the rich red wine swirling as if an invisible spoon stirred it.

He transferred his gaze from daughter to mother and not for the first time marveled that they were related. "Sure." He was looking forward to having it over with and her out of his life again.

"You were quite the talent before you…took off on your little adventures," she drawled.

Oh, she liked to play. Bastian slid on the ice shield all witch nobility learned in the cradle. "Everyone follows their passions. Some for travel, others for ambition. You'd know about the latter, Clarissa." His implication of her status-climbing was veiled thinly enough to be arrested for indecent exposure.

"Goddess knows my daughter doesn't," she said with some disdain. "She could've done something useful with her life, but no. She had to go mingle with the humans." Her nose wrinkled and he saw Emma cringe from the corner of his eye. "And open a bar, of all things."

Bastian was beginning to understand why Emma had chosen a bar, a place full of laughter and emotion, as the setting for her new life. And he approved. "It's impressive she owns it," he countered with a light smile, spearing an asparagus with his fork. "Working hard shows good character." He paused before slipping the vegetable into his mouth. "What is it you do with your time again, Clarissa?"

If possible, her mouth thinned further. It was delightful, Bastian had to admit, though he mainly wanted to hold her down and make her confess what she'd done to him and his. Still, his parents had raised him better—nothing so gauche as torture at the dinner table unless it was done with a few skillful words.

"Getting back to the Exhibition…" Clarissa's study sent a chill through him, likely done with a spell. "Have your powers grown much in the years and years that have passed?"

Subtle she was not, but she got her point across. "I guess you'll have to wait and see."

"How mysterious."

"Or maybe you don't want to admit you're weak," Christopher joked, slinging back his third glass of wine.

Bastian pitied him and let it show. "Maybe."

"What is it that you specialize in?" Kole asked, cocking an eyebrow.

"Mind magic."

"Hmm." Kole leaned in. "Can you read my mind?"

It didn't take a warlock adept with mind magic to pick up on the violent images flickering in there. As Kole was clearly Emma's favorite brother, Bastian obliged his request.

"I'd say the rake is a bit excessive." He shrugged. "But the other weapons would do the job."

Kole smiled.

"Impressive," intoned the eldest brother, Johannes. He didn't look impressed. He looked as if he'd sat through a six-hour lecture on the best plants to use for potions. "Is that what you plan to do at the Exhibition?"

"No." Like with a magnet, his gaze was drawn back to Emma. She looked even paler, if that was possible, and she'd barely eaten anything on her plate. Concern added an edge to his words. "I'm going to be doubling up with your sister."

"Mouse?" The second-eldest chimed in with a snort. "What can she do?"

Mouse? Bastian's eyes narrowed. "Plenty" was all he allowed himself to say. After all, he couldn't get into a fight with Emma's family. She'd clearly been terrified of this dinner not going well; she'd barely been able to get the invitation out.

He was here to help, not to torture her mother or punch her smirking brothers. Or to telekinetically drop them in the swamp. With some come-get-me gator bait.

"Emma has told me what she plans to do for the Exhibition," Clarissa interrupted. She sipped her wine, a queen presiding over her court. "I think it's best if she identifies her power away from you."

Emma's eyes went to the table and he saw the white bones of her knuckles as she gripped her fork tighter.

"I'm sure she appreciated the advice," he said, taking care to sound casual as concern blended with temper, "but that isn't really your call to make."

Every sound in the room muted as suddenly as if a vacuum had sucked out the noise.

Emma's eyes were wide and so dark, he couldn't tell where the black pupil ended and the brown iris began.

Well, fuck it. He wasn't scared of Clarissa.

Bring. It. On.

He picked up his glass of wine, his stare direct. He sipped calmly.

"I'm her mother," Clarissa said, stiff. "I know what's best for her."

"She's not a child anymore," he pointed out, enjoying the shifting from the Brothers Dim across the way. "She's going to be a wife."

"Yes, a position of responsibility. I've been training her for it but, as you must have noticed, she is lacking."

His jaw tensed. Goddess, her daughter was sitting right there, staring at her lap. Kole stiffened beside her, opened his mouth.

Bastian slapped a mental hand across it and Kole's eyes bulged with annoyance.

But Bastian wasn't letting this go. He may have had his doubts about Emma's allegiances, but he would be her husband, her teammate in this game, and there was no way he was letting an enemy player sack his teammate and get off unscathed.

"In what ways?" He cocked his head, his tone a perfect balance of warning and inquiry.

Clarissa's eyes didn't move off him. "A Higher family wife must be poised, resplendent, articulate and gracious: a shining example to those beneath her. Emmaline, try as I might to have her do so, has never risen to any of those traits."

What a bitch.

He took the mental hand away from Kole but sent him a

steady look. Kole was furious, but he tipped his chin up with a smirk as if he didn't believe Bastian would go up against Clarissa.

The old him might have run from the challenge. Taken the easy path. But what did he have to lose now?

"I disagree." Bastian put his glass on the white tablecloth. "I've never found Emma to be less than charming."

A hint of a glacial smile tipped Clarissa's mouth. A passing resemblance to a smile, really; it was more of a sneer. "It's gracious of you to say, Bastian, but we all know you're contracted to marry her. We all know she was fortunate to have a mother looking out for her interests—or are you saying you'd *choose* to marry her? That you came back from Africa because you couldn't bear being away a minute longer?"

He seriously wanted to put the hurt on this woman, even without the hex and Joining stuff. Maybe he could conjure a nightmare. He hadn't done it since he was a prank-loving kid, but some things were like riding a broom.

When he failed to say anything after a couple of beats, Clarissa spread her hands. "So, we see, Higher families are all about responsibility."

Emma avoided his gaze.

Damn it.

"I'm pleased to marry Emma," he said, infusing his words with sincerity. "She'll make a perfect wife." It was only because he was watching her that he saw the flinch. Saw and wondered at it.

Clarissa hummed in her throat. "Regardless, I think it best if you both follow my advice. A couple's Exhibition just isn't done. What would your parents say, for example?"

"That I'm a man who can make his own decisions."

"How modern of them. But Emmaline comes from a traditional family. Bluewaters have always exhibited alone. No matter how lackluster a performance it may be."

Just one nightmare. Nobody would blame him. He was owed.

He stole another look at Emma. She was just sitting there, letting her mother attack her.

He'd have liked her to jump in and stand up for herself, but in lieu of that, he'd step in.

And enough was enough.

"Clarissa," he said with a genial smile. "Thank you for your opinion. And while I applaud your familial loyalty, here's my opinion: you're a coldhearted bitch."

He heard a sucked-in breath that resulted in a coughing fit, but he didn't check who it was. He kept his gaze focused solely on Emma's mother. Not that this icicle deserved the title.

"Emma is warm, loving, funny and smart. Smart enough to judge whether she wants to exhibit solo or with me. She was definitely smart enough to move away from you and your acid tongue and for that, I have to applaud her. If I'd lived with you, you'd have woken up trapped in a nightmare." He let an edge settle over his expression. His magic sparked around his fingers, a display only the more powerful warlocks and witches could do. It was nothing more than show, really, but it made a statement. *Try me.*

When she didn't, he inclined his chin, almost disappointed. "Thank you for dinner." He rose to his feet and walked around the stupidly large table to where Emma sat. Chester was leaning against her leg, the doggy equivalent of support.

She blinked up at him but took his hand when he reached out to help her up.

"We'll see you at the Exhibition—and the wedding," he added, having no intention of letting this witch near the planning, even if it meant he had to get involved with the damn thing.

He didn't want to open a portal in the room, so keeping Emma's hand clasped in his, he strode toward the exit. Chester's claws skittered after them, a couple of low woofs voicing his displeasure at the tension. As they passed Kole, Bastian heard the brother snort with laughter. A seal of approval, hopefully.

Emma walked docilely along next to him. Like a good Higher family wife. Or like someone in shock.

He paused at the door, glancing back to where the family remained frozen in place. A lot of flies caught in those open mouths, he thought, focusing on Clarissa.

She looked as if she'd swallowed a lemon and a grapefruit, and then got bitch-slapped for good measure.

He allowed another smile. "And Clarissa? Emma is going to be my wife. A power in this society. I suggest you think of a better way to talk about her in the future." He didn't need to finish the sentence. All he needed was to hold her gaze as it sparked and darkened with anger. The glass nearest her wobbled, a telling display of how ferocious her emotions were.

His magical protections were the strongest they'd ever been; still, he reminded himself to add another layer to his shields when he had the time. Someone as potent and pissed off as Clarissa was someone to watch, especially now that the veneer of civility had been ripped away. Hex me once, shame on you, et cetera.

With one last encompassing hard stare, Bastian nodded to Kole—who saluted him with his wineglass—and ushered Emma out of the room.

They were in the hall when he heard Kole say, "Best dinner you've ever had, Mother. Great entertainment."

CHAPTER 17

*E*mma was pretty sure she was dreaming. Surely Bastian hadn't just thrown aside the rulebook of witch society manners and told her mother the truth.

The truth. Holy Goddess. He really had changed.

A shiver worked its way down her body and she hugged herself. They were walking in the manor gardens, mainly it seemed because Bastian wanted to pace off the tension. He practically hummed with it, that and the magic he'd called to the surface in that impressive display of power. Chester gamboled ahead, paying little attention to Bastian and Emma as he sniffed every tree and investigated every hedge.

The Bluewater gardens weren't as imaginative or creative as the Truenote ones; no hidden follies or woods, just regimental hedges and lawn and a flower garden at the bottom of the hill the manor sat on. It was there that they seemed to be headed.

A chill skipped down her bare arms and she chafed them again. She could have used telekinesis to warm the air currents around her, but that would take concentration she didn't have. Plus, she kind of wanted to feel the cold. Cold meant reality.

Which meant Bastian really had told Clarissa off like an impudent child.

Glee burst into being like a ray of sunshine, followed by a claw of tension that threatened to rip the satisfaction away. Would she be paying for that in the next few weeks before the wedding? After?

Bastian finally stopped by a bench, sank onto it. He sprawled in the seat, long legs outstretched, spine a curve against the wrought iron back. He let out one long sigh.

"I should probably apologize, right?"

She looked down at him. "Apologize?"

"For snapping at your mother." He rubbed the back of his neck, and his expression turned from rueful into a grimace. "But, Goddess, Emma, the woman's a pill."

"You don't have to tell me."

He huffed a laugh, then shoved his sweater sleeve up and showed her his wrist. "Earned me a new tattoo, though."

In stylized font, *loyalty* was now branded into the skin.

Just looking at it made her giddy. Like she'd suddenly launched into the air and her stomach hadn't yet registered it had left the ground.

At her silence, he covered the tattoo. "I guess I lost my temper."

"I guess you did." He never used to have one, but she'd seen the hints of it lately, and where there was smoke… "It's okay."

"It's not. Push enough buttons and it's a jack-in-the-box. A bad new habit."

"Maybe." She hugged the memory of her brother's coughing fit. "Thank you, though."

"No thanks needed. I enjoyed it. I kept waiting for you to jump in."

Something hard stabbed her in the throat. "I, ah, can't talk back to my mother."

Shadows crept into his eyes. "She's always been tough."

"Stalin took his inspiration from her."

Warmth banished the shadows and he patted the seat. She sat next to him, settling her hands into her lap.

He gazed at her. "I didn't realize how bad it still was. Your brothers don't help?"

"Kole will if I don't interrupt." She lifted a shoulder. "It's fine."

"No. It's not. But I'm understanding the move to Chicago and why you bought the bar even more now." He nudged her knee with his. "You did it to piss her off."

Emma didn't confirm or deny, but she did allow herself one satisfied smile.

He settled back and threw an arm along the back of the bench. "Think she'll give a toast at our wedding?"

"It would be an ode to herself."

"We'll have to mute her then. Tia's handy with hex bags, right?"

She wasn't sure if he was serious. But he did need to know: "You've made an enemy."

He sobered and there, there was the flash of something dark. "Bring it."

"She's not a good enemy to have."

"Let's just say, this one's been coming for a while." Before she could decipher that, he added, "And she shouldn't treat you that way." He lifted a hand, caressed her cheek, the shell of her ear. "Nobody should. And you shouldn't let them."

His eyes were so navy in the dim light of the garden lamps, they were black. She breathed in his familiar scent, went giddy for another reason. "I know. I'm working on it. I have a list."

His mouth quirked. "Practical Emma. What's step one?"

"Talk."

His smile grew. "You talk to me."

"You're easy."

"Don't spread that around."

She tried to hold back the smile, but it wouldn't be contained. "You're ridiculous. And sweet. Thank you for standing up for me."

He cupped her cheek, the action startling her. "I'd do anything to make you smile."

The humor of the moment drained, leaving behind stillness and a growing tension that was darkly sexual. Amidst the lush flowers that hummed around them, they were alone. Away from the world.

Just the two of them.

Giving her plenty of time to say no, he leaned toward her and brushed his mouth over hers. Unlike last time, it wasn't a race for pleasure or a desperate need for each other. This was a sampling, an intimate tasting that made Emma hum in her throat.

"I've been thinking," he said against her lips. Each small movement made tingles chase across her skin. "We said we'd forget the past, right?"

She managed a nod.

"I think we need to really wipe the slate clean. Look forward." He pressed his mouth to hers briefly, enticingly. "Let our mistakes lie."

That got to her. She inched away to stare at him. "All our mistakes?"

His smile was faint. Knowing. "Keep your secrets, Em. For now. I'll make you trust me again."

The idea tantalized as much as it terrified. To be unleashed…it was a heady prospect. Guilt faded under the patience she saw, desire rattling at the chains. Still… "I don't know what you mean."

His response was to capture her mouth with his again.

As he kissed her, Bastian wound an arm around her waist, slid her willing body the last few inches. She leaned heavily into him, lost to the slow dance of lips and tongues and little nips. Her skin hummed along with the flowers, and a ball of need twisted in her stomach.

"Bastian," she murmured. Her fiancé. The man who'd apologized to her, who was making amends, who'd faced down Clarissa. Who made her laugh. Who made her feel joy. Who made her feel so many other things.

"You're projecting," he murmured back. His lips kissed along her cheek to her ear as she reactively stiffened. "Some of the images…well, Emmaline Bluewater, I'm shocked."

Her muscles relaxed. Her secrets stayed hers. Just as he'd promised. "You ain't seen nothing yet." She caught his mouth again, a little harder, a little needier. Her free hand slid down his chest, sensitive to the muscles that jumped at her touch. When she dragged his shirt out from his pants and slid her hand underneath to graze bare skin, his hand on her back flattened and pressed hard.

Despite the urgency that wound between them, they kissed like they had days to spare, weeks. Long, lazy kisses that fueled the need boiling inside both. Or inside Emma anyway, she thought, faint as her body writhed against Bastian without permission.

He dragged his mouth away. His eyes glittered, his breathing as heavy as if he'd got an extra job working at a phone sex company. "Emma."

And Goddess, with that voice, he'd make millions.

Then: "We shouldn't."

At first she thought she'd heard him wrong. Because the man who'd just been kissing her so ardently, the warlock who'd been sliding an invisible hand up and down her thigh, would not have said that they *shouldn't* keep going. He would have created a portal and whisked them to her apartment, where they'd fall onto her bed.

But he *had* said it. And he was serious, if his creased brow and flat lips were anything to go by.

"We shouldn't?"

"No." He stood up abruptly, forcing her hands to drop away, and turned to whistle for Chester. "We should go."

"Okay…"

She didn't understand, him, his words, why he'd change his mind, but pushed slowly to her feet. Her cheeks flamed when she saw the surge of flowers around them, how lush they'd bloomed thanks to her uncontrolled magic, but she waited for her dog and stepped through the portal Bastian created in silence.

Her apartment seemed small after the manor. Normal. As though everything was the same. Always the same.

"I'm going to turn in, if that's okay?" He didn't look at her.

"Okay." She turned for her bedroom. She'd taken one step before she twisted back to him. "Why shouldn't we? I mean, you asked me to think about…" And now he'd given her permission to keep her secrets and not feel as guilty, she was all aboard that train.

"It's been an evening," he said, all but vibrating with tension. "You're probably feeling all sorts of emotions. I don't…" He trailed off to shove both hands through his hair. His gaze was raw and searching. "I want you, but I want you to want me. When you're not feeling…everything."

Emma wasn't sure whether to be insulted or relieved for the reprieve. She didn't know what she felt. It was safer just to repeat: "Okay."

She called for Chester as she headed for her room. Her familiar landed on the bed, turning on his back for a belly rub, his expression hopeful as she shut the door behind her.

She obliged, sinking down next to him, scratching his belly. Chester's back leg went into ecstatic midair scratching as she hit a good spot, but she barely noticed. Her chest was tight as she stared at the door.

He wanted her to want him when she wasn't "feeling everything"? He picked *now* to be a good guy?

But…maybe he was right, the practical her pointed out. She was anxious about how Clarissa might seek revenge, giddy from Bastian going all white knight, needy from his kiss, still a little guilty about keeping secrets from him, no matter what he said…actions and reactions, emotions and logic swirled in her like a cocktail from Toil and Trouble.

All she knew was that she wanted him.

She *wanted* him.

Need shoved everything to the side and she fisted a hand in the covers. Screw sensible. She knew the score, and so did he. Why couldn't she have some fun with her fiancé with the understanding that he'd leave after the ceremony and she'd only see him from time to time? As long as everyone knew the rules, it would be uncomplicated. It was time to take some chances.

Wild Emma.

Chester nudged her hand, yipped. He jumped off the bed and went to the door.

"You're right," she murmured, standing. Then stopped.

If she was going to take the risk, she was going to do it as herself. Not as the image her mother had made her into.

She did a turn, replaced the green sundress with a navy number that cut low in the front and had more in common with a nightgown than a dress. She'd seen Tia in something similar once and had admired how brave she was to wear something that bold. Now it was her turn.

She pulled her hair down, ran her hands through it, wincing as her scalp prickled, sensitive from being held back for so long. A good metaphor for her, she thought, crossing to the mirror. Restrained so tightly, now set free. And okay, it was a rush, sensitive, kind of painful. But it felt good.

All she had to do was walk through the door.

She didn't give herself a chance to talk herself out of it, just opened the door and barreled through. "I want you," she said, breathless at the sight of him standing on the other side of the couch. "I want you, and it's not because you stood up to my mother and it's not because of how she makes me feel. It's because of how *you* make me feel. Prettier, smarter, funnier, more desirable than anybody has before." She swallowed, hands fisting in her dress as she watched him. "When I look back on my life, I want to see color in it. So, kiss me, Bastian. Turn my world Technicolor."

She'd run out of breath toward the end, and it was maybe the longest speech she'd ever made. But she didn't focus on that fact. Her attention was all on the man staring back at her.

The man who strode forward, sliding the couch out of his way with a breathtaking show of telekinesis. The couch skidded to rest against the breakfast bar.

And then he was on her.

CHAPTER 18

$\mathcal{E}$mma's breath caught in her throat as Bastian hauled her against him, his lips urgent against hers, his hands tangled in the dress.

She met him eagerly, rising up on her toes to catch his mouth, to slide her hands into his hair. He tasted like the wine they'd drunk with dinner and a flavor that was uniquely Bastian, addictive and sweet and enough to have her gripping his hair tighter.

He dragged his mouth from her lips across her cheek. "You're sure?"

She tugged him back to her. "Stop playing the perfect gentleman."

She felt his smile as he kissed her again. The zing in her blood brightened, heart quickening as his hands moved with strong, confident movements to her hips to press her against his lower body.

"Did you take a gun to my mother's?" she murmured against his lips.

He stifled a laugh. "You should never take a loaded weapon

into that kind of environment. You never know if it might go off."

"As long as it doesn't go off too soon."

"Emma Bluewater." He drew back, eyes sparkling. His cheeks were flushed. "You constantly surprise me."

"Shh, don't tell anyone."

"They're all missing out." Affection bunked up with the desire as he slid a hand up from her hips, down her bare arm in an action that left goose bumps in its wake. He tangled their fingers and began to walk her backward toward her bedroom. "The truth is I wanted some extra padding in case things got dicey."

She flicked a look at the area in question, noted the bulge. And, okay, yes, blushed. "You're telling me that's padding?"

"Are you sure you want to find out?" His grin was darkly seductive.

In other situations, flirty banter was not her strong point. But it had rarely been a problem with Bastian. She let the truth roll off her, mind fixed on other things.

"I'm a big girl. I can handle it."

They passed through her doorway. She was very aware the bed was behind them.

His cheek dimpled even as he pushed her gently onto the mattress. She scooted back, aware of how her dress's hem had flipped up a few inches higher on her thighs. His eyes went there.

"Goddess, I hope that's a promise."

Chester padded in, looked at both of them, Bastian standing in front of the bed, Emma half reclined on it.

Her cheeks boiled as she pointed. "Out, Chester."

He looked at her, cocked his head. Enquiry came down the bond, a hopeful question of play.

Goddess. "Out," she said again, voice high-pitched. "Later."

He hung his head and slunk out. Bastian chuckled. "You're embarrassed because your dog knows we're having sex."

"Well." She covered her eyes with her hand, flopped back. Resignation filled her, and not a small amount of disappointment. "I guess the moment's over."

"Oh?"

She pressed her lips together, tried not to sound miserable. "I ruined the mood."

"You should be ashamed of yourself."

That was a bit far. Her hand moved off her eyes and she levered up. "I'm—"

Whatever she'd been about to say strangled in her throat. In the time she'd been lying back, he'd shucked the jacket, vest and shirt, standing before her in his trousers and nothing else.

And Goddess, the man was built. All the digs he went on had hardened his stomach and chest, molded his biceps, creating layers of rippling muscle until he was a walking advertisement for what a man could achieve with physical labor.

Her mouth went dry. A cliché for a reason. And the only thing that could quench her thirst was the tall drink of water passing a considering gaze over her.

"Since you ruined the mood," he said, voice husky. "You need to help me get back into it."

"I do?" His words said one thing, but the way he looked at her... A shiver skipped along her skin, followed by rising hope. She hadn't ruined it by being a dork?

"Yes." He jerked his chin. "Lose the dress."

Her hands went to the material. "My dress?"

"Or the scrap of material posing as one."

Nerves scraped along the underside of her skin as she slid the dress up, lifting her hips to get it past her butt. She was paying attention to him so she saw how his eyes dilated, how his breath quickened at the small, unintentionally sexual movement.

Having him at her mercy was a thrill. His eyes were locked

on her every motion, so she slowed down, even as her hands trembled, inching the dress higher, pausing at her breasts.

"I'm starting to feel it." His voice was raw. It created an echo inside her. "A little more."

She crossed her hands over, allowing the dress to fall back like a curtain over a peep show. Then, with a breath, she lifted the dress over her head. It dropped from her fingers as she dragged in a breath. An attack of shyness made her hesitate to meet his gaze.

"Oh, hell, Emma." He swore. "I'm not going to last two minutes."

Dizzy relief made her head spin as she looked to find his hands unbuckling his belt, unzipping his pants. Nerves tried to crowd back in, but she held them back, put up a no-entry sign.

Enough. She wanted this. He wanted this. It was obvious in the way he looked at her, all black eyes and tight jaw and the way he fumbled to drop his pants.

She felt her nipples bead in her lacy navy bra, felt his eyes drop to them. She'd never been that large, but the way he stared, she felt as desirable as any movie star. He made her feel that way. For that alone, she could love him.

But as a friend, she assured herself, eyes glued to the boxers that were revealed. His erection was obvious, but he didn't make a move to lose the underwear.

As if sensing the small amount of nerves that remained, he crawled onto the bed and half over her, pausing at her breasts. His breath hit her skin and she shivered.

"So pretty," he praised, lifting one hand and propping himself up on the other. He shaped her with one strong palm, squeezing.

A rush of breath left her and her head fell back on a small moan as he tweaked her nipple through the lace. He thumbed it, seemingly transfixed as his hand swept back and forth. Her legs moved restlessly under him. Then, as her hands gripped the sheets, he bent his head and sucked the nipple into his mouth, tonguing it as her back arched.

He moved his attention to her other breast, palming the first as he kissed and nipped the other. She was a mass of sensation, zero to sixty in three seconds.

Tension built inside her. She released the sheets and caught his hair, tugging him. He complained but came willingly enough for her kiss. He relaxed more of his weight onto her as their mouths clashed, a heated kiss this time with teeth and tongue that only built the black hole of sensation that screamed inside her.

Her skin shuddered as she felt his telekinetic touch ease up her thigh. As his hand continued to manipulate her breast, he eased a telekinetic finger under the scrap of panties she'd conjured, cupped her.

She cried out, losing his mouth, quaking.

He made a growling kind of noise. "That's it. Go on. Go over, Emma."

He pressed harder, finding and plucking her clitoris in a rhythm designed to make her insane. Back and forth, squeeze, release, squeeze, release, *squeeze...*

The black hole swallowed her, chewed her up and spat her out the other side, shuddering, weak, damp. Books from the shelf on the wall had flown off onto the floor, heaped in a display of loss of control.

Bastian was tense above her, obvious appreciation across a face drawn taut with passion. "Yes" was all he said, before he kissed her hard. "Again."

She couldn't find her words, but it seemed she didn't need them as he set about taking her back up to the peak again, sliding his hands—real and not—over her body, learning the few curves she had, tasting her skin until she was quivering again, his name a litany in her head.

Bottles on the dressing table rattled and she cast a desperate glance at them.

Bastian caught her gaze. "Trust me?"

She hesitated, then nodded. A familiar scent wrapped around her mind a second later. She bucked instinctively but he shushed her. "Just the surface," he reassured. "No deeper."

Her instinctive panic receded as she realized her guard was still up, that he couldn't get through. She probed it with a mental finger as he soothed her, as he kissed her neck, her collarbones, her breasts. It was a shield of some sort, she thought, calming. To keep her escaping magic under control. He didn't know about Sloane, about anything else.

"Okay?"

She caught the uncertainty. Her thudding heart gave an extra kick to the ribs. She nodded, and then drew him back for another kiss.

Their bodies came back together, pressing firmly. Emma couldn't keep her hips still, rubbing against the hardness in Bastian's boxers, a hitch in her breath every time it knocked the right place. The exquisite friction made something wild appear in Bastian's eyes.

Suddenly his boxers were gone—so were her panties and bra. He drank her in with his eyes and she forgot to be nervous or worried about what he'd think of her. Why should she when it was written all over his face?

"Goddess," he choked out, tracing her body with his eyes. "Emma…"

"Bastian." She stared down at him, swallowing. He was larger than she'd thought he'd be. "That wasn't padding."

"No, it fucking wasn't."

A condom appeared in his hand and he ripped the packet open with his teeth, sheathing himself in the next second. Sweat gleamed over his chest as he crawled back over her body. His heat was amazing, and the feeling of him against her, skin to skin, was like nothing Emma had ever felt before. Intimate and awesome and terrifying, and it made her crazy.

He watched her, dark eyes rapt on her face.

She shifted, restless. "Now, Bastian."

Powered by the words, he positioned himself and pushed into her body.

It was not an easy fit, even with how wet she was. She wriggled to ease the small sting even as he released a string of swear words she wouldn't have associated with Bastian Truenote.

"Fuck," he rasped. "You're so tight."

She choked out a breath as he thrust the rest of the way, nails biting into his back as she lifted her hips.

His chest was heaving and sweat beaded on his forehead, but he stopped. "Are you okay?" he gritted out.

"Yes." It was a hoarse word and she wasn't sure if it was the truth.

He was just so big inside her, so hard, so…

He shifted, hit a spot that made her clutch at his back reflexively. "Oh," she gasped.

A pause. Then he eased his hips back and sank into her again, hitting the same spot.

She moaned.

He did that for a minute, shallow thrusts that slowly made her lose her mind, her nails surely drawing blood as her hips began to move, to meet him, to urge him to go faster.

As ordered, he picked up the speed, withdrawing and thrusting back in, their bodies dancing in a rhythm designed to make minds insane.

He caught her mouth with his, a rough, fumbling kiss that knocked teeth together. She didn't care, fully focused on his hands on her skin, his cock hitting the sweet spot inside her, hips pistoning, and Goddess, his telekinetic touch that circled her clitoris in time with his hips.

Black swamped her and she cried out, waves of pleasure flooding her, sending lightning bolts up her skin, setting her body on fire.

"Yes," she heard him say through the haze. "*Emma.*"

His hips continued the motion, becoming more frantic as he reached his peak. He said her name again, once, drawn out on a groan, before his body tautened.

Then, as if someone had reached out and stolen the bones from his body, he fell half onto her, catching his weight with a hand.

She wouldn't have cared if he'd squished her, little aftershocks continuing to zig and zag in her blood. She quivered, sweat coating her body.

After a moment, Bastian raised his head. He stared at her in silence before pressing a soft kiss to her lips. They clung to one another, damp, pliant.

When he drew back, she smiled, utterly relaxed.

Then, he lifted his eyebrows. "Why didn't you tell me that was your first time?"

Emma's warm, pliable body stiffened. Bastian kept his relaxed, even as his mind raced to fill in the blanks.

He'd never stopped to question whether she would be a virgin or not. To be honest, he hadn't wanted to think of it, her with another man, and he'd known that was a touchy subject, since he was the one who'd left. *For a good reason.* Their engagement contract was technical, so until it had been officially locked down, she had been free to date. Technically.

But she hadn't. Or if she had, it hadn't got so far as the bedroom.

He knew the satisfaction he felt placed him vaguely in the

same category as a caveman, but just knowing he was her first lover was shockingly powerful. It made him want to…hell, he didn't know. Do things for her. To her.

And the fact that she'd trusted him with that gift? It went a long way toward healing old hurts.

He'd been honest earlier when he'd told her to keep her secrets. The more he knew her now, the more he was sure she couldn't have betrayed him then. And the few things she was keeping from him would only be sweeter when she grew to trust him again and shared them voluntarily.

Her eyes were wide now, the brown dappled with black as she stared up at him. Her hair was tousled, her cheeks flushed, and she looked adorable.

Unable to resist, he dropped a kiss onto her nose.

She startled, eyeing him. "What makes you think— I mean, maybe I might be a bit rusty, but— I mean, why would you say it was my first time?"

"Apart from the fact that you're rambling again?" He stroked a free hand down the side of her body, ostensibly to calm her but also because she had the softest skin. "You were tight. And your reactions…"

Her eyes flashed up to his. "I did it wrong?"

The chuckle flowed out of him and continued even when storm clouds gathered on her face. "It's okay," he soothed, still laughing. "Practice makes perfect. We'll just do it again." He kissed her neck. "And again." Her cheek. "And again." Her lips, and this time he lingered, nudging her to kiss him back.

Annoyed, she resisted at first, but as naturally responsive as she was, it took only a few seconds before she sank in, opening her mouth for long, lazy kisses.

When he broke away, it was with some difficulty. He looked into hazy eyes. "You were incredible, Emma. I just wish you'd told me."

Pleasure at his words dimmed. She didn't meet his gaze, instead focused her attention on his chest. Her hand reached up and she traced the line of his pec as if needing to occupy herself. "It wasn't important."

"It was to me. I could've…" He struggled. "Gone slower. Been less rough. Or something."

Her smile was faint. "I liked it."

His chest grew two sizes. He wanted to pound it, but best to wait for a private moment.

He settled where he was, enjoying her petting. Their intimacy. In no rush to run away, he was content to be close. But then, he reasoned, Emma always had been his place to rest.

"Why me?"

She still didn't look at him, her busy fingers now stroking over his nipple. Sensation was uncurling in his belly, but he didn't let it distract him.

"Emma."

She lifted a shoulder. "It never seemed right before."

"And it did with me?" That chest-pounding was looking more and more likely.

"We *are* going to be married. It was sensible that the first time be with my husband."

Disappointment popped the caveman feeling. He put it away to examine later. For now, he wanted to keep it light. To see her smile again. "Sensible and wild at the same time. A whole new Emma."

"Darn straight." She finally looked at him, and there were the brown eyes he craved. They were careful as she flattened her hand against him. "I'm guessing it wasn't yours?"

Alarms rang and he shifted. "I know this is your first time, but this isn't exactly pillow talk."

She didn't smile, just continued to stare at him.

He sighed, stroking her, needing the contact. "Honesty, right?" He forced the words out. "No. It wasn't my first time."

She didn't stiffen, just nodded. "You've been with lots." Her expression was pure Switzerland, neutral to a fine point. He couldn't tell what she was thinking, and he wouldn't invade her privacy by seeing if he could catch any impressions at the top of her mind.

But he also wouldn't let her believe he'd been sleeping around for seven years. "No. Not lots. One." One too many.

Doubt replaced Switzerland. "One? But you're..." She skimmed her eyes up and down.

Under normal circumstances, he'd have reacted to such a flirty comment. Now he needed her to believe him. "One," he repeated firmly. "And it was a disaster." He let out a breath, cupped her waist. "You sure you want to talk about this? Can't we talk about how you have a few freckles on your hip that look like Cassiopeia?"

She watched him for a minute, then shrugged. "You're right. We don't need to talk. Casual, right?"

It was her easy capitulation that did him in. That and the fact that he was being a coward and running again. And he'd already told her the worst of it.

He rolled to his back, grabbing her hand, tangling his fingers with hers and bringing it to rest on his chest. He stared up at her ceiling, aware of her gaze on his face. "It was with an exchange student I met in the first six months after I left." She'd been human, British and a lot more experienced. "She was with a group I was hanging around, and she pursued me hard. I didn't put her off. I...liked the attention. I liked that she wasn't after me because I was Bastian Truenote, heir to a Higher family, perfect warlock and son." No history between them, no suspicions of betrayal, no complicated love. "She just thought I was hot and funny and she wanted a fling on her holiday. I'd left witch society behind, convinced myself that this was me being my own man, not playing into what was expected of me. So I went to bed with her." He cringed inside as the words left him. "It was awkward and I felt like shit. Sick to my stomach. I left halfway through and didn't speak to her again."

Emma was quiet. Then she said, "Doesn't that count as half a time, then?"

No judgment in her voice. No hurt, betrayal. He dared a look at her. She had a faint, but unmistakable, smile on her face.

He grabbed on to that, hope a tight ball inside. "You're not..."

"What?"

"Angry? Betrayed? Hurt?"

"Bastian." She readjusted her head on the pillow, squeezed his hand from within what he realized had become a death grip. He gentled it. "We were kids when the contract was drawn up. It wasn't your choice or mine...it was just what it was, and we didn't question it. We weren't responsible for it." At the mention of the contract, his gaze shot to hers, examining it for any indication. If she was insinuating something, he couldn't tell. "You didn't ask me to marry you. We weren't a couple." She traced his face with her eyes. "It wasn't cheating."

"Then why did it feel like it was?" The question was ripped out from where it had grown, nurtured by guilt and self-loathing. Because even with his suspicions and hurt, he'd felt like he'd betrayed *her*.

Her smile kicked up the corner of her lips. "Because you were brought up to be the perfect man."

He shook his head, serious. "I'm not, Emma."

"I know." She inched closer. "I kind of like the less perfect version. Makes you more..." She struggled for the word.

"You're not mad?" he asked again, needing to make sure.

"Some might say I betrayed you. Shouldn't betrayal be punished?" So much he couldn't say there.

She cast him a semi-exasperated look. "Sure, if it was true betrayal, but sometimes it's in your head, and that needs to be let go. It wasn't. *We* weren't a couple. *We* didn't make promises. All that existed back then was a piece of paper neither of us signed."

A piece of paper neither of us signed.

Emma had been a bystander, a victim, he thought. Just like him.

"Fresh start," he said now, adding emphasis to cover all past actions. "But we have more between us than a piece of paper."

"Not right now." Now she smiled, one full of mischief. "And Bastian, really. You could have told me it was practically your first time."

"What?"

"I could've been…" She shrugged, a coy copy of him. "Slower. A little less rough. Or something."

Affection and desire made him dizzy, and he lunged for her. She squealed as he caught her, rolling on top. So happy he felt it flood from his grin, he put everything he was feeling into a kiss.

"What I want to know," she said, breathless when he lifted his head, "is how you knew all those moves."

He cocked his head. "You know how I told my mom I learned to like some books? There are some great books out there." Not to mention movies, but he didn't need to go into that right now.

"Romances?"

He evaded. "All kinds of books." At her steady look, he sighed. "Yes."

She laughed, delighted. "Goddess bless romance writers everywhere."

★ ★ ★

Emma woke to the desperate urge to pee. Grumbling, she lifted her head from where it was using Bastian's bicep as a pillow. Weariness swamped her and as she moved, soreness in new places made her wince.

Then Chester sent another *please, please, please* request down their bond and she groaned. "Sorry, Ches. I'm up."

She maneuvered herself into a seated position, wincing as she swung her legs around. She caught sight of the clock. Nine a.m. No wonder poor Chester was dancing around.

But it had been a late night. A secret smile curled her lips as she tossed a greedy look over her shoulder at the gorgeous male sprawled in her sheets. He slept like the dead, oblivious to her rolling away, utterly exhausted from a night of learning each other. In the bed. On the floor. In the shower. After that, Emma had had to regretfully say no, but she'd sated his and her curiosity by exploring his cock with her hands, with her tongue, until he'd been shouting her name.

Yes, she felt like a femme fatale this morning. Wild Emma. Unabridged. Nothing practical about bedding her fiancé.

She couldn't believe he'd bought the whole "sensible to sleep with my husband" thing—but then, maybe she'd been overthinking anyway. She'd done it, slept with him, and woken up no closer to falling back into her old pattern of adoring him and putting him up on a pedestal. She saw the flaws. She saw the man. And she was more than happy to take things as they came. Keep them casual.

On her way back with Chester, she decided to pick up two coffees and muffins from the coffee shop three blocks away from her apartment. As she waited in line, she texted Sloane a good-morning message, with a link to a story about the teenager's favorite actress. She might have been playing a little kiss-ass, but when they saw each other later, Emma would bring a batch of doughnuts to make it up to her.

It didn't take long, though, before her thoughts zeroed back to Bastian's confession the night before.

She'd told him the truth—she wasn't mad that he'd been with someone else. She'd assumed he'd slept his way across the globe, and while it wasn't pleasant to think of the man you're attracted to dating others, she'd figured that they weren't a couple and things happened. As she'd said, *they'd* made no promises. She'd never thought of him as hers. Not really. He'd been too…above her.

Now he'd been below her, too. She snickered at the thought and wondered at how far she'd come. No longer the lost little girl hoping for scraps, now she felt every inch a strong, sexy woman and that had as much to do with taking control of her own life as with being intimate with Bastian. Her first. And she was kind of his first, too, considering he'd stopped before out of misplaced honor. He really was a good man.

A stab of guilt had her eyes closing for a second before she purposefully moved past it.

They still needed to discuss what would happen now, whether it was a one-night thing or a casual affair until they were married and he left.

But not this morning, she decided as she smiled brilliantly at the barista who handed her a paper sack and two coffees in a carrying container. This morning she felt too good to be serious, especially when Sloane messaged back with a bunch of emojis, excited about the new movie her actress was shooting. For once in her life, Emma didn't want to think ahead. She just wanted to focus on the now, and the now involved going back to the incredible man in her bed.

Except he was at the breakfast bar fully clothed when she walked in, looking at his cell. He glanced up when she closed the door behind her and a hunting expression slid across his face. Desire and the memories of last night all played into the dark smile aimed her way. "Good morning."

Like the prey she was, she'd frozen midstep. Now with her heart thudding wildly, she crept closer. "Morning."

He'd moved the couch back into position, so it wasn't in his way when he stepped forward, wrapped an arm around her waist and hauled her close to kiss her.

It was greedy and lush. The man liked kissing, she was realizing. And it clearly wasn't a one-night thing. A glow warmed her as she dropped the coffee on the countertop, the sack on the floor and knotted her hands around his neck.

He lifted her with ease, two solid hands under her butt. Walking them to a wall, he continued to kiss her, long, slow, teasing.

"Well." She blinked as he released her mouth. Her throat was tight due to lack of oxygen, but who needed that. "Hi."

"Hi." He grinned at her. "I woke up and you weren't there."

"Coffee." She lifted her chin toward the breakfast bar. "And—oh, *Chester*." Her dog had investigated the sack and nosed out a muffin.

If dogs could look guilty, Chester did as he scurried behind the couch with his stolen treasure.

At least it was blueberry and she wouldn't have to chase him down like the time he'd got his paws on a double chocolate. That had been a fun trip to the vet.

"So." Bastian cocked his head, bringing her attention back to him. "Thoughts on last night?"

He was feeling her out. Making sure she wasn't suddenly in love with him. The Virgin's Curse, or what every man assumed would happen when a woman lost her virginity to him.

"Five out of ten," she answered with a straight face. "A little shaky on the dismount."

He squeezed her butt and she bit back a yelp. "Smart-ass."

"You'd know, you're grabbing enough."

He squeezed again. "You're okay? Not too…sore?"

Instant heat rushed to her cheeks. "Some. The walk helped." Not to mention the quick healing elixir she intended to stir up and add to her coffee.

He attempted to look chagrined. "Sorry about that."

"Yeah, right."

"I am. And to prove it, I am willing to give you a nice massage to ease out all the…" His hands shifted and she twitched in reaction. "Kinks."

"Hmm." She closed her eyes as his fingers pressed. Her teeth bit her bottom lip. "What kind of kinks?"

"Damn it." He swore and moved his hands back to a semi-respectable position. She opened her eyes in protest. Turned out after one night, she was an addict. "I didn't mean to start it. But you walked in and…" He shrugged. "That was about it."

"You're not fussy."

"On the contrary. Your legs in a skirt could make any man forget his mind."

"Funny, they've all managed to do just fine." She stroked one hand down his chest, loving how hard he felt beneath her. Against her.

"They might not have done something, but trust me." He kissed her once. "They all thought it. Now. Quit distracting me." He set her back on the floor, held out a hand. "Hands off. Restrain yourself."

"Oh, I'll try."

A flash of a grin. "I had a missed call from my mom this morning."

Emma took a step forward. "Is she okay?"

"She's as fine as she can be. Thanks." He held out a hand, twisted his fingers into hers and drew her toward him. She didn't bother reminding him of the hands-off rule he'd just implemented. "I called her back while you were out. Seems someone doesn't trust us to pick a wedding planner."

The penny dropped. "She called someone?"

"Yep. A Ms. Tamsin White. Apparently she's all-singing, all-dancing and needs only one afternoon with us to pick flowers and crap like that."

"You make it sound so romantic."

"Call me Cupid." He brought their joined hands to his lips, kissed the knuckles. "The appointment is in half an hour."

She knew him well enough to know that even though this was his idea of hell—maybe hers too—because his mom had asked it, he'd face the hazards of place settings and seating charts to please her. So, she surrendered without grumbling. "Let me change."

"Why? I think you look perfect." He ran his free hand down her side, gaze following. His fingers bunched the skirt's hem, started to slide it upward. "You got any of those lacy panties on under here?"

"Of course. I wouldn't go out without my underwear." That was a little too wild. And cold. Not to mention stupid in Chicago, aka the Windy City.

The brush of his fingers on the sensitive skin of her hip made her eyes half-close, her body lean toward him.

"So practical." He teased around the edge of her panties. "About that massage."

"Bastian." She swallowed as his knuckle pressed against her. "We'll be...oh, Goddess...we'll be late."

"We can portal there. It'll take five minutes tops." He cupped her, tutted even as she shuddered. "You're soaked, Emma. Don't you know it's not practical to walk around like that. Here." A telekinetic hand nudged her until she pressed right up against him. His eyes gleamed. "Let me help you out of those wet clothes."

CHAPTER 19

$\mathcal{I}$t didn't take Emma two minutes to realize that Tamsin White could have taken over the world if she had a free hour between clients.

With ruthless efficiency, she'd taken in the couple that had portalled into the hotel conference room in downtown Chicago, ignored their rumpled clothing and parked them in two seats directly in the center of the room. She'd conjured two clipboards with two questionnaires and handed them off to each of them. With instructions to fill them out, she'd walked to the back of the room and begun conjuring grand tables, each with a different theme. Her magic clearly lay in conjuring; Emma wasn't even sure she could do small "fetches," let alone pull off such grand designs. Tamsin wasn't even breaking a sweat.

Her body felt like melted wax after Bastian's "massage"— and that was all it had been, despite her pleas, because he thought she'd still be too sore for "the main event," a phrase that had obligated her to bean him with a pillow—Emma had relaxed into the chair despite her shyness around strangers and snuck glances at Bastian as she ticked a, b, or c for questions relating to flowers and themes and music. She didn't really care. It wasn't a real wedding and everybody, including her mother, would be judging her for everything anyway.

Finished, she watched as the long-legged redhead with eyes of smoke tapped her painted red lips with her French manicure, surveying her last creation. As if feeling Emma's gaze, Tamsin glanced up with the air of a dog scenting prey.

"You're done?" Her voice was cool, calm and clipped as she and her four-inch stilettos briskly walked back to them.

"Crap." Bastian hurriedly ticked the last few without even looking.

Emma stared at him. "Are you *scared* of her?"

"Duh. Aren't you?"

"I don't like talking to anyone I don't know," she pointed out sotto voce. Especially not witches that were gifted with powerful magic, beauty and efficiency. Her mother would have loved her. Emma just found her intimidating.

"We got this." Bastian gave her a nod. "Just keep saying yes."

"Of course that would be your advice."

He grinned. He kept doing that. The no-holds-barred grin he used to wear around her. It was a jolt to her system every time.

Tamsin held out a hand and their clipboards jumped to her. She ran her eyes down both pages, looked up with a stern expression.

Emma tensed. Had they done it wrong?

"Well," Tamsin said. "Your choices are a little...out there for a Higher match, but I love a challenge. You'll be an experiment."

Bastian's gaze flickered. "Thank you?" he tried.

Tamsin nodded, gifted him a smile. It looked genuine and actually made her seem more normal. Friendly, even. "I'm sorry if that came out wrong. To tell you the truth, you get sick of precious stone-studded floral arrangements and five-piece orchestras. From these—" she waggled the clipboards "—I can see you're both hoping for something more casual?"

"We just want it to be something fun. Emma is particularly into being wild. Right, honeybear?"

Emma shot him a *die* look.

Tamsin blinked, taken aback, but rebounded quick enough. "Okay, I can try and work in something…wild."

Emma sighed. "He was kidding. I'm not… I mean, I'd like to— Not that that's…" She trailed off and her shoulders reared up as if in defense.

The wedding planner's expression softened. "Shy, right? I get it. My baby sister is this mad blast of sass and energy, but park her with someone she doesn't know and she can't get a word out. It frustrates her to no end."

Emma's head came up. "Yes. That's it."

"Bet this whole hoopla is your worst nightmare." Tamsin tapped her nails on the clipboard. "If it helps, brides don't have to speak much and if you plan it right, a lot of attention can be on the pair of you, instead of just the bride. Would that make you more comfortable?"

Suddenly she was really warming to Tamsin. She should have known Diana Truenote wouldn't send them to a carbon copy planner.

"Hey, it can be all about me, if you want." Bastian smiled with innocence as both women eyed him. "Big photos of me everywhere, on the cake, a choir as I walk down the aisle to Emma and a special dance celebrating the wonder that is Bastian."

"You can ignore him," Emma informed Tamsin.

Who eyed both of them with interest. "I think I'm going to enjoy this." She clapped her hands together, disappearing the clipboards. "Right. Let's get to it."

CHAPTER 20

*E*mma walked out from the shower to find two males on her bed. It was a different experience.

Bastian eyed her towel with interest as he stroked Chester's ears. "Hey good-looking, come here often?"

"I did last night."

He turned his attention to the dog. "I've created a monster," he told Chester. "Scram. Mommy and I have some business."

"No, we don't," Emma corrected as she turned to her dresser. She hesitated, looking back over her shoulder. She felt a little awkward getting dressed in front of him. But then, he'd seen everything she had and didn't seem to have complaints. "How's your mom?"

Diana had called just as they'd arrived home from wedding planning.

"Fine. She said she'll talk to Tamsin, help with some of the arrangements going forward."

"Good. That's good." Tamsin seemed to have a natural sense of what the pair of them liked. She'd assured them that she'd take care of the minutiae, though she had convinced Emma to come back to try on the dress. Guess that was inevitable.

She opened the top drawer and selected some underwear, wishing they were more exotic than white cotton, like the lacy underwear she'd conjured before.

Hmm. With a murmured command, she lifted out a violet satin set and crossed to put them on the bed. Silly, really, considering she was going to a shelter and not on a fancy evening out.

She collected jeans and a T-shirt and then hovered by the bed.

Screw it. C'mon. Wild Emma, remember?

She dropped the towel, focused on the panties as her cheeks blazed. She reached out and drew them on, sliding them up her thighs as if she dressed in front of a man every day.

The bra was a front clasp and she adjusted herself properly before she felt like she could look up.

She almost took a step back at the desire pulsing on Bastian's face.

"C'mere," he commanded.

"No."

"I think your strap is twisted."

"No, that's you."

He clearly fought a grin, his eyes roving across her body. Now, though, she stood a little taller. What woman wouldn't feel confident under such an approving gaze?

"I've thought of something we can try." He patted the bed. "Beat it, Chester."

"Chester, stay."

The poor dog looked at her and then cocked his head, tongue lolling. Down their bond came the feeling of happiness. He was happy they were both here.

She blinked. *Both?*

No, she told him. Bastian wasn't part of the pack. Sloane, maybe, but Bastian? *No.*

Chester sat up, scratched his ear. Very unconcerned.

She frowned.

"Don't tell me you're sick of me already," Bastian joked.

Her eyes shot to him. Then she realized how silly she was being over a dog's feelings. Chester loved everyone—the mailman was also part of the pack sometimes.

She brushed it off and refocused. "What can I say? Thanks for the ride."

"Come here and say that."

A shiver skimmed her skin at the huskiness of his voice. "I don't have time. I'm volunteering at the shelter this afternoon."

"The one Leah works at?"

She nodded, reached for her jeans and dragged them on. Hesitating, she then added, "It's until five if you want to get dinner after?" Maybe he could meet Sloane before they left the shelter, and she could get it over with.

Wait, *what*?

Her heart thudded at the uncharacteristic thought. She wanted to keep them separate, remember? Uneasy, she rubbed her chest and clamped down on any runaway thoughts.

"Got a shift at the bar, but you could come, keep me company. Practice for the Exhibition. It's coming up fast."

She grimaced, dropping her hand. Something on her skin caught her eye. The bottom fell out of her stomach. "Oh, my Goddess."

"What?"

She jerked her arm out, appalled. "Look at that."

He twisted his head to read the new tattoo on her wrist. *Passion*. A grin lit up his face. "Huh."

She shook it as if it would erase itself like a Magic 8 Ball prediction. "How am I going to explain this?"

"In great, flattering detail." He shoved up his sleeve, looked. "Hey, I have one, too."

She covered her eyes. "I'm going to have to move. How can I face your mother with *that* on my arm?" A thought occurred and she dropped her hands, appalled. "What is *Tia* going to say?"

"'Lucky you'?"

She groaned and flopped onto the bed.

Bastian was in love. The feeling washed over him as he stared into eyes so perfectly echoing what he felt. He'd thought he might be more alarmed when he fell in love for the first time, but this was just right, a click inside him.

He twisted his head to look at Emma. "I'm in love."

The double take she gave him was amusing enough to have his lips tilt into a grin. "What?" she choked out.

"I want her." He pointed at the three-legged tabby sitting politely in its enclosure. Unlike the others, she didn't parade in front of the glass, meowing for attention or scratching at the door.

Emma looked between him and the cat. "Oh. Hallie?"

Hallie. "Can we get her out?"

"Ah...sure." Emma slid the bolt from home and swung the glass open. "Hey, Hall. Want to see a gentleman caller?"

Crooning to the cat, she slid her hands under the body and scooped her up. The cat was on the small side and went easily, solemn eyes regarding them both. Emma held her out.

Bastian took her as carefully as a bomb, stroking a hand along her back. A deep purr vibrated through his hand.

He'd walked Emma into the shelter, asking for a tour, not really because he wanted to see the sad faces of all the unwanted animals, but because he'd been weirdly reluctant to leave her side, enjoying spending time with her.

She'd been weirdly negative and had tried to shoo him off, then when it had been clear he wouldn't be shooed, had been twisting this way and that all tour. She'd hustled him past all the workers and had pushed him through a lot of areas.

Amused by her awkwardness, which he could only assume was fueled by embarrassment, he'd been ready to let her be and head home, until he'd felt the spark. Like seeing a match flare across the room. He'd followed it and it had led him here.

She was his. He knew it. He could already feel a bond, shadowy but there. All it would take was the small ritual and the cat's acceptance and they would be forever linked. She would lend him support, both emotional and magical, and he would offer her safety and love.

Emma's smile was affectionate as she looked at him cradling his soon-to-be familiar. "She likes you, and she's particular."

"I have a way with particular females."

Emma only arched her eyebrows.

He continued to stroke Hallie, an odd emotion tightening his chest. "I want her," he repeated.

"As in to adopt?" Surprise flashed in Emma's eyes.

He nodded. "I can feel her, Emma. She's mine." Even saying it made the tight feeling expand.

"As a familiar?" A small frown nestled in between eyebrows now drawn low. "Are you sure?"

"Yes."

"But… Bastian, she's not…" Emma pursed her lips, waved a hand at the cat's small body. "She's not a familiar most Higher families would have."

"Why?"

"She has three legs. She's not…perfect."

Goddess, he hated that word. It made him bare his teeth at Emma in a grin. "Good. Then she'll suit me fine. Won't you, Hallie?" The cat bumped her head against his chin, rubbing her soft ears against him. His heart melted.

"What will your parents say?"

"My mom'll love her. My dad will complain about another cat even as he sneaks her sardines." Bastian cocked his head. "I wouldn't have pegged you as someone who cared about that."

"I'm not." She leaned back against the enclosure. "Chester isn't exactly a purebred. But people don't think a lot of me anyway."

He frowned at that.

She ignored his expression, watching Hallie. "People might judge you for her supposed defect."

As he stared at his complicated fiancée, the fiancée that he knew thought of her shyness as a flaw, that tight feeling in his chest constricted to the point where dragging in a breath was a great achievement. His luck, he was allergic to his damn familiar.

"I really don't give a shit what people think of me," he told Emma honestly. "Let them say what they want—their funeral. And I don't see imperfection when I look at Hallie." His eyes caressed Emma's downturned face. "I see strength."

Emma swallowed, leaning back against the cages. "Oh."

Bastian scratched Hallie's ears as a small pause fell between them like a cloth preserving the moment. "Is there paperwork?" he nudged when Emma didn't seem inclined to say anything further.

"Yes, but… She was abandoned, Bastian. Like a lot of animals, she doesn't do well with change. She needs a stable environment for a few months." She hesitated, scuffing her shoe on the floor. "I'm not sure she would do well in Egypt or wherever it is you're going next."

"She's stronger than you think," he told her. "But that's fine. Maybe I'll stick around for a bit after the wedding."

He'd only said it offhandedly, but alarm—and it *was* alarm—sparked in Emma's eyes. "What?"

Taken aback by the emotion, Bastian paused in his stroking. "Unless that's an issue…"

She straightened away from the enclosure. "I thought we had a deal. Marry and split, remember?"

Noting the flush that rode her cheeks, Bastian took a minute to think of what to say. To wonder why she wanted him gone so quickly after the wedding. "Well, you just said Hallie might need some time. And besides, I don't want people judging you if I leave immediately."

"I thought you didn't care what people thought."

"Well, no, but you do. And I don't want them talking about you."

"I'll be fine. We agreed you'd go so that's fine. You can go."

"You sure know how to flatter a guy's ego," he drawled, trying not to let her practically kicking his ass out her door bother him. But it did, damn it. Not to mention, the suspicions he'd buried in the name of letting go were clawing back up. "What's the big deal? It's only a few extra months."

"It's not. A big deal. We just…had a plan. And I can take care of myself."

His jaw tightened despite his attempts not to get annoyed. "I feel like you're trying to get rid of me, Emma. Why do you want me gone?"

She rubbed a hand along her neck, looking at the sterile white walls, the concrete floor, Hallie, the other cats—anywhere but him. "I'm not trying to get rid of you. I just don't want you to feel like I need you. To stay."

He relaxed. So, that's what it was—her insistence that this was casual so she didn't feel like the old Emmaline. She needed to realize she didn't need to go back to being the old her to open up to him. Just a little.

Maybe she needed a nudge. "Well, would you like me to?"

She chewed on her lip. Shrugged. "It doesn't matter to me."

Okay, now he was getting annoyed. He gently loaded Hallie back in her enclosure for the moment, pausing to chuck her under the chin. Then he rounded on his pain-in-the-ass friend, bride-to-be and lover.

"We'll make it easy. Do you like me?"

"Please. I'm not going to feed your ego."

"It's a simple question. And considering we were in bed last night, a damn pertinent one, I think."

Color blossomed in her cheeks and her shoulders went up. "Of course I like you."

"Good. I like you, too. A happy coincidence in a marriage. Emma, we said honesty." He touched her hand. "What's the deal here? Why are you so adamant about me leaving?"

Tell me, he all but willed. *Trust me.*

She stared at where they connected. An inhale lifted her shoulders and her head came up. She smiled, a shade rueful. "I'm not. Honest," she insisted at his doubtful expression. "It just surprised me. It's a change in plan. I thought you couldn't wait to leave."

"Well, I have gotten fond of Chicago." He altered the contact to a gentle grip, using it to reel her in until he had his arms around her. He inhaled the scent of Emma, felt something settle inside him as her arms slid around his waist. He rested his chin on her head. "I'm not in any hurry to leave." Not when his life was starting to feel…right.

Her breath stirred his shirt. "So you're staying," she said into his chest. "For a bit longer."

"Yes." He dropped a kiss on her head. "I'm staying."

She didn't say anything, but her hands tightened on his waist. After a moment, she lifted her head. The tension had mostly disappeared, leaving behind a smile that reached into his soul and cast away any lingering shadows. "Hallie's glad to hear it." Something behind him caught her attention. She lurched back, quick enough to give him whiplash. Or maybe that was from her change in emotions as she lost her smile and strode past him.

"Hey, Sloane. Where're those going?"

Bastian turned to see a young girl, maybe twelve or thirteen, coming toward them with her arms full of boxes. She peered around the boxes with brown eyes that were both curious and cagey.

Manners jolted him to move. "Let me take those."

"I got it." Her voice was super quiet, but he'd been raised with Emma, so you could say his ear was tuned for it. She had retreated when he'd moved toward her, so he stopped in place.

"You sure? They look…awkward."

"She's fine." Emma stepped in between them. She nudged her chin to the back. "I think Leah's in there if you're taking those to her."

Bastian looked back and forth, then raised a hand. "Hi. I'm Bastian."

The girl's eyes widened. "*You're* Bastian?"

He raised his eyebrows and glanced playfully at Emma. "Been talking about me to everyone, I see."

Red flagged up on Emma's cheeks as she herded the girl backward. "*No.*"

He didn't see if the girl had tripped or if the top box had just been too heavy, but suddenly with a clatter, the boxes were on the floor.

"Excuse me, ma'am?" called someone from out near reception. A guy with a baseball cap on waved cheerfully. "Can we have some help real quick?"

Emma looked visibly torn. "Sloane, why don't you go help?"

"Oh, no." The teenager smiled so sweetly, Bastian could practically hear the birdsong. "I have to pick up all of this. Don't worry, I'll be fine." Some kind of undertone threaded her words.

"I can help her." Bastian shooed Emma with a hand. "Promise I won't get to the bottom of all your secrets."

Emma's smile was tight. A look passed between her and the girl before she turned on her heel and hurried to help the customer.

Bastian knelt and began to stack the scattered items back in the box. "So, it's Sloane, right?" When she gave the barest hint of a nod, he said, "You been volunteering here long?"

The girl's hair swung forward as she ducked her head. She was crouched, concentrating on putting items back in the box precisely. Her shoulders were lifted, a sign Bastian recognized. Shy now that the person she knew had disappeared. A mini-Emma. Good thing he had years of experience. "A while," she said.

"It's a nice place," he continued, smoothly dropping the last pencil into the box. He stayed kneeling, figuring his height would intimidate. "I'm adopting today, as a matter of fact."

She glanced at him, blinking as they made eye contact.

"Hallie," he supplied as if she'd asked. "Took one look, fell in love."

A smile bloomed on her face like ink in water. "I love her," she said in a quiet voice that was oddly melodic. "She doesn't get cross like some of the others."

"I've heard some of them yowl like grumpy grannies," he said, and smiled when she did. "I picked a good one, then?"

She nodded seriously. "Hallie always lets you stroke her, especially if you've had a bad day."

"You have a lot of those?"

She shrugged. "Not so much anymore. Leah pays me some to help out here, and I get to hang around with people I like."

"Shouldn't a nice kid like you have loads of friends?"

"Emma's my friend. Well—" she changed her mind "—she's my big sister so she kind of has to be my friend."

His heart thumped. "Big sister?"

She glanced at him and smiled widely again. "The volunteer group thing."

"Oh." He didn't even know why he'd gone there; the idea of Clarissa bedding down with a human was crazy. Even if, as he'd thought, the girl did behave and look kind of like a mini-Emma. "And you know Leah?"

Sloane nodded. "She's cool. She has loads of animals. When I'm older I'm going to have five cats and four dogs."

"That's specific."

"You have to consider these things."

Bastian hid a smile. "Very practical. No wonder you and Emma get along."

"Yeah, she's cool, too. She, ah…" She shot him a look. "She's teaching me all sorts of things about where you guys came from."

"New Orleans?"

"Yeah. Was it awesome? It must've been amazing."

"It's a cool place. You've never been?"

"No, Emma says it's not time."

"Not time?"

Pink ran up the girl's neck. "To, ah, visit."

Weird, but maybe Emma just didn't want to take a human near the witch world. Understandable. "It can be dangerous, too."

"Yeah," she said glumly. "They keep telling me that. But I think some things must make up for it."

Some things? "Beignets can save a bad day," he agreed.

She cocked her head. "What's a beignet?"

He choked. "What's a— Oh, sweet mistreated child. Tell you what, I'll bring you a beignet next time you're working here."

She gave him a shy smile. "I'd like that. Maybe we can talk more about New Orleans. Emma says you're leaving and I have a bunch of questions before you do."

"She may be wrong about that. I'm happy to answer any questions you have."

She beamed at him, and he could definitely see how Emma fell for the human. "We can have milkshakes as well."

"Now you're talking my language. I'll answer anything for a milkshake."

"Me, too! Emma always gets boring old vanilla."

Bastian shook his head. "Chocolate's the only way to go."

"Right? She says I must have a cast-iron stomach since I never vomit."

"You're either born with it or you're not."

"But she says it'll come in handy when we go traveling." Animation leaped into her face. "Emma says we can go wherever we want, but she's saving 'cause airplanes cost money. Which is stupid since…" She stopped talking and then shrugged again.

Very expressive, those shrugs. But he thought he'd finally stumbled onto why Emma hadn't traveled, at least recently. It was…unbearably sweet that she wanted to take a young girl who she'd met through volunteering around the world. Almost like giving herself a second chance at it through Sloane.

"Where do you want to go?" he asked and was treated to a laundry list of places Sloane had seen in movies.

Seeing as he'd been to a few, they managed to have a decent conversation, which stopped abruptly when Emma hurried back over. She looked pink, like she did when—

Not suitable around a child, he reminded himself. Even if seeing one more side of her giving, caring nature made him crazy.

"What're you guys talking about?" she asked, out of breath. "Sloane, Leah's gonna want those."

Bastian helped Sloane up with the boxes. "We were talking about Rome," he said.

Sloane turned to Emma, eyes shining. "Bastian says he's been to the very top of the Vatican. There's a staircase that turns around and around and around and you feel like you're going to hurl."

"Lovely." Emma nudged her. "Go to Leah."

"'Kay." Sloane hesitated, shooting a quick look at Emma, before saying, "It was cool, like, meeting you."

"Same." Bastian watched her go and with a grin, turned back to Emma. "She's great."

"You guys were talking for a while."

"Just getting to know your little sister." He laughed as she shot him a half-frozen glance. "I know; when she said it, swear to the Goddess, my head just kind of went thick. But Sloane explained about the volunteering group."

"Right." Emma nodded, looking down the hallway where Sloane had disappeared. He thought he saw her eyes narrow. "Right."

Emotion lapped at his feet like a gentle wave. "It's nice you do it. She clearly worships you."

"She's great, like you said."

"She reminds me of you, a bit."

Emma did a weird laugh and folded her arms around her middle. "Why would you say that?"

"She's shy with strangers, but once you get her talking, she won't shut up." A shot of telekinesis where he was most ticklish made him jump. "Play nice, Emma."

"How about we go home and I'll show you nice?"

All thoughts of Sloane disappeared. "Let's sign what I need to sign and get out of here."

CHAPTER 21

A few days later, Emma clinked glasses with her friends and Sloane in the bridal boutique owned by one of Tamsin's contacts. The wedding planner had marched off in search of the perfect dress for Emma, leaving the four of them to drink the free champagne (and OJ for Sloane) and pretend to be happy about the upcoming wedding. Well, Leah wasn't pretending, Emma didn't think. If this was a ball game, she'd have a big foam finger and would've cheered anytime Bastian came onto the field. Was it a field in baseball?

She pushed that aside. "You should see him with this cat," she told her friends, curling her legs up beneath her on the champagne velvet seating and smiling. "This big strong man dragging a string along the floor for his cat to play with."

"Big and strong, huh?" Leah waggled her eyebrows.

Sloane made a face. "He didn't look that big and strong to me."

Tia shot her an approving look. "That's my girl. So he has a cat. Big deal."

"Hallie likes him."

"If Hallie likes him, it means he's good people," Leah informed Tia. "Remember that one woman who looked at her, Sloane? She got all sniffy and asked for a discount since Hallie was deformed. Hallie's ears went back and she snarled. Definite higher intelligence—like all animals."

"Higher than yours at the moment." Tia sipped champagne as Sloane giggled. Unfortunately, she idolized Tia. Emma dreaded the day when Sloane discovered her true potential for sass. "He's found his familiar. Okay, I wouldn't have pegged him as the type to choose anything not purebred, and that's to his credit, but the bond is strong enough to overcome it."

"He's not bothered by the fact she has three legs," Emma insisted, remembering his deep voice saying *I see strength*. "And he coos to her." She couldn't help the silly smile.

"Oh, no." Tia sat up straight. "Don't do that. None of that."

"What?"

"The whole gooey bit. I thought you were keeping it light and friendly."

"We are." The man had made love to her in the shower last night before carrying her to her bed and kissing every inch of her body. What was that if not friendly?

But she got Tia's point. She bit her lip. "We did get into a bit of a...thing," she decided on, with a quick look at Sloane, who was listening intently, "when he adopted Hallie. I pointed out she needs stability and he said that he was thinking of staying for a bit longer."

Leah bounced, almost spilling her champagne. "This is *so* exciting."

"Does that mean I have to pretend I don't know about magic longer?" objected Sloane at the same time. "Or can we finally tell him that I *know*?"

"No, he's not to be trusted," Tia answered for her. "Why does he want to stay around?" she demanded in the next breath. "To make sure you start to rely on him before he skips town?"

Emma would scoff if that wasn't exactly what had run through her panicked mind when he'd said he'd stay. She didn't want to need him in her life. Didn't want to rely on his being there, so that when he left, her heart wouldn't crack along those old stress lines and break all over again. And despite what he said now, he would leave. He wasn't designed for one place. Itchy feet.

Not to mention the whole Sloane issue. When she'd seen them with their heads together, her chest had seized. Especially with the whole "little sister" thing. Sloane insisted it wasn't as incriminating as he'd made it sound, but now she knew what a heart attack felt like.

She wouldn't lie—she had found herself wondering if she could let him in on the secret. All her secrets. But just the idea gave her a chill. The idea that she'd lay herself so bare, reveal everything...

Maybe if they were in a relationship that was actually going somewhere, it would be different. She'd push past the fear of what he'd think of her, of what he might do, because there'd be an expectation of commitment. They'd be a true team.

But part of her, a large part, held back. It was easier to keep him in the dark—maybe cowardly, but easier. Safer. What he didn't know couldn't hurt him. Literally, thanks to the ring Kole was having created.

"He probably wants to stick around to be with his mom when she's better," she pointed out. "It's got nothing to do with me." And she needed to remember that whenever her softer side tried to lead her down the tempting path toward feelings.

"How do you know that?" Leah tipped back the rest of the champagne, put the flute on the floor and grabbed Emma's arm. She shook, impatient. "He might just be trying to see how you feel about him."

"How *do* you feel?" Tia watched her face as if she held a flashlight up to it and was demanding the codes for a bank vault heist.

Sloane piped up. "She had this gooey look when she was talking to him at the shelter."

"Traitor." Giving her a tickle telekinetically and wincing at Sloane's loud shriek, Emma shrugged, uneasy. "I like him." True. "We're friends." Also true.

"Oh, come on," Leah complained, letting go of Emma's arm. "You can't tell me you don't look at that man and think about…" She widened her eyes meaningfully. "You forget, I've seen you together. Sparks city."

Emma spluttered. "I… He… No…"

Both her friends' eyebrows shot up. Leah's with delight, Tia's with suspicion.

"Sloane, honey," the latter said with a tight smile, "can you go find Miss Tamsin and ask her to look for dresses in peach and apricot too?"

"Aren't they the same thing?"

"Go ask her and you won't believe the long-winded answer you get." Tia smiled and watched as the young teen left the room. Then folded her arms. "Show us your wrist."

Emma recoiled. Almost put her arm behind her back. "Why?"

"I have a theory."

"Find a new one."

"Why don't you want to show us?"

"Because a woman's wrist is her own."

Tia snorted. "Don't make me grab you."

Emma could've argued more, wanted to on principle, but Sloane would be back any minute and ripping off a Band-Aid was supposed to be the best approach. Resigned, she turned her wrist to face the light.

All three read the word that was written at the bottom of the chain.

"Emma." Tia's voice was flat. "It says 'passion.' Why does it say 'passion'?"

Leah's grin took up half her face. "You had *sex* with him and you didn't *tell* us?"

Someone flipped the temperature dial to Sahara and Emma began to sweat. She blinked, as if that was an answer.

A small scream from Leah covered Tia's cursing—luckily not the magical kind. "You had sex with Bastian!"

Emma put a finger to her mouth, glancing over her shoulder for a hint of Sloane.

"How was it? Was it good? It was good, wasn't it? He just looks like he was born with the knowledge of how to make a woman scream." She caught the flicker in Emma's eyes and crowed with delight. "Oh, my God, he does. When was the first time? Were you okay? Did he take care of you? How many times? What does this mean?"

The questions made her feel like she was in front of a firing squad and she inched back with every one thrown at her. "I, ah…" In a way she was glad the truth was out, but she wasn't comfortable with the attention.

Or with the look on Tia's face. "You're falling for him," she said tonelessly.

"No." The word blasted from Emma, followed by a definitive shake of her head. "I just… Haven't you ever wanted to do something crazy?"

"Sure, that's why I buy shoes that cost six hundred dollars. I didn't sleep with the man I once loved and who abandoned me, who could find out about a secret sister and tell the world."

She reached for her throat, rubbed. "I've got a bad knowing, a lot of black clouds on your horizon."

Emma's scalp prickled. "Sloane?" Her stomach squeezed.

"I don't know. What I do know is you're setting yourself up for a fall, Em."

"No, I'm not," she insisted. Tia's "knowing" was rarely wrong, even if it was vague. "I know we're not going anywhere serious. He's leaving and I'll wave him off with a smile when he does. It was time, Tia. And I wanted to sleep with someone I trust."

"You trust him?"

Emma shrugged. "With my body." Her heart and her sister were different matters.

Tia reached out, covered her hand with hers. "I'm just looking out for you. If you're happy, I'm happy. But I don't want you to fall into the trap of thinking he'll stick around and love you like you deserve. Because he won't."

Ouch. "I know." Emma exhaled. "I'm not twenty-one anymore. The rose-colored glasses are gone. My heart isn't involved."

"So, this is a friends with benefits situation?"

Leah eyed her. "From the look on her face, really big benefits."

Emma covered her face before it gave any more secrets away, and she heard Leah laugh.

"Personally, I think you're both nuts. Maybe it's a witch thing…"

Both Tia and Emma hushed her.

"…but as a human, I see a man who's so into you. And you're *so* into him. You're going to be married. Where's the harm in trying for the happily-ever-after?"

"You're so cute sometimes." Tia patted her on the head and then laughed as Leah flipped her off. "Witch society doesn't work like that. We don't marry for love. Well, most of us don't."

"Well, that sucks. And it doesn't mean you couldn't try."

Emma tossed back her remaining champagne. "Maybe for some. But Bastian is always going to leave. And I... I can't let myself depend on him and then watch him go. Again." He'd already sent a tidal wave through her life once; she was taking all the precautions this time so she'd survive the coming storm. "The most I can do is enjoy him while he's here and let him go with a kiss goodbye."

"And you'll be fine with him leaving? Even though you've slept with him."

Emma nodded firmly. "Yes."

Leah held up her hands. "You're nuts, but I concede. It's your life and you know him better." She wriggled her shoulders in anticipation. "So, come on. When did it happen?"

"After the dinner at my mother's." She bit back a smile, remembering. "He told her off and we left early."

Tia's mouth dropped. She sat as if her legs had been cut out from under her. "He told *Clarissa* off? Like, in so many words?"

"He told her she was a bitch."

That sent Tia into a breathless laugh. "Oh, to be a fly on that wall." She shook her head, amazed, and settled back into the cushions. "Good for him."

From Tia that was a gushing review.

Leah waved that off impatiently. "Yes, that's very brave, but how did it happen? Did he grab you? He strikes me as the grabbing kind."

"Actually, it was me."

Two sets of eyes looked at her blankly.

"I grabbed him," Emma said to help them out.

Still blank.

"I told him I wanted him. That he made me feel things. And I said I wanted him to kiss me." She considered. "Then he flung the couch out of the way and grabbed me, so I guess in a way…"

Leah stomped her feet, for all the world acting like a giddy teenage girl. "Oh, this is too good. First, last of the die-hard wallflowers, Emma Bluewater—"

"Hey," Emma objected.

"—seduces a man, and then said man moves a *couch* just so he can grab you?" She sighed wistfully, hand to her heart. "You really need to introduce me to some warlocks."

"No," Emma and Tia said together.

"One day."

"No."

Looking disgruntled, Leah narrowed her eyes, but let it drop. Until a later time, if Emma knew anything about her friend. Probably around the same time Sloane started begging to be introduced to teenage warlocks. Then there'd be two of them.

Goddess.

Leah considered her. "At least tell me, was it everything you thought it would be?"

"Was he gentle?" Tia asked from the other side.

Unbidden, Emma moved her fingers to her lips, grazed them. "Yes," she said softly. "He's…" Memories slid in front of her like slides on a screen, images of them learning each other's bodies. The shower. The chair. The floor. His mouth. On her. "…amazing."

When she glanced up, Tia's features were strained.

"I'm not falling for him." Exasperation made her voice clipped.

Tia opened her mouth, but Tamsin fortunately chose that moment to bustle back in with a gown draped across her arms, Sloane and the shop assistant in tow. If the witch wedding planner wondered at the presence of two humans, she didn't voice it. Another reason to like her.

"I've found the *perfect* dress," she announced. "The ladies are short on champagne, Helen."

Helen, the shop assistant, flicked her hand and Tamsin caught her eye, shook her head with a tilt to Leah. Who pretended not to notice the flute by her foot had filled and emptied again. Sloane hadn't noticed, luckily. She was terrible at playing it cool, as any kid around magic would be.

"I'll go get the bottle." Helen hurried off.

Tamsin jerked her chin. "Up. Come try this on."

"Does she scare you?" Sloane wanted to know as Tamsin headed to a dressing room.

Emma flashed her a grin and followed. Sloane rounded the coffee table, where bridal magazines fanned out, and dropped next to Tia. "Tell me a story," Emma heard her say along with Tia's answering laugh—because all Tia's stories were drawn from actual witch culture, her way of educating Sloane and making Emma despair at the same time.

Tamsin closed the white shuttered doors behind them. "Now, it's not what you indicated you might choose on your questionnaire, but I think it'll look gorgeous. See these small straps that flow into a sweetheart neckline? Very simple, very elegant, and then the skirt—" she reached out, fluffed it out "—a hint of sparkle and volume, but not so much you'd feel all eyes were on you. The back has these pearl buttons, again, classy, understated. And we can make this any color. I know other witches have opted for crimson, violet, emerald…"

"Bastian likes blue," Emma heard herself saying.

Tamsin floundered for a second. Odd. Maybe other brides didn't take their partners into consideration. "Okay. Navy would look lovely against your skin tone. Or if you wanted to go more jewel, we could try a teal."

"Yes…" Emma remembered well his reaction to her teal dress. "Teal."

Tamsin pulled her clipboard out of thin air and made a note. "Just making sure to have teal accents throughout the ceremony," she explained and the clipboard disappeared.

She stroked a hand down the wedding dress and color followed in its wake. "I'll leave you to try it on. If you need help, just yell."

Alone, Emma stared at the most beautiful dress she'd ever seen. It was just a dress, she reasoned. No need to feel partly scared of it. It didn't represent anything more than a nice dress to wear to an event that would tie her to Bastian. That was it. The vows were big; the dress was just another cog in the machine of the day. It didn't matter.

It all sounded good in her head until she had the dress on and looked in the mirror.

"Well?" Leah called out, excitement threading through her voice. "Come out, let us see!"

Emma dragged in a breath. A strange tingling feeling was happening in her fingers. Her heart beat against her ribs in a rhythm usually heard when breaking through a door.

She opened the doors and made her way to the main area. She saw Tamsin first, the wedding planner's face curving into pleased satisfaction.

Sloane was next and she was gaping. "You look like a movie star!" she announced excitedly, before her expression fell half a degree. "I wish I got to wear a dress."

Emma winced, as it was a sore point that her sister couldn't be a bridesmaid. For them both. "Maybe we'll have our own party and get you one to wear," she said.

Her sister beamed. "I like that idea."

"Me, too."

As her friends hadn't said anything, Emma turned to them expectantly. Both looked struck dumb.

"Oh, Emma." Leah got misty as she stood up, hands clasped at her heart. "You're beautiful. Bastian won't be able to believe his luck."

The glow in her chest brightened as she smoothed a hand down the material. "Tia?"

The silent witch stood and strode to her side, very serious. Emma was about to make an awkward joke when she was unceremoniously hauled into a tight hug.

When she drew back, her friend had tears in her eyes. "He had better not hurt you," she choked. "You're gorgeous, Em."

Uncomfortable, Emma rolled her shoulders. "It's just a dress."

Tamsin came forward. "I don't think a veil," she said, studying her. "The back dips low, and with that pearl button detail, you want to show that off. A tiara would draw too much attention, so maybe hair up and with a diamond hair clasp." She nodded to herself, probably making mental notes.

Emma caught sight of her reflection in the mirror. Her chest squeezed.

She looked like a bride.

It was just a dress, she reminded herself, pressing hard against the rapid beat of her heart. It didn't mean anything. Except that at least she'd feel pretty on her wedding day. She couldn't ask for more than that. She wouldn't.

After one last look, she turned away from the mirror.

Emma put the wedding dress and how it had made her feel out of her mind, compartmentalizing as she and Bastian continued their practice for the Exhibition—and as they continued their affair. If you could call sex between an engaged couple an affair.

But she didn't think of them as engaged. Not really. Engaged meant you had chosen each other. Partner, best friend, lover. The soul that would join seamlessly with the fractures in your own broken one. She and Bastian fit well—anyone could see that—but the fit was loose. Eventually, over time, they would slide away from each other.

Knowing that, she could enjoy him as he did her. No expectations. He made her feel free to be sensible or wild, to try new things or to sit in her PJs on the couch watching reruns of *Friends*. It was what had led them to be friends before, she thought as she walked up the flight of stairs to her apartment after a dinner at a sushi restaurant Bastian had dragged her to. That easy nature of his that made her feel safe to be, to try. To live.

"Admit you liked it," he was saying, one hand on her hip as they walked up.

"It was interesting" was as far as she'd go. "I think I'd try the California roll again, but not the wasabi."

He laughed, tiny lines around his eyes. "I don't think I've ever seen your face go so red."

"Remember that time you convinced me to join the Mardi Gras parade?" She twisted her head to grin up at him as she put her hand on the doorknob. "You pushed me into the lineup and suddenly I was wearing a cheerleader outfit. My face was *definitely* redder, then."

His expression turned cautious.

"What?" She turned the doorknob. "I'm not still mad."

Chester ran at them like he was in *Jurassic Park* with a T-Rex chasing him. Behind him, Hallie trotted best she could at a sedate pace. Safe to say, Chester had no clue how to deal with the curious cat that had invaded his home. He wanted to be friends, but always seemed to lose his nerve.

Emma bent to hug him, shooting warm, safe vibes down their bond. "Big baby."

She pushed to her feet. Bastian was still standing in the doorway, the same expression on his face.

She paused. "Bastian? You okay?"

He shook himself, stepped in, shut the door behind. "Fine. You just... We don't talk about the past. It threw me off, I guess."

Emma set her clutch on the breakfast bar. No, the past had been a verboten subject since they'd made up. One of the unspoken conditions that had let them move on. She hadn't even fully realized that they'd both taken a giant step away from it until now.

But their friendship had meant a lot to her, and it was part of their history.

"You were my friend." She leaned back against the counter, considering him. "Before I hated you, you were one of my only friends. It meant a lot. It still does."

"It meant a lot to me, too." He came forward, stuffing his hands into his jeans pockets. "I know it might not have seemed like it, but I always knew I could talk to you or go to you and you'd be happy to just...listen."

The words did something to her, punched her chest so her breath evaporated and her lungs strived for air. It put her off-balance. She didn't like it.

"Then why did you make me do all that crazy stuff?" She aimed a mock-threatening look his way, pushing through, lightening the moment.

His grin flashed. "Because you needed to live a little. And it was always fun watching you." He frowned, suddenly. "You were mad about the Mardi Gras thing? You looked like you were having the time of your life."

"Don't make me say it." She rolled her eyes, stepped out of her heels. "I wanted you to think I was cool, not a loser who didn't want to freeze her ass off in skimpy shorts."

"Ah." Humor danced in his eyes and the sight was enough to stop her breath. Again. She should probably get that checked. "But you wore them so well. Almost as well as the Jasmine costume I got you to wear for the Perritons' Halloween party."

Still sore about that, Emma drilled a finger into his chest. "You told me you would go as Aladdin if I wore that. And then you showed up with your friends as the Three Musketeers." She'd have cheerfully melted back into the wall when she'd seen him. His friends had jeered until he'd cut them off with a look. Ever her hero.

He adopted a wounded expression. "I forgot. And I did dance with you."

She remembered. It had been a highlight of the awful night. "Blue Paige cornered me about wearing half a couple's costume. All her lackeys made fun of me. One dance wasn't enough."

"I'd have beaten them up if I'd known," he declared and pulled her against his chest. He began to sway them, and music drifted into the air from her sound system. Frank Sinatra crooned as Bastian bent his head to murmur in her ear. "I was an idiot. But not enough of one not to have my hands on you in that Jasmine costume."

She smiled into his chest before tipping her head back. "You can't fool me, Bastian Truenote. You kept your hands respectably on my hips and watched Kerry Whitestar the entire time."

"Kerry… Oh. The blonde."

"Lady Godiva."

"Right…" He gave her a sheepish smile and turned them, dipped her. "I was a teenager, Emma. And she wore a long wig and a glamour."

She rolled her eyes, surprisingly hard to do upside down. "I was crushed."

"I was an idiot," he repeated, then lifted her back up, nestling her closer. "If I could go back, my hands would have definitely slid to your bare back…waist…breasts…"

"I was fifteen, you pervert. And my mother almost fainted when she saw that costume."

For a moment the only voice was Frank's. Bastian leaned back, watchful, then said, "She punished you, didn't she?"

Emma's gaze slid to the side, remembering the lock, the key. No food for two days. "I don't want to talk about her." She patted his back. "I want to talk about your wearing an Aladdin outfit for me."

He scoffed, falling into the light mood at her whim. "Never happening."

"Not even for me?" She batted her eyes.

"You could talk me into a lot of things, Bluewater, but not a Disney prince costume."

She smiled, rested her head against his chest as they danced.

His hands skimmed her back, down, resting on the curve where it met her butt. A shiver stole over her as he rubbed his thumbs there through the silky material of the cami top she'd worn for him.

"I was such an idiot, Emma," he murmured into her hair, before he pressed a kiss to her temple. "How did I not see you?"

She wasn't sure what the words meant; she only knew the way they sank into her, twisting and toying with the old feelings she kept hidden away.

Not wanting to dwell on it or ruin the mood, she lifted onto her toes, turned her head and caught his mouth. The kiss was soft but determined, one of her arms lifting up to hook around his neck.

They'd had so many kisses in the last week or so, and yet they never failed to spark inside her, humming beneath her skin. His tongue slid inside her mouth, deepening the kiss. He tasted like the chocolate from dessert.

One of his hands stroked down over her butt and anchored beneath it. He lifted her, likely using telekinesis, she knew, but still the display of strength made her melt. Her arms tightened around his neck as he walked them into her bedroom before falling with her onto the bed. Around them, a dozen candles suddenly blazed to life.

He levered himself up on one elbow and stared into her face. With light fingers, he brushed her hair out of it, caressing her cheek. Dipping his head, he brushed her lips with his, intensifying the kiss as she moved restlessly underneath him.

One of his free hands slipped under her cami top, writing sensation on her skin as he dragged his fingers to her breast. He tweaked her nipple and she jumped, tasted his smile the next instant.

She bit him. Then shoved until he rolled onto his back, displayed like a feast laid out for her. Rumpled and gorgeous and all hers to touch.

For now, she reminded herself, a pang brushed aside as she trailed a fingertip down his sweater.

"I want to taste," she said into the candlelit room.

Moving slowly, Bastian sat up, drew his sweater and shirt over his head. He watched her with the intense focus he had in bed, where she knew only she existed for him. It was heady. Thrilling.

Emma flattened a hand on his hard chest, pushed so he lay flat and then climbed on top. She settled back on his erection, pleasure dropping her head back as it hit a sweet spot. Her back bowed as he lifted, almost by habit, to nudge her again.

"No," she said, breathless. She'd been working on her telekinesis, and had practiced concentrating bursts of it on small areas. It was her turn to play.

With a sly smile, she gestured. Bastian's hands flew back up to the bedpost where they hung as if suspended by handcuffs.

His expression made her smile widen into a grin. Dumb-founded, he looked at his hands, then back at her.

"I want to touch you," he complained. His narrowed gaze drifted to her breasts. Lower. "I need to touch you. Where you're warm. Wet."

Her thighs clenched against his. Still, she shook her head. "My turn first."

Silence crackled like static electricity. "Turnabout's fair play, my dear Emma."

She shivered at the dark, sensual threat. Then she set her hands to his chest.

She'd touched him before, but always he had been in control. Now she gave in to the pleasure of touching him, sliding her hands across his strong muscles, making them jump. She bent and followed the caresses with her mouth, an action that made him swear and his wrists jerk reflexively, especially as she settled more heavily onto him.

"Emma," he gritted out, as she rubbed herself on him, her mouth moving down. "You done playing yet?"

"No." She paused. "Unless…you don't like it?"

Sweat beaded on his temples. "Do you?"

She ducked her head, smiled.

A purr of laughter came from him. "The lady likes to be in control. Why am I not surprised?" His head fell back on a groan. "Fine. I might die, but it's your game."

She liked the sound of that. Minutes flowed into each other, the only sounds erotic and darkly whispered. They were soon both naked. Emma wasn't trying to restrain his wrists anymore, her concentration splintered by the incredible feeling of having him at her mercy.

He was cursing, one hand in her hair as she licked him into her mouth, sliding him in and out, nipples drawn tight in arousal as she listened to him losing his mind.

"Emma," he grated out. "Please...let me...*fuck*...touch you."

It was hard to concentrate. Her body was a mass of pleasure points, even the sheets rubbing against her skin a turn-on. Making her whimper.

"*Emma.*"

She couldn't wait. With a thought she released his magic bonds. "Yes."

She was hauled upward over his body. Pure sensation gripped her as he caught her mouth in a devouring kiss, one hand determinedly finding the center of her body, sliding his fingers in, thumb finding her clitoris with unerring accuracy. She cried into his mouth and he initiated a rhythm that made the dresser drawers rattle. Before she could worry, his mind was there next to hers. Protecting her. Letting her be free. But not going too deep. *Thank the Goddess.*

"I need you inside me," she said into his mouth.

His eyes were black. "Yes."

She sat up, unsure exactly what to do next. They hadn't done it in this position before, her on top. He waited, his patience so clearly stretched to breaking point, but he let her do it her way. Hunger made his grip tight on her hips and she relished it. Holding his gaze, she reached back and took him in her hand. His body jerked, head crushing the pillow on a hiss.

Levering up on her knees, she positioned herself and took him into her body. He felt bigger in this position, harder. Black spots danced in front of her eyes as her back arched, as a shudder pulsed through her. When her hips met his, they both gasped. Sweat gleamed on both of them.

"It's your game," he ground out, fingers digging in. She'd have bruises. "Finish it."

Yes. On a moan, she lifted almost off him, before sinking back down. Sensation streaked up her back. She quaked, a whimper slipping free.

"That's it, baby." His hand tangled in hers, and he brought it to his mouth, kissed the knuckles. "Ride me."

She was lost in pleasure, one hand braced on his tight belly for balance, the other tangled in his as she rode him, listening for his groans, finding the spots that made her cry out. Up and up she went, her fingers tightening on him, her hips slamming back down now.

And then she was there on a strangled cry, back bowing as intense pleasure fried her from the inside out. She felt her body being pushed to the bed, blindly widened her thighs as Bastian thrust back into her on top. He dropped his head, kissed her hard.

She'd thought she was done, but as his hips pounded into her, the dark pleasure began again and she shifted, legs locking around his hips, joining him in the rhythm they'd learned together.

Telekinetic fingers pressed her clitoris in time with his hips, his own hands locked to her waist for better traction. Emma sobbed into his mouth as she was flung off the edge a second time, joined by him a moment later.

Their breaths were as tangled as their bodies, raw, aching, satisfied. Bastian stroked damp hair off her forehead, kissed it. The tender gesture made her heart clench. She told herself to enjoy the moment, not to overthink, not to worry.

And she didn't until an hour later when, after talking idly of the past and sharing memories, he tucked her close and said, "Tell me about having Clarissa as a mother."

CHAPTER 22

$\mathcal{B}$astian watched the tension creep into Emma's muscles. He had one arm flung over her waist and he rubbed it over her skin in comfort. He regretted her reaction, but he had to know. It was eating at him. With everything he now suspected Clarissa of, what more had swum under the surface that he hadn't seen?

He had to know.

She didn't look at him. Maybe she knew what he did—that those brown eyes of hers were an open book. "Why?"

"Because." He bent, brushed a kiss over her bare shoulder. "Because we're going to be married. Because we're partners. Because we're lovers. Because I'm your friend. Because you need to tell someone. Because I want to know. Pick one, they're all true."

She tried to laugh, but it came out more as a sad sound. "You're thinking about my mother right now? I knew you were a pervert, but that's low even for you."

He didn't speak, just waited.

"You know what it was like. You were there."

"I thought I knew. I saw that she was controlling and bossy and always strove for perfection. I know we joked about her being the Wicked Witch. And I know sometimes I didn't see you for days." Not to mention, a lot more she didn't know about, like the Joining clause or the silencing hex. "I didn't think much of it at the time. Now I am."

Her eyelashes drifted down, veiling her thoughts. Her skin was chilled and with a thought, he moved the duvet to cover them.

"Clarissa wanted a perfect daughter," Emma finally said, her voice matter-of-fact. "And she got me. I'm awkwardly shy, I'm too skinny. As the lastborn, I don't have strong magic. I'm not beautiful or charming. I was her greatest failure."

"Emma."

"No." She rolled to look at him. "It's the truth. Until she saw us playing and worked out how to make the engagement happen, I was the disappointment. And when the contract was signed, suddenly I was useful. But she needed to mold me into the perfect Higher family wife." She swallowed and her hand pressed the arm that was around her. "It wasn't easy."

"She's a bitch," he told her, just as matter-of-fact, resentment for both their sakes simmering in the pit of his stomach. "There's no such thing as a perfect Higher family wife."

"She thinks there is. For as far back as I remember, I had to take lessons."

"In what?"

"Everything. Magic. Beauty. Charm. How not to be awkward." A line appeared in between her brows. He kissed it. "When I did anything she didn't approve of, she locked me in my bedroom without food or magic."

The tight feeling of rage in his chest was new. Unsettling. A monster roared inside him as he curled his free hand into a fist so tight the knuckle would be white. He breathed deeply through the red haze, needing to stay calm. To hear all of it.

He didn't ask how her mother had restrained her magic. She'd likely used a magical barrier of some kind, but that wasn't the point of the story, even if it was unbearable to think of your magic being taken. He should know.

"I never knew it was that bad." And, though it wasn't logical, he blamed himself for that blindness. "Didn't your dad get involved? Your brothers...?"

"My dad wasn't a strong man. In any way, really. But when she tried to do worse, he threatened to tell your family. I loved him so much for that," she said in a soft voice. "I'm sure she made him pay, but he never backed down. He'd travel sometimes but only when necessary, so I'd be as protected as possible. Then he died."

Grim, Bastian stroked a thumb across the dip in her waist.

"I wasn't allowed to mourn him. She said he was weak. Kole and I had our own service." A smile touched her lips. "I was terrified she'd find out, but he said he'd handle her. He was still a boy, but I believed him. We always planned everything together."

"Did he get involved after your dad died?"

"As much as he could, but he was away at boarding school. And I'd learned how to play the game by that point." At the lift of his eyebrow, she continued. "I did what she wanted, spoke very little. Didn't laugh, didn't draw attention. The only time she let me go away from her was when I said I was meeting you."

He connected the dots. To her young self, he'd represented freedom. And then he'd left her alone.

Pain, sharp and swift, stabbed him in the gut. His hand tightened on her.

"She thought she'd done as good a job as she could. There

was no getting around the shyness, so that was always a thorn in her side, but I was quiet, demure, nonargumentative. The only time I got into trouble was when you convinced me to sneak off, so even then her punishments were half-hearted."

"Fuck. She *punished* you when we snuck off?" He wanted to throw himself at her feet, beg her forgiveness. It felt like he had broken glass in his throat when he swallowed. "Emma."

"I loved every minute," she said, hitting him with a direct glare. "Don't apologize."

"I wasn't going to," he lied. He hesitated, braced. "Did she ever hit you?"

"Not really. Used her magic sometimes."

Now he felt sick. "I'm going to fucking kill her," he said with a grim note in his voice. "Next time I see her—"

"You'd never hurt a woman," Emma interrupted. "Besides, it's done. I got away."

"I still can't believe she let you go. How the hell did you convince her?"

He felt the fine line of tension hum through her body. "You'd gone and I was the pitied Bluewater again. I…made a case that out of sight was out of mind and she allowed it—on the condition I came back if called. I left as soon as I could."

"I can't even…" He fought to find the right words, gut churning. "I'm just so damn sorry, Emma." He pressed a kiss to her temple, lingering there to speak the truth against her skin. "I never should've left. I—" On cue, the silencing hex wrapped around his throat, squeezed until black spots danced over his eyes.

"You didn't know," she was saying as his vision swam. He gave up, chest rising and falling in frustration. "And we've been over this. Old history." She patted his arm. "I'm going to get some water. You want?"

"You know what I want?" Using a fine tendril of telekinesis, he skimmed a mental finger over her thigh.

"You're gonna kill me," she said with a groan, collapsing back.

"What a way to go, though."

"Oh, yeah. Death by dehydration is super sexy."

"I think you've been living with humans too long." He conjured a bottle of water and pressed the icy surface to her skin, just to hear her squeal. And to see the shadows lift from her eyes.

Now they flashed. "Are you insane?"

"You like it."

"You *are* insane. I get it. Shall we call the nice warlocks with their white coats?"

"Only if you want an audience." He covered her smiling mouth with his, determined to wash the past away.

They had to go to a party in New Orleans the following night. Leah took over the bar so all three could attend, though she bitched and moaned about having to miss out on the opportunity to play dress-up.

"One of these days…" she'd threatened. Sometimes she sounded remarkably like Sloane, Emma reflected with a sigh. Goddess knew how many fights she had like that in her future.

Emma wished she could be the one to stay home. Her mother was keeping a distance, still plainly furious over Bastian's dressing-down, but that alone wasn't enough to allow Emma to relax. Not even Bastian's presence next to her could do that.

Not when they were being bombarded by people who wanted to see their Divining tattoos to see what traits they'd exemplified so far.

By the tenth bemused stare at the "passion" that scrawled

across both her and Bastian's wrists, Emma's face was the exact temperature of the sun. And he wasn't helping, merely smiling lazily in response to the questioning looks they received.

"You need to stop," she hissed, drawing him away from an older woman and her friends who now stood huddled in a tight group, no doubt gossiping about their licentious behavior. He might be a Truenote, but she wasn't yet, and she didn't need the extra gossip.

"Ah, forget the old crones. You look amazing. Want to find a closet to make out in?"

She choked on a laugh. "*No.* We've given them enough gossip."

His dimple winked. "Can they ever have enough gossip?" His thumb idly stroked the satin material of her dress.

Mindful of the criticism she usually received, she hadn't felt up to trying a brightly colored dress, but under duress, she'd agreed to wear navy. It was a simple sheath and bared too much of her shoulders.

She touched a hand to her collarbones again, wishing she'd worn a high collar. Without her usual armor, she felt naked in front of this crowd.

Everyone had turned out, or so it seemed, for the charity gala hosted by the Graysons. A whirl of bright colors, expensive jewels and haughty expressions, all accompanied by a quintet.

Bastian's parents had declined their invitation—Diana not feeling well enough to attend—but had asked if the two of them would come in their stead.

To represent the family? Emma had asked.

To get all the gossip, Bastian had corrected, knowing his mom well.

Otherwise, anyone who was anyone was in attendance, all dying to see the marks on her wrist, how she was preparing for the Exhibition next week, and what kind of wedding they were planning. All sickly sweet in front of Bastian, his old friends crawling out of the woodwork to pal around with him, punch him in the arm, try and get him to leave her and go drinking in the library. To his credit, he looked as uncomfortable around them now as she felt. Another indication they'd both changed.

She longed for a break, but their chance to duck out was sunk by the impending arrival of a witch in peridot green.

"Maybelline, incoming," she murmured to Bastian.

To his credit, he smiled warmly when the shorter woman stopped in front of them. "Maybelline. How are you? You're looking stunning tonight, as always."

"Hush, you charmer." Maybelline brushed the peacock feather in her curled hair, face crinkling in pleasure. "I've come to see the tattoos that everyone is talking about."

"Oh, but—" Emma began, falling into resigned silence as the older woman grabbed her arm and turned her wrist.

Maybelline's feline smile was full of approval. "Just as I suspected. And you, young sir?"

Bastian promptly gave her his wrist for inspection.

She crowed in delight. "My, my. Seems like you two have been getting along just dandy."

Mortified, Emma took a drink of champagne, the bubbles chasing down her raw throat.

Bastian just laughed, hugged Emma to his side. "Always direct, Maybelline. Have some pity on my Emma."

"*Your* Emma, is it?" Shrewd eyes dipped to the possessive hand he curled around her waist. "Well, well. How nice it is to see. I always liked you, dear."

Emma managed to mumble a thank-you.

"But take it from me, don't let Bastian get his way all the time. Men like a bit of spice, that's what my first husband used to tell me. A bit of salt and pepper can keep anything from being bland."

Emma refused to look at Bastian. "I'll remember that."

"Where are you two planning on living after the wedding?" Maybelline glanced between them, the feather in her turban quivering as she was, eager to get the inside knowledge first. "Are you planning on moving to Chicago?"

"We, ah…"

"I'll stick around Chicago for a while," Bastian answered easily. "It's Emma's home and I want her to be happy."

"Well, aren't you two sweeter than a bug in sugar." Maybelline tapped a manicured finger on her chin. Emma couldn't help but notice that her nails shifted color, like winking Christmas tree lights. "And to think you've found your way back to each other after all these years."

A stab of uneasiness slid between Emma's ribs. Maybelline talked like they were a love match on the path to eternal togetherness. And okay, they were lovers and maybe even friends, but that didn't equate to happily ever after.

Fortunately, Bastian stepped in. "Your drink looks empty, Maybelline." He released Emma to gesture to the bar. "I work in Emma's bar now, did I tell you that? Let me show you how to whip up one of their Cauldron cosmos."

"Well, don't mind if I do. I've always liked to see a good-looking warlock shake it." Maybelline winked. "Enjoy the party, dear. And don't worry, I won't keep him from you too long."

Emma made herself smile. As they walked away, Bastian shot her a teasing look over his shoulder. His lips moved and words brushed her ear, as if he'd whispered directly into it.

You owe me.

It made her smile widen. As soon as they disappeared into the crush, Emma drifted backward until she reached the walls.

Her aim was the terrace and with her old stealth, she managed to make her way there without encountering any more curious witches who were dying to know how the Divining was going.

A cool breeze flowed over her naked skin as she propped herself against one of the columns near the doors, melting into the darkness. The stars were bright against the dark sky, and she stared up at them, chewing over Maybelline's words.

And to think you've found your way back to each other after all these years.

Well, in a way, yes, they had. While their friendship had been real all those years ago, she could see now it hadn't had a chance to develop into maturity. Bastian had been so busy trying to be perfect for his parents. And her crush on him had been sweet but innocent. Hard for any man to develop feelings for a woman who said yes-sir-no-sir-conjure-three-bags-full-sir.

The party continued behind her, but the dark quiet surrounding her kept her apart, allowed her mind to drift back. To other parties, other nights. Some full of promise, some… not so.

She didn't like to think of it. Or talk about it. She still wasn't sure how Bastian had convinced her to share about Clarissa. What good would it do now?

He'd looked…sick, she thought, shifting from one heel to another, the shoes pinching. Furious. And quietly guilty. It was disconcerting how much it had touched her.

And tonight, he'd been lightly possessive, a touch to her lower back, a skim of fingers across her bare shoulder, a brush of her hip with his. It could easily go to a girl's head. Bastian Truenote and expensive champagne—both needed to be taken in small doses to stay sensible.

Because she had a very *unsensible* urge to share more. To

trust him, with at least some of her secrets. He'd gone all in, and knowing she was holding back so much had nausea sliding greasily up her throat.

Voices coming from the other side of the wraparound terrace made her shrink back into the shadows, not ready to face another onslaught about the damning "passion" tattoo.

A group of young married witches, the same posse that had never failed to sneer about "poor Emmaline" and her running fiancé, turned the corner.

Shrinking back into the shadows had been an excellent instinct. Now she just had to stay quiet and hope they went back inside before they realized she was out here.

"Did you *see* Bastian Truenote?" Lyssa Garden, blonde, blue-eyed and a strong firestarter, waved her fan in front of her face energetically. "Traveling agreed with him. He looks even better than he did seven years ago."

"I heard he works in graveyards," another of her group, Blue Paige, spoke up. "Digging up corpses."

"Why would he do that?"

Blue shrugged, adjusting the dress she wore so it hung lower on her spectacular cleavage. "I don't care why if it's given him arms like that. My Frederick is nice enough, but he doesn't look as good in a tuxedo."

"Blue, you're terrible." The third out of the four, Macy Roarke, giggled. "Though you're right. Bastian only looks better since he went away. A shame he's wasted on poor Emmaline. We've all said it."

Emma stiffened.

"He doesn't seem to mind." This from the fourth, Betsy Lakeland, a brunette in emerald. She'd used to be one of the main witches who had ridiculed Emma in the first months after Bastian had left. Her words came as a surprise, which only continued when she added, "He barely take his eyes or his hands off her."

Lyssa looked down her nose at Betsy. "That's ridiculous. If he is watching her, it's probably to make sure she doesn't do anything to embarrass him and the Truenote name. He's stuck with her, after all."

"He could have stayed away," Macy said in wonder. "Maybe he likes her. She does have that whole doe-eyed innocent thing."

Blue waved that away. "Please. He came back because he's a good son. He knows his duty. Do you think if he had a choice, he'd have willingly come back and married that puddle?"

Emma's stomach twisted.

Betsy lifted a shoulder, uncertainty on her face. "Well... I don't know. He laughs a lot when he's with her."

"Betsy, you sound like an idiot." Lyssa's words carried the distinct ring of a slap. "Please. Bastian Truenote choosing to marry someone like Emmaline Bluewater is like a dog with a cat. And not even one of those purebred Siamese, but a ratty street cat abandoned in an alley."

"I..."

"Betsy, you really need to shut up." Blue adjusted her hair. "You're not here for your opinions. You're here to make us look good by comparison."

Ouch. Even Emma winced at that.

"Why don't you stay out here, get some fresh air? Maybe that will sort out these idiot ideas of yours," Lyssa suggested. "Macy? Blue?" Without another word, the three walked off into the party.

Betsy fisted her hands by her sides, her eyes swimming as she stared after the rest of her group. Her chest heaved. With a sharp motion, she turned and stumbled for the railing, bracing her hands on it.

Emma argued with herself, but stepped forward. "Nice women."

Betsy stiffened, turned her head with cool precision. "Did I ask for your opinion?"

"No." Seeing that familiar derision, Emma almost turned tail and scurried off. But she'd been on the receiving end of similar insults, felt them eat away at her like acid. So, she hesitated, fingers awkward at her side. "Why do you hang around with them if they talk to you like that?"

"At least they talk to me." Betsy looked back out. "It's better to be inside than outside. You should know."

Emma wavered, then slowly walked to join Betsy at the railing. "My friends wouldn't talk to me like that."

"Well, lucky you." Color rode Betsy's cheeks like flags, visible even on the shadowy terrace. "I live in society. This is what it's like. Maybe you've forgotten."

Maybe she had.

Betsy continued, scorn biting at the air. "It's dog-eat-dog. You have to be the predator to survive."

"How do you think the prey feels?"

Betsy gave a jerky shrug. "This is their world. We're just living in it."

And looking at her old tormentor, a witch who had stood in front of umpteen people and declared that "poor Emmaline" would need stronger bait to catch her man and haul him to shore, Emma felt the strangest feelings of pity. Ask her before and she'd have said Betsy had it all, riding with the celebrated witches. She was attractive and had a decent handle on magic.

Yet she was miserable, trapped in a world Emma no longer had to be part of. Emma might be awkward and not fit the mold of what a witch should be, but she had the freedom of her own business, she had great friends, a perfect sister, and she had a man who treated her with respect and desire.

"You could get out," she said. "Leave."

"Why would I want to do that?" Betsy stared into the night. "I have it all."

Emma didn't comment. Instead she wrapped her arms around herself, the cold air beginning to raise goose pimples on her skin. "If you ever feel like you need to talk about it—"

"Please. I don't need poor Emmaline pitying me." The words were harsh but lacked heat. "I have it all." She repeated it as if speaking the words would make it true.

Emma's lips parted but she couldn't think of anything to say. The best thing for her to do, she realized, was walk away. Her wrist tingled as she went, familiar and alarming. She paused in the doorway to read. *Compassion.*

She huffed an amused breath as she was absorbed back into the throng. In the witch world, that was like being described as "nice." Better "ambitious" or "ruthless" than a washed-out version of being a pushover. Just another example of her being different.

But for perhaps the first time, Emma acknowledged that that was not always a bad thing.

Bastian had managed to lose Maybelline after ten minutes and a strong cosmo, which he feared would come back to haunt him as she'd declared she was switching to her danc-ing shoes and had been on her way to badger the band into playing "something she could shake her hips to."

He'd lost sight of Emma in the crowd; hardly a surprise, but he didn't feel comfortable leaving her alone in this pool of sharks. His Emma could go toe-to-toe with him, but under these lights she seemed to lose her nerve. He'd promised him-self he'd make this night fun for her if it killed him, but he hadn't anticipated Maybelline. Who did? He had to grin as he spotted the waving feather determinedly approach the band.

If he hadn't caught Emma's fleeting projection of kill-me-now embarrassment, he'd have stuck it out and wouldn't have left his fiancée at all. But he had and, after her childhood revelations, he wanted—no, needed—to…make her happy. Stupid, he told himself, head nodding to acquaintances as he continued his search. It wasn't like he could change the past, but he was resolved to affect the future. Give them a chance.

He thought they might have one. Not that he'd told Emma, but he was picking up more and more of her emotions, some good, some bad. He could only assume it was because he instinctively wrapped his mind around hers now when she threatened to lose her control over magic during sex. She'd let him in.

It had led to the beginnings of an idea that had at first seemed ridiculous and now… Hope glinted, just out of sight.

He wanted to mind-meld with her.

Merging minds with another witch was dangerous, and took great skill. Only those very experienced with mind magic could even attempt it. But it was one way to see inside someone's mind.

Or have them see inside yours.

When Emma had told him what she'd gone through, what she'd really lost when he'd left…it was as if she'd reached in and clawed long bloody scores down his insides, leaving salt in her wake.

He needed her to know he hadn't left of his own volition. Not entirely and not because of her. *For* her. For them. And if he'd known then what he knew now, he wasn't sure what he'd have done. The silencing hex forbade him to speak of it, but if he merged minds with Emma, she'd finally know the truth.

And maybe they'd have a shot at a real future.

He'd caught how important Sloane was to her, even the few comments in passing, the odd calls and texts now making sense. And yet, she hadn't told Sloane about the wedding.

Emma was still not thinking of it as a real marriage. A real husband. A real future.

He wanted her to believe in him. In them.

He'd spoken at length to Ethan this morning, both friend and go-to researcher for these types of old casts and spells. Ethan had warned that the meld, if done incorrectly, might go wrong. He could lose pieces of himself, get stuck; there were a number of risks for the caster if he fucked up. Bastian was willing to take that chance.

But that was for later. Tonight he needed his wits about him.

His eyes slid over Tia, who'd abandoned the two of them—with a disdainful look in Bastian's direction—to go talk to her parents. She wasn't with them now, instead standing hipshot, arms crossed. She was talking animatedly to a tall man with a shock of platinum hair and a scowl.

He felt the man's pain. When Tia decided she didn't like you, changing her mind was like trying to reverse the earth's rotational direction. He knew he deserved it—especially in light of what Emma had shared with him about what had happened after he was gone. But the key to getting Emma to see him as more than a fling was to get her friends—her true family—on his side.

The warlock was talking back now, pushing his body closer to hers.

A faint tingle of alarm ran through Bastian and he altered his direction to plant himself by Tia's side.

"Is there…?" he started and then grinned. "Henry Pearl-matter?"

His old friend—possibly the only true one he'd had here, besides Emma—dragged his annoyed gaze from Tia. Startling green eyes lightened and he grinned back. "Bastian. I wondered if I'd see you at one of these before the big day."

"Mom wanted me to show my face since she couldn't make it."

"Is Emmaline with you?"

"Somewhere."

"I haven't spoken to her in years."

"That probably has something to do with you being a jackass," Tia intervened, her tone snappish. Her eyes sparked dangerously. "Falling in with the rest of these dicks when *he* abandoned her."

Henry's jaw tightened. "I didn't—"

"Whatever." Tia folded her arms, radiant in blue that glowed against her skin. "I'm just glad I found out what you were like before I made a huge mistake."

"You ostracized Emma?"

A muscle in Henry's jaw jumped. "No," he bit out at Bastian's question. "I stayed out of it."

"Not man enough to help her." Tia's sneer was purposefully goading.

Henry took one heated step forward and then halted. With one last silent glare for Tia, he nodded at Bastian and turned.

"That's it, walk away. It's what you're good at."

Henry's gait was more like a march as he stormed away from her.

Tia's eyes were still dangerous when she rounded on Bastian.

He held up his hands. "Peace. I thought you might need help."

"He's a coward. I knew he'd walk away." Her expression turned disgusted. "He always does. Like you in that respect." She exhaled, looked past him. "You ditched Emma?"

"You really don't think much of me, do you?"

"Not really."

His jaw set, but with effort, he unclenched. "Fair enough. She told me what it was like, how bad it was. I can't change that, but I'm here."

"For now." Tia leveled a challenging look on him. "What

are you doing, Bastian? Cozying up to her, flattering her, making her feel things—"

He perked up. "She has feelings for me?"

"It's not fair to her."

"Has it occurred to you that I might not leave?"

"You were born to leave. Some men just do."

"I came back."

"For your mom. Not for Emma. And trust me, that is an important distinction for her. For me. I'm her best friend. I picked up the pieces before. I don't want to do it again. So I'm warning you to be careful with her."

"I..." She hammered him. He wasn't sure what to say, how to put it into words. "I care for her, Tia. I don't want to hurt her." That was the last thing he wanted.

She didn't soften. "She wouldn't want me to say this, but she's fragile where you're concerned. You've always been her weak spot." She firmed her jaw, a commando in silk. "Don't mess with her. I'll admit you've been good for her, but that only goes so far. You might be okay with casual sex, but she's never done that."

She made it sound like he was purposely out to break Emma's heart. Like he was using her. "It's not like that between us."

"So, you're saying you're in love with her, that you'll always be here for her? You'll trust her, forgive her, protect her, whatever baggage she comes with? Forever?"

He swallowed, the words slapping him upside the head like a frying pan. "I, ah..."

"Exactly." Tia sighed, lifting a hand to rub her temple. "I don't hate you, Bastian. But until you can say those words, the best thing you can do is not give her expectations you'll stick around. And leave before she starts falling for you any harder."

CHAPTER 23

$\mathscr{T}$ia's warning played on a constant loop in Bastian's head as he took orders the next night in the bar. He'd shrugged it off during the day, spending time with Emma as she baked in the back, sampling the cookies and her mouth whenever the feeling struck him.

She'd looked beat only a couple of hours into his shift, so he'd sent her home to referee poor Chester and Hallie. Maybe even to hang out with Sloane, though she'd tensed when he'd mentioned the teenager's name. He already wished he was home with Emma instead of up to his elbows in booze, but he'd promised to help out and truthfully, he enjoyed chatting it up with the regulars. Even on karaoke night, although if he never heard a drunken woman warble the Pointer Sisters again, he'd be okay with that.

He was chatting easily with Leah and confirming that hell no, he'd never do karaoke, when Kole strolled through the doors.

Leah waved him over, patted her knee. "Best seat in the house?"

"I don't think my fragile male ego could take it," Kole drawled. "What're you doing here? I thought you had a hot date."

She made a face. "He took me to one of those tiny portions, weird sauces kind of places and then got embarrassed when I asked to supersize my meal." She rolled her eyes. "I was *joking*. Unless, of course, they'd agreed, in which case, I'd be a genius."

"I swear, you attract losers." Kole shook his head. "Em told me about the pharmacist who kept picking cat hair off you all night."

Leah caught Bastian's curious glance. "I thought it was sweet at first," she told him, "until he brought out his own personal lint roller."

Bastian laughed. He slid his gaze between the two. "You two never dated?"

"My stud muffin here is firmly kept on the bench, on account of the fact he's the brother I never had."

"Goddess help me," Kole muttered. "Stud muffin? Why not whack off my balls and wear them as earrings?"

"Because I don't like small earrings."

Kole gave her a narrow-eyed stare, switching to Bastian as he choked with laughter. "I'd murder her before I dated her."

Leah grinned and jumped up. "You're so easy. You here for the Cubs tickets?"

"You sure you don't want them?"

"Of course I do, but Sonny can't find anyone to work the shelter that night so..." She shrugged. "I'll go grab them, not that you couldn't just snap your fingers and—" Her gaze shot to Bastian and she stuttered to a stop. "Ah, get me to go grab them," she finished lamely. Then scurried off.

"So." Kole leaned on the bar. "I heard you were all over my sister last night."

Bastian considered him. "So. Leah knows witches exist."

Kole didn't move. Didn't breathe. "What?"

Bastian just lifted his eyebrows.

"Damn it." Kole planted his hands. His eyes turned stormy and sparks of magic began to dance. "If you tell anyone—"

"I wouldn't. I'm not going to." He'd suspected for a while. Little slips, the odd comment, pieces of memory from the night Tia slipped him the truth potion. But the fact that Emma had broken the rules had given him a lot to think about. "She's Emma's family. And I wouldn't hurt Emma. Or Leah," he added with a small smile.

"I won't even ask how you guessed." Kole grimaced as the magic sparks subsided. "Jane Bond, none of them are. It's why they try and keep witches out of this place. Leah has the worst poker face."

"When did you find out?"

"A couple of years ago. I mostly try and pretend I don't know. I'd advise you do the same."

"Why?"

Kole's smile was rueful. "Our Leah is...curious."

Their Leah bounced back in with the tickets and a pout. "Go, enjoy, I hate you."

"I got time for a beer before I clear off." Kole reached out, tweaked her nose. "You old enough to serve me?"

"You young enough not to let it go to your head?" So saying, she busied herself pouring him a beer and then leaned her hip on the counter. "So, what were you guys whispering about?"

"Men don't whisper," Kole said with lofty emphasis. "They discreetly discuss."

Bastian had to grin. He could see how Kole and Emma were related. "You," he told her, against advice. "And the fact you know."

"I know." Blank, she looked at Kole's face, then Bastian's. "I know?"

"You do."

"I know. I know…oh." Her face froze. "Uh. No, I don't."

"You don't what?"

"Know. I don't know anything." She tried a laugh, then slumped. "Shit. Emma and Tia will kill me. Or Tia will. Emma will just stand there looking disappointed and terrified, or if I'm lucky I'll get the sarcastic comment to end all comments."

"I won't tell them."

Kole gave him a slitted stare. "You'll lie to my sister?"

"Shut up, Kole." Leah studied Bastian, her earlier concern melting under interest. "You won't?"

"It'd stress Emma out if she knew I knew you know." He frowned. "Or something like that. Anyway, she's stressed enough. I'll let her know after the Exhibition and the, ah, wedding."

Kole grunted. "Acceptable answer. What do you think, Leah?"

"I like it. I like him for her."

"Hmm." Kole considered. "Not too pretty?"

"No such thing, but don't feel sad because you're not." Leah patted his cheek. "You've got such a good personality."

Kole, who'd never had trouble with women, just grinned. "And he went after my mom—which I have to tell you was a beautiful thing," he said to Bastian, who sat there feeling like he was a steak on a shelf they were thinking of picking.

"I *so* want to meet her."

"Not going to happen."

"Seconded," Bastian added, with a shudder at the idea.

Huffing, Leah pointedly ignored them. "Emma laughs with

him." She picked up the threads of the conversation. "And apparently the sex is *hawt*."

Kole blanched. "Ah, man. Leah. I don't want to know that."

"Well, it's a factor."

"Shit." Kole rubbed the back of his neck. Bastian felt like rubbing his, as awkward as Emma's big brother. "There is the whole leaving thing."

Okay, that was enough. "Sorry to interrupt." Bastian cut a gaze between them. "What in the hell are you two doing?"

"We're discussing whether you get our vote with Emma." Leah lifted a hand, shushed him. "I vote yes, provided he promise not to hurt her."

"Do I get to be part of this conversation?"

Kole ignored Bastian's irritated question. "The fact is that he abandoned her before and he's planning on leaving again at some point. Emma told me about his archaeology work." Bastian found himself the subject of stern blue eyes. "Right? You're into that stuff."

"Yeah. But I'm not planning on going anywhere. Not yet. And when I do, I'll talk to Emma."

Leah and Kole exchanged a look. Finally Kole turned to him. "Promise not to hurt her."

Annoyance washed over him. "I'm getting tired of people assuming I'm going to hurt her. What about if she hurts me?"

Kole looked interested. "Could she?"

Bastian thought of Emma and his heart constricted.

"O-*kay*." Kole drummed his hands on the counter. "So, I came here tonight to tell you to back off. She's been hurt by you before and I don't want to watch it happen again."

Bastian opened his mouth, indignant.

Kole lifted a hand and a telekinetic force slammed Bastian's mouth shut.

"Fair's fair," his soon-to-be brother-in-law said mildly. "I *was* going to tell you that. But the gooey look on your face just now has me questioning things. So, here's the deal: I want to like you. Leah likes you."

Leah gave him a thumbs-up and sauntered over to a beckoning customer.

"She's a good judge of character. For a human. My sister seems lighter this visit. Could be age, could be you. But she's happier. I want her to be happy. You know how to work hard—for a Higher son, anyway—you don't brag about your magic, you can shoot the shit. And you can stand up to my mother. That's important. Emma can trust you to be there for her. I just don't know if that's temporary." Kole exhaled. "So, I guess we'll see." He paused and, very carefully, said, "She say anything to you about Sloane?"

"The human? Yeah, I met her. Why?"

Kole examined him and a muscle popped in his jaw. "Nothing, I guess. Just… Emma loves that kid, she's important to her."

Bastian had no idea what this was about, but he did know Emma loved Kole. As with Tia, it would be good to have Kole on his side.

"Okay," he said slowly.

"Have you had the contract discussion?"

He straightened, on high alert. "What about the contracts? What do you know?"

Kole settled back, head tilted. "What do *you* know?"

"Don't play around," Bastian all but growled. His hands itched to haul Kole to him. "Do you know…anything?"

"What would I know about engagement contracts?" Kole eyed him without expression. "I just wondered if there was a way to get a better deal for Emma. My dad wrote it, yeah, but if I know my mother, she had her claws in it."

Oh, she had. "Trust me," Bastian muttered. "Emma's getting a good deal." Access to his magic, for one.

"Always worth taking another look." Kole shrugged. "So, minus the point for the weird factor, I still say a temporary yes."

"I kind of like a weird factor" was Leah's comment as she returned.

"That's why you pick losers."

Letting the tension from the reminder go—what was the point in holding on?—Bastian cocked his head at Kole. "What would it take to get a firm yes?"

"You ever get to go full-out Indiana Jones in hidden tombs?"

"Sometimes."

Kole's grin flashed. "We'll talk."

Leah sniggered. "Like you'd do well in a tomb. Emma told me how you used to fling spells at spiders to make them run away from you."

Kole scoffed. "She exaggerates. And I was eight."

"Uh-huh." Leah turned to Bastian. "When did you find out I knew?" she asked, as if the interim conversation hadn't happened.

He tried to keep up. "I've known for a while."

"Huh. You'll have to let me know my tells in case any others come snooping. Kole refuses to discuss it." She pouted his way.

He sent her a stony look in return.

"Ah, sure," Bastian said, drawing back her attention. "Why not."

"Great. And while we're at it, maybe you could talk to me about mind magic? Emma says that's your specialty. Oh! And telekinesis. And potions, we must discuss potions because mine keep blowing up on me."

Bastian blinked.

Kole laughed as he pushed to his feet. "Good luck, man."

Bastian caught up with him outside. "Hey. I just want you to know." He thrust his hands into his pockets to defend against the night's chill as Kole eyed him. "I'm not messing around with her. It's not like that." He huffed a disquieted laugh. "I can't tell you what it is, but I care about her."

Kole's breath came out in a white plume. "Okay."

"It's not just a fling." Bastian didn't know what had compelled him outside. What drove him to continue. "She told me about your mother. How she used to lock her up."

True surprise made Kole's posture change, harden. He turned grim. "Our mother is a stone-cold bitch, as you called it," he said. "I did as much as I could, but I was away at school a lot. Not that that's an excuse." The last was added with a healthy dollop of self-loathing.

"She said that. Emma. She said you tried."

"For what good it did. We were always a team, but that didn't mean we always handled things well." Kole scowled at the sidewalk, ignoring the people swarming around them like fish in the sea. "Clarissa has this idea in her head of what Emma should be to live up to the Bluewater name. Some name," he snorted. "My dad was the least of a Higher family. We're barely respectable in society. Emma is Clarissa's way in."

"I know."

"She was harder on her than any of us. Any perceived fault she took out on her. When you left, Clarissa took it out on her."

Bastian flinched. "I know."

"I'm not trying to make you feel bad. I'm just…" He trailed off, rocked on his heels. Light from the bar caught his thoughtful expression. "She told you, huh?"

"Yeah." Bastian jingled change in his pocket. "She still thinks I'll leave."

Kole paused for a couple of seconds. "Emma grew up thinking she was flawed. And when you left rather than marrying her, that only emphasized it. She's had to be by herself—fend for herself—a long time. She's never felt wanted."

A gaping hole opened in Bastian's chest. "I want her." The words were raw and honest.

They were lost on Emma's brother. "If you really do, you'll have to find some way of proving that to her or she'll always think you have one eye on the door." And just when things had reached a new level of intensity, he added, "Ask her about the ring."

"The ring?"

Kole's smile was faint. "She'll kill me, but it's important. When she gives you the ring. Ask her."

CHAPTER 24

The days leading up to the Exhibition could be described as some of the happiest of Emma's life.

Days filled with laughter, smart-ass remarks, teasing and wedding prep; nights spun away as she and Bastian hung out at the bar, shot pool, judged the karaoke singers and challenged each other at drinking games. Tia had woken up one morning with blue-and-silver-striped hair—a shot of karma, Bastian had said with an easy smile. Tia had just warned him to watch his back for her revenge.

And of course, nights were also for just the two of them, when they more than made up for the time lost, each addicted to the other. And he was always surprising her by being quippy one moment and then hauling her in to hold her. Just hold her, with one strong hand cupping her neck. It was those moments that made her unease deepen, but also what fed the endless hunger to be near him.

Of course, the days were not all light. Emma, frazzled from stress, had failed five times in a row to perform their trick as Bastian had envisioned. Close to bursting, she'd announced that she was quitting, changing her name and fleeing the country. Since she'd never yet left the country, the threat was fairly empty.

Still, Bastian had taken her seriously, badgered her into going for a drive with him. And then coerced her into using her magic to create the illusion of a siren so they could speed their way through downtown. Laughter had shoved the panic aside as they'd flown through the city, Emma's knuckles white on the steering wheel, feeling free and reckless and in definite lust for the casually rumpled man laughing beside her.

Just in lust, she assured herself. Who wouldn't be?

It wasn't just the siren illusion. He nudged her to break the rules wherever, reminding her of when they were young and he'd cajole her into pulling pranks that she'd never got away with. One rude woman in Starbucks had her jeans split when she bent forward; a spoiled child had to run after his floating ice cream cone. When Emma had told Sloane that one, her sister had almost cried with laughter. But her pleas to hang around with them had led to reminders that Bastian didn't know—and couldn't know—about Sloane. At least, there was no point in telling him. He'd be moving on soon.

She'd catch him looking at her sometimes with an odd expression, but he always just smiled when she demanded to know what was up, caught her hand, kissed the knuckles and moved them on. She sometimes worried he was reading her mind, but knew he'd never purposefully broach her privacy. Not to mention if he really did read her mind, well, she'd know. By the explosion that met her at the door.

No, her secrets were safe. Some she had to keep, but some…

Kole had lived up to his word and passed across the barrier ring days ago. She'd hidden it in her jewelry box, barely able to look at it, let alone think about how to give it to Bastian. What she'd say.

How could she lie to him again? She'd lied so much already, and with each sunset and sunrise they saw together, the need to crack open the door, to let him in a little, mounted. She had to give him the ring. She just didn't know if she should cross the line she'd drawn and admit why she was giving it to him, what it had been created to shield him from. The agony of indecision left her spinning.

She'd heard him on the phone talking to his friend Ethan, the one who lived near the Nile. She'd been folding laundry in her bedroom, but had paused when she'd heard the interest in his voice.

"A new find?... Oh, that soon? Yeah, I'm not sure... Yeah, right. I'll see what I can do."

She knew what that meant. He was already being asked to join a crew, to go on a dig. That reminder had been a harsh slap, but one she'd needed. He might say he was sticking around for now, but it was just for now. Eventually he and Hallie would go back to his old life.

But the ring...the more she thought about it, the more her desire to admit the truth grew. He'd already seen for himself what a poisonous family she came from, excepting Kole. No illusions there to maintain. And she really liked that if she did this, told him this truth, it could be a gesture that showed how much she cared for him—as one did for a friend. For someone who was important in that way. He'd opened up to her; this could be her way to bridge the gap. She couldn't tell him about Sloane, not without jeopardizing her sister, but she could tell him about the leeching power of the Joining clause.

If only she could find the right time. Amazing how there never seemed to be one.

Like a clock counting off minutes, the days passed, and then it was the night of the Exhibition.

Bile churned in her stomach as she stared at her reflection.

Muttering, she tried on outfit after outfit, spinning in one circle after another until dizziness made her flop backward onto the bed.

Bastian came in, saw her. "Don't mind if I do."

Before she knew what was happening, he'd crawled on top of her. He kissed her, his heavy weight helping to ground her. "Hi."

"I can't do this."

"Yes, you can."

"No, I actually can't."

"Yes, you can."

"They'll laugh at me."

"Then I'll kill them. Wonder what the tattoo for that will be."

She hadn't thought a smile was possible but one nudged at her lips. "What if I make a mistake?"

"Then you make a mistake. I'm not going to leap to my feet and scream *stop the wedding*. Mainly because I don't leap. Not becoming of a Truenote."

Yeah, and because he had no choice but to marry her, she thought, uneasy. She stared into his eyes. "You seem calm."

"I do, don't I. Must be because I know you can do it." He kissed her nose, then levered himself up. "I need to move before we're late."

"Why would we— Oh." She huffed a laugh and sat up, raising her knees and hugging them as she watched him check his reflection in the mirror.

Hallie came jumping in with her three-legged version of a skip, straight to him. She purred as he scooped her up.

"She's settled well," Emma commented. She slid off the bed and knocked her feet together. A pair of black heels with a thin ankle strap appeared on them. She thought they'd suit the black-and-white fifties-style dress she'd decided on. And they complemented Bastian's dark suit well. They almost looked like a couple.

Of friends. A couple of friends. She pressed a soothing hand to her belly and ordered the butterflies to chill.

"Hasn't she?" Bastian scratched Hallie under the chin, softening as she leaned into him. "Better than I expected. She'll make a good site cat."

"Site cat?"

"Yeah, on digs and stuff. I don't think anything fazes her. Unlike Chester, the big baby."

His teasing went over her head. *On digs.* Her heart squeezed. Well, she'd expected it, hadn't she?

Willing herself not to react, Emma kept it light. "Don't even start. My poor baby."

On his laugh, she crossed to her jewelry box on the dressing table. She stared blindly at the contents. It was good, she told herself fiercely, banishing the pressure behind her eyes. A good reminder. The masculine ring, a simple platinum band, mocked her as she took a breath.

Now. It had to be now. She picked it up. "Good thing Chester isn't your familiar. He'd be a terrible site dog."

"Oh, I don't know." Bastian came over, pressed a kiss to her bare shoulder. "He's in love with everyone. After a couple of days, I think he'd be just fine." He worked his way to her throat, then spied the ring. "What've you got there?"

Panic was an ice ball in her belly, hard and hurting. She forced herself not to shake as she turned and held it out. "It's for you."

He took it from her. "A ring." He turned it in the light, confusion chased by a jolt of something else. His gaze shifted, pinned. "You got me a ring?"

"Yes." She straightened her shoulders, fighting the very real urge to run. To pretend. Emmaline might have cowered but Emma would do this. "I need to tell you something."

Everything about him stiffened in degrees until his face was like granite. He closed his hand around the ring.

She didn't want to look at him, so forced herself to. "I wasn't sure how to tell you this, not when my family has already done so much to you."

A hunted expression claimed his face. Wary. Expectant. "Yeah?"

"There's a clause in the contract that—that means when we say I do, I could call on your magic." He made an odd sort of choking noise and she hurried on before he could speak. "The minute I found out, I told Kole. That ring—he called on a warlock to create it. It'll block the curse. As long as you never take it off, nobody can call on your magic. So...yeah. That's...that's the deal with the ring. I'm sorry that I didn't tell you before. I'm really sorry for it all. I was just...scared of what you'd think."

She waited, her shoulders tight, her stomach drawn in as though she'd pulled a pin on a magic grenade and was braced for the fallout. He didn't speak for twenty full heartbeats. She knew because she counted them.

And then he smiled. It pierced her heart how bold and beautiful it was, how it affected everything in his face. His eyes danced bright blue.

"Okay," she managed, speaking around the heart that was still lodged in her throat. "Not the reaction I was expecting."

"Thank you." He swept in and pressed a long hard kiss to her mouth. She sank into it, arms lifting to his shoulders, pure freeing relief drowning out the guilt for once. Telling him had been the right thing to do.

After a drawn-out moment, he broke off and nudged a piece of her hair out of her eyes. "Thank you for telling me everything." She must have spasmed or something because he studied her face. "That *is* everything?"

Her throat dried out in the waiting silence. His question howled through her mind, rattling the doors to the secrets she still held.

She couldn't tell him about Sloane. She just couldn't. He was leaving and not telling him, shielding him in one sense from the secret, was for the best. For him, for her, for Sloane. For everyone.

She gave him one short, firm nod.

He cupped her cheek. "Right." He let out a breath. "Before we go, I want to do something for you. For us."

"I don't think we have time for sex."

"I like where you're going with that. Maybe later. But this is a bit more…intimate."

More intimate. She nudged him away, curious. "What?"

He took her hand with the one not holding the ring and held it, looking intently into her face. So much so she felt awkward under the probing stare. "You let me in just now. I want to do the same." He squeezed her hand. "I know you still believe I left because I didn't want to marry you."

Oh, Goddess. She managed a weak smile. "Water under the bridge, Bastian. Come on, we're gonna be late."

He held firm. "There are things I want to tell you, Emma. Things I'm longing to tell you. But I can't."

"Okay then." She tugged her hand. "Why don't we—?"

"Emma," he half scolded, half laughed, but she heard the nerves that rode under the two syllables. "Would you just stop for a sec? Just listen." He took a breath. "I can't tell you them because…" He froze as if he'd slammed into a wall. Annoyance made the navy of his eyes shimmer. "Well, you'll see in a minute."

"See what?"

"The truth. Please." His gaze devoured her, pleading. "Trust me."

"Bastian…"

"Emma." He lifted her hand, kissed it. "*Trust me.*"

Her heart threw itself against her ribs in rapid movements. It was crazy to consider, stupid when they had somewhere to be, except… "Okay," she said before she could think better of it. "I trust you."

"This will make it right." As nerves trickled into her belly, he pressed his forehead to hers and whispered, "See into my mind. *Leviatus aperta.*"

Emma had no idea what he was doing as the spell words dropped from his mouth but all of a sudden she was flooded with thoughts and feelings that literally slammed her back against the wall. When she opened her eyes with no idea when she'd closed them, she saw Bastian across from her, but they were no longer in her bedroom.

They were in one of the society gardens in New Orleans, she realized, disoriented. Party music played in the background and Bastian was slouched against a wall, except he looked younger. He still had the touch of innocence age robbed you of, his face open and vulnerable to anyone looking. He looked troubled.

What the hell…?

She began to ask the question. And heard the voices.

"…don't know what to do," a female voice hissed, the tone so low it was hard to tell who it was.

Emma watched as young Bastian's head came up, not threatened but annoyed his solitude had been invaded.

She was beginning to understand what was happening. Bastian had allowed her into his mind to witness whatever it was he thought she should see. But why not just tell her? This magic came with risks for the one casting it. Worry for him clashed with fascination as she edged closer.

A male voice rumbled, but she couldn't make out the words.

"I'm telling you, it's in there," the female insisted. "When Sebastian Truenote and Emmaline Bluewater wed under the full moon, there will be a Joining and the Truenote magic shall flow into the Bluewater veins."

There was a pop in Emma's ears and her stomach dropped away. Ice sheathed her completely as her head swung to the inner garden where the conversation was taking place. The figures were hidden but Bastian had heard what mattered.

He looked as sick as she felt. Stunned. His hands had fallen to his sides, both of them faintly shaking. Eyes glassy, he took a step back, as if in denial.

The voices were muttering, snatches of conversation but no real meaning. Either Bastian hadn't heard them or they hadn't been loud enough, but either way, he hadn't heard what followed it.

He took another step back and stumbled on a decorative display of rocks. His feet hit the pebbles loud enough to shatter the intimate moment.

The voices cut off.

As if regaining his senses, young Bastian suddenly threw himself into motion, charging forward as if to confront them. Emma trailed him, sickness sour in her mouth as she knew what he'd find. Nobody.

She was tugged along behind him as if on a string as he whirled and ran to the house, searching for someone. His mom, she realized, when they came across a glowing Diana, a heartbreaking memory compared to her current state.

Bastian grabbed her arms. "Mom, I'm—In the garden, I just heard—" His chest jerked with ragged breaths and his expression could only be called wild.

Diana put her arms around her son. "Shh. Calm yourself. We'll go somewhere private."

"No." Bastian pulled back. "I just heard…" He cut off abruptly, one hand flying to his throat. He opened his mouth, wheezed, shut it again with a look of horror.

"Silencing hex," Emma whispered, horror sinking into her bones. "Goddess."

Everything was coming together in excruciating detail.

And suddenly she was ripped out of the memory, a tornado of sensation hitting her as she once again felt the slight give of the carpet beneath her feet, the sturdiness of the wall at her back. The cold, though, the cold stayed with her. She wondered if she'd ever be warm again.

She summoned her courage and lifted her head to see Bastian staring at her, denial alternating with horror on his face.

"I didn't mean to," he said hoarsely. "But the spell…it drove me into your mind."

The chill of the past slid one finger down Emma's nape.

He shook his head, one hand passing over his mouth. "I saw the night again…but I saw it from your side. Because you were there." He dropped onto the bed as if his knees would no longer support him. But his eyes, his eyes locked on her face. Almost pleading with her to tell him he was wrong. "It was you. You cast the silencing hex."

Emma squeezed her eyes briefly shut before opening them to face the consequences of what she had wrought. "Yes."

CHAPTER 25

Too many thoughts and feelings assaulted Bastian, like he was being stoned to death with them. Each hit with different pressure, each felt like a burn that wouldn't end.

Emma stood braced against the wall, a lovely slip of a woman he'd let down his final wall for because he'd thought she'd finally told him everything. Bitterness washed up his throat. What an ass he was.

"Why?" he managed, the word more of a raw sound.

She flinched but continued to face him. So brave, he'd once thought. Soft petals disguising steel. Now he marveled at the idea she had anything soft about her at all. She deserved an Oscar for the way she'd played him all these years. The way she'd played him moments ago, giving him just enough without revealing the whole truth.

"Your mother would be proud," he said, sending the darts of poison her way and delighting when she cringed. "Playing me so well."

"I didn't play you." Her voice was like a sigh, utterly quiet. As if she was the victim.

He wasn't having it. "You did this to me. You know, my parents still think of me as selfish because of you. Poor Emmaline," he sneered, ignoring the way his gut twisted as she whitened. "You have society fooled as well."

"Can I explain?"

"You mean lie to me some more?"

"I didn't lie."

"You sure as hell didn't tell the truth." He exploded up and gripped his head, almost wishing he'd never done the mindmeld. Wishing he could go back to ten minutes ago, when he'd been happy. Looking forward.

He heard a plaintive meow and looked down to see Hallie had bravely entered the fray. Their bond was new, but he must be pumping distress out like a generator. He picked her up and cradled her, allowing the small vibration of her purr to keep him centered.

"Fine," he said, sitting again, curling his lip at the way Emma placed one hand on Chester's head. As if she needed comfort. "Spin me a story."

She bit her lip and looked away, but the next second brought her gaze back. It was haunted and he didn't like what it did to him, seeing her like that. He refused to feel sorry for her.

"It all…" She took a breath. "It all started when our dad died. You remember my mother refused to mourn or let us grieve. Well, Kole and I decided to make a project, a tribute of sorts, of going through his papers, finding his hidey-holes where he kept things from Mother. We all had them, but my dad was the best—next to Kole, who has a talent for finding lost things." Bastian remained silent as one of her hands lifted to toy with her necklace. "About a month before…before," she finished with a flicker of guilt, "we found a letter to Dad which he'd concealed with a lockpicking spell—only obvious if you know what to look for. I did. The letter was from a woman. A human. She was writing to tell Dad that her sister had died in childbirth." She met Bastian's gaze and took one long breath. "The baby was his daughter."

The truth clicked into place. "Sloane."

She nodded slowly. "Our half sister."

"A human." He blinked, trying to wrap his mind around that. There hadn't been a half human, half witch that he knew of in decades. "Does she know?"

"Yes. Her aunt told her who her dad was, and he used to write her letters, contact her through the mirror. Secretly, of course, because of my mother."

Yes, he could only imagine what Clarissa would do if she learned of a child from an affair with a human. He didn't know what Clarissa would find more offensive—the half-human child or the implication that Emma's dad had found Clarissa so lacking he'd sought a human for comfort. He released a long breath. "Goddess."

"When we discovered it, we knew we had to keep it from our mother. We weren't sure what she'd do—maybe nothing, but…" She shrugged. "Without Dad, we felt Sloane was vulnerable. Not only to outside forces but inner ones. What if she came into magic? She wouldn't know what to do. Kole could get messages to her, but it wasn't a long-term solution. I was constantly monitored. But I wouldn't be…" She hesitated. "After we married."

"Which was why you didn't raise a fuss when Clarissa pushed for a quick wedding," he said slowly.

"I'd hoped you wouldn't mind having a half-human sister-in-law, but I didn't want to risk you refusing to marry me if you found out. A quick wedding was the answer. Once out of Clarissa's house, I could help Sloane more. And then…"

Bastian felt his eye tic. "You found out about the Joining—if you didn't already know."

"I didn't, I swear," she said in a rush, one hand lifting as if in plea. "I was reading over the contract, trying to see if I could protect Sloane once I was married, and I found the clause that stipulated that a Bluewater could Join with Truenote magic."

"It's something I've never understood," he said tightly. "If you weren't behind that clause, why bother? Did Clarissa think she could intimidate you after we married and use my power that way?"

Emma moistened her lips. "Like most witches, Clarissa keeps back some of her gifts from public view. Years ago, she learned the art of leeching magic."

His head came up, distaste plain. Hallie yowled in protest as he jostled her, and he immediately cradled her again. "That's disgusting. She drains people of magic?"

Emma looked at Chester as he nudged his bulk onto her foot. "It's more like she can take a sip. I don't know what would happen if the cup ran dry."

"She's done this to you."

She jerked a shoulder, unwilling to say the words.

He battled with too many emotions, his head ringing with revelations and so much that he didn't understand.

"So she wanted to access Truenote magic through your marriage bond to me," he gritted out. "If you didn't know, why the…" His throat closed up and he snarled. "Why do what you did?"

"That night in the gardens, I was freaking out. Not only because of what the Joining meant for you, but because of what it could mean for our plan."

He looked at her blankly.

"Our plan to help Sloane," she elaborated. "Me and Kole. If you found out about the Joining clause, you might stop the wedding. We needed—I needed to help her."

"And you didn't think to just tell me?" His voice lifted in volume.

"I was scared you wouldn't go through with it," she threw

back, adding a little more volume herself. "If you'd learned about it, you'd have stopped it. You wouldn't have wanted your family's magic joined to mine."

"You made sure I didn't get a say in it," he muttered and then forced a nod. "Fine, I would've stopped it. Because it's our fucking magic, Emma."

"And she's our fucking sister, Bastian." The fast words slapped him. She looked at him, a plea spread across her face. "She came before everyone. So when I heard someone listening to our conversation, I panicked. I thought someone had heard about Sloane. We portalled out and I cast a silencing hex. I didn't know it was you, I swear. I… I don't know what I'd have done if I knew. We were young. I didn't know what I was doing. I reacted. I wanted to keep her safe."

He didn't know what to think. He was bursting with so much anger that it sparked everything it touched, like wildfire. She'd betrayed him worse than he'd ever dreamed and it was clear she didn't even really regret it.

"When you left," she continued as if he wasn't about to explode, "it seemed like we'd done it for nothing. But it became clear there was an opportunity here I could use to actually get away, out of New Orleans fully. So I did. I worked on my mother until she let me go to be rid of me, I came to Chicago and I took Sloane on."

Everything made so much more sense—why Emma had rebelled to the extent she had, why she'd looked desperate to get married those last few weeks. Why he'd never felt like she'd told him everything, let him in.

"Why is it still active if you don't need me anymore?" he ground out.

She looked shamefaced at that. "I didn't know who it was in the garden. Or what they'd heard since we'd mentioned Sloane. I didn't realize you'd barely heard anything. I'll undo it."

"Gracious of you."

She flinched. "I'm sorry."

He looked at her with a bone-deep tiredness. His rage burned out, leaving blackened ash of what had once been alive. "Are you, though?"

She looked away.

He put Hallie on the floor, watched as she stubbornly refused to leave his side. Loyalty. Bitterness soaked into him. "You didn't even think it might be me when I ran?"

"You…you'd put in your note to Diana that you couldn't marry me. Specifically." She swallowed. "It hit my vulnerabilities and I didn't think past that." She looked up. "Why didn't you do the mind-meld thing with your parents?"

"It's not something people do every day," he said somewhat caustically. "Some casters never wake up or the other person interrupts something in their mind and the caster wakes different. Not to mention it expends a great deal of power. Don't worry though—" and this time he was definitely caustic "—I'll still perform well at the Exhibition for you."

She stroked Chester for a few seconds. "Does it help at all that we found a way around the Joining?"

"You mean when you lied to me just now and told me there were no more secrets?" Abruptly he felt wrung out. "You weren't going to tell me." He looked at her. "Still? After everything."

She pressed her lips together. "Bastian…you're leaving anyway."

He found he did have energy for anger after all. "I'm leaving, therefore I can't be trusted with the truth?"

"No, it's not that. It's… I just… What's the point in baring our souls? It's not like we're…you know…"

"Getting married?" he forced out. "Spending our lives together?" *Falling in love?*

"But we're not," she pointed out quietly and his heart

stopped. "We're spending our lives apart, even if we're married. What was the point in telling you everything?"

"Maybe because I fucking deserved it." His voice shot across the room like a slap. "You don't get to decide what I should know."

"You're right. It's just… I needed to keep Sloane safe. All the lies, all the secrets, they all unravel and lead back to her. I had to put her first."

"You thought I would reveal her to Clarissa? You know what, Emma." He shook his head in disgust, climbing to his feet. "Screw you."

"No." She shot forward, dislodging Chester. "No, I didn't. I don't. Not really. But it's just safer for her with less people knowing. And you're leaving. Why bring you in on this when you could be unaware and better for it?"

Like he believed she'd done this for his benefit. "You don't trust me." He barked a laugh that was empty of anything. "My Goddess. You forced me to run in the first place and yet you don't trust *me*."

"I told you, I know you wouldn't tell Clarissa…"

"It's not even about that, though, is it?" he demanded. "You don't *want* to trust me. You don't want to let me in."

She'd lost all color and her eyes were shiny, but she jutted up her chin. "You're leaving," she repeated.

His jaw hardened and so did everything else inside him. Goddess, he hurt everywhere and not even Hallie's soft purrs helped. He lifted her to the bed, giving her a stroke with a hand he refused to acknowledge was trembling. "We have to go." He didn't look at Emma as he conjured a portal. "Can't be late for our own Exhibition."

CHAPTER 26

The Exhibition was a roaring success. Just as they'd practiced, Emma and Bastian had conjured a large seed forth
from nothing, through which Emma had dramatically flash-
grown a rose. With his mind magic, Bastian had created an
illusion of a thousand roses as if Emma had grown many instead of just the one. Synchronized, they'd both used telekinesis to pluck the petals, one by one, off the real rose until
they lay suspended in the air. The illusion roses followed suit
with eight thousand fragrant rose petals hanging still before
Bastian fired them upward to burst into a red firework that
brought gasps and exclaims of delight. Applause had thundered, with many witches looking at Emma in a whole new
light. No more "poor Emmaline."

Emma could barely stir herself to care as she watched Bastian move away through the crowd. He hadn't even bothered
to say more than "you did it" before he'd walked away. He
was back to being solemn Bastian, the one she'd re-met weeks
ago. Tense, unsmiling except for the society smile she hated.

And she deserved it.

Her heart wept as she forced her own smile to the surface and accepted a stranger's well-wishes. It was for the best, in a way, she told herself. At least now he wouldn't be tempted to stick around. And she wouldn't be tempted to share herself with him.

"Come with me now."

Emma barely had enough time to focus on her mother before she'd caught hold of Emma's upper arm and towed her in the direction of one of the private rooms.

She should've known a criticism of her performance would be forthcoming. Emma thought of breaking the hold, but her emotions were already wrung out. She could sit through Clarissa's autopsy and then go home, curl under the covers and wait to see what happened when Bastian came back.

If he came back.

Her mother entered the Blue Room and pushed her toward one of the chairs. "Sit. And tell me exactly why Bastian isn't at your side."

"Because you dragged me in here," Emma muttered, seating herself.

"What was that?"

Emma blanched, realizing she'd said it aloud. She plucked her skirt. "We had— Well, it's like this." Why was this still so hard? She bore down, despising her own weakness. "We—before the Exhibition—kind of had a—a disagreement."

"A fight." Her mother paced up the Persian rug and back. The cocktail dress swished with silk and fury. "Why would you do that to us?"

Us? Emma stared at her blankly.

"Emmaline. Don't play dumb. You know what happens with Bastian affects all of us. We are this close to securing this marriage. We don't need you killing the deal right before the handshake."

Of course her mother would assume it was her fault.

Okay, it had been, but for the right reasons.

Right?

A headache drilled behind her eyes and she ached to close them. "The marriage is still happening, Mother."

"Yes, it is. And on your wedding night, I'll be able to finally relax."

Will you be climbing into bed with us? So badly did Emma want to say it, but she knew there was no point. She tried changing the subject. "Everyone seemed pleased with the Exhibition."

"Mm." Clarissa waved that away. "Bastian carried you, but I can't say I expected much more. At least you didn't embarrass us. The trick was…okay."

"It was *great*." Emma tensed as the words popped out, but Goddess, her mother could just not give a compliment. About anything.

"Don't let a little applause go to your head."

"It was good, Mother," Emma repeated, bunching her skirt in her fists. "I was good."

"You were adequate, although I still say you and Bastian should have performed separately. But we all know what that arrogant warlock thought of that." Her face mottled with color at the memory. "If he thinks he can speak to me like that after you're married, he has a hard lesson coming."

Emma wondered what she'd say if she learned of the ring Kole had had crafted to prevent Clarissa from doing what she was imagining. It would almost be worth telling her, but Emma didn't relish the thought of getting witch-slapped across the room. Clarissa not only killed the messenger, she sent him back in tiny bits to make her point.

"The disrespect he showed… Well, it's clear that he's been spoiled all his life. What else can you expect from a Higher son, especially one who ran from his responsibilities?" Her lips pinched. "And did we get an apology? No, all we got were excuses and prevarications. Cuts from other families and whispered jokes about us. I endured it all."

Such a heroine.

"I knew he'd be back. I knew he'd toe the line eventually." A feline smile that sent chills down Emma's spine settled on her face. "With his precious mother falling victim to the curse clause, how could he not?"

Emma felt it ripple through her. "You knew about the curse." She'd suspected, but to have it confirmed...

"Of course I did. I helped your father write up the contract, though the weak-minded fool tried to talk me out of it. Kept on and on about choices. Having the right to choose. We had a shot at securing an invitation to the upper ranks of society and your father chooses to grow a conscience?" She all but spat the word. "So weak."

"Dad was a good man."

Cold eyes flitted to her. "Weak," she repeated. "And I was proved right. You think Bastian would be back if it wasn't for the clause?"

Pain stabbed Emma in the heart. "No." And he might not have left in the first place if it hadn't been for her choices.

Choices. It was all about choices.

"That's right," her mother declared. "No. I engineered it all. And on and on your father went about wanting you to be happy, to choose, to have veto power—"

Emma's chin snapped up. "Veto power?"

Clarissa's eyes flickered. "Nothing. A whim of his. I put a stop to it."

"He wanted me to have veto power?"

"As if you would exercise it."

"Did he put it in the contract?" Her throat was tight, echoing her chest. Had she missed something? Breathing became a struggle as she half rose. "Did he?"

Clarissa glared at her. "That doesn't matter because even if he did add it, you would *not* be exercising it."

"What happens if I veto the marriage?" Tiny drummers drilled a beat inside her head. "Would Bastian's mom be okay?"

"Emmaline..." The answer was mingled with warning.

"But..." Emma felt her insides shrink as Clarissa turned the queen of all black looks on her. The pounding behind her eyes was quicker, harder, a rapid heartbeat. Her hands shook as she swallowed back the need to obey.

Not now. *Not now.*

She forced the question out. "Is there— Are you saying there's a clause in the contract that allows me to v-veto the engagement with no consequences?"

Her mother hissed like a spitting fire. "You will not speak of this. You are getting married to a Truenote. We will become a Higher family. I will have that power."

Dizzy, Emma dropped back to the chair. A hand fluttered at her throat. "I could end it?" She could give Bastian back his life. His choices. To be free of her and her family.

"Emmaline, I am warning you. Put it out of your mind." Clarissa turned calculating, waving a hand in the vague direction of the ballroom. "I see the way you look at him. You've fallen for him. Do you think he would choose to be with you if he didn't have the engagement contract? You want him? This is the way."

She felt sick. And she needed to get out of here. Look at the contract. Stick her head under cold water. Try not to cry.

Emma rose, making for the door. Her hand was on the doorknob when Clarissa stayed her with a slashing gesture, the telekinetic vise clamping down and crushing Emma's ribs.

She made a pained noise, hand spasming around the metal handle. "Let me go."

"I knew when I'd discovered what your idiot father had done that you'd ruin this. I'm not having it. Promise me you will forget any idiotic ideas about vetoing this match."

Thoughts turning jumbled, needing to get out, Emma did something she'd never done before. Reaching out through their link, she pulled on her bond with Chester. His love, joy, strength wrapped around her as her familiar's small gifts combined with her own magic. Power flooded her veins for one hot, bright second. It was all she needed. With a thought, she broke through her mother's hold.

It was more luck and surprise than skill, but she didn't pause as she created a portal and escaped through it, her mother's threats echoing behind her.

Emma didn't go home. She had no idea what she'd do if she saw Bastian, not with this knowledge tumbling around in her head.

Was it true?

She needed a copy of the contract. Fortunately, both families had one as per the arrangement. Her dad's arrangement. Had her dad really given her the option to veto the contract when she was of age?

It was something he'd do, she admitted as she stole upstairs in the Bluewater manor to her mother's office. Go against her mother's wishes without being overt about it. The last laugh. Quietly triumphant. That was her dad. Especially if he'd seen the Joining clause written in. After all, he'd been trapped in a loveless marriage. It had taken her time, but Emma could now be happy he'd found some small measure of joy with Sloane's mom. Anyone stuck with Clarissa deserved it.

A twist of love and longing powered her through the office

door and to the family safe on the wall. Clarissa hadn't bothered to hide it because it was keyed to family magic only—and it didn't house anything of extreme importance. Emma was sure there were other safes she didn't know about. Clarissa probably had the Hope Diamond and Amelia Earhart locked away somewhere.

She placed a hand on the cold metal of the safe door. "*An-electum.*"

An electric shock buzzed her skin and the safe clicked open. Emma sorted through the papers, keeping her mind on task, wanting to get in and get out before her mother thought to look for her here.

She grabbed the black folder when she saw it, the gold shimmer of Emma's and Bastian's family crests on the cover. Packing the papers she'd moved out of the way back in, she shut the door and relocked it.

Then she stood still, unsure where to go. Home was out, at least until she knew what was what. The bar was the next place someone would think to look for her. It left only one place she could think of.

It was past midnight when she emerged from a portal onto the quiet beach she'd last been to after her blowup at Bastian. She'd wondered then how they'd move forward. Things had got so good and in the space of an evening, now they were...

Refusing to continue that thought, Emma dropped to the ground, tucking her legs under her as she sat cross-legged. She conjured a small ball of light after a quick look to make sure she was alone and then stared at the black folder in her hands.

"Just do it." Rip the Band-Aid.

Twenty minutes later, the folder was next to her and she had her knees drawn up, arms resting on them, head propped on her arms as she stared out to Lake Michigan.

It was true. It was couched and hidden, only noticeable if

you were looking for it—and if you'd grown up with him as a father.

He'd made it into a game when she was little, she remembered, gazing at nothing, empty inside. Giving her a note that said one thing, letting her work her way through a lockpicking spell to the words hidden beneath. She'd thought it fun, clever, a childish game to fool her mother.

He'd used it when she was older, too, when his need to hide his other daughter had driven him to hide the truth on the papers she and Kole had discovered, the ones that had told about Sloane.

She'd known all of that, had known how her father's mind worked. But she hadn't thought to check the contract.

And it was there. She could call off the engagement with no repercussions.

She could make this right. And all she had to do was let Bastian go once and for all.

The knowledge was a howling roar in her head, but she felt numb. Even the cold wind didn't touch her as her eyes tracked the ripples on the water.

Choices. It all came down to choices.

It had been two days since the Exhibition and Bastian had played the coward and hadn't been back to see Emma.

He brooded in a chair overlooking the Nile. Ethan had put him up for the past two nights with minimal questions, a blessing when Bastian didn't even know if he could get the answers straight in his head.

Emma had put the silencing hex on him. But she'd done it because she'd been young and stupid and had thought whoever had overheard her was a threat to Sloane. She'd thought she'd needed to trap him *to help her sister.*

Hadn't he also been young and stupid when he'd fled? Should that excuse her?

The whole thing made his head hurt. Logic was down and insanity was up and right meant left and two wrongs made a right. And he was just so *tired* of it all, the whole messed-up thing. At least Emma had finally lifted the silencing hex; he'd felt it dissipate the night of the Exhibition. And even now, he hadn't said the words aloud to anyone back home—just Ethan. Who'd blown out a long breath, said how screwed up it was and had offered his spare room for the duration. Bastian knew whenever he wanted to talk about it, Ethan would listen, but he didn't know if he'd ever be ready.

"Okay," his friend called from behind him, as if reading his mind. A frosty beer bottle was thrust into his line of sight. "I'm calling it on the brooding time. Either talk it through like a modern man or get the hell off my continent."

Bastian grabbed the bottle and took a swig, glad for the cool drink. He'd forgotten how hot it could be out here, even if it was a kind of cleansing heat that baked the pretentiousness out of a man. Or woman.

Emma would love it. He thought about those picture frames, thought about her traveling with Sloane. Wished he could be there as their guide.

To hell with it.

"I see we're sticking with brooding." Ethan threw himself into a chair he conjured seconds before he fell on his ass and stretched like a human cat. Sunglasses appeared over his eyes. "Where's your head at, Bas?"

"My head? Fucked," Bastian said succinctly.

"Well, sure. The woman you're about to marry lied to you, hexed you and blamed you for leaving her when actually she was the reason you left."

Bastian shifted. All true, but he didn't like the scathing tone that Ethan used. "Yeah, but she did do it for her sister."

"And she didn't talk to you like a normal person because…"

"She was scared. And maybe she's right." Bastian swept his thumb through the condensation on the bottle. "Maybe if I could've talked, I would've got the contract suspended."

"Maybe?"

Bastian cleared his throat. Looked off to the distance. "Moot point. Look, I get why she did what she did. But it's that she didn't tell me, even after we…" He stopped.

"Made sweet, sweet love?" Ethan yelped as Bastian made best use of his telekinesis. "Easy, bud. Take it out on your lady love, not me." He shifted again and lifted his own beer to his mouth. After a swallow, he glanced over. "Why do you think she didn't?"

He didn't know, and that was what was killing him the most.

Bastian couldn't sit anymore and surged to his feet, bottle left behind. He took a few steps away toward the powerful river. Fall in there, get swept away pretty damn quick, he thought. He knew what that was like.

"Gotta say, kind of sad not to have met her," Ethan said. "She sounds unusual if she's brought Bastian Truenote so low."

Bastian quirked his mouth. "She is. Smart, funny, pretty."

"Putting the looks in third, must be serious."

"She's got this way of insulting me and making me laugh at the same time." Bastian smiled even now, even when he was feeling so wrecked. "And she's so reluctant to break the rules, but then she'll do something so unexpected. Impulsive. And the way she cares for everyone, her familiar, her friends, her sister. She gave up everything for them and puts herself down when she's…amazing."

When there was silence, he turned back to see Ethan staring at him. "What?"

"Nothing. It just makes sense now."

"Makes sense?"

"Why you're so torn up." Ethan shrugged. "You're in love with her."

The breath stole from Bastian's body with one swift kick. He lapsed into silence, heart tripping over itself in his chest as the words were spoken aloud.

Unsettled, he struggled with the power they unlocked. The sheer force of what he faced. But hadn't he skimmed the idea before? Never landing, not ready for that, the knowledge tucked away in a corner for when he was ready. When she was ready.

Damn Ethan. He just had to drag him kicking into the sunlight to face the truth.

Emma was his best friend. His lover. His…

His.

"Shit."

"Now, that's romance." But Ethan didn't laugh. His eyes sober, he considered his friend. "What're you gonna do?"

Bastian passed a shaky hand over his face. Hell if he knew. Because even though he loved her, if she didn't trust him, as Emma would say, what was the point?

"Emmaline! Sorry. Emma." Diana looked up from where she was reclining. A tired smile tugged at her mouth and she struggled to lift her frail body into more of a sitting position.

"Please, don't." Emma held out a hand, taking a few steps forward. "I won't be here long, but I had to talk to you."

"Okay." Curiosity and a hint of concern drifted into the eyes that reminded Emma so much of Bastian's. Diana looked from Emma to her husband, who'd let Emma in and escorted her.

Finding no answer forthcoming, she waved a hand at a chair. "Please, sit. Is Bastian not with you?"

"No." And she knew she was a coward for doing this, especially this way, but she just couldn't handle seeing the relief that would creep into his face. When he found out that he was free from her.

He'd have been a gentleman, she knew that. And for all their faults and the contract that forced them together, they had become friends. Lovers. But Bastian had freely admitted he'd come back for his mom. He'd abandoned everything he knew because of Emma and her family, had suffered through everyone thinking he was selfish because of her actions.

She'd waited the last day and a half for him to appear. For them to talk, maybe. To see where this left them. And when he hadn't come back, she'd had her answer. He'd only been making the best of things. He'd had to get married to her so he'd decided to throw his lot in, but it didn't mean he really wanted her. If he really wanted *her*, wouldn't he have talked to her?

It was better for everyone to just set things straight while he was away and save him from a messy conversation, especially when she knew how much he hated those.

His parents were the logical choice. Not only because she knew they were suffering because of her choices, but also so they could understand how unselfish Bastian really was.

She glanced at Alistair. "I need to speak to both of you."

"Is something wrong?" Bastian's dad perched on the arm of the couch, his hand making its way into Diana's.

She cut right to it. "There's something you need to know—about the engagement contract. Why Bastian left the way he did."

She told them everything, omitting Sloane's name, and, even though she stammered at times, didn't pull her punches when it came to owning her own actions. Even when Alistair surged to his feet, and only the smallest touch from Diana stopped him.

"My Goddess," he said, covering her hand with his. His face was pale. "My boy...our boy."

Emma pressed her lips together so they wouldn't tremble. It took her a minute to speak. "I know my actions are unforgiveable."

Diana shared a look with her husband as he went to say something. "Emma, we understand why—"

"No," Emma interrupted with a slight lift of her hand. "You don't have to do that. The polite graceful thing. I know you must hate me now." She took a breath and plowed ahead. "But there is a way out. My mother told me about a clause in the contract which gives me veto power over the engagement." She swallowed past the emotion. "It's true. I've looked."

Both parents absorbed this, a slow kind of stunned realization spreading over them like sunshine appearing from behind a dark cloud.

Emma curled her fingers into her palms. She wished she'd brought Chester. "I'm going to exercise it."

If they'd been stunned before, now they looked an inch from fainting.

Diana shook her head weakly. "I'm sorry, this is news to me. I thought it was locked in."

"My dad hid it from my mother. He wanted me to choose." Her lips lifted and fell. "Or maybe he wanted Bastian to be able to choose."

One eyebrow lifted. "And you're not choosing our son?"

Land mine. *Swerve, swerve.* "I'm choosing to let him go."

Alistair rubbed the back of his neck, troubled. "Have you spoken to Bastian about this?"

"He doesn't know."

A fatherly look of disappointment settled on Alistair's features. "Seems to me he should be told."

"I know he'll be happy. This gives him an out without having to admit that he's ready to be rid of me."

"Emma," Diana began.

"He shouldn't have to deal with me," she burst out and stood in one hurried movement, unable to sit still. "Or the wedding, or any of it. It's better for everyone if he leaves now."

Diana laid her head on her husband's thigh. Something in her eyes made Emma uncomfortable. "I see. And you don't even want to see if he can get past what you did?"

Emma couldn't face her, them, any longer so swiveled to the fireplace. She spoke to the flames. "Bastian deserves a woman he wants, not one that has lied to him, betrayed him, made him feel like a fool."

"You really don't think he could see past that?" Diana hummed in her throat. "I've seen him look at you, seen how much he cares for you."

Emma's eyes closed. "I think he doesn't know how he feels," she said, the words barely audible above the soft crackle of fire. "He's been told he'll marry me all his life. It's fact to him. He knew it would be easier if he cared for me, so maybe for a while he convinced himself that he did. But if he really had feelings for me, he'd have come back after the Exhibition."

"Why come to us?" Diana asked. She'd regained a bit of color in her cheeks, but it was more the flush of an ill person, not a healthy blush.

She at least would fix that for Diana, Emma thought.

"To set the record straight." Emma half smiled, though there was little funny about the situation. "My mother will be furious, Goddess knows, if word gets out, but if you need to tell people to restore Bastian's reputation, I understand. I just ask that you keep my sister out of it."

"Of course," Alistair said softly. "My dear, if I may say so, you don't look happy, for all that you're saying you're about to right a wrong."

"It doesn't matter if I'm happy; only that Bastian is finally free of me."

Alistair looked ready to argue, but Diana stilled him with a squeeze of her hand. She was studying Emma, and though it made her stomach churn, Bastian's mom obviously saw enough to convince her of the wisdom in Emma's plan.

Emma just wished she felt better about it.

CHAPTER 27

*B*astian's heart stopped in his chest. "What?" he croaked, then cleared his throat. "What?"

His mom—who looked healthier than she had since he'd returned—stirred the coffee she'd made them. She slid a mug over to him, concern marking her delicate features. "I put a calming potion in it."

"You can't be serious."

"It has jasmine and ginseng and—"

"Not the calming potion, Mom." He shoved it away. He didn't feel like being calm. Raking a hand through his hair, he held on to his patience. Barely. "The other thing."

"Oh." Diana let go of her spoon, but her coffee continued to stir itself. "Emma has released you from your engagement."

That was what he'd thought she'd said. "Not possible."

"Her dad put a hidden veto clause in the contract." Diana picked up her coffee, blew across it. Like she'd taken a freaking calming potion herself. "Emma told us her mother let it slip at the Exhibition."

His stomach turned over. That fucking contract was the gift

that kept on giving. He pushed away from the table to pace, needing to eat up the ground. "Why wouldn't she talk to me first?" He gestured out of disbelief. "This is the kind of thing you talk to someone about first."

Although she sure had made a habit out of making these decisions on her own. Maybe he should be grateful there were no hexes involved this time. He braced his hands on the mantelpiece and hung his head as he stretched out his body.

"Would you have talked her out of it?"

"Yes. No." He closed his eyes and smacked the mantelpiece. "Damn it. I don't know."

"Did you want to get married?"

He turned, frustration bleeding from him. "It's not that simple."

"It could be." His mom took a moment. "You never asked why we signed the contract."

Well, that had come out of left field. He jittered in place, unsure what to do with that.

"Bastian. Come sit with me." She waited until he was sitting before indicating the mug of coffee she'd conjured. A healthy color lived in her skin again and he was split in two, with one half overjoyed that his mom was well and the other losing its mind.

She held her mug close to her. "We said at the time it was for the financial advantages the Bluewaters could bring to our family. That's something Clarissa understands."

"It wasn't, though?"

"No. I had a...knowing, I suppose you could call it, the first time I saw you and Emma playing together."

Shock made him lean back. Knowings were an erratic power and not every witch or warlock could get them.

"I'd never had one before, and I haven't had one since," she went on. "But I looked at you both and this...tight feeling crushed my chest and hope bloomed inside. Warmth and a glow and a feeling of home. I knew Clarissa Bluewater had her eye on marrying off the next generation and I didn't stop to think before I made the deal. Clearly," she added with a face, "Clarissa did, because she sure had her fun with it, didn't she?"

Bastian was still stuck on the knowing. "You think we were destined for each other?"

Her face softened. "I don't know. It wasn't romance I felt— just a sense of belonging. You might only have been destined to be the greatest of friends. But I hoped with that as a basis you might form something of an attachment. I've seen how other society sons can grow up and be drawn to the same cold arrangements for power. I thought this might avoid that, hoped with her in your life from a young age, a marriage would be the best thing for you. I never dreamed it would hurt you both to the point where you ran from each other."

His heart twisted. "Emma didn't run," he pointed out. He hesitated but even with the silencing hex destroyed, he didn't say anything about his reasons.

His mom's mouth quirked. "Not then," she said somewhat cryptically, then put down her mug. "She told us about the other clause in the contract."

Shock made him mute. His eyes apparently said volumes as his mom took one look and smiled. "Yes," she said to whatever she saw in them. "I was surprised, too, and so was your dad. She gave us permission to tell everyone."

"Don't." It was a whiplash of sound, as he reached to touch her arm.

She glanced at his hand. "Your reputation…"

"I don't care. It's not important."

"Then what is?"

He struggled with an answer. "It's… It happened. Did she— did she tell you everything?"

"The silencing hex, the 'important person' she was trying to protect." His mom sipped her coffee, keeping her eyes on him. "Do you think that justifies what she did to you?"

It was that question that had consumed him for the past seventy-two hours. And he'd finally come to the realization that if it had been his sister, he'd probably have done the same thing. "Yes," he murmured. And yet...

"And yet she didn't tell you sooner," his mom finished, demonstrating the eerie mind-reading thing singular to moms. She put down her mug, took his hand. Already it was a stronger grip. He linked their fingers as she said, "You know, it's funny how we protect ourselves. For example, instead of staying to dissolve the contract, you ran away. Why do you think that is?"

"Because it was easier. Because I *am* selfish."

His mom squeezed. "I think it's because you couldn't face the idea of a life without her, and you didn't want to have to admit it."

He made a few noises of dissent, unsure what to say.

"Answer me this: Are you happy that she's ended the contract?"

"No," he snapped, anger sweeping back over him like wildfire.

"Why not? Her family has caused you nothing but pain. She lied to you."

"Only for her sister," he pointed out. His foot tapped impatiently, but his mom still held his hand. "And she'd found a way to stop the Joining. Of course, she didn't tell me that either until the last minute," he muttered.

"So, why aren't you happy?"

"Because we need to talk." He scowled at the carpet. "I need to talk to her."

"Why?"

He moved his scowl to his mom. "I care about her."

"Do you?"

"Of course I do!"

"There's no need to shout."

"I'm not shouting," he shouted, then felt foolish. "Sorry. She just makes me insane. She always thinks she knows what's best."

"Reminds me of someone else."

His scowl made a reappearance.

She smiled. "You say 'of course' you care, but she deceived you. Nobody would blame you if you couldn't get over that."

"It's not that I can't…understand. It's why she didn't tell me when we…" He broke off. Even he, a grown man, couldn't discuss sex with his mom. "When we…got serious." A muscle popped in his jaw. "I shared myself with her."

"Sweet child." She cupped his cheek with her spare hand. "You grew up in a home where you were nurtured. Your ideas and thoughts and opinions mattered. You learned to trust. Emma… I don't think she had the same childhood."

He thought of her mother, what Emma had shared. Something dark flirted inside him. "She didn't."

"So maybe trust doesn't come easily to her. Maybe…" His mom cocked her head. "Maybe her first instinct is to hide and protect herself."

"Why does she need to protect herself with me?"

His mom stroked his cheek before taking her hand away. "What greater threat is there than falling in love with someone who can't love you back?"

It was like his mom had calmly flung a crushing curse at him. He struggled to breathe as he dropped her hand. He searched her face. "Why would you say that?"

"Over a century of loving and learning. I saw that young woman as she bared herself to us. She's scared."

"Of me." The idea had ice forming in his gut, stabbing into his skin.

"Of you not loving her," his mom corrected. Then, she threw him one more curveball. "I think she was right."

"*What?*"

"You've always known you'd marry her, and you do have a habit of going along with things when it's easier." She lifted a hand when he went to speak. "Thanks to Emma, now you both have the freedom to choose. Time to consider what it is you want. What you could build together."

The last month bloomed in his mind, ink in water. He thought of Emma's hidden sassy side, her generous nature, her constantly surprising him, even if it sometimes wasn't exactly for the best. How pretty she looked first thing in the morning or when she was baking, with flour on her cheeks, how flushed she got in the middle of an argument. How devastated she'd looked when she'd admitted the truth to him. When he'd turned his back on her at the Exhibition.

"I'm crazy about her," he admitted. He lifted his gaze and found his mom beaming at him.

"Sweetheart. I know."

"Then why did you let her break off the engagement?"

"Because I still think you need time to decide if you can learn to trust her. And," she continued when he went to speak, "I think she needs time to decide if she can learn to trust you. Bastian, she has always known you were forced to be with her. Never chosen. It would be easy for you to go to her, but she needs to realize that it's not about you choosing her; it's also about her choosing you."

"I don't understand."

His mom reached up, kissed his cheek. "Just trust me. If she's what you want, this time, we do this the right way."

* * *

A tornado exploded into the bar, whipping glasses off shelves, cracking the mirror and scattering napkins and peanuts across the floor.

In the part of Emma's head that could still joke, the Wicked Witch of the West's theme tune played with shrill, dire notes. *Duh duh duh duh duh duhhhh, Duh duh duh duh duh duhhhh.*

Fortunately, the bar had already closed for the night, a fact that wouldn't have escaped her mother, or else she wouldn't have made such a dramatic entrance.

Emma knew she should feel panicked, terrified, a baby rabbit frozen in the field where a fox bore down on her with gleaming white teeth.

Instead she felt numb, packed in ice, as she had for the past week since she'd ended her engagement officially. She'd known Clarissa would find out sooner or later. She'd thought about telling her, but just hadn't had the energy. She didn't have the energy for much else but baking and milkshakes with Sloane these days. Who had made no bones about the fact she thought Emma dumping Bastian was a sucky decision.

Tia had also surprised her. When Emma had told them she was no longer engaged, she'd expected streamers to suddenly sprinkle through the air, a mariachi band to appear, castanets to appear in Tia's hands and her friend's booty to start shaking in the well-known victory dance.

Instead Tia had asked her if she was sure this was the right decision. And even though Emma had insisted it was, her friend hadn't stopped casting her concerned looks ever since. Leah had been more vocal in her belief it was a mistake; she thought Emma and Bastian belonged together, but even she'd backed off after Emma refused to discuss it.

So, she kept busy, ignoring Chester's worried whines and

her own idiotic desires. Better to be alone than trapped in a marriage with a man who couldn't forgive her.

She'd asked Diana and Alistair to keep Bastian away, but a part of her had still hoped he'd come after her. Convince her they needed to talk. Maybe even confess how much he cared for her, that he wanted to be married. That he did forgive her and understand why she'd done it.

Because that was the cruelest thing of all: she was in love with him.

And it was because she loved him that she'd let him go. Yes, a small part of her had violently hoped to see him come rushing through the bar's doors, but the facts were that he hadn't tried to see her or make her change her mind. It was enough proof she'd done the right thing. Kole had even reluctantly told her he'd heard Bastian had left again and that society was already whispering. She couldn't find the energy to care.

Just as she didn't care now as Clarissa blew in, a towering witch of formidable power with one pissed-off attitude.

"No ruby slippers here," she said, dropping the cloth she'd been disinterestedly rubbing along the counter. "Dorothy already left."

Her mother glowered. "Tell me it's not true."

Emma didn't bother prevaricating. "It is."

The mirror behind Emma shattered in a controlled burst of power. Instead of fragments flying out, they all collapsed into a heap of shrill music.

Emma eyed it, impassive. "That's seven years, right there."

"I can't believe you did this."

"Why? Just one more disappointment in a row of them." Emma released a breath. "Why are you here? It's done. There is no engagement."

"We can still make this happen."

"No."

A strong current of electricity ran through Emma's body at the word.

Clarissa stilled. "Excuse me?"

"No." The tremor was the first good feeling she'd had for days and she relished it. "No."

"You don't get a say."

Emma's laugh would have cracked the mirror if it hadn't already been shattered. "I'm not a kid anymore. You can't control me. And I'm done letting you." The words were out before she'd even thought them through.

They fell between mother and daughter like a challenge.

Clarissa's eyebrows lifted, dangerous. "You're my daughter. You are a Bluewater."

"I'm Emma." She spread her hands on the bar, needing to ground herself. "I'm just Emma."

"Listen to me. You will go to the Truenotes and you will make them recall their nomadic son—"

"*No.*" Each time was its own giddy thrill. "I'm done trying to please you. Because I never will. And I shouldn't have to try."

"Nothing in this world is free."

"Dad didn't think so."

"Your father was a fool."

A flash of anger lit up inside her. "He was better than you. He gave me a choice."

"Which just shows how weak he really was." Clarissa sneered. "He was always weak. A slave to his feelings."

"He fooled you," Emma shot back. "He added the clause under your nose."

"He got lucky. And it's no matter now." Clarissa fisted a hand at Emma in threat. "I will have the power I was promised."

"No, you won't," Emma shot back. "And you know, while

we're sharing, you never would have. I figured out how to stop your leech power from taking magic from any Joining."

Clarissa stilled, a moment of silence before a scream. Everything went to hyperawareness.

"I will never let you take from me or mine again," Emma said. Shakily, but she said it. Behind the counter, her hands curled into combat position, just in case.

"If you mean that bastard half daughter of your father's, you can keep her."

The words hit with an impact she hadn't seen coming. Emma swayed as if struck. "Wh-what?"

"Please. As if I didn't know what your father was doing." Clarissa eyed her with disdain. "As if I didn't know why you were so desperate to leave New Orleans."

"Then why help me?"

"I didn't *help* you." As if the very idea gave her a churning stomach, Clarissa recoiled. "I needed the situation managed. I couldn't have people asking questions, questions that might bring shame to the family name. Not when we're so close to getting everything I have worked for."

Still reeling from the idea that Clarissa had known all this time, Emma fisted a hand on her stomach and forced herself to keep on track. "You need to look elsewhere, because Bastian is gone."

"As if we could get anyone better than Bastian Truenote."

Well, that was true.

Seeing that agreement on her face, Clarissa stepped forward. "This is the only way you can have him, Emmaline. No warlock of his caliber would choose to be with you."

Words she'd heard all her life. From outside the manor and from in. She had to do this to please Bastian, do that to fit in, to look powerful, to hold up the family name.

"Maybe," she managed, throat raw. "But why should I have to change for him?"

"Don't be an idiot."

"I'm n-not an idiot!" The exclamation exploded from her, a quick tug on the knot that held back her emotions. They tumbled free, rushing through her, her blood pumping as she smacked the counter. Nearby the register drawer burst open. "All my life, you have always put me down and made me feel small. And I let you. That's on me. But no more. Do you know what I felt when I stood on that stage at the Exhibition? Freedom. To be me, to realize that I am enough."

Clarissa's jaw tightened. "Bastian obviously disagrees."

Her mother had thrived in witch society long enough to know where to stick her daggers. She drew blood.

The sudden scratch of claws was the only warning before Chester suddenly sprang forward from the passageway. Instead of his customary dopey look, his fur was ruffled, ears up as he stalked forward, eyes intent on Clarissa.

Emma's smile was soft. "That's what you don't get," she said, turning back to Clarissa. "You shouldn't have to be a certain way to have somebody love you. Love isn't love if it isn't freely offered." Something she'd struggled to realize in her childhood. Hell, even when she was an adult. "Love isn't selfish. Bastian had the right to be free."

"Weakness. It's always been in you." Her mother was the essence of cold, her face ugly in its twisted expression. "I should never have believed you could succeed at even this. You've failed again. This is the last time."

Emma nodded, taking a breath. "You're right. It is." She flicked a finger at the doors which opened on command. "Goodbye, Clarissa."

Her mother was used to getting the last word in, but as she failed to stare her daughter down, her eyes flashed. A portal that roared its fury tore open near a booth and she stalked toward it. Then she looked back over her shoulder. If Emma didn't know better, she could have sworn there was a glint of unwilling pride there. "I hope you know what you've done."

Then she was gone.

Emma bent to run shaking hands through her familiar's fur, letting him lick her cold cheeks.

Leah came out of the back, her own cheeks pale. Her eyes showed a bottomless excitement. "Now, that was awesome."

Another week passed and Emma's tattoo grew fainter by the day. Her stubbornness to refuse to talk never did.

And yet, despite that, Emma found herself dragged out for milkshakes off schedule with one chatty teenager.

She lifted her straw and poked at the helluva amount of whipped cream on the top of her milkshake. "I could do without the heart attack."

"Jeez." Sloane rolled her eyes and lifted a spoon to scrape the mass onto hers.

"Not sure I should be condoning that either." But Emma couldn't really care. People were gonna do what they were gonna do.

"So, we've been talking." Sloane leaned back in the booth and folded her arms.

"We?"

"Your coven."

"I told you, we don't have…" Emma trailed off, suspicion lifting a wary head. "Who are you talking about?"

"Who else? Tia and Leah." She scrunched her nose. "You ever think how funny it is that their names rhyme?"

"Constantly."

Sloane sucked up some shake. "Anyway, we've decided you need to do something about it."

"About what?"

"The whole dumping Bastian situation."

"I didn't dump him."

"I thought you said you broke the engagement."

"Well, yeah, but—"

"Dumper." Sloane pointed at Emma. "But it was clearly the wrong choice since you're all mopey and everything."

Emma raised her eyebrows. "How much of this is you and how much is Tia?"

Sloane avoided the question. "If you're not happy you dumped him, why not get back with him?"

"It's not that simple."

"Sure it is. If he likes you back. And since you guys were having sex—"

"Sloane."

"—then he must like you a bit. Unless you were bad at it, I guess."

"It's not happening. It's a dream," Emma told herself.

"Is there ever a way to tell?" Sloane wondered. "Like, can you ask?"

"Sure, when you're of legal age and you're ready and in love."

Sloane snorted. "Because those are the parameters."

"They should be."

"Did *you* wait until you were in love?"

Emma opened her mouth to say yes and then sort of just hung there because she was damned if she did or didn't answer.

Satisfaction smiled back at her. Sloane already knew.

"I told you about the contract," Emma said after a couple of seconds. She stabbed her straw back into her shake. "He was forced into that, then he was forced to go through with the engagement because of me and my mother."

"Leah says she's fascinating." She shifted, uncertainty crossing her face. "Will I have to, like, meet her?"

Emma reached across the table and touched her hand. "Only if you want to. She might think she has a say in when or if you ever come into society, but she doesn't. Only you do."

Relief appeared for a brief moment and Sloane nodded. "Was he mad when he found out about the hex?"

Emma gave her a look.

"So, you dumped him before he could dump you?"

"In a way, I guess."

"Are you sure he was gonna dump you?"

"What's with all the questions? Why're we still talking about him when we could be talking about your new friends?"

"Tia said you'd try to change the subject."

"Tia doesn't always know what's best." Emma ruffled her hair with an agitated move. "Look, I waited for Bastian to come back after the Exhibition and he didn't. That was my answer. It was easier the way everything played out. And it's done."

"Seems to me you could've at least talked about it. Isn't that what you're always going on about to me—talking?"

Emma aimed a glare her sister's way. "Well, we're done talking about this. It's over. He's gone, like he always was going to be."

Sloane pounced like a rat on cheese. "You kind of pushed him away first, though. Like, you didn't actually think he'd stick around. You said that's why you didn't let us hang out—because he was gonna leave, right?"

Emma softened at the flash of uncertainty the teen still had. "Right. I didn't want you to get attached to someone who was going to leave us. And the less people who knew about you, the better—though with Clarissa knowing, I guess that may change, depending on how we approach it."

"But he said he wanted to stick around a bit," Sloane persisted, dismissing that. "He told me. Leah told me."

"Are you guys having meetings or something?"

"So, if he wanted to stick around, why didn't you just tell him about me and all of it? You must have liked him to have had sex."

Emma groaned at the return of the subject. Her face burned as a passing waitress shot them a startled look.

"And if you liked him that much, why not just tell him? Unless you thought he would tell on me."

"No," Emma said swiftly, now knowing it to be true. "Bastian would've never 'told on you.'" She fiddled with the paper napkin that came with her "drink," scrunching it up into a ball. "Some people stick and some people leave. You know that. So, why should I share the most important part of my life with someone when he was always going to go away?"

Sloane studied her, and Emma didn't know if it was the light or the thoughtful way she cocked her head, but suddenly she saw the resemblance to her dad so strongly it brought her heart to a standstill.

For a moment there was only the clink of silverware and the hushed chatter from the diners around them.

"You want to know what else Tia and Leah said?" her sister said in a soft voice. "If it helps, I think they're right."

Emma sighed and gave in. "What did Toil and Trouble say?"

Sloane grinned at the nicknames. "They think you were scared that he'd hurt you when he left so you built a wall and you kept things—like me—behind it. And then you could use them as an excuse to push him away."

Emma blinked, shook her head. "No, I… I gave him freedom. From me and all of it. I did it for him." She had. Right?

She hadn't deliberately held herself back. It was just… She fumbled for the answer.

Sloane heaved a breath. "Okay. Plan B." She lifted her cell, punched in something.

"What're you doing?"

"Sending for backup."

"Sending for…" Emma slumped as the diner door opened and Tia sailed in with Leah walking along behind her. "Great."

"Fancy seeing you here. Sloane, scoot a bit, would you?" Tia plopped down next to the willing teen and folded her hands as Leah crowded Emma on the other side of the booth. "I thought you'd hear the truth from your sister, but clearly the blunt approach needs to be used for someone with such a thick head."

Sloane watched with interest as she scooped some cream into her mouth.

Leah gestured. "Gimme a try?"

"Okay." Sloane pushed her drink across as Tia and Emma squared off.

"I don't need any approach," Emma gritted out and stood. "I'm fine and I don't appreciate being manipulated."

Tia barked a laugh. "There's irony, and sit your prissy ass down. We gave you time to get over it. You didn't. Goddess, if I'd known you dumping him would've brought down the mother of all mopes…"

"I didn't dump him—I gave him the *choice*," Emma spaced out, planting her hands and leaning in.

"Did you ask him?" Tia's eyebrows slammed together. "Did you go to him, explain the veto and ask if he wanted to be set free?"

"I didn't need to."

"So, now you're clairvoyant as well? That's a new power. Congrats."

Emma scowled at her. "Harsh, Tia."

"You need it," her friend—although that was a debatable term right now—retorted. "Someone's got to slap you awake. What you did was cowardly."

Emma gaped at her, then Leah.

Leah shrugged, smiled in apology. "I agree."

"I set him free," Emma insisted. "He didn't come back when he knew the truth. I let him have the choice."

"But you didn't," Leah pointed out. "You chose for him."

"No, I— It wasn't like that." Unease slithered into a coil in her stomach. She fisted her hands. "I did this for him."

Tia held her gaze. "You did it for yourself, Em."

It was a slap and Emma flinched.

But Tia wasn't done. "You've been so scared about him coming back into your life and falling for him again—"

"I seem to remember someone else worrying about that," Emma shot back.

Tia grimaced. "So, I can be a bitch. Sue me. It doesn't change that you've been so certain he'd leave you, that you left first."

"*I gave him a choice.*" Or had she chosen for both of them? It was all tangled in her head now.

"You left him," Leah said in her optimistic, peaches and cream voice, sunny and yet stern. "You ran."

The words knocked Emma off her feet and she dropped to the seat. Her ears were ringing. "I didn't run."

The three sets of eyes looking back at her were serious.

"I didn't," she insisted, mind tumbling over the facts. "I... I wanted to..."

"You were scared and you ran," Tia said. "You wanted to leave before he could leave you. And at first, I thought it was fine. If that was what you wanted. But it's not." Her lips pursed and sympathy stole into her features. "Is it?"

Emma stared at them blindly. Their words circled her, jabbing out, forcing her to face them. Her chest heaved and she drew unsteady hands down her face. It was all true.

"Oh, Goddess," she breathed. "How did I not see that?"

"Duh." Tia reached across the table, flicked her forehead. "Because you're stupid." But she grinned to ease the moment. "Luckily you have us."

"I voted for the subtler approach, just so you know." Leah gave Sloane a wink. "Clearly you needed a witch slap and your sister is more human than bitch. Sorry, I meant witch."

"Clever," Tia said dryly as Sloane giggled.

Emma ignored the byplay, absently rubbing her aching heart. "It doesn't matter though, does it? He did leave. He's gone. He didn't want me." The raw wound hissed at the salt she poured into it.

But Tia was only exasperated. "The man might have a smidge of pride, Emma. You ended the engagement and then asked his parents of all people to keep him away from you. He probably thinks this is what you want." She rolled her eyes, muttered something under her breath. No doubt something flattering to both Emma and Bastian.

Sloane licked her spoon. "We think you should go after him."

"I don't even know where he is."

"Egypt." Tia conjured a piece of paper, held it out. "This location was bought at great expense, so use it well. And mention me in your vows, I think I'd like being known as a cupid."

"I can't just go to Egypt."

"I'll go with you!"

"Nice try, kid," Tia said, "but this is something your cowardly sister needs to do herself."

Emma shot her a glare.

"It'll be very romantic," Leah assured her. "You can sweep

in and tell him you love him and then you can fall into each other's arms."

"Or he'll cringe awkwardly and have to gently tell me he's not interested anymore." The idea of that made panic bubble to the surface. "No."

"Yes," her friends chimed.

"Or I could go with you," Sloane insisted. "How could he say no to *this* face?" She framed it with her hands, deliberately hamming it up.

But Emma wasn't in the mood to laugh. "I *can't*. I can't see his face and hear that."

"You might not," said the human eternal optimist.

Tia leaned in. "Emma, you finally stood up to your mother. You can do this."

Emma closed her eyes, said the weakest thing she'd ever said. "What if he says no?"

"Then at least you'll know for sure." Leah's hand covered hers. When Emma opened her eyes, she smiled. "You're a fighter, Em. Don't surrender now."

"And if that bastard doesn't want you…" Tia slid a hex bag across the table, batting Sloane's curious hand away. "That's what this is for."

CHAPTER 28

Egypt proved to be hot with gritty air that felt like sandpaper when she gulped it in.

Or maybe that was her screaming nerves as she navigated her way through the dig site Bastian's friend had directed her to after she'd thrown herself on his mercy two hours ago. It had been mortifying to come clean to a total stranger, but she'd promised herself that she was going to fight this time. And at least if Bastian turned her away, Egypt was sufficient distance from Chicago that she wouldn't have to worry about bumping into him getting groceries.

Scents rode the air peppered with exotic languages, but she couldn't enjoy it, her eyes fixed on the row of white tents toward the back of the site. Or maybe it was the front.

That was where she'd find Bastian.

Her heart hammered twice for every step she took. It had been a bad idea to come here. She could have called him—except she knew her tongue would have been too tangled on the phone and she'd have massacred every sentence. Not that there wasn't a real threat of her doing that now.

Her foot slid in the sand and she took a moment, reminding herself that this wasn't life or death. She was just delivering on her promise to let him choose.

She might have made a mistake and chosen for both of them when she ended the contract, but now it was his turn.

Oh, Goddess.

Just as she was reaching a reasonable level of hysteria, a flap on one of the tents pulled back and a familiar golden head emerged.

Her foot glued to the spot it had just touched. Her heart tripled its beat even as it gave a painful leap in her chest like a dog that had spotted its owner.

He wasn't smiling. His hair was a little longer, rumpled and streaked with highlights from the sun. His skin was browner, too, but it only made his blue eyes more breathtaking. In short, he didn't look like he'd suffered from the same ice cream binges she had in the days since he'd left.

She was relieved when he spotted her before she had a chance to rabbit. His face froze, fierce emotion playing with his features like pinball.

She began to move again, hesitantly picking her way through the dig site, ignoring the shouts and noises of the work behind them. Her eyes drank in his movie-star looks until they were only a few yards from each other.

He didn't speak.

"Hello." A good opener.

He pushed his hands into his shorts. "Hi."

Good. Then she panicked. Was she supposed to continue? How was she going to lead into it? Should she just blurt it out or should she have prepared a speech? She'd tried, but everything sounded so utterly lame that she'd finally just jumped into a portal, figuring she'd know what to say when she saw him.

Great plan.

The silence was charged as she searched for the right words.

"Lost your way?" he finally asked, the timbre of his voice striking the right note in her heart.

"You know how it is," she said nervously. "You take the wrong turn and end up in Egypt."

His navy eyes were shuttered. "So, you took a wrong turn?"

As she gazed at him, everything inside her boiled up. Love and lust and apology and need. "No."

"No?"

"I mean, yes." She huffed an impatient breath. "I took a wrong turn. Before. But I'm on the right path again. Now."

He looked confused and she didn't blame him. Speeches really weren't her thing.

So, she decided plain speaking was best. She longed to close her eyes so she didn't have to look at him, but that was the cowardly option. Emma Bluewater was no coward. Not anymore.

She looked him dead in the eye. "I love you."

He blinked. He looked shocked. He didn't look like a man happy to hear a declaration of love.

Panic swamped her and she opened her mouth and let herself babble. "I've made bad choices all my life with you. I forced you to silence and I forced you to marry me and I kept secrets and didn't trust you. You—you shared yourself with me in every way you could, and I was the coward. I was the one who was too scared to admit how fast I was falling and how much it would hurt if you left me again.

"I thought if I kept secrets between us, I could keep part of myself safe, so that when you left, I would survive. But then you found out and I realized it didn't matter, I'd fallen for you anyway and it hurt like hell. When I learned that I could end the contract, I convinced myself it was the right choice for you, I was doing it for you, but really I thought if I left first, it wouldn't hurt as much."

The breath she took scraped her throat as she drank him in. "But I was wrong," she admitted, broken. "It hurts more. I know you might not forgive me, or that you might not even love me or want me in that way, but I'm done being a coward and I'm done not believing I'm enough. So, I came here to tell you the truth." She swallowed, bracing herself. "I love you. I want to be with you. I had to tell you, even if it's a no." A tiny nervous smile quivered. "It's your choice."

If she'd scored it, there would have been crescendoing music in the background. If this was a movie, the hero would light up, take her in his arms and dip her into a sweeping kiss.

But life wasn't a movie.

And as her words fell into the chasm between them, her every cell sensitized and painfully exposed, Bastian pursed his lips. Turned. And walked back into the tent.

Well. She blinked back tears as pain clamped vicious jaws around her heart. Okay. That was her answer.

But as she turned blindly to walk away, to quietly go bury her head in the sand somewhere, the flap of the tent rustled and he came back out, holding a stack of letters in his hand.

She hesitated, hope even more painful than the heartbreak. Maybe he'd thought she'd left and needed to post some mail, and she looked even more of an idiot by thinking it was for her.

But his eyes were all about her, intense and serious enough to make her stomach jitter.

He handed her the stack.

A slight frown marred her forehead. "I don't…" She looked down. At her own name.

Emmaline Bluewater.

She glanced up. "They're for me?"

He nodded, jaw tight. But he didn't explain.

She had the feeling of being in a play and having forgotten her lines. She hesitated. "Can I read one?"

"They're yours." His voice was as gritty as the air.

She looked around for somewhere to sit, settled on a chair that was in what passed for shade. A small table sat next to it and she placed all but the top letter on it. Sliding her fingers into the unsealed envelope, she pulled out the contents.

A birthday card?

She didn't know if she looked as confused as she felt, but she soldiered on, flipping open the card.

"'Dear Emmaline,'" she read in an unsteady voice. "'I'm not sure if I'm going to mail this to you. I can't even write down why I left you. Maybe you know, maybe you don't. I can't think about it. But I've always given you a birthday card, so while it might not be the best birthday, I hope you find some small way of being happy. I want you to be happy. I know it might not seem like it now, but I do. Have a cake for me. Bastian.'"

She lowered the card, stared. His chin dipped, indicating the stack.

Taking the hint, she picked up the next envelope. Another birthday card. "'Dear Emmaline,'" she read. "'You're twenty-two and pissed I'm sure that I'm still not back. Or maybe not. I'd hoped I might be able to tell you everything, but still I can't find the words. I know whatever you've done, you'll have done for good reason. I'm not coming back yet; I haven't found a way. But I want you to be happy. I hope the birthday is good and that someone is giving you cake. Bastian.'"

The stack got smaller as she read each one. The cards got longer, filled with descriptions of what he was doing, the places he was visiting, the obvious undertone of a secret he longed to share but couldn't, a secret he struggled with deciding if she'd been part of or not. The fact that he missed her so much. He composed whole paragraphs to childhood memories, writing on paper that he included in the cards when he ran out of room. Sometimes he'd write of how much he ached to be with her again, but how he felt trapped. The troubled young man torn between duty and emotion. And throughout it all, it became clear that he'd never considered her a burden, only a friend he craved to speak to, except he thought they might never get back to where they'd been.

The birthday card for her most recent birthday was the final one. She flipped it out. It was short, like his first. "'Emmaline,'" she said. "'I'm coming back. My mom is sick and it's because I ran instead of facing everything, facing you. All I want is to have my sweet, shy friend look at me and welcome me home, but I know it's more complicated than that. I just hope one day we can be friends. I've never stopped believing in you and I doubt I ever will. I'll be seeing you. Bastian.'"

Pain was a dull thudding inside her as she carefully put the card on the top of the stack. He couldn't have told her more clearly that he'd considered her a friend, but just a friend.

"I understand," she said with quiet dignity. "I'll go."

But as she went to rise, a telekinetic force pushed her back down. Even as she gasped, Bastian said, "There's one more."

Her eyes went to the table. Empty.

When she looked back, he held out one last birthday card. Had he already planned ahead for next year?

She didn't want to take it. All it would say was how great a friend she'd proven to be, that he'd enjoyed them as lovers, but thank you for setting him free.

Maybe not, the hopeful part of her whispered. *Courage.*

With an unsteady breath, she took the card from him. Their skin grazed with an electric shock.

She fumbled to open the card and saw three words.

I love you.

When she looked up, he was kneeling in front of her. "Huh?" was all she managed.

He took her free hand. "I never stopped," he said in a tight voice at odds with the tenderness in his face. "I never stopped caring about you. Thinking about you. Every year, I wrote you a card I'd never send, hell, I don't know why. I just knew I needed to wish you happy birthday. I always had." He gripped her hand tighter. His eyes had never been so blue. "I never stopped loving you, Emma. Despite the contract, the hex, everything, I never stopped missing you, wanting you. I could yell at you for putting up that wall, for not trusting me, for being a coward and sending me away, putting us both through this, instead of being a reasonable adult and talking to me."

She sent him a squinty-eyed look that was probably lost due to the tears that were gathering. And also, he was right. Not that she'd say it again, or he'd lord it over her for the rest of their lives.

For the rest of their lives…

"I could," he continued, "but I did the same thing, so what would be the point? I could've stayed and figured out a way to break the hex, a way around the clause. Hell, Emma, I'm almost a master at mind magic. I could've stalled until I broke it. But I couldn't face what it meant if I had to talk to you, accepted that you knew, what that meant for us that you'd betray me."

"But I did, didn't I."

"No." He gripped tighter to her hand. "I want to be very clear about this—I don't consider what you did a betrayal. You were stupid and you should've come to me, but I understand why you didn't. I didn't come to you either. We were young, forced into something beyond us. Puppets. But you were stupid again when you were an adult and deliberately didn't tell me the truth just to shut me out."

A tear slid down her cheek. "I know. And I'll never do it again. I vow it."

He looked at their tangled fingers. "I want you to know you put me through hell."

Her heart ached. "Bastian…"

When he looked up, *his* heart was in his eyes. "I thought you didn't care about me. Wanted to be rid of me."

"Never."

"My mom told me I should take some time to think, and that I needed to let you think as well. I wanted to give you time, give us time, so that when I came to you, you'd know that I wasn't reacting—I was *acting* out of my own free will. That I was choosing you, Emma Bluewater, stubborn, sassy, shy, all the incredible, infuriating sides of you." He brought their hands to his lips, pressed a fervent kiss there. "The only person who made me feel like being imperfect was enough. How could I choose anyone else?"

Emma slid off the chair, almost boneless, in the process just missing Hallie, who'd emerged from the tent.

"It's always been you," she whispered, tracing his features. "I've never met anyone who challenges me, who scares me, who amazes me or makes me feel the way you do. Like I could take on the world. Like I'm the best version of me."

"Stop, you'll make me blush."

She laughed, a bright sparkle of noise in what had been tragic gray. "Imperfect," she said. "But perfect for me."

He gathered her close and kissed her, hard, needy. A kiss that was legendary. A kiss that told her everything she'd ever need to know.

"I love you," he said against her mouth. "Be with me. Stay with me."

"In Egypt?" She blinked.

"For now." He kissed her nose, her cheeks, his hands tight around her. "Then maybe Cambodia, Milan, Paris…"

She weakened with every kiss.

"Let me show you the world," he murmured. "And be my home."

"I come as a package deal," she reminded him. "Two for one."

He paused. "In that case, it's a no. I'm sorry, I can't face Tia every day."

She snort-laughed and hit his shoulder with her palm. "I'm talking about my sister. I can't abandon her."

"So, we'll bring her along."

"She has school. She can't skip class because you're not thinking straight."

"And you're thinking like a human. Portals, Em. She can come here after school and go home before they even miss her. And when school lets out, we'll all go traveling together."

"You'd do that?"

"The kid likes milkshakes. What wouldn't I do for a fellow sweet tooth?"

"You're serious?"

"Yes. Emma." He kissed her. "I liked her. I want to get to know her. I want both of you. So? Will you be with me?"

She didn't even have to think about it. "Always."

Of course, Bastian—being Bastian—couldn't let it end there, which was why in ten months and change, witch society found themselves attending a party at the Truenote mansion. Nobody noted the date; after all, parties were thrown for all sorts of reasons. It was a masquerade, which everyone loved and wholeheartedly threw themselves into. Ghouls and goblins and fairy godmothers abounded, drifting around to the music that played.

And at midnight, Bastian Truenote took off his mask, and so did the woman at his side.

There had been whispers about Emmaline Bluewater, how she'd shamelessly traveled to fetch Bastian back, even after she'd broken the engagement contract. Of course, there were rumors that if they'd completed the Divining, the rings the magic would have created would have been platinum forged with diamonds for eternity, the strongest of all bonds, but it was so easy to brush that aside and consider Emmaline to be another woman who'd had to chase after a man who didn't want her.

But when Bastian got down on one knee and proposed with that very ring, even the most cynical among them found themselves clearing their throats at the love he shamelessly displayed for the witch nobody had thought he'd choose.

The applause that rang out when she accepted was genuine, as genuine as it got in society, and everyone noted how pleased Diana and Alistair Truenote were. Clarissa Bluewater merely looked smug, as if she'd engineered the entire thing, though everyone knew her daughter had cut her visits down to twice a year. Not to mention there were whispers about a human love child, though not many put stock into that. Clarissa would surely have taken care of it.

Only those closest to the happy couple saw Emma's blush as she pulled away from Bastian's soul-crushing kiss. These included a beaming Maybelline, who proclaimed she'd always known they'd end up together, an eye-rolling Tia Hightower, and a woman and what may have been a teenager wearing full feathered masks neither would take off, though both were eagerly looking around at everything but the kissing couple.

And only the kissing couple heard Bastian's loving whisper. "Happy birthday, sweetheart."

★ ★ ★ ★ ★

ACKNOWLEDGMENTS

This book marks the end of an era and the beginning of a new chapter for Team Morgan. After five years, I've had to say goodbye and good luck to my first agent, Lizzie Poteet, as she returned to her roots as an editor. She was one of the first people to believe in my worlds and champion my characters, and I hope she's proud of this, the last book she helped sell. Lizzie, I want to say thank you for all your hard work, dedication and enthusiasm, and I know the authors you're now nurturing are incredibly lucky.

I'm also grateful that you left me in the equally enthusiastic and more-than-capable hands of the new Team Morgan, Cole Lanahan and Julie Gwinn. To quote Bogart (as we all should whenever possible), "I think this is the beginning of a beautiful friendship." Let's go get 'em, ladies!

I want to say an additional thank-you to Stephanie, editor extraordinaire, whose commitment to bringing out the best in these characters (and me) and who excitedly shook the pom-poms from even before we signed, has been so appreciated. You've helped shape this book into something I hadn't expected when writing it. It just goes to show—never underestimate a woman who owns a spaniel.

And, finally, thank you to everyone who took a chance on this book and gave their heart to Emma and Bastian's story. We'd all be nothing without you!